Praise for *Sparrow Hill Road* and
The Girl in the Green Silk Gown

"Hitchhiking ghosts, the unquiet dead, the gods of the old American roads—McGuire enters the company of Lindskold and Gaiman with this book, creating a wistful, funny, fascinating new mythology of diners, corn fields, and proms in this all-in-one-sitting read!"

—Tamora Pierce, *New York Times*-bestselling author of
Battle Magic and *Bloodhound*

"Seanan McGuire doesn't write stories, she gifts us with Myth—new Myths for a layered America that guide us off the twilight roads and lend us a pretty little dead girl to show us the way home."

—Tanya Huff, bestselling author of *An Ancient Peace*

"The best ghost story I've read in a _____ while."

Green Man Review

"An evocative and profound___ ___ ___stantly wraps around readers' imaginations . . . ___ ___stently surprising collection of adventures is al___ ___ ___t to the power of American myths and memorie___ ___ —*RT Book Reviews* (top pick)

"Beautifully written . . . ___ ___ing, richly imagined story of love and destiny features an irresistible heroine and is one of the accomplished McGuire's best yet." —*Publishers Weekly* (starred)

"McGuire's twilight America contains some strikingly strong mythic resonances." —Tor.com

"The author takes a deliberately lyrical tone with this series, making the story feel like a folk song. She has a gift for putting her heroines in danger and finding creative ways to return them to see them out of it. . . . McGuire's fans will relish this ghostly treat."

—*Library Journal*

**DAW Books presents the finest in urban fantasy
from Seanan McGuire:**

°*Coming soon from DAW Books*

SEANAN McGUIRE

ANGEL of the OVERPASS

Book Three of *The Ghost Roads*

DAW BOOKS, INC.

DONALD A. WOLLHEIM, FOUNDER

1745 Broadway, New York, NY 10019

ELIZABETH R. WOLLHEIM
SHEILA E. GILBERT
PUBLISHERS

www.dawbooks.com

First Printing, May 2021
1st Printing

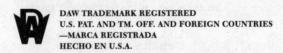

For Amber and Sarah, the very best of road trip buddies.

Editor's Note:

The majority of urban legends form around a small grain of truth, however misinterpreted or misunderstood. In the case of Rose Marshall, more commonly known as "the Girl in the Green Silk Gown" or "the Phantom Prom Date," we are well aware of the documented events behind the legend. It began with the death of a teenage girl on Sparrow Hill Road in Buckley Township, Michigan, and has since spread across North America, carried by people who heard and retold her story, changing it in ways both great and small.

Like Rose herself, the story of the Girl in the Green Silk Gown is a hitchhiker, borrowing from those around it. Yet no matter how far the tale travels, this grain of truth remains: Rose Marshall lived. Rose Marshall died. And as of the time of this writing, Rose Marshall does not yet rest in peace.

—Kevin and Evelyn Price, ed.

Book One:

Eumenides

Lady of shadows, keeper of changes, plant the seeds of faith within me, that I might grow and flourish, that I might find my way through danger and uncertainty to the safety of your garden. Let my roots grow strong and my skin grow thick, that I might stand fast against all who would destroy me. Grant to me your favor, grant to me your grace, and when my time is done, grant to me the wisdom to lay my burdens down and rest beside you, one more flower in a sea of blooms, where nothing shall ever trouble me again.

—traditional twilight prayer to Persephone

Hitchhiking ghost stories can be found in cultures across the world. While the details of the haunting will change depending on cultural markers and local norms, the core remains the same: someone appears on a road or trail where they shouldn't be, either a stranger or a familiar face who is somehow presented as "out of context." The girl in the prom dress on a winding country road; the grandmother on the path in the middle of the forest; the soldier by the side of the highway. They may be confused or disoriented, but they are not, at this stage, hostile. They request help getting home. They say that someone is waiting for them.

In some hitchhiking ghost stories, this can be the end of the tale. If the traveler refuses to help the stranger, they are able to move on, no harm done, and continue with their lives. In other stories, this can be the cue for terrible vengeance on the part of the wandering spirit, who is only able to harm those who have refused to help. (It should be noted that stories of the type "traveler refuses aid, suffers no retribution" are rare, presumably because they are uninteresting to the storyteller. A story in which nothing happens is merely an anecdote, and those have little staying power in the oral tradition.)

American hitchhiking ghost stories—like the tale of the Phantom Prom Date, which we are here to make sense of—tend to follow a predictable model. Traveler encounters stranger; traveler agrees to provide transportation; stranger gets into car, taxi, or other conveyance; stranger complains of being cold; traveler provides stranger with coat or sweater or even cloak, depending on the provenance of the original story. This is where the two types of American hitchhiking ghost story will diverge. In the first type, the traveler will continue on to the address provided by the stranger, and either find a cemetery at that location, or a house in which the stranger has not lived since their untimely death. In either case, the stranger will disappear upon reaching their destination, most often leaving their borrowed outerwear behind.

(On the occasions where the borrowed garment is not discarded on the seat, it will be found either draped across a tombstone or folded neatly on the bed of the deceased. In either case, the traveler will be able to retrieve it later, although most stories fail to detail whether or not it will ever be worn again by the living.)

The second type of American hitchhiking ghost story is far more sinister. In this version, once the stranger enters the traveler's vehicle, the traveler's fate is sealed: they will not be returning home. Instead, they will meet the end so many others have met—including the stranger who now rides with them. It is the paradox of the Phantom Prom Date that her tale so often bridges the gap between these two, raising the question of when, exactly, a teenage girl unable to find her way safely home was transformed into a spirit of unending vengeance . . .

—*On the Trail of the Phantom Prom Date*,
Professor Laura Moorhead, University of Colorado.

Chapter 1
Rubber Meets the Road

FUCK BOBBY CROSS.

"Hey, asshole!" I shout over my shoulder as I run down the side of the highway, only half-present, the coat that had been loaning me flesh and material substance long since fallen away on the side of the road, one more skin to be discarded. I've shrugged off two bodies and more outerwear than a hundred years of New York Fashion Week, and I'm getting tired of it.

Normally, this is when I'd be dropping down into the twilight, the land of the dead nearest to the world of the living, but there are two big things stopping me. One, ever since my honorary niece, Antimony Price, decided to screw around with the crossroads, the twilight has been a little unpredictable. That's putting it nicely. The parts of the twilight that don't see a lot of regular use have been doing their best to recreate one of those fucked-up surrealist horror movies from the 1970s, the ones that replaced my good, dependable giant creature features with acid-trip hallucination sequences and gimmicky serial killers. Not wanting to spend another three days finding my way out of a maze made of mirrors, chainsaws, and disemboweled farm animals is a great incentive for playing haunted house a couple miles more, at least until I get to familiar ground.

The second big thing is a little more ordinary, by my definition of the word: I hate Bobby Cross more than I hate anything else, living or dead, in the entire universe. If I disappear, he'll turn around and go back to the restaurant where he found me, and there are people there I care about. I need him to follow me into the twilight, although even the chainsaw mirror mazes don't deserve to spend any more time with him than absolutely necessary, and once he follows me down, I need him to *stay* there. If I drop down in hostile territory, he'll just bounce straight back out again.

The third big thing that I don't want to admit as a factor is that as soon as I leave the daylight, he'll know he has me scared.

I'm tired of letting Bobby scare me. I'm tired of letting Bobby chase me. Really, I'm tired of Bobby, full stop.

My name is Rose Marshall. I'm both the first girl who dies in the horror movie and the one who refuses to stay buried once she's dead. I've been sixteen for more than sixty years, and I think I have some pretty good reasons to be pissed.

"Hey, *asshole*," I repeat, as I stop running and whip around to face the man who's been making a night out of chasing one pretty little dead girl down a stretch of deserted Alabama highway. I'm not winded in the least. One of the perks of being dead. "You know, when I come from, we have a word for creepy old guys who have a weird obsession with teenage girls."

I know he can hear me. That man never drives with the windows up if he can help it, and since he's basically immune to the laws of physics, he can always help it.

But he doesn't slow, and he doesn't swerve, just keeps barreling down the road toward me like I'm the finish line and he's running the Indy 500.

Motherfucker.

This seems like as good a time as any to get you caught up on the situation, since if we go much farther down this road, we won't have any-place left to turn around. Yes, road metaphors. You're going to get a lot of them if you hang around here. Road metaphors are sort of where I exist—not where I live, because if the "sixteen going on seventy" line up there didn't tip you off, I don't live anywhere anymore. I haven't lived anywhere since 1952, when a man named Bobby Cross decided to run me off the road on the way to my high school prom.

I was just a kid.

I was young and scared and not sure what was happening to me, just that I wanted it to stop; just that I had never done anything to deserve this. I stand by that feeling. I died in 1952, and after all these years of afterliving, I still say that the girl I was didn't deserve what happened to her. She was innocent. She'd never done anything truly wrong in her life. Oh, she'd lied, and she'd stolen little things from her parents and brothers, and she'd cheated on a couple of math tests, but none of those were crimes worth dying for. She should have had the chance to grow up and figure out who she was actually going to be. She should have had a *life*.

Instead, she got a short, brutal fall from Sparrow Hill Road, and when she woke up, she was me. A dead girl who didn't get to rest in peace, who had to keep on running for her life from a man named Bobby Cross, who thought other people only existed to make things easier for him. Rose Marshall died that night, and the Phantom Prom Date, the Walking Girl, the Angel of the Overpass, and the Girl in the Green Silk Gown all rose from her broken body, ready to carry on, ready to become the person she'd never been given the chance to be.

But I'm getting ahead of myself.

This is a story about the dead. A ghost story, if you will, because any story with me at its center is inherently going to be a ghost story: I define my reality by my very presence. If you don't like ghost stories, if you don't like spending time with dead people, if you'd rather pretend life goes on forever and nothing ever goes wrong, you can still put this down and walk away. I'm not going to haunt you just because you don't feel like listening to the ramblings of an octogenarian teenager. There are always better reasons for a haunting.

But if you're still here, here's how it works: when people die with unfinished business weighing them down, sometimes they stick around for a while. Days or centuries, whatever it takes to accomplish what they're hoping to achieve. I've known ghosts who flickered through the twilight and vanished in a single evening, moving on to the next stage of existence as soon as they knew their organs were being donated according to their wishes, or as soon as the other person who'd been in the car with them breathed their last and caught up. I've also known ghosts who lingered for centuries. I'm somewhere in the middle at this point, established enough to be impressive to the new ghosts, new enough to be treated like a child by the old ghosts.

It used to bother me. Then I figured out that most old ghosts are homebodies, more interested in haunting whatever battlefield or descendant has caught their eye, and I'm . . . well . . . not. I'm what's called a road ghost: I died in an automobile accident, I died with no thoughts more prominent in my mind than "get away, get away, get away," and so I became a spirit whose entire existence is tied up in motion. Nothing pins me down. Not for long.

I know, this is a lot, and you're probably more interested in the man who's trying to run me down right now. But time is a funny thing for the dead. We exist permanently in the present tense, not quite clear on what's past or future, and everything I'm telling you now is something you need to understand if you want this story to make sense. I promise we'll get back to asshole Bobby in a second. There's nothing wrong with making a dick wait a little while.

Anyway, there are people who think it's not fair that the circumstances of your death will determine what kind of ghost you become, but I don't honestly see how it's any different than existence among the living. So many of the things about you are decided by who your parents are and where you're born, and if you can change some of your circumstances later, well, you can never change them all. Even if I haunt the twilight for another century, I'll always be the ghost of a poor girl from the bad part of town, a girl whose mother both mourned her and was silently, secretly relieved to have one less mouth to feed.

Life is determined by the way you enter it. So is death.

Road ghosts haunt roads and house ghosts haunt houses and family ghosts haunt families. There are countless forms of haunting, some more common than others. Some ghosts spend a lot of time in the lands of the living, while others are content to stay in the twilight until it's time to move on. For every ghost a living person sees, there are a hundred on the other side of the veil, dead haunting the dead, and most of them are incredibly talented when it comes to getting on my goddamn nerves.

But the twilight isn't just ghosts. The twilight is a kind of skin around our reality, protecting it from the big bad emptiness of eternity, and if it's the natural dwelling place of the dead, it's also a comfortable home for all kinds of other things. The routewitches build their bolt holes in the twilight, scattering them along the length of the Old Atlantic Highway, which time and the alchemy of distance have elevated into something barely shy of divinity—or maybe not shy at all. The Ocean Lady is their patron goddess, and they heed her will above all else, even when what she wants isn't precisely what they wanted to give her.

The world is full of witches and sorcerers and wanderers trying to find their way out of this daylight existence and into the twilight right next door. When physicists talk about the missing pieces of the universe, they're actually talking about the twilight, even if they don't know it. It's the balance to the scales, the shadow that proves the object exists, and without it, everything would fall to pieces. The dead are the immune system of the living. Even if they never see us, we keep them safe, and for the most part, all we ask in return is to be left alone. No exorcisms, please. Let us rest. And if that resting takes the form of hitchhiking to a diner in the middle of nowhere to enjoy a slice of strawberry rhubarb pie, that's our business.

But all that's the twilight. Below the twilight comes the starlight, which is stranger and deeper and harder to explain; it's where nonhuman intelligences tend to go when they die, seeking an afterlife that's a little less accessible to the sort of people who might have tormented them when they were alive. I've met dragons in the starlight, whiling away the happy hours of their afterlives in caverns filled with the memory of gold and the laughter of the hunted who have found themselves finally, mercifully safe. I've seen unicorns. I don't go there very often because it isn't for me, but part of me will always be grateful to know it exists—that somewhere, everyone gets to rest.

Below the starlight is the midnight, which houses those spirits who may never have been alive at all. I don't necessarily understand how that works, and I'm absolutely sure I don't want to: that's not my place, and trying to claim it wouldn't just be colonialist, it would potentially be deadly. The midnight doesn't care for intrusions. When I have to travel there—and I do have to, sometimes, to get to where I'm actually supposed to be—I always do it as quickly and as unobtrusively as I can. It doesn't do to linger. Not when you're so deep that even the memories of stars have burned out, leaving the sky as black as tar and twice as unforgiving.

And through them all, like a cold breeze working its way through the foundations of a manor house, run the ghostroads.

No one built them. They built themselves, coming together an inch at a time as people in the daylight carved roads into the body of the world. Distance is a kind of vitality, and gradually, those roads became living things. They followed the same cycle as everything that lives: they grew, strengthened, flourished, faded, and finally died.

But nothing that's really loved is ever totally forgotten, and when they lost their hold on the daylight, those roads solidified in the deeper levels, connecting all the layers of the afterlife, crisscrossing the twilight like the strands of a spider's web, keeping us tethered to the lands of the living. Every ride on the ghostroads is a katabasis of sorts, a journey from the land of the living to the lands of the dead, because the roads remember what it is to be alive and they know what it is to be dead and they keep us from forgetting where we come from.

I will never forget where I come from.

I know, I know, asshole with a muscle car trying to run me down back in the part of time that probably feels a lot more urgent to you, because you're alive. I'm not. Urgency isn't as big a deal for me, and these are all things you *need* to know if you want everything else to make sense. So be patient just a little longer, and you'll get to see a fucker get what's coming to him.

I'm originally from Buckley Township, Michigan, which isn't the sort of community that wants to draw attention to itself. Just a little town surrounded by woods, water, and the occasional monster. I could have grown up and old and died there if not for a teenage girl named Mary Dunlavy. She was before my time, but people who knew her said she was sweet, and kind, and gentle, and didn't deserve to disappear like she did, slipping out of sight shortly after her father passed away. He wasn't murdered; Benjamin Dunlavy was tired, and sick, and he died in his sleep. It happens sometimes.

Mary wasn't murdered either. She was just on the wrong road at the wrong time, and she met the business end of a Buick driven by someone who was going too fast and had maybe had a little too much to drink before climbing behind the wheel.

Here's where I got off better than Mary: I know who killed me. She never found out who was driving that car. They hit her and they moved on, off to the rest of their lives, while Mary choked to death on her own blood in the corn out by the Old Parrish Place. She was just a kid. She didn't want to die. She begged the universe not to let her die.

And something answered.

Up until real recently, the crossroads were the greatest danger in the twilight. They didn't belong there. They didn't belong to the midnight or the daylight, either. They didn't belong anywhere spirits like us are intended to go or gather. They were a wound in the walls of the world, a ripped, rotten place where something ancient and toxic and unspeakable leaked through, changing the rules to suit itself, remaking reality in its own image. But Mary didn't know any of that. Mary just knew she was scared and dying and leaving her father alone. So when the crossroads came to her and asked what she'd do if it meant she didn't have to go, she said "anything." That's exactly what she said. "Anything."

Never tell something you don't understand that you'll do anything if it means you get what you want. "Anything" is a blank check against the foundations of the universe. "Anything" lies.

The crossroads took Mary and made her their own, their little crossroads ghost, intended to lure innocent people into their devil's deals, to convince girls like she'd been that the crossroads were playing fair, even though they weren't. Even though they never could have been because they didn't know the meaning of the word. The crossroads never met a bargain they didn't want to bend in their favor or a loophole they didn't want to exploit, and Mary was their perfect kind of patsy—young and scared and brilliantly naïve in the way that only sheltered daughters ever get to be. It's a blessing and it's a burden. Mary lived and died before my time, but I knew girls like her, shared classrooms and community centers with them, and they were always innocent and easy to take advantage of. So the crossroads took advantage.

Mary and I were both born in Buckley Township, and our bones will rest there until they finish the long, slow process of returning to dust, but that's all we have in common. We're different kinds of ghost, with different rules and desires to bind us, but our stories are inextricably tangled together all the same, because one of the first deals Mary helped the crossroads broker was with a man named Bobby Cross, who wanted to live forever.

And there's the asshole with the road rage issues, finally joining the narrative for keeps.

Diamond Bobby, boy-king of the Silver Screen, a man so scared of getting old and fading away that he was willing to stage his own death and render himself irrelevant. He could have been one of the greats. Now he's just a footnote for film buffs to obsess over, another James Dean figure who never had the chance to grow up and show the world what he could do. People think he crashed out in the desert. People think his body is rotting on the rocks of some canyon somewhere, waiting to be discovered by an unlucky hiker. People think a lot of things.

They couldn't be further from the truth. Bobby Cross tricked the routewitches into telling him how to find the crossroads, and he scored himself an inexperienced crossroads ghost who couldn't talk him out of making a deal, and he sold his soul to live forever . . . technically. As long as Bobby's behind the wheel of the car the crossroads gave him, he won't age, he won't die, he won't ever run out of time. But that car runs on ghosts instead of gasoline, and the best way to guarantee someone leaves a ghost when they die is to kill them. Violent deaths lead to unquiet spirits, and that's where Mary and I slid onto the same track. She made Bobby; Bobby killed me. Ran me right off the road in my green silk prom gown, broke me at the bottom of the ravine.

I got away. I shouldn't have. I was a scared teenager running through the night, leaving my body behind, still in that unformed liminal state most ghosts settle into for a little while, not sure what I was going to be, not sure who I was going to be when I got there. I was easy pickings for a man like Bobby Cross.

But my boyfriend came looking for me when I didn't show up for prom. He saw me by the side of the road, and he wrapped his coat around my shoulders, and he made a hitchhiking ghost out of me. I guess I should be grateful—I like what I am; I'm good at it—but part of me will always wonder how I might have settled if not for Gary's intervention. What would the twilight have made of me if it had been given nothing but my own wild desires to work from?

We'll never know. I got away, thanks to luck and timing and Gary, and Bobby Cross has been on my ass ever since, determined to claim what he thinks of as his, regardless of my own ideas about the matter. I got away. I'm still running.

Spend as much time on the road as I have, and people will do their best to hang an urban legend around your shoulders like a borrowed coat. Like a borrowed coat, those stories never fit quite right. Unlike a borrowed coat, they may, given time, start making changes to the person you think you are. Am I still little Rosie Marshall, who wanted nothing more than to graduate from high school and watch Buckley dwindling in her rearview mirror? Or am I the walking girl of Route 42, the girl in the diner, the phantom prom date . . . the girl in the green silk gown.

When the line between story and history begins to blur, very little remains certain. But I'm certain of this much:

My friends still call me Rose.

So that's a lot to bring you up to the present, where Bobby Cross is once more trying to run my sweet ass down with his crossroads-customized car. He still thinks all he has to do is get me to touch the paint or chrome and our decades-long game of cat and mouse is finally over; that thing drinks ghosts like sunburnt skin drinks lotion. Dude's been driving around the twilight for a long time, but he's not dead, and he doesn't make many friends, so people don't necessarily sit down to explain things to him the way they otherwise might.

See, I have a big-ass tattoo covering most of my back, given to me by Apple, the current Queen of the North American routewitches. It signifies that I walk under Persephone's protection. The Lady of the Dead isn't all-powerful, nor is she always kind, but what belongs to her, she keeps, and she protects. As long as I have that tattoo, Bobby can't take me.

Doesn't mean he stops being a pain in my unaging backside. I'm his white whale, the girl who got away, and he blames me for basically everything that's gone wrong for him since the night he failed to kill me. Which is, to be honest, quite a lot. And things have to be even worse for him since the crossroads died. Whatever Annie did to them, it didn't unmake the bargains they'd put into place—no sudden losses of fortune, no new lineages springing up because their ancestors hadn't all died under mysterious circumstances—but it rendered them unable to do anything *more*. Bobby thrives on *more*. So he's pretty pissed. Pissed enough to risk angering Persephone, the dick.

Being a hitchhiking ghost means I spend a lot of time in the land of the living, since that's where the rides are. The rides, and the roadside dives. I'd started my night with a hankering for real white-gravy fried chicken, the kind you only get at Sunday church suppers or at run-down little holes in the wall off the Alabama highway, cooked by old men whose arteries have long since solidified into a solid mass of butterfat and flour. I'd hauled myself up into the daylight, flagged down a ride, and got my sweet ghost ass dropped off at one of my favorite fry shacks, borrowed coat on my shoulders and hunger burning in my belly.

Pretty sure the cooks here know I'm dead, given I've been coming to their place since it was their granddaddy's joint and they weren't even born yet, and here I am, still sixteen, while they've gone gray and wizened. But they can cook like a dream, and before their daddy gave them the deed, he told them what the rules were with me.

Told them I would never pay for a meal in their place, and that it didn't matter, because one guest wasn't going to break them. Told them I would never order or ask for anything, either, just say things sounded good or smelled delicious. Everything had to be given to me freely, without payment. And he told them that as long as I kept coming, they'd stay open, no matter how hard times got, which was sweet of him, if a little bit stretching the truth.

See, routewitches take note of the places where the hitchers like me tend to gather, and they follow us. So as long as I keep stopping by for a plate of cheesy grits and fried chicken, the routewitches will keep coming for the same, and as long as the routewitches keep coming, they'll always have a guaranteed clientele. The road is an ecosystem.

It's always nice to be back in familiar surroundings. The brothers who run the place these days have kids of their own, and I've been watching for years to see whether it was going to be Frank or Breanna who decided to take over when their fathers retire, and it's been looking more and more like it's going to be Breanna. She enjoys the cooking and the business side of things equally, and she loves Alabama in a way that makes me suspect she might be a routewitch.

People hear "routewitch" and assume they have to be nomadic. Even the Queen feels that way. The routewitches who serve her bring her offerings of distance, because her role in the community means she stays on the Ocean Lady and never gets to see the world with her own eyes. But that's just one extreme. The other extreme is people who love their land so much they never want to leave it, the sort of folks who tend to become homesteads when they die, because they can't imagine living or loving anyplace else. They get their distance from the stories people bring them, and they thrive on it.

Breanna's pies have always had that little extra edge that whispers route magic to me, and if she takes over for her father, this place will last at least another generation. If she and Frank run the place together, it may never close its doors.

She smiled when I came in the door, and her call of, "Rose! It's been an age," was colored with genuine pleasure, even knowing that my presence didn't mean so much as a tip for her. People are sometimes willing to slip a few small bills to a hitchhiker, but it's not a reliable thing, and most nights all I have in this world is the coat on my back.

"Hi, Bre," I responded, returning her smile with one of my own as I bellied up to the counter and claimed a stool. About half the tables were occupied, some by regulars I recognized from other visits, some by travelers who'd stopped for a quick bite and found themselves astonished by the quality of the food. You could tell the difference by looking at their faces. The ones who looked like kids on their first visit to Mr. Wonka's factory, those were the newcomers.

"We have fried chicken legs in white flour gravy, baked cheese grits, and peach pie tonight," said Bre. "That all right with you?"

"That's just fine with me." I flashed her a smile and settled in to wait for an excellent dinner. My death doesn't have a lot of novelty in it, but I'm a regular in enough different sorts of places not to need it. I get fed, I get to see familiar faces, I get to feel like I'm not losing touch with the world of the living—important for someone in my line of "work." Hitchhiking ghosts who fall too far out of touch have a hard time getting rides, and the consequences for that can be . . . bad.

I was still waiting when a new smell eeled its way through the air, sinuous and repulsive and clearly not present for anyone else in the room. Wormwood and ashes. Bobby Cross was coming.

Ashes usually mean someone's going to die. Not always, unless they're accompanied by a second scent that identifies the means of death—lilies for a death on the road, honeysuckle for a death *of* the road, and the two aren't always the same thing. Red cherry syrup for a death at the carnival, empty rooms for a death by old age. Everyone's death is unique and everyone's death is the same, and only Bobby carries wormwood on his skin. The bastard.

He's not as unique as he wants to be, of course. Ashes and wormwood are the smell of a crossroads death, and while he's not dead yet, he set the means of his own end in motion when he sold his soul for the chance to live forever. He wears his death like a shroud, a foul perfume that seeps from his skin and won't ever wash away. Makes it harder for him to sneak up on ghosts who know what that mixture means. Must be part of why he preys on the young and innocent the way he does.

I turned on my stool, fixing my eyes on the door, and waited. Breanna dropped off the plate of grits and cheese, and I barely remembered to thank her. I could have run then, I supposed, but I wanted to know what he wanted, and it wasn't like he could do anything to hurt me.

Bobby wasn't worth letting my food get cold. I turned back to my plate. Cheesy grits are proof that humanity is worth preserving, no matter what it may have done. They rolled hot and buttery down my throat, and—for a moment—they were enough to wipe away the smell.

Then the door swung open behind me, and the smell of wormwood became unbearably strong. I swallowed, reaching for the coffee Breanna had also dropped off, already doctored the way I liked it. Familiarity has its perks.

Footsteps approached my seat, echoing on the old linoleum. I sighed.

"Hello, Bobby," I said and took a drink of coffee.

Chapter 2
Unhappy Reunions

H E SETTLED ONTO THE STOOL next to me without a reply, grabbing a fork and sticking it into my grits without so much as a by-your-leave. Man was lucky I didn't have my chicken yet. The grits were amazing, but I'd break the fingers of any man who tried to mess with my white-gravy chicken legs. I made a sour face and shoved the plate toward him.

"Why, thank you, Rosie," he drawled. "I didn't know you cared."

"I just don't want to find out if you have something contagious enough to pass along to the dead," I snapped, turning to look at him.

Bobby Cross hasn't aged a day since 1950, the year when he decided to drive out of the daylight and into the dark. He's short by modern standards, five foot eight at most, with a compact dragster's build that's still as taut and sculpted as the studio trainers could make it. He's a bug in amber, and nothing he does to his body changes it from what it was when he sold his soul. Lucky bastard. All the benefits of being alive, and none of the consequences.

Except for the part where it's a conditional immortality, and one day he'll die, and while he waits for that day to come, he gets to watch his legacy wilt and fade away. As Diamond Bobby, King of the Silver Screen, he'd been a panty-wetting playboy, draped in women any time he crooked his little finger. These days, the smart girls avoid him, and the ones who aren't smart wise up damn fast. He's rotting from the inside out.

But that's opinion, and what I saw was a man with dark hair that hung loose and careless in a modern, tousled style. He'd slick it back into its customary duck's ass as soon as he was behind the wheel where he belongs, but when he walks among the living, he makes an effort to blend in. It's one of the few things I can't fault him for, because I do it, too. No one wants to be an anachronism.

His eyes gave him away. His eyes always gave him away. They weren't—they aren't, god, I hate trying to use the past tense—remarkable, pale brown and plain, but something about them made the living shy from him. Mary's eyes have the same effect. The crossroads have to leave their mark somewhere, and they left it in Bobby's eyes. Now they were gone, but their bargain, and Bobby, remained.

He was simply dressed, white shirt and tight jeans. No jacket. I've never borrowed a coat from Bobby, but he's alive, and I probably could if I wanted to—if he was willing to offer me one. I think he likes showing off his arms too much to cover them.

He smiled, lowering his lashes and watching me seductively as he slipped another bite of my grits between his red, red lips. I wrinkled my nose.

"You do realize that in this era, people don't like it when men your age leer at girls my age, right?" I asked.

"Sugar, I'm ninety-six and you're eighty-six," he said, and took another bite of grits. "Me seeing you for the pretty thing you are is only natural."

"What the fuck do you want, Bobby?" I don't have a lot of patience under the best of circumstances. Having Bobby in the room dropped it to less than zero.

"That's a harsh way to talk to your oldest friend," he said. Breanna approached with my chicken and gravy. He turned his award-winning smile on her. "Hello, beautiful."

"Um, hello," she said, clearly dazzled and unnerved in equal measure. She put my plate down in front of me, pulling out her notepad. "What can I get for you?"

"I'll have what she's having, and I'll cover both checks," he said.

Breanna didn't like that reply. Her glance at me carried a question I'd heard many times before: "Are you all right with this?"

And the answer was, of course, no. No, I was not all right with this. No, I was not happy to be apparently having dinner with Bobby Cross. But being the kind of man who felt like he was entitled to everything he wanted, no matter how many people got hurt along the way, meant it wasn't safe for me to tell Bobby to go away. He couldn't hurt me. He could come back tomorrow and burn this place to the ground with two generations locked inside the kitchen, and even as the thought formed, I caught a whiff of burning dust, like a car heater turning on for the first time after a summer of indolence. Death by fire.

The potential was here. Still forming, not yet fixed; still something we could easily avoid, if I played nice.

"Thank you, Bre," I said, and gave her what I hoped would be a re-assuring smile. As she walked away, I glanced back to Bobby. "The food here's amazing. I've been coming since the seventies, when a trucker dropped me off on his way to Huntsville. What do you *want*, Bobby?"

"You," he said, so bluntly that it was a shock, even though it was the only answer he could have given. "I want you, Rosie. You've been run-ning from me for a long damn time, and I'm tired of it."

"You're scared," I said, with slow wonder. "You're *scared* right now. What the hell do you have to be afraid of? You still have your car. I assume the damn thing still puts itself back together when you wreck it, and you don't look like you're getting any older."

Not that I'd be able to tell. It hadn't been long enough yet.

I understand the fear of getting older. I was resurrected for a little while not all that long ago, thanks to Bobby, and I could feel myself rotting with every moment that passed. Finding a way to become dead again without actually dying had been a new and unpleasant challenge.

"I just need to keep my tank as full as possible until I've worked out everything that's changed," he said, with the slow, deliberate pa-tience of a man who was barely holding himself together. "I thought you, being the altruistic sort that you are, might be willing to help a fellow out."

I blinked, slow and deliberate. "What the hell makes you think I'd ever help you?"

"This place. All the other places like it." He waved his hand expansively. "Because you never quite got over that little girl need for human connection. You want people to *like* you. And that means you wind up liking them in return . . . which makes you vulnerable."

The perfume that swirled around him in that moment was indescribable, a horrific, rotting blend of every type of death I've ever been close enough to identify. Cherry syrup and lilies and honeyed mint candies and burning dust and wormwood, wormwood, wormwood over everything. His smile was a narrow blade, designed for slashing through the dark. He leaned forward, a fork laden with cheesy grits in his hand, and pointed it at me.

"You like to brag about how you've stayed clear of big bad Bobby for so long," he said. "Like to say it makes you special. Well, it does, in one regard: it makes you high-octane. I stuff you in my tank, I keep rolling for a few years, while things in the twilight settle out and the new boss gets things under control. I don't have to hunt. I don't have to worry. It's easy riding for ol' Bobby."

"You can't touch me," I managed. "Persephone—"

"Only protects the faithful." He smirked, gesturing with the fork again. "Repudiate her and her works, and that little doodle on your back won't mean anything at all. I can take you freely, the way I should have from the start."

For a moment, I just stared at him. I was still staring at him when Breanna arrived with his grits and my chicken, placing them on the table. He favored her with another of those oily smiles, and pushed his plate of grits toward me, making it look like I'd given mine to him voluntarily. I mustered a weak smile of my own for Breanna, trying to convince her everything was all right.

It didn't quite work—she looked uncertain as she turned and walked back to the kitchen—but she left, and that was good enough for me.

"Do it, and you'll save a lot of lives," said Bobby. "Not just the ones I'd be hunting normally, but the people you claim to care about. The ones I would never have noticed without you. Refuse me, and I'll take them all—even that weird-ass family you share with sweet Mary. She was my first, you know. You could be my last."

It wasn't just what he was saying: it was the tone he was saying it in. I pushed the chicken and grits away. He smirked. "Lose your appetite, Rosie?"

"Fuck you," I snapped and threw my coffee in his face.

And then I ran.

Bobby's car was parked right out front, the color of moonlight glinting off a poisoned lake, black and silver and iridescent all at the same time, revolting and beautiful in equal measure. I gave it a wide berth, feet pounding down the dive's rickety wooden porch, and leapt to the gravel parking lot, nearly losing my balance and going sprawling. I managed to recover and keep running.

Running's something of a skill of mine these days.

There's one simple, consistent rule for dealing with Bobby Cross: don't ever, ever touch the car. Bobby's the driver, but the car is its own entity, a creation of the crossroads that does whatever it wants to do, only nominally under his control. Persephone's blessing should be enough to keep it from consuming me unless I break faith with her, but my faith isn't *faith*, not exactly. I don't believe in her divinity. I do believe in her. Hard not to believe in someone who's saved your soul from burning eternally in the engine of a muscle car, after all.

But with the crossroads gone, who was to say the rules binding Bobby's car were still the same? Better not to risk it. Bobby didn't get any special powers out of his bargain, save for the ability to walk in the twilight without dying for his trespasses, and since any routewitch can do that, within limits, it's not like that's the kind of gift that could shift the balance of power between the living and the dead. For all that he's my murderer and personal bogeyman, the important word in all of that is "man." He's still just a living man, albeit one with more access to the dead than he deserves. But the car . . .

Whatever it was to begin with, it never rolled off an assembly line. It wasn't born in Detroit, no creation of American steel and human ingenuity. There's nothing human about it, and if there's one thing I have to thank the crossroads for, it's that they didn't steal some innocent car's chassis, didn't force their demon dragster into the shape of a good Chevrolet or Ford. They gave it the right lines to fool someone who doesn't know their cars the way I do, gave it white-walled tires and sleek, shimmering tail fins, but they kept their design vague enough that I can still look at real cars without feeling my stomach turn over. Touching the car is a good way to get caught, and more importantly, to get fed into its eternally hungry engine. Ghosts who go into the car's inner workings don't come back out, not even in fragments.

Persephone's blessing is supposed to keep me safe. But I didn't survive more than fifty years in the twilight without it by being careless, and so I made sure I was well away from the car by the time Bobby came running after me, fury in his face and thunder in his eyes.

"Rose!" he hollered. *"Rose Marshall, you come back here, or I'll come after you!"*

Well, I wasn't going back there, so that left him with only one real choice in the matter. Instead, I kept running, feeling the coat I'd borrowed from my earlier ride drop through the suddenly insubstantial substance of my shoulders, leaving me a flickering outline of a girl whose clothes were already starting to unspool into a green silk prom gown, racing down the lonely road toward freedom.

Bobby followed. Of course he did, and that's what brings us to where we started, which I'll repeat for good measure:

Fuck Bobby Cross.

I don't have a plan in the moment, except for getting Bobby as far away as possible from the people I care about. I'm not as attached to this particular family as he thinks I am—I'm not a *beán sidhe*—but they're good people, and they don't deserve to get hurt because they made the mistake of feeding me. Getting him away should be enough, at least for a while, because Bobby is a spoiled child. If I did all my growing up after I died, he never did his at all. He went from being a pretty, reasonably attractive teenage boy to a Hollywood star who got everything he ever wanted handed to him on a silver platter, and when that wasn't enough, he managed to convince the universe itself to break the rules to give him his heart's desire.

Bobby Cross was never going to be a good person. I could almost feel bad for him because of that if he hadn't taken "spoiled and a little selfish" as an excuse to become a complete and utter monster. If I lead him away, he'll follow, and while he might still torch the place if he winds up back here, he won't necessarily take the time to come back of his own accord. As plans go, "get him to chase me and hope he forgets what isn't right in front of him" isn't a great one, but I'm a hitchhiker. Running away is sort of what I'm made to do.

So I run, and I keep running when his headlights flicker into life behind me, running as hard and as fast as my phantom legs allow. Every time my feet hit the road, they dip briefly below the surface of the daylight, little ghost girl skipping along the membrane around the twilight, and I can feel just how fucked up what's beneath me really is. I can't blame Annie for the chaos currently consuming my home. This is all on the crossroads. Fuck them, too. I don't want to drop down here.

I'm not going to have a choice. On a straight run, a car will always beat a person. I could go off-road, run into the soybean fields spreading out to either side of the road, but Bobby's car doesn't follow normal rules, and I'm afraid he'd just follow me, tearing up some poor farmer's crops, doing as much damage as he can before running me down.

I can keep running forever. Being dead will do that for a girl. But he'll catch me before forever comes, and he's gaining ground steadily enough that I already know how this will end. So I stop running. I plant my heels, turn around to face him, and raise both hands, middle fingers pointed toward the sky.

"You're a fucking coward and a bully, Bobby Cross!" I shout. Then I smile, slow and mean, and add, "And your movies weren't that good. Your pants were just extremely tight."

I drop down into the twilight before I see his response, or even know that he heard me. It doesn't matter either way. I'll always know I finally said it where he could hear.

Some people think that it's never daytime in the twilight. Those people have the right spirit but the wrong idea, like dogs barking up the tree next to the one where the squirrels have made their nests. Words have meanings, absolutely. That doesn't mean they're absolute, unbreakable laws. We have days in the twilight. Most of them are short, perfunctory things, sometimes lasting no more than a few hours, but they exist.

Homesteads and outfielders and cornfield ghosts can make those days last for years, stretching them out like bright banners, filled with blue skies and sunbeams and the golden dance of wheat chaff in the air. We have nights, too, and those are just as varied, just as variable, because there's no version of reality that works for every possible kind of haunting. The world of the dead gets to be as complicated as the world of the living—maybe more complicated since we're not devoting ourselves to the business of getting on with life.

But remember, the sun sets in the daylight. People see the night sky before they die, and that's a good thing, because if every new ghost was also confronted with their first nighttime, there would be a lot more screaming. Finding out you're dead is hard enough without adding a whole level of "oh and by the way, sometimes the sun goes away." So the sun sets in the daylight and rises in the twilight, and that's the way things are meant to be. Change is one of the only universal constants I know.

There are people who say the sun even rises all the way down in the midnight. I'm not sure I believe them. The midnight is chaos, chthonic and cruel, and it doesn't feel the need to brighten up its terrifying corners. But what do I know? I'm just a road ghost, after all.

I'm pretty indifferent to the distinction between night and day. It's easier for me to get rides when the sun is down—people worry about a teenage girl walking down the highway shoulder with her thumb cocked heavenward when the world is dark and cold and filled with wolves. Only some of those wolves are driving the cars. It's easier to get *safe* rides during the day, rides where no one puts a hand on my thigh or produces a knife from inside their conservative camel hair jacket.

Do people even wear camel hair anymore? Ugh. Things change so quickly in the lands of the living. I think that's the real reason most older ghosts choose to let go and move on. There's only so much trying to keep up with the times that the mind can handle when everything is happening on what feels like fast-forward.

It was nighttime in the daylight when I released my hold on the lands of the living and dropped into the land of the dead, landing in what should have been the safety of the twilight, which isn't currently living up to its name. The sun is a blazing orb overhead, and to make it worse, someone has equipped the damn thing with eyes and a mouth full of jagged teeth. That sounds like something out of a children's cartoon, and—for an instant—my brain tries to interpret it that way, to make it something soft and sweet, and maybe it was, once, but now it's monstrous and mean.

The sun narrows its eyes and hisses like a cat, flame licking from the corona of light around it, and the air grows hot enough that I feel my skin trying to remember how to burn. "Nope," I say, and turn around, taking three long strides before I drop down to the next level of the twilight, which may still be in murder-chainsaw-maze-mode, but will hopefully not be occupied by a hostile celestial body.

The twilight is infinitely divided and subdivided. Each level has its own rules and laws, which are far from being the same thing. Some levels have hundreds of occupants, even thousands, spirits who have chosen to share their afterlives in a sort of communal dream. There are heavens and hells and from the outside, they can look exactly the same. Resting in peace is very much in the eye of the beholder.

Other levels have one, maybe two occupants, people who didn't like company when they were alive and have found they enjoy it even less now that they're dead. Finding those levels can be virtually impossible, and sometimes when an outsider stumbles into them, they're already deserted, their creators having gone into the ground or the sky or whatever waits for us when the twilight no longer pulls hard enough to keep us here.

I barely have time to adjust to the change in temperature, which goes from "the sun is actively trying to kill you" to "pleasant summer evening" in an instant, before a little girl, maybe seven years old by time spent among the living, races out of the corn and slams into my side, throwing her arms around my waist.

Her hair is long and dark and tied with ribbons, and that's the only reason I recognize her, because her face is buried against my side and her lacy white dress is gone, replaced by jeans and a shirt blazoned with the face of the latest Lowry princess.

"Corletta?" I ask.

She lifts her face and looks at me, and yes, it's her; it's the homestead I met last year, when I was struggling to regain Persephone's blessing. The banked fire that always burns in the back of her eyes is only embers. She's calm, for all that she's crying.

I don't understand how she's here. Corletta's a homestead, a ghost who loved her home so much that when she died, she kept it with her in the twilight, haunting the ashes after the fire had consumed them both. She can't leave her own borders. She's the polar opposite of a road ghost, immobile, fixed . . . and she was nowhere near Alabama when she died.

"Thank you," she says. "Thank you so much, thank you, thank you."

"For what, sweetie?" I don't actually know her very well, certainly don't harbor any misplaced affection for her, although I'm grateful that the last time we met, she didn't try to keep me pinned on her property forever. And that's where I am now. I can feel it in the soles of my feet. I just didn't realize it before, because her farm was built and burned in Oklahoma, and I was in Alabama when I dropped out of the daylight.

Distance is always sort of funny in the twilight. I guess right now, with everything else that's going on, it's even worse than usual. This is the closest to normal anything's been since Antimony pulled her little stunt, and there's nothing I've ever seen among the living or the dead that could change a homestead when they didn't want to be changed.

"You sent the ever-lasters," she says, and her face is innocent and bright. She looks like the child she was when she died, not like the sullen spirit she'd become. "I have *friends*."

In answer, eerie giggles come from the corn all around us, and I relax as much as I can when I'm standing on a homestead's property, which admittedly isn't all that much.

Ever-lasters are the spirits of dead children who can't handle whatever happened to them, but don't have something specific to haunt.

They can't cope with their new condition, and so they go back to school, to a familiar structure and rules they can understand. And sometimes, the rhymes they chant on the blacktop at recess tell the future.

They creep me out. They creep most adult ghosts out, though the ones who don't find them unnerving tend to become their teachers, helping them get over the trauma of their deaths and move on. But I meet a lot of them on the road, and sometimes even dead kids need a summer vacation. I had told several of the larger schools about Corletta's place after meeting her, after she'd said she wanted visitors.

Well, apparently, they listened, and they came, and now she's beaming at me, bright as a summer sky.

"My friends say things are weird as weird gets out in the rest of the twilight," she says. "But everything's normal here, so they've been coming for campouts until it gets calm again. Their teachers came, too, and I'm learning my letters proper. I'll be able to write you soon."

"That's nice." It was, too. Homesteads are less likely to turn toxic when they have people to talk to. I glance around at the endless corn. "Are you playing hide-and-seek?"

"Some of my friends don't like it when adults they don't know see them," she says, and pouts. "They look a little funny, I guess, but that doesn't mean they have to *hide*."

"They can come out. I don't mind."

The corn giggles again, but no children appear.

Corletta scowls, then focuses on me again. "They told me you were coming," she says. "They tell the future sometimes."

"I know. I've heard them."

"But we told this future about you," says a high, clear voice, and a little boy steps out of the corn, one end of a jump rope in his hands and a bullet hole in the middle of his forehead. He looks like he was about Corletta's age when he died; looking at him hurts my heart.

The little girl behind him, holding the other end of the rope, is covered in scabs that never had a chance to heal before the infection carried her away. Children are resilient, right up until they're not, and too many of them wind up here.

"Corletta, will you skip?" asks the boy, and she nods eagerly, pulling away from me and running to the rope. It begins to turn, and I fight the urge to do the same, to turn and run into the corn, to escape whatever fate they've seen for me.

I don't. Hitchers are made for running, but sometimes the right thing to do is stand and see.

"Better be careful, better stay calm, girl in green who missed her prom. Bobby's on the corner, Bobby's on the trail, Diamond Bobby's out to chase your tail." They spin the rope as they chant, and Corletta jumps, fleet and happy and ignorant of the chill that's running through me. "Things are getting harder, things are getting strange, everything you think you know is gonna change. Ocean Lady's counting apples, one two three, go and take your questions to Persephone."

Corletta claps her hands as the chanting stops, and the boy turns to look at me, expression grave.

"I think it's clear what you have to do," he says. "I don't think you have a choice."

I bristle. "I always have a choice."

"True," says the girl. "You could choose not to listen."

"You could choose to lose," says the boy.

"You could choose to be foolish."

"You could choose to let the twilight burn."

Then they turn and walk into the corn, leaving me alone with Corletta, little homestead whose need for me to get this message yanked me here from Alabama, little girl who'll never grow up.

She looks worried. "I don't like fire," she says, the ribbons in her hair beginning to blacken and curl. "I don't want the twilight to burn."

"Don't worry," I say. "It won't. I'll listen." Because the ever-lasters are right, dammit: I really don't have a choice.

No matter what level of reality I'm on, the sun rises and the sun sets, and I like that part best of all. The horizon is a blazing dance of colors when I step back into the daylight, reds and pinks and yellows and oranges, all trending into purple before they deepen into the bruised blue-black of the darkening night sky. I pause to blink at it for a moment. I wasn't in the twilight for all that long, and it looks like I've lost an entire day.

Emma and Gary will be getting worried by now. Emma's my best friend, the *beán sidhe* who currently owns and operates the Last Dance Diner. Gary's my boyfriend.

He's also my car. Things can get weird fast in the lands of the dead.

Well, if they're going to worry, they're worried already, and dwelling on it won't change anything. My skin is tight and tingling, like I've just stepped out of the shower and drenched myself in something astringent, witch hazel and peppermint drawing my flesh taut as a bowstring. I rub my elbow with one hand as I start to walk down the road. It doesn't help. The feeling persists and sharpens, seeming to run all the way down to the surface of my bones. I rub harder. It still doesn't help.

Hitchers are like ferrymen and gather-grims: we're a form of psychopomp. We move between the lands of the living and the lands of the dead with relative ease, and by doing so, we continually stitch those lands together, like a needle stabbing into stacked pieces of felt. It's not good enough to stitch a permanent seam. It still makes a difference. Because I'm a ghost with a job, when I don't *do* that job for too long, reality punishes me. It usually starts small. I lose focus, I lose the ability to control what I'm wearing, I lose my sense of time. It's like being alive again and sleep-deprived at the same time, so everything begins to go fuzzy around the edges. If I keep refusing to rise into the daylight and cock my thumb out for the unwary, it gets worse. I'll start slipping out of phase with the twilight, jumping forward by days or weeks or even months as I lose the right to be here.

If I stayed deep for too long without coming up for the metaphysical equivalent of air, I'd fade, becoming one of those indistinct, indescribable haints that haunt the long stretches of the ghostroads. They're cold spots of air and patches in the grass where nothing grows, where everything is sere and withered even down here in the lands of the dead. They're lost. I've never heard of anyone pulling a haint back into themselves after they've faded, and I've been rambling around for long enough to have heard just about everything.

Fading would mean Bobby Cross could never have me, and that's a good thing. But everything else about it would be horrible. The haints are aware. On some level, they *know* what they've become, and they know it's too late for them. They can't go back to what they were. They can't move on to whatever they were supposed to do or see or become next. They're stuck.

Not me. Rambling roadside Rose doesn't go out like that.

So I'm out of the twilight, and it's still telling me I was deep for too long. Makes sense if I'm losing time. I would have thought the ride I caught in Alabama was enough to take the edge off, but apparently not. I sigh and start walking down the side of the road, thumb cocked high, gravel crunching under the soles of my shoes.

The sun keeps setting, casting everything around me into deeper darkness, but I know this is Ohio. I'd know these endless fields of rippling corn anywhere. If boats could sail on crops instead of water, the cornfields of Ohio would be an inland sea, carrying cargos back and forth on the cornsilk tide.

It's a fun image. I play with it as I walk along the highway verge where I've found myself, hoping to catch the attention of any passing motorists willing to take a chance on me. People are less inclined to pick up hitchhikers than they used to be. I blame it on the horror movies, which have made every person walking across America seem like some sort of calculating serial killer, out to paint their name along the highways in the blood of nice suburban housewives.

Not that all hitchhikers are angels—far from it. Bad things can happen when you let a stranger into your car, whether or not that stranger's alive. People have been assaulted, things have been stolen, drivers have found themselves dumped in the former hitcher's place as their new "friend" roars away in their car. Living people are hungry people, and hungry people make mistakes.

The dead get hungry, too. It's just that our appetites tend to be a little different.

Me, I hunger for rides, for the feeling of a borrowed coat or sweater settling on my shoulders and granting me the illusion of flesh for a few hours. I'm always cold when I'm in the world of the living, even when I'm walking down a country road in the middle of the day. The ice of the grave breeds in my bones where the marrow used to be, and I freeze, and I freeze, and I freeze. When I borrow a coat, I borrow a little of the warmth that comes with it. Sure, it's all symbolic, and yeah, I'm always happy when the coat drops away and I drift back into the twilight, free from the chains of petty mortal flesh, but in the moment, the warmth of the living is my drug of choice.

That, and cheeseburgers. There's some decent food in the twilight—Emma at the Last Dance Diner, especially, makes a mean chocolate cherry malt—but it's not the same as what I can get in the daylight. Cheeseburgers in the twilight are always a little bit too perfect. There's never any char on the onions, never any gristle in the meat. Ghosts eat the platonic ideal of a cheeseburger instead of eating the cheeseburger itself, and while I'm all for the platonic ideal now and then—where by "now and then" we understand that I mean "five nights a week, because I'm dead and don't need to worry about clogging my arteries"—there's nothing like the real thing.

That's why I love Ohio. You can get a decent cheeseburger anywhere in America and almost anywhere in Canada, but there's nowhere on the continent that does frozen custard the way Ohio does. I keep walking, daydreaming of pirates sailing on waves of corn, their holds filled to the bursting with sweet, creamy custard, and feel the weight of the living world settle more and more heavily on my shoulders, like a weighted blanket keeping me anchored to the ground. Yes. This is what I needed, what I went to Alabama looking for, before stupid Bobby came along and ruined everything, the way he always does. I needed to walk the world of the living, to fill my stomach with mortality and cover my feet in honest dirt.

Let the ever-lasters make their prophecies about me as much as they want, and yeah, I'm going to find a way to talk to Persephone, because I take ominous omens seriously. But I'm going to get that cheeseburger first.

A few cars flash by, not slowing down or stopping. I keep walking.

The point for me isn't always *getting* the ride: it's asking for the ride, it's being willing to climb into a stranger's vehicle and put my destination, however briefly, in someone else's hands. For a road ghost, this is the closest thing there is to prayer.

Except for actual prayer, I guess. But now that I know the gods are definitely real and definitely paying attention to me, I find that I'm not very fond of praying. It was a lot more appealing when I thought I would be safely ignored. These days . . .

The consequences of prayer could way too easily be worse than whatever situation I'm praying to get out of. I'll take my chances with functional atheism, thanks.

I don't know how long I walk. Time slips away, dulled into the pleasant background whistle of the wind blowing through the corn and the occasional hum of tires on the pavement, driver after driver passing me by. Eventually, I'll have to come to a rest stop, someplace with bathrooms and soda machines, and it's always easier to find someone to drive me from one of those. People feel more like they have to engage when they're face-to-face with a lost girl like me. Or maybe I'll come to a neon-and-chrome oasis in this verdant desert, a truck stop diner where I can convince some soft-hearted trucker to buy me a plate of fries. Doesn't matter which it is, not really. Both have their charms, and both are somewhere up ahead of me in the great wide somewhere else, waiting for my arrival.

I'm so deep in my own thoughts that I don't immediately notice when the red pickup truck pulls up next to me. It's a relatively recent model, introduced to the roads in the last fifteen years; it has that dully generic look I've come to associate with pickups. They're all individuals, of course, but it takes someone who really loves them to tell them apart. This one is the bright cherry red of arterial spray, a comparison that's strengthened by the patches of rust the color of dried blood that dot its flanks and fenders.

The passenger side window rolls down. The driver leans across the cab so she can see me, so I can see her.

"Hey," she says. "Going my way?"

Her hair is black and streaked with faded lilac, shoulder-length and somehow windswept even though the warm air escaping from the cab tells me she's had her windows up for miles. She's wearing jeans and a black T-shirt with silver foil printing on the front, so cracked and faded that it forms a runic scrawl instead of the name of the band it was originally intended to advertise. She looks like she's about the age my mother was when she died, which means she's so much younger than me that it's ridiculous. Time is a toll road, and it never gives back as much as it takes.

Her accent is Irish, like my friend Emma's, and her smile is sunshine on a country road, wrinkling her nose and exposing the gap between her front teeth.

"Bon," I say, only half-surprised. I tend to attract routewitches when we're in the same area. I would have been one, if I hadn't died the way I did. Between that and their natural affinity for road ghosts, they're well-inclined toward me. But the last time I saw *this* routewitch, she was standing sentry on the Ocean Lady, and we're nowhere near that ancient, august thoroughfare. "What are you doing here?"

"Offering you a ride, of course," she says. "Unless you'd like to turn me down?"

This smells like a trap, or like the next step in fulfilling the prophecy seen by the ever-lasters. Bon shouldn't be here. I'm in the middle of nowhere, Ohio, and while a random routewitch would be an understandable coincidence, a routewitch I already know is a stretch. But oh, everything I am aches to get into that truck. I hitchhike. It's what the twilight crafted me to do. That means I ask for rides, and it means I accept them when they're offered. To do anything else is to say that I know better than the road.

"I guess I'm going your way," I say, and open the door, climbing into the truck. Bon already has the jacket in her hand, a light windbreaker almost the exact green of my prom dress. I slip it on and feel the gravity settle over my bones, weighing me down.

"Next stop, adventure," says Bon, and hits the gas, and—wow—do I hope she's wrong.

Chapter 3
Under the Cornfield Sky

I'LL GIVE BON ONE THING: she knows these roads as only a local or a routewitch can, finding an unmarked offramp that takes us through a farmer's field on our way to a narrow frontage road lined with apple trees. They're not fruiting right now, but we crack the windows to let the sweet smell of sap and apple blossoms work its way inside, until we're bursting out of the orchard and onto a slightly wider, equally bumpy street that takes us into something that looks more like a time-slipped frontier outpost than an actual town.

There are ten buildings, maybe fifteen if I'm generous with the way I count garages and rickety farm stands. Two gas stations, a bait shop, a pawn shop . . . and a diner, grimed gray with road dust, neon sign not even bright enough to attract moths, barely clinging to fitful, flickering life.

I give Bon a dubious look. She laughs.

"Best Shaker lemon pie in the county, I swear," she says. "Their cheeseburgers aren't bad either."

I want to be suspicious, but the promise of cheeseburgers *and* pie from someone I already know to be, if not a friend, then at least an ally, is too much for me. "Works," I say, and open the door, sliding out of the truck.

The air changes when my feet hit the pavement. The smell of lilies and ashes drifts by on the wind, and even though I'm still draped in borrowed mortality, I feel a needle of cold lance through my bones. I look across the hood of the truck in open-mouthed dismay, radiating betrayal. Bon meets my eyes and shrugs.

"Sorry," she says. "If it helps at all, I wasn't kidding about the pie. It's the best I've ever had, and I've had a lot of pie."

Somehow, this time, pie doesn't help. Pie feels frankly inconsequential, maybe even insulting, when compared to the weight of the storm I can feel bearing down on me. Whatever this is, whatever it means, I don't like it.

"Shall we go inside?" asks Bon.

I want to say no. I want to strip off the coat she gave me and use the last of my corporeality to fling it at her as I drop into the twilight, getting myself the hell away from whatever this is and whatever it's going to mean. I close my mouth, eyes narrowing.

The ever-lasters found me in their playground rhymes. Bobby Cross is desperate enough to threaten everyone I love. Whatever's happening here, it's something I have to see through to the finish line, whether I like the idea or not.

"Yeah, okay," says Bon. "I guess we're not chatty friends anymore. That's fine, but I don't get to move along until I've delivered you safely, so if you could go inside, I'd appreciate it. I can't be standing around here all night long, not when I've things I need to be doing."

She still looks utterly relaxed. Whatever dreadful doom is hanging over my head isn't hanging over hers. Still, she might be able to give me a little more information before I walk into my own doom. "What's in there?"

"Pie," she says. "Cheeseburgers. And someone who wants to talk to you, badly enough to be willing to pick up the check. She said this felt like neutral ground to her. More so than that diner you're usually haunting."

The Last Dance Diner is a landmark of the twilight, and not only because it's as mercurial as everything else you'll find along the ghostroads. When true danger looms, it has a tendency to change its neon sign from green to red, and shift all of its menus from the Last Dance to the Last Chance.

The pie at the Last Chance is no good, but the cheeseburgers are to die for. Possibly literally.

The current owner of the diner, whatever face it's wearing at the time, is my friend Emma—I've mentioned her before. The American ghostroads are a long, long way from the green hills of Ireland. That didn't stop her from following the family she keened for across the ocean several generations ago, and when they died out, she stopped haunting the living in favor of feeding the dead. It's something to occupy her time until she figures out what she's doing next. People like Emma, they're not ghosts. They're not alive, either. They're something else altogether, part of the strange ecosystem of the twilight, born deep in the midnight, and it's best not to ask too many questions. There's always a chance they'll be answered, and that's not going to work out well for anyone.

It's not hard to see why someone would look at the Last Dance and see it as other than neutral territory. Emma and I have been through a lot together, and at this point, well. It's hard to say "ride or die" when you're already dead. "Ride or exorcism" might be closer. There's not much she wouldn't do for me. There's not much I wouldn't do for her.

Which makes this whole situation stink like old gym socks. "I'm not sure I want to talk to anyone who wouldn't be welcome at the Last Dance," I say.

Bon shakes her head, strolling closer so she's not shouting across the hood of the truck. "It's not that she wouldn't be welcome. You'd be welcome in her places. It's that she wants this meeting to happen in a place where neither of you is necessarily in a position of power over the other. It's a mark of respect. Please, let her respect you, and let me get on my way. I'm supposed to be vending at a swap meet in Florida first thing in the morning, and it's already going to take bending the rules of the road in some inadvisable ways for me to get there on time to set up."

When a routewitch says she's going to bend the rules of the road, she doesn't mean breaking traffic laws. She means changing the way distance works, twisting it back on itself until she's traveling in the sweet embrace of a tesseract, miles blurring into feet, feet becoming inches, delivering her to her destination in a fraction of the time it should have taken. It's not cheap, warping the road like that. It's not *easy*. I eye Bon with wary respect. If she can make it to Florida by morning, she's stronger than I assumed she was, and a lot more dangerous.

She sees the change in my demeanor and sighs. "Is there *any* chance we could do this like civilized people?" she asks. "You keep company with a *beán sidhe,* and I'd rather not get on her bad side, which means avoiding yours."

"How would civilized people do this?"

"They would agree that standing out here arguing doesn't do any good." She looks at me solemnly. "I didn't lure you out of the twilight, you came on your own. Saints and angels know it's possible to summon a hitcher to somewhere she doesn't need or want to be, but that doesn't make it a good idea. We know enough of how you operate to know that when the air clears, you tend to appear where you need to be. No interference, no magic, just plain and simple need put you into my path, close enough to the diner as to be a short and easy errand. I've done you neither ill nor evil, nor interfered in the natural way of things. So please do me the immense favor of getting your eternally underaged ass into this damn diner and letting me go on my way."

I raise an eyebrow. "How long were you workshopping that?"

"A little while," she admits. "I'm particularly proud of 'eternally underaged ass.'"

"Poetic," I agree. "All right. We could be here all night, so I'm going to just ask you: the person inside absolutely means me no harm, is not going to attempt to magically compel me, and is not secretly working either for or with Bobby Cross, correct?"

"Correct," says Bon. "You're a suspicious spirit, Rose Marshall."

"I have good reason to be."

She can't argue with that. The last time I intentionally met someone in a diner, she turned out to be Bobby's patsy. I don't blame her anymore. Laura Moorhead had been mourning her boyfriend and blaming me for his death for decades by the time Bobby had approached her and offered her what must have seemed like the deal of a lifetime. And it *was* the deal of a lifetime, really, because trying to keep it—and seeing the light and breaking it—had been the end of her. She'd died in my arms, like so many others before her, and the last I'd seen her, she'd been tucked safe in Tommy's passenger seat, his eyes on the horizon as he drove them both toward whatever waited on the other side of the ghostroads.

I hope they're happy now, wherever they are, and if they're not, I hope that they're at least together. They deserve that much. Laura and I may have had our differences, but I never once doubted her love for Tommy, and they didn't get the life they should have had with each other. They should get a gentle afterlife.

"I swear to you that the person you're here to meet means you no harm, harbors no ill will toward you, and is absolutely *not* working with Bobby Cross in any capacity, willing or unwilling." Bon raises one hand, fingers folded in a complicated pattern that's something like a scout's prayer and something like a Vulcan salute and something like an anatomical violation. They seem to waver where they cross over one another, as if they don't want me looking at them.

So I stop looking at them. I mean, hey, I'm as curious about the world around me as the next dead teenager, but I've been on the ghostroads long enough to understand that when something doesn't want to be seen, it's not my place to try and force the issue. That's the sort of behavior that gets people shoved into spirit jars and forgotten about for a couple of decades. Not my idea of a good time.

"Fine," I say.

Bon blinks at my sudden capitulation. "Fine?" she echoes. "Just fine?"

"You're clearly going to argue with me until I go in. I'm tired, I'm cold, you would not *believe* the day I've had, and I want a cheeseburger. So fine. I'm going inside, and you're going to Florida."

Bon smiles, sharp and sudden, and bends to embrace me before I have the chance to step away. She smells faintly of asphalt and lemon-lime soda, the cheap generic stuff they sell in truck stops around the country, the kind that tastes the way little kids think floor cleaner will taste, sweet and bitter and artificial and somehow addictive.

Lips close to my ear, she murmurs, "You should have been the best of us, Rose Marshall. You should have been the one who caught and kept the damn horizon."

Then she's letting me go and stepping away, heading back to her truck, back to her destination, back to whatever journey she was on before she was pulled loose and set on hitchhiking ghost duty. She doesn't look back. Routewitches very rarely do. They learned their lessons from Orpheus.

When you look back, you lose your heart's desire.

I shiver a little at the thought, remembering my own time in the Underworld, which is a very different place from the afterlife. Twilight, starlight, and all the levels in-between, they're essentially mortal places. Not human—not all of us were human when we were alive, and even if we were, not all of us stay human after we die—but *mortal*. We know what it was to be alive. To walk in the light and breathe in the air and believe in our own immortality.

The Underworld is different. Oh, it houses the spirits of the dead, just like the twilight does, and it's tied inextricably to the lands of the living, because it matters too much to ever be fully sundered, but the forces that craft it never belonged to anything mortal, and the Lord and Lady of the Dead . . . they're like Emma. They were never alive. They're ancient and terrible and beautiful and I would lay down my soul for them if they asked me. I wouldn't have a choice in the matter. Which makes them terrifying.

I turn toward the diner. Diners aren't terrifying. Terrible things can happen in diners—I've been present for some of those terrible things, have been witness and participant and unwilling psychopomp of the aftermath—but the diners themselves stay essentially the same. Solid and welcoming, way stations on the road between here and hereafter.

The door sticks a little when I push against it, scraping on linoleum too old and too worn to be slippery, to shine. The air is overly air-conditioned for the evening chill. It tastes stale against the back of my throat, but it smells like grease and fried potatoes, like butter and whipped cream from a can. All the best things the world of the living has to offer, all the things that would keep me coming back over and over again, even if the road didn't demand it.

The bell over the door jingles as it swings back into position. I don't move.

The waitress says something to me, a greeting, maybe, or an invitation to sit wherever I like, she'll be with me in a moment. She's wearing a uniform so perfect that it's practically parody, belled sleeves and hairnet and a white apron just stained enough around the edges not to look like a prop. I don't move.

Someone calls for a refill. I don't move.

The reason for my stillness tilts her chin upward in invitation. The neon streaming weakly through the filthy windows sparks glints of gold and silver off her hair, like she's dressed in all the riches the world has to offer. It throws a robe of dancing dust motes around her shoulders, haloing her in light, and she's beautiful, and she's terrible, and she's not supposed to be here. She's not supposed to be anywhere in the daylight because the daylight is *dangerous*. The daylight has death and time and all those other natural forces that she's supposed to be exempt from, for as long as she keeps her place, for as long as she wears the crown.

I don't move, until the Queen of the Routewitches—definitely of North America, maybe of the whole damn world, and how is this happening? This can't be happening—raises her hand and beckons me forward, and maybe it's the coat around my shoulders, the coat that belonged to a routewitch, that drapes my borrowed bones in phantom flesh, but I start walking. I don't want to. It doesn't matter. I was supposed to be a routewitch, would have been a routewitch if Bobby Cross hadn't decided I looked like a girl he wanted to swallow whole, and right now I'm technically alive, and that means she's the boss of me. I don't have a choice. When she calls, I come. When she calls, I'll always, always come.

"Hello, Rose," says Apple once I'm close enough that she doesn't have to raise her voice. "Care to join me?"

"Not really," I say. I slide into the booth across from her anyway. The vinyl is cracked and flaking, as old as the diner around it, or maybe older. Some of these roadside dives are built from the bones of the

diners that lived and died before they were conceived of by their owners. I wouldn't be the least bit surprised to hear that all these booths
were scavenged from somewhere else, that I'm sitting in an American
graveyard, surrounded by the ghosts of a thousand late night cups of
coffee and a couple hundred slices of pie.

Food doesn't usually leave actual ghosts behind. I'd eat a lot better
if it did.

"Sorry about that," says Apple.

I eye her. "No, you're not."

"No, I'm not, but it seemed like the polite thing to say." She picks
up her milkshake. The glass is thick and heavy. That's an old trick. It
looks so much bigger than it is. It's also about half empty, although I
can see enough to know that it was chocolate, and that it was probably
delicious.

Apple swirls the straw in the brownish sludge, ice cream streaked
with whipped cream, and it looks amazing, and I've never wanted a
milkshake less in my entire death.

"Sorry," she says, glancing at me. Maybe she can see my discomfort
in my eyes. Maybe she even cares. "I know you don't want to be here,
but this seemed better than, you know." She makes a gesture with one
hand. Presumably, it's meant to indicate "having you kidnapped and
dragged onto the Ocean Lady so we can have a talk."

She's done that before. Sent her goons to sweep me away from
whatever I'm doing and haul me off to do what she *thinks* I should be
doing, which is mostly whatever she wants. She feels responsible for
Bobby Cross' existence: she was there when he went to the crossroads,
and she didn't do anything to stop him. And that's all well and good,
and I would be one hell of a lot happier if she'd take her guilt somewhere else and leave me out of it.

"Right," I say. "You know. What I don't know is why I'm here. Why
am I here, Apple? What can the Queen of the Routewitches possibly
want from dead little ol' me?"

She puts down her glass and looks at me solemnly, not saying a
word.

This is Apple, Queen of the Routewitches, possibly the most

powerful living person I've ever met: she's tiny. She looks like she's the same age I am, which is a neat trick, since she's never died and we're both decades older than the faces we wear. Apple's been sixteen longer than I have, but not by all that much; she took her place on the Ocean Lady shortly after World War II. Before that, she'd been hitchhiking her way across America, gathering power with every mile she traveled, pulling it out of the air, out of the water . . . out of the road beneath her feet.

Routewitches get their power from distance. Apple started in California and ended up in Maine, trading one ocean for another, until the highway she walked along somehow slipped out of the daylight and into the twilight. Humans don't belong on the ghostroads—not living humans, anyway—but the Ocean Lady makes her own rules and takes what she wants, and back then, she wanted Apple. Wanted her real, real bad. I've never been sure how a road can want things. Not that it matters, because the Ocean Lady isn't only a road. She's a goddess. Man-made, sure, weaker than Persephone, absolutely, and a goddess all the same.

It's never a good idea to argue with the divine. The consequences can be pretty dire.

I don't know what Apple's name was before she took the name she wears now, but she's lovely, Japanese American with brown eyes and black hair and lips that always look like they're on the verge of smiling. She probably wasn't that pretty when she stumbled into the twilight, not after all the miles she'd traveled, not after the travails of Manzanar, where she'd been imprisoned before she broke loose and ran away. And sometimes I look at the way the world of the living has gone since my death, and I wonder if maybe where she came from isn't part of why the Ocean Lady wanted her so badly. Apple has already experienced some of the worst of what people can do to each other. There aren't many surprises left on her side of the grave.

"All right, I'll bite," I say. "What was so important that you had to order Bon to track me down and bring me to you?"

"Don't you want me to order something for you first?" she asks. "Anything you want. My treat."

Food almost always tastes better in the lands of the living. It's something about the air. Maybe it's something about *needing* air. But there's a catch to keep us hungry ghosts from devouring the world in our eagerness to fill what can never be filled: we only get to taste our food when someone gives it to us willingly and without being somehow forced. Bobby ruined my dinner. My stomach grumbles. My throat is dry. I could kill for a piece of pie and a cup of coffee, and I could kill time consuming them, stretch out the moment before she tells me what mattered this much until the idea of answers frightens me a little bit less.

Or I could say to hell with it and rip the bandage off.

"Tell me," I say.

Apple sighs. It's a deep, mournful sound. One of the truckers at the counter goes pale, his eyes raising from his eggs and bacon and fixing on a point somewhere outside the horizon, like he thinks he can see eternity from here. The waitress drops a coffee mug. It shatters when it hits the floor. It's the loudest thing I've ever heard. Whatever's coming, it's not something I'm going to enjoy. But then, I knew that when I sat down.

"The crossroads are dead," she says.

Silence falls across the diner like a shroud, muffling everything, wrapping me in a quiet so profound that it's like returning to the grave. I frown at her, trying to figure out why she's telling me something that's patently obvious to anyone who's set foot in virtually any layer of the twilight since Annie and her friends left Maine. I wasn't sure up until now whether the crossroads were actually *dead* or just severely damaged—I'll have to let Annie know she did the job right. She'd been asking herself the same thing the last time I saw her, but when you're limping away from the monster's lair to lick your wounds, you don't necessarily want to go back in to poke the corpse.

So they're dead. The balance of power in the twilight has shifted in a permanent, profound manner, and Bobby's panic over how he's going to keep paying his share of his devil's bargain suddenly makes a lot more sense . . . as does the ever-lasters' exhortation that I go and speak with Persephone.

Apple regards my lack of surprise with baffled concern, and neither of us says anything. The silence stretches out like a thread of
pulled taffy until she leans to the side and flags down our waitress, who
is probably twenty but looks forty, although she might be sixty—forty
is the sweet spot for truck stop waitresses, and something about the
place will age them either up or down at its whim, until it settles them
in that eternal, somehow desirable degree of middle age. The ones who
stay teens or age past forty are only ever here to go, on their way to
some position of permanence, while the ones like ours seem to last just
shy of forever.

Apple casts a sweet smile at the waitress, and says, "My friend
would like a cheeseburger, rare, with fries and a vanilla malt. Please
excuse her. She's just had a bit of a shock."

The waitress shoots me a sympathetic look and bustles off to place
the order, which will be up in minutes if I'm right about the kind of
place this is. Diners that look this rundown and still keep the lights on
are very, very good at what they do.

Apple returns her attention to me. "You don't seem as surprised as
I thought you would," she says.

"There's a reason for that," I reply. "Even if there weren't a reason,
have you *seen* the twilight recently? It's like a fucked-up Halloween fun
fair in there. The sun just tried to eat me. The *actual sun*. So no, I'm
not surprised."

"If you knew—"

"If I knew, then what? I don't belong to you, Apple. Even when I'm
wearing a coat, I'm still dead. And you made it very clear to me when
I was alive that we could never be friends with the way things are."

Routewitches pull power from distance. I've been hitchhiking for
seventy years. You do the math. The way things stand right now, I'm the
only person who potentially has the power to unseat Apple from the
Ocean Lady, and she knows it. When I was rendered temporarily
among the living by a plot of Bobby's, Apple didn't hesitate to assert her
dominance and make sure I remembered who was really the one in
charge. As Queen, she can spend the distance of others. She spent some
of mine. I didn't approve. I still don't.

Apple frowns, worrying her lip between her teeth. She looks like she's about to speak when the food arrives, picture-perfect cheeseburger and hot, crispy fries, along with a tall glass of vanilla malt and the metal cup that holds the overflow. Milkshakes and malts have gotten a lot bigger since I was alive. One of the few things I can absolutely and unreservedly say has improved about the world during my death.

Apple waits until the waitress walks away to solemnly say, "This food is for you, the honored dead, and the living have no claim over it," which is the fanciest way of saying "you can have this" I've ever heard, but it works: the food is ritually ceded to me, and the smell of grease, melting cheese, and sweet vanilla snaps into focus. My stomach rumbles. Stupid, traitorous stomach.

I take a fry. It's hot enough to almost burn my tongue, crisp exterior giving way to mealy interior, almost liquid in that way potatoes have when they're fresh from the fryer and haven't had time to remember that they came from the dirt, came from a place of stillness and solidity. They'll be awful when they're cold, all limp and soggy, but right now, they taste like what I assume the air is like in Heaven, if Heaven exists. Hot French fry wind and vanilla malt clouds, that's paradise. If I knew for certain that I'd end up there, I might be willing to move on.

I swallow and reach for the cheeseburger. Apple is still worrying her lip between her teeth, expression torn between hurt and confusion.

Finally, the silence is too much for her. "What do you know?" she blurts.

Apple looks genuinely upset at this point. She's not the boss of me, but she's still the boss of the routewitches, and I'm a road ghost; she could make my existence fairly unpleasant if she wanted to. I grab my milkshake and take a fortifying gulp, malt and sweet ice cream running down my throat like a blessing. Malts are something Apple and I have in common. I'll never understand how they were allowed to fall out of fashion.

"I didn't know they were actually *dead*, so thanks for confirming that for me," I say, and put the glass aside, grabbing another fry. "I was a little worried they'd just been seriously hurt and were going to come back pissed. Dead is better. Most of the time, dead is better."

"I didn't ask you what you *don't* know, I asked you what you *did*," she snaps, and winces, looking briefly, terribly weary. "I'm sorry, Rose. I'm so accustomed to dealing with routewitches who don't question me that sometimes I forget other people might not be so understanding."

"Forgiven," I say. It doesn't matter whether I mean it or not. What matters is moving forward, ploughing ahead down this strange, dark road, toward whatever unseen destination is waiting for me. "I really need you to explain what we're doing here, though. I get that this is a big enough deal for you to be willing to leave the Ocean Lady, but why am I here? Why *me*?"

"Because where you go, chaos tends to follow," says Apple. "You're not an ordinary hitcher, Rose Marshall."

"Never got the chance to be." It's hard to keep the bitterness out of my voice.

I don't even know if I was supposed to *be* a hitcher, and I never will. Maybe I wasn't supposed to linger at all. Was my unfinished business—a grieving but relieved mother, a heartbroken prom date, an untaken math test—really enough to keep me here? I should have been a route-witch. Should have been a wife, a mother, a whole lot of things . . . and if I became a ghost, I should have been the one to set the shape of my haunting.

Not Bobby when he ran me off the road, and not Gary when he slung his coat around my shoulders. *Me.* So many of my choices were stolen by men who should have known better, or who didn't know any better themselves. And that's never going to happen again.

Apple seems to realize she's struck a nerve. She pauses, taking a breath, and says, "There a lot of ways to kill the dead. You've experienced some of them."

She's not wrong. I take another gulp of my milkshake to cover my annoyance. Once I've swallowed, I say, "I'm one person. Weird or not, I'm not even the most dangerous kind of ghost. Hell, a white lady or a gather-grim would be a lot harder to take down than one little hitch-hiker. Killing me is easy. If you called me here because you think I killed the crossroads, you're wrong. I've never had that kind of power."

"And yet it happened," says Apple. "We're still trying to find out exactly how, both so we can thank whoever was responsible, and because if someone out there has figured out a way to kill *ideas*, we have to be sure they won't be coming for the Ocean Lady." Her expression hardens, becoming something much older than her apparent years. "Every routewitch in the world would answer to me if they allowed any harm to come to Her."

So she doesn't know that Antimony was the one who struck the killing blow, and I don't think I want to tell her. The Prices are no blood kin of mine, but they're deeply important to Mary, and I've had a few generations to grow fond of them. They call me "Aunt Rose," and I feel responsible for their well-being. Not always the most comfortable position to be in as regards a family of monster hunters with no common sense or belief in their own mortality, but still, I'll be damned if I'll put Antimony in Apple's crosshairs.

Especially because while the crossroads weren't a god, they held similar levels of power. Big power, too big for the world as we know and understand it to easily contain. Something that could kill them could absolutely threaten the Lady. Even being moored in the twilight wouldn't be enough to protect her, because the crossroads were never a part of the daylight. Reaching them, rendering them vulnerable . . . it took travel. I've led more than a few people to the crossroads in my time, when I didn't have a way to tell them "no."

The thought hits me like a rock striking a windshield. I sit up straighter, eyes going wide as I stare at Apple. "Bethany—"

"Your niece is on the Ocean Lady, being kept from dissipating until I've had the chance to talk to you."

Of course she is. I scowl as I slump back in my seat. "You mean you're planning to use her to blackmail me."

Apple shrugs. "Only if you don't leave me any other choice. I think you will, honestly. I think you're enough of a routewitch to want to help."

I don't say anything.

I died at sixteen. My brothers didn't. They grew up, they mourned me, and they moved on. They left our childhood home to molder— good riddance—and they had lives. They had big, tangled, wonderful, messy, *human* lives. They had children, and those children had children, and one of those descendants, my brother Arthur's grand-daughter, was a girl named Bethany. Bethany, who heard the call of the road the same way I did but didn't have the power to reach for it. Bethany, who *wanted*. Every day of her life, that girl wanted. She wanted to be strong and she wanted to be free and she wanted to put Buckley Township behind her.

Poor, confused, terrible, sad Bethany.

Bobby Cross—see how he keeps popping up over and over again, like the world's worst jack-in-the-box? My life would have been so much easier if he had never made his way to the crossroads—had been looking for a way to hurt me, and he'd stumbled across Bethany, little girl with a blood tie to the ghost who got away. He managed to convince her he could give her everything she'd ever wanted, if only she'd give him what he wanted most. Me. She offered him me and he offered her the world, and when she couldn't deliver, he did what Bobby always does. He took the balance out of her soul.

Bethany was a stupid teenager when she ran afoul of Bobby Cross. He left her old before her time, ripping her youth away and feeding it into the engine of his damned car. He would have done worse if not for the fact that the very thing that attracted him to her—our blood relationship—insulated her from the worst of his assault. Persephone's blessing travels down bloodlines, and it protected Bethany's soul from his machinations. Not thoroughly enough, but it was something.

Not something Bethany could live with. She went to Apple and petitioned for an escort to the crossroads—a position that had, due to family relationship and a sliver of responsibility, fallen to me. I took Bethany to the crossroads. I did my duty as a psychopomp and her great-aunt.

I couldn't protect her from the crossroads. I could never have protected her from the crossroads. They were bigger and stronger and more terrifying than me, and they took what they wanted. They took her life. They made her a teenager again, sure, but a teenage ghost, just like me, the aunt she hated, the aunt she betrayed, and they took her into their service, bound to them the same way Mary was, reshaped in their image, designed to test and broker the bargains made by desperate souls like she had been, like Bobby had been, like so many others still were.

I didn't save her. I never had a chance.

"Bethany is our guest," says Apple, snapping my attention back to her. She's watching me, not wary, not exactly, but careful, like a lion tamer watches a lion. It's anyone's guess whether I could actually do her harm here, with the Ocean Lady miles and levels of reality away from us. I'd have to be a fool to try it.

On the Old Atlantic Highway, Apple's power is effectively limitless. She doesn't travel. That's strange for a routewitch, but it's necessary for their ruler, who is supposed to be accessible at all times, which means stationary. The other routewitches bring her offerings of distance, and she squirrels them away, growing in power, solidifying her position, capable of using them to do virtually anything. Given the right place to stand, Apple could break the world.

But she's not from *this* world anymore. She's a voluntary exile, and she doesn't understand how things really work because she's not a part of them. This is my world more than hers. She doesn't belong here.

"What do you mean, 'dissipating'?" I ask.

"Bethany is the newest crossroads ghost we've been able to find," she says. "There may have been others her age, but I think she's probably the newest to survive. She was unwinding around the edges when we stumbled across her. I know that must seem convenient to you, that your niece should be the sole survivor, but I swear on the interchanges that it wasn't intentional. We felt the crossroads drop away. We felt something new rising up to fill their place. We went to investigate—we had no choice, given our relationship to the roads—and one of my people found her, clinging to the fabric of the twilight with fingers already beginning to fray. They wrapped her in a shell of offramps and wrong turns, hiding her from reality's eyes, and they brought her to the Ocean Lady to ask what could be done."

I want to call bullshit. I want to say there's no way her people "just happened" to stumble over Bethany while they were out there investigating the enormous, unwanted question of where the crossroads had gone. I want to throw my milkshake in her face.

I don't do any of those things. Because the fact of the matter is that the routewitches serve the road and the road serves the routewitches. It's a perfect symbiosis that flows in both directions at the same time, and if Bethany, who was a potential routewitch when she was alive, didn't want to vanish into the ether, the road would have done its best to help her hold on. It's professional courtesy as much as anything else. As for the living routewitches, their relationship with the crossroads has always been strained at best, like people trying to live in a house occupied by a hostile wild beast that attacks anyone foolish enough to stumble into its path. They went looking because they had to. They found Bethany because the road wanted them to. It's as simple, and as complicated, as that.

Apple sighs as she looks at me. "Because Bethany is so new, she doesn't have anything else tying her to the ghostroads or to the twilight in general. She might be able to find a new calling. She might not. If she can't, she's going to move on. She doesn't have a choice."

Meaning my niece could find out real soon whether or not there's anything beyond the afterlife where we've been existing since our respective deaths. "That sucks for her," I say.

Apple blinks. "I thought you'd be more concerned."

"Why? Because she's family?" I don't have to force my laugh. "She never gave a damn about me. The first time we met, she did her best to bind me to the daylight long enough for Bobby Cross to shove me into his gas tank. We're not exactly friends."

"She was his victim as surely as you were."

"No." I pick up the cheeseburger, turning it around in my hands, admiring the symmetry of it. No cheeseburger is perfect, but some of them come closer than others. This one is pretty close. The bun is lightly toasted and golden brown; the cheese is dripping seductively down the sides, already starting to solidify, not yet congealing. I take a bite. It tastes better than it looks. I chew, I swallow, and I look at Apple again.

"No," I repeat, with more confidence this time. We're not talking about the crossroads anymore. We're talking about my family. "She made a choice. He hurt her, absolutely, but she wasn't his victim like I was, because I never did *anything*. Not to him, not to her, not to the crossroads. I was innocent. I was a kid. Bethany brought this on her own head."

"She was a kid, too," says Apple. "She didn't understand what she was doing."

"That excuse has never worked on a natural disaster. The crossroads were a natural disaster. Bobby Cross *is* a natural disaster."

"Unnatural disaster might be more accurate, but point taken." Apple dips one of her own fries in her milkshake and sighs. "I thought this would be easier."

"Because my love of Bethany is *so* well documented?"

"No. Because your hate of Bobby Cross is so well documented." Apple looks at me across the table. "The crossroads are dead. Their ghosts are fading. Bobby Cross has no patron. That's why I'm here. That's why I've had my routewitches watching for you for the last week."

I stare in silence as she continues.

"Bobby Cross is vulnerable. Without the crossroads to protect him, I think he can be destroyed. So will you do it, Rose? I could call on the world's expectations of the Phantom Prom Date, I could invoke the Walking Girl and see what wearing her story would do to you, but I'd rather go straight to the heart of the matter. I'd rather ask you, as kindly and as clearly as I can. I think I owe you that much."

"Why?" I whisper.

"Because if anyone can do it, you can. So will you? Will you go to where the crossroads were, and find the trail, and finish the job? Will you kill Bobby Cross?"

Chapter 4
The Hard and the Easy

HER QUESTION RINGS IN THE DINER air like a bell, silver and dull and sweet and broken, all at the same time. I stare at her across the table, unable to find any words that would suffice to answer her. Finally, just as the silence turns truly awkward, I realize what they have to be.

"Fuck you," I say, and pick up my cheeseburger again. It's cooled a bit, but it's still delicious. I focus on shoving as much of it as I possibly can into my face, interspersing bites with snorting slurps of milkshake, and it's all amazing, and that's a good thing, since I figure there's a non-zero chance that this is going to be my literal last meal.

Routewitches can manipulate the twilight to a certain degree. It's not their primary role in the universe, but since when has that stopped anybody? They're still human, which makes them petty and vindictive and all those other awesome things people excel at being. A baby routewitch can control when and where I pop into the twilight, warding roadways and cities against me, making my afterlife a lot more difficult than it has to be. They generally don't because it's hard on them—it takes a lot of energy, and since most ghosts don't go out of our way to cheese the routewitches off, we all sort of keep our professional distance from one another. I've been summoned a few times as well as warded out of a few homes that didn't feel like they were in the market for a haunting, but on the whole, we're big into staying out of each other's way.

Of course, again, petty and vindictive, and I've met more than a few routewitches who would be *happy* to deny the dead access to the lands of the living if they had the power to do it. Some of them think they'd be doing the right thing, encouraging us to rest in peace instead of cropping up in truck stops and shopping malls and wherever else our phantasmal feet take us. Others don't give a crap about the right thing. They just want the dead to remember who's in charge here.

Apple has that kind of power.

Apple has the power of all the routewitches in North America and some of the routewitches elsewhere. She sizzles with strength. She can bend the world any way she wants, and when she does, it listens. She could have pulled me out of the twilight any time she wanted to. She could have sent living routewitches down roads the living are never supposed to see, all for the dubious pleasure of hauling me to her throne. I know what happens if I decide to tell her "no."

Ghosts whose nature doesn't require them to interact with the living in order to maintain themselves can deal with being cut off from the daylight. They may not enjoy it, but they'll be fine. Me . . .

I'll fade away. I'll disappear into the haze of screaming spirits that haunts the path between the Underworld and the rest of reality, and I guess that's a mercy because, while they're aware of themselves, they don't remember who they were, which means they can't remember everything they've lost. I keep eating, mechanically, methodically, stuffing my face as fast as I can without choking. If this is the end of me, I want to go out the way I've always gone on: with a cheeseburger in my hands and a cynical expression on my face, daring the world to do its worst.

I don't know why I keep doing that. The world is always happy to oblige.

"You don't have to eat like a dog expecting to be kicked," says Apple. "I'm not going to do anything to you."

I cock an eyebrow as I swallow. "You'll forgive me if I don't believe you," I say. "It's not like you hear the word 'no' very often."

"Oh, I do, it's just usually paired with 'please,' not 'fuck you.'" Briefly, Apple looks amused. "Sometimes I wish you'd survived to come to the Ocean Lady on your own. We could have been really good friends in a world where we both had a heartbeat at the same time."

"I doubt that."

Apple waves a hand, like she can brush my doubts away. Hell, maybe she can. I don't know what all comes with being a Queen in the sense she is, and I've never been overly interested in finding out. "We couldn't be friends when you were suddenly alive again in this time period because you've traveled too far. You're a threat to my dominion. But if you'd escaped the wreck and found your way to the Ocean Lady, like you were meant to do, we could have been teenagers together, forever. You could have been my most trusted adviser."

"Yeah, and we would have done each other's nails and gossiped about everyone we'd ever had a crush on, I know the drill," I say. Maybe she's right and maybe she's wrong and maybe it doesn't matter even a little because that world never got the chance to come to pass. I died. It's as simple as that. Apple ran away from home—if a concentration camp set up by the United States government for its Japanese-American citizens can really be called "home"—and I died, and we were never teenagers together, even though that's exactly what we look like to the people around us.

Daylight people. They may understand that they walk on a thin shell of normalcy above an endless well of weird, but if they're lucky, they'll never crack it, never fall into the dark places they spend their lives trying to avoid. To them, Apple and I are two kids sneaking out after curfew to get milkshakes, little hooligans in training but not really their problem. They don't look at us and see a routewitch so powerful that she's stepped outside the flow of time for personal reasons, or a ghost wearing borrowed flesh and filling her phantom stomach with offerings. They're normal, so in their eyes we get to be normal, too, if only for a little while.

Then one of the men in the booth next to ours gets up, leaving a handful of crumpled bills on the table, and sneers at us as he heads for the door. "Dykes." He spits the word like a stone, like it's something he can throw.

I'm halfway to my feet before Apple grabs my arm, pulling me back, keeping me from going after him. It would be a pleasure. I know this kind of man, this kind of bigot; I know how to goad them into throwing the first punch even before they realize they're going to make things physical. We have so many witnesses here. He could break my jaw, maybe, or my nose, beat me to the pulp his inner demons demand, and then by the time the police show up, I'm gone.

Bigotry is a weed that takes root wherever it finds fertile soil, and there's no way this man is the only one here who thinks Apple and I are somehow violating the rules they keep in their heads, the rules that tell them how teenage girls are supposed to live and love and act and be. But this man was foolish enough to voice it, and they all want to think they're better than he is. I'm young—forever young—and pretty and delicate, with the refined bone structure that only comes from child-hood malnutrition. I'm white, too, and that's a weapon that can be used in places like this one, however horrible that feels to admit. If he hits me, he loses.

"No," says Apple, voice low and tight and wire-sharp with need. She needs me to stop, so I stop. She needs me to sit, so I sit. It's not her power over the twilight. It's not that she's the Queen and I was sup-posed to be her subject. It's that she sounds strained and sad and some-how lost, and while we're never really going to be friends, that doesn't mean I want to hear her suffer.

The man sneers one more time before he leaves, and then the waitress is coming to bus his table and ask whether we need anything else. Her eyes are hard. She heard what the man said, I realize, and while she might not have thought it before he spoke, she thinks it now; she's holding the cloth he cut up to our outlines, and she doesn't like the shapes it makes.

Apple digs money from her pocket while I smile at the waitress with all my cold psychopomp's heart in my eyes.

"Local girl," I say. "Thought you were going to be the first one in your family to get out, and then you found a job here, after school at first, only school ended and the job didn't, the shoes fit your feet better every year, and the apron strings tied themselves so tight around your waist that you forgot how to take them off. The smell of coffee and grease is in your hair. You could have been a priestess, you know. These places, they're temples to the gods of hard work and distance. Hermes loves diner waitresses, keeps them as safe as he can, protects them from the dark. Not you, though. Because Hermes also loves the transgressors of boundaries. He loves the outcasts. He loves me. He loves my friend. But love isn't always enough. Even if he loves you—and he has a lot of love to give—he doesn't *like* you. You are a disappointment to the god you have unwittingly served for your entire life, and I hope you remember that when you try to sleep. I hope you remember that when he comes to take you home. And if I were you, I'd pray he's more forgiving than I am when it's time to pay the ferryman's fee."

I stalk for the door, leaving the waitress gaping behind me, Apple close on my heels. Bon is long since gone; the parking spot where she'd briefly stopped her truck is open. Apple didn't drive here. We exchange a wordless look and break into a run, crossing the narrow local highway without looking back. We're not teenagers, even though we look the part, and sometimes form dictates function. Sometimes a teenage girl, faced with the disapproval of adult authority, just needs to *run*. Together we dive into the waving wheat on the other side of the road. It's tall enough to brush our shoulders, and we run and run and run until we come to a trail cut through the growth, where we duck down, fully out of sight.

Apple claps her hands over her mouth to muffle the sound of her breathing, and I crouch, hands and head dangling between my knees, trying to remember how air is supposed to work. Being dead means I don't actually improve my physical condition, no matter how much I run from danger, and when I'm draped in borrowed flesh, I tire easily. Some things about the spiritual condition suck.

Apple's shoulders shake. I'm briefly afraid she's crying, and then I realize it's something else she's trying to keep pinned behind her lips.

She's laughing.

"Hey." I jab her in the side with my elbow. I've been credibly assured that my elbows are unreasonably sharp. From the way she jumps, the people who told me that were being entirely truthful. "Don't laugh at me. I was just defending your honor." Another thought occurs to me.

"*And* I left the rest of my milkshake back there. If you're about to pin me in the twilight forever for disobeying you, that was probably my last milkshake. So a little gratitude would be nice."

She lowers her hands, laughter fading as she gapes at me. "You thought I was going to . . . for the Lady's sake, Rose, I'm not a *monster*."

"You want me to go hunting for Bobby Cross. You called me here to ask me to kill a man." I shrug, the borrowed coat heavy on my shoulders. "That feels pretty monstrous to me."

"Yes, because you *know* him, and he's your monster if he's anybody's. He's mine, too, but I can't hunt him."

"Why not?" Her answer might change my mind.

Then again, it might not. I've put too much time and effort into keeping myself out of Bobby's gas tank to go chasing him down now, not without a damn good reason.

"He can go as deep as he wants." She looks at me, eyes solemn and clear. I'm pretty good at knowing when people are lying to me. She's not lying to me now. "I've had reports of him from the midnight on up. I can't go that deep."

"You're the—"

"Yes, and that's *why* I can't go that deep." Apple shakes her head. "I'm the Queen of the Routewitches, I'm the chosen of the Ocean Lady, and I've promised to keep my post until there are no more Manzanars. That man, back there? The one who looked at us, hurting no one, doing nothing wrong, and decided he needed to turn a word into a knife so he could stab us with it? He's the reason I can't go down. I need to guide my people. I need to be able to know, absolutely, that no one can challenge me for my place and turn the Ocean Lady from a haven into a prison. She needs me. My people need me. I don't risk myself until the world changes."

I start to answer her. Then I pause, looking at her more carefully. "How many routewitches do you have watching us right now?"

Her smile is a small, tired thing. "The younger waitress back in the diner is one of mine. She's very disappointed in her coworker right now. Where did you even *get* all that about Hermes?"

"Pulled it out of my ass," I say cheerfully. "I have no idea whether he has opinions about diner waitresses. I bet he does, though. Persephone is way too interested in ghosts like me for Hermes to be sitting out the game entirely."

"I see." Apple smiles a little. "Two of the other patrons were mine, too. They'll be somewhere in this field by now, giving us space but staying close enough to get here quickly if I call for them. I never get to go anywhere by myself. That's not what a Queen does."

I tilt my head. "I've never seen you in the daylight before."

"This was a special situation."

"Are you . . ." I can't figure out how to ask this nicely. But I remember the feeling of my body defying me when I was brought back to life for just a little while, the knowledge that every cell of me was older than it had ever been before and was never going to take me back to what I'd been. I wave my hands in the air, indicating as much of her as I can encompass.

Apple looks at me with faint amusement. "If you talk, I can answer."

"Are you aging? If you stayed out here long enough, would you grow up?"

"Ah." She shakes her head. "The Ocean Lady is firm but fair. I came to her as a child. I promised her my future if she'd give me a place to belong. I wasn't Queen then, but I think she knew I was going to be. Causality is negotiable when you're a goddess. She took my adulthood. The woman I might have become, the people I might have loved when my hormones finished whirling around and tripping over themselves, all of it belongs to her. If we ever reach the point where I feel like I can walk away, she might be willing to give it back to me. Or she might not. Growing up, for me, might mean crumbling into dust and blowing away. Assuming it's even an option."

"Yeah," I say glumly.

The past wasn't perfect. People tend to don their rose-colored glasses when they're talking about times before today, like the fact that something isn't here anymore makes it somehow morally superior. But it was easier, when I was a kid, to pop up out of nowhere and make a life for yourself. Runaways happened. Orphans. Lots of things more terrible than that, too, but a teenager had a chance of showing up in town, making a few polite excuses, and putting down roots.

It's not like that anymore. Apple would be in for a hard road if she left the Ocean Lady. She's a girl out of time, the same as me only, unlike me, she still has needs. Food, and drink, and a safe place to sleep. She can't just drop down into the twilight and know she'll be taken care of.

Only maybe I can't either, not if Bobby Cross is nearby. The smell of white asphodel tickles my nose, a reminder of Persephone's blessing, which hangs around me like a shroud. As long as I belong to her, he can't touch me.

Maybe I can do this after all.

"I belong to Persephone the same way you belong to the Ocean Lady," I say. Apple quiets, looking at me attentively. I don't meet her eyes. Instead, I look at the grain around us as I say, "If she doesn't like this, if she threatens to withdraw her blessings, I can't. Bobby isn't my fault. He's my problem, yeah, but I didn't create him. The crossroads and routewitches did that. But the ever-lasters already told me I had to go and talk to her, and Bobby's running desperate. He's threatened to hurt what's mine if I don't go to him willingly."

"I know he's not your fault," says Apple. "It's why I came to you myself, instead of bringing you to me. This is our shame and our burden. I'm sorry we can't survive the depths long enough to hunt him down. I'm sorry I have to ask you, as his victim, to be the one who cleans up the mess we've made. It isn't fair. But I can tell you that if you give me a list of names, I'll set my people to protect them for as long as I can."

The idea of spending Apple's foolish promise on protecting a hundred little diners and dives across the country is appealing. The idea of protecting the people I consider my own is even more so. "If you'll protect them from him while I go hunting, then I'll try." I finally sit all the way down, nestling my butt into the hardpacked earth of the trail. "If Persephone says I'm allowed to do this—and I have no clue how I'm going to ask her, since it's not like I got a manual for 'how to be bound to a Greek goddess of the dead' when I asked her to let me complete my katabasis—then I'll at least try. I'll go to the place where the crossroads used to be and follow their bones to Bobby Cross. But I need you to agree to do one more thing for me."

"If it's within my power, you know I'll do it," says Apple. "You have my word as Queen of the Routewitches."

"Never been quite sure what that's worth," I say, tilting my head back, until I'm looking at the star-specked sky that stretches from one end of the horizon to the other, like a blanket drawn across this farming country, covering and comforting everything beneath it. I lived and died under skies like this one. It's familiar and cold at the same time. This is not my home. Never really was, no matter how hard I once tried to pretend. Rosie Marshall was only ever here to go.

I take a breath, air cold in my borrowed lungs, and say, "Gary loves me. I mean, he really, *really* loves me. He would never have been able to pull off the stunt he pulled to slip into the twilight as my car if he didn't love me all the way down to the bottom of his bones. But sometimes I wonder whether he loves the me I am now, after all these years in transit, or whether he still loves . . ." I trail off, not quite sure how to finish the thought.

"Whether he still loves a girl in a green silk gown standing by the side of the road, waiting for a hero to save her," says Apple.

I glance at her, startled. She smiles, ever so slightly, as she shrugs.

"The thing about being connected to the road is you hear a lot of stories," she says. "He featured pretty heavily in yours back when people were just starting to tell it. The helpless hitchhiking damsel, the handsome boy who saved her and took her home. He dropped away, though, around the time they started calling you the Girl in the Diner and the Phantom Prom Date. It was like once you had a name of your own, the people who told the stories didn't feel like they needed him anymore."

"Yeah," I say, and look at the sky again. "It's a lot like that. He grew up without me. He got old. He died. That's the only thing we both got to do. We both got to die. And he . . . I want to say he looks at me like I'm still this lost, helpless kid, but he doesn't look at me at all, because the road doesn't want him unless he's in a shape it understands. So he surrounds me. Sometimes it feels like he smothers me. Finding a way to stay in the ghostroads was a big, romantic gesture, but it's not like he asked me first. He didn't say, 'Hey, Rose, I know you loved to drive when you were alive, and I know you've been a hitchhiker for more than fifty years now. Are you cool with me turning myself into a car?' You know? My whole being is bound up in being the person who asks for a ride, and I don't need to do that anymore."

"He's chipping away at your identity without even meaning to," says Apple. "I get it, I honestly do. There was this whole wave of route-witches in the nineties who'd roll into town, find their way to the Ocean Lady, and then say things like 'wow, it's so great to see someone like you running the show,' and when I asked for details, would get defensive and tell me they didn't see color, they didn't see me as a Japanese person, they just meant that it was cool to have something as big as the Ocean Lady speaking through me instead of another white guy."

"White guys run fucking everything," I say.

Apple smiles wryly. "Only in the lands of the living. Haven't you noticed that by now? Once you're dead, the old privileges fall away, and suddenly it's not about money or connections, it's about how much work you're willing to do. That's the way it's always been."

"I wonder if that's why so few of the ghosts I know died happy, rich, and attended by their third wives," I say.

"Probably," says Apple. "Routewitches trend female, too. Men hear the road just as clearly, but they're more likely to be happy where they are. They're more likely to believe they can stay and see things get better. So women wind up slipping through the cracks in the world, leaving their daylight America behind. I'm pretty all right with that. It was always the men who said, 'someone like you,' and then quietly tried to take over, because I'm too young and too female and too not exactly like them. I asked one of them once if he could go and tell the United States government that he didn't see color, and so he'd like them to restore all the lands and property seized from Japanese Americans during internment, since if color isn't real, we were imprisoned for no fucking reason. He left pretty quickly after that."

"You *were* imprisoned for no fucking reason," I say.

"Preaching to the choir," says Apple. "I am who I am because of the wounds the world inflicted on me before I turned my back on the things I was supposed to want. I traded my name for a crown, and I'm not sorry. But I didn't sell my skin. I have my mother's hands and my father's eyes and I never saw Japan and I probably never will, but her dust is in my bones. Someone who 'doesn't see color' is telling me that nothing my family has ever done counted for anything. It doesn't matter if they're trying to help. It doesn't matter if they're trying to be kind. They're still chipping me away."

I let my eyes drift from the sky to the waving wheat. "If I do this for you, if I go looking for Bobby Cross—even if I don't succeed in getting him off the road—I want you to try and find a way for Gary to be a person in the twilight."

"He's not a road ghost."

"I know. He didn't die the right way for that." Even dying in an accident wouldn't have guaranteed him the ghostroads because he would have died with thoughts of me dancing behind his eyes. That's the sort of thing that makes a homecomer, when the person they're dreaming of is among the living. Since he'd have been dreaming of the dead . . .

An accident might well have slung him straight into the actual afterlife since, statistically, that was where I'd be. The me in his mind wouldn't have been enough like the me who actually exists to tell the road what he wanted. He would have moved on.

"I'll have to figure out a way to bend things, so he doesn't just drift off to whatever anchor he should have had in the first place. You sure he wouldn't be happy just staying on the Ocean Lady?"

As the most powerful highway in North America, the Ocean Lady sets her own rules. She's part of the daylight, part of the twilight, and part of the midnight, all at the same time. When I walk there, I'm always in my green silk gown, and when Gary crosses her borders, he finds himself back on two legs, with hands to hold me and lips to kiss me and to be honest, it's confusing as hell. It's a lot easier to be angry with him for making my choices for me when he's a car, silent and somehow managing to brood at the same time.

Regretfully, I shake my head. "Part of the problem is he wants to be with me, *constantly*. He sulks when I spend too much time in the Last Dance, and he can see me from the parking lot. He's not going to agree to anything that puts us in different places full time. It's just not . . . it's not going to work. I need him to be a person again, all the time, so I can figure out whether he's capable of loving *me*, not only the idea of me. So that's what I want from you. I want you to find a way to make Gary human again, out on the ghostroads."

Apple chuckles. "It's poetic, in a way. Bobby took Gary away from you when he killed you. Now you're going to try and stop him, and you want me to give Gary back."

"Do we have a deal?"

She nods. "We do."

"Then I'd better get started." I shrug off the jacket Bon gave me and let go of the daylight, of the phantom force that lets me steal life and temporary vitality from the world of the living, of everything but the need to go, to go, to go.

The last thing I see before I drop into the twilight is Apple's face, surprised but not displeased. Then I'm descending through layers of mist and infinite nothingness, and there's nothing to hold onto but the cold.

I just hope I don't wind up in another chainsaw murder maze.

Navigating the twilight is one of those things that never gets easier if you stop to think about it and is as effortless as blinking if you let go and allow your instincts to guide you. I fall, and I trust the sky to catch me. I fall, and I trust my heart to know the way.

There was this book I read back in elementary school, about a world where everything was flat. Two dimensions only. To the creatures that lived there, people were these weird, impossible monsters because we had a third dimension they couldn't see or fully comprehend. Sometimes I feel like I'm a Flatlander and a normal person at the same time when I'm dropping into the twilight because everything around me is a world smashed flat and compressed for ease of passage. Every drop of mist, every scrap of fog holds its own level of the twilight. All of them are ready to be opened and explored, eager for a new potential citizen.

Come home, they whisper. *I could be your home, come home, come home to me.*

I shut out the clamor of their voices and keep dropping, moving farther and further from the daylight at the same time—farther in distance, further in spirit. I can't quite reach it anymore. I would need to have something pulling me, or I would need to be on the ghostroads, ready to walk my way back into the light.

My destination is a deep one. I'm leaving the twilight behind me, and it doesn't want to let me go because it knows me too well, and it misses me when I'm not there. The stretches of ghostroad that I travel the most frequently are tangled in the twilight, and their familiar ground is both anchor and burden to me, making it harder to move on. I do it anyway, focusing on the fall, letting the mist wisp by around me, dropping down, down, down, like Alice in her rabbit hole descending into the darkness.

I'm in my green silk gown, have been since the instant I left the daylight behind. It flutters around me, blown by the wind created by my fall. The air only a few inches away is deathly still, filled with swirling fog that moves in every direction at once, paying no attention to the laws of physics. Physics aren't really spoken of here because they belong to the living; the dead have other constants by which to measure our existences. We don't name them. We don't need to. Also, it doesn't work. Most of the dead I know personally were human once, and humans like to have names for things. Not the laws that govern our existence; when people try to pin them down; they twist and change and slip away.

Very few people try to name the laws more than once.

I fall, and I breathe in the fog of a thousand layers of the twilight, and I focus on the place I want to go, refusing to let my image of it waver. Under the twilight, above the midnight, lies the least understood of the layers of the transitory afterlife.

The starlight.

I drop through the fog. Everything is gray and misty one second, and the next, everything is light, dazzlingly bright without being blinding, twinkling and glimmering and glittering all around me. It's like falling through a waterfall of broken glass, each piece sparkling for everything it's worth, turning the world into a beacon. I close my eyes. This is the hard part.

In the twilight, I am familiar. In the twilight, I *belong*. Here in the starlight, I'm a tourist at best and a trespasser at worst, walking where I was never meant to be. I force myself to relax and let the brightness flow over and through me, until I feel ground beneath my feet again, until the air is sweet at the back of my throat. There's a constant feeling of itchy *wrongness* from the world around me trying to cast me out. I push it aside.

I open my eyes.

I'm standing in the middle of what looks like a station on the London Underground—something I shouldn't be able to do, since I never saw one when I was alive, and the starlight can be strangely strict about only showing people things they already know. But I've been alive *twice*, and the second time, I managed to travel all the way to Europe in order to use the marbles in the British Museum as a doorway to the Underworld. Capital U, as in "you better not do this if you have any other option." I've been here before.

A train is pulling up. I step back, away from the doors, and wait. They slide open with a soft hiss, releasing a wave of heavily conditioned air. A single passenger steps out.

She's shorter than I am, and heavier, with the kind of curves I used to dream about back when I was a starving beanpole of a high school student. Her waist-cinching corset only exaggerates them, giving her a silhouette that could sell a thousand hungry Goths on paying the door charge at a club they've never heard of before. The corset is black, like the ruffled shirt above it and the skin-tight miniskirt below it. Her fingerless gloves, her fishnets, her high-heeled shoes, everything about her is Goth chic, except for the choker around her throat. That's pink, so pink it hurts my eyes, pink as a warning sign, as a "do not touch" writ clearer than nature ever managed, no matter how hard it tried.

Matching streaks striate her hair, which is otherwise dyed a flat, unrelenting matte black and cut in an old-fashioned style that neither matches nor clashes with everything else about her. She's wearing too much makeup, black and pink and silver glitter. Her lips are the only exception, the color of fresh blood and so glossy that I wouldn't be surprised to hear that she's been slitting throats all day in order to get the look just right.

She stops dead in her tracks when she sees me, eyes going very wide in their rings of mascara and eyeliner and bubblegum baby-doll brightness. "What are *you* doing here?" she demands, accent as thick as Ulster peat.

She'd sound a lot more impressive if she could learn not to squeak when she's surprised. I consider telling her so. I decide it would be a very bad idea.

"I need to get a message to Her Ladyship," I say. "I figured I'd find you in the starlight and, hey presto, here you are." I spread my hands, indicating the train station around us. "Why is this a train station?"

"Underground has lots of ghosts," she says, watching me warily. Her hands twitch, like she's resisting the urge to lock them around the handle of some sort of swingable weapon.

Dullahan have a reputation as reapers of souls. I'd really rather not find out the hard way that it's been honestly earned.

"So this is what, a dead station?"

"Something like that. One that never got built. The funds were allocated, the plans were drawn, everything was designated and de-signed, and then the temper of the planning commission changed, and someone decided we didn't need a station where this one would have gone and what the sweet, suffering fuck am I even on about right now? You're not supposed to *be* here, ghost." She pauses. "Ghost. You're dead again. You did it. You actually did it."

"I did," I agree. I don't really want to argue with her. I have no idea what kind of a timeline I'm working with here, but I know what's riding on my success: Bethany's existence, Gary's freedom, the safety of the living people I love, and yeah, my vengeance. I do this and maybe Bobby Cross goes away forever. I do this and maybe I can get a little peace.

"How?"

"It's a long story."

She folds her arms, cocking one hip out with the insouciance of the arrogant and the attractive. In her case, I think it's probably both. "I have time."

I don't, necessarily, but I still take a breath and say, "I went into the Underworld with Laura. We managed to navigate the traps between us and the garden, and I met Persephone."

"You met the Lady?" Her eyes go wide, and her head seems to wobble slightly, although that could be the wind from the departing train stirring her heavily shellacked hair. "She let you go?"

"She did."

Dullahan are better known as headless horsemen, although from what I understand, they don't appreciate the nickname, especially since most of them don't have horses. They're like *beán sidhe*, creatures who were never alive, never human, no matter how much they resemble humanity. *Beán sidhe* are born in the midnight and thrive in the twilight, among the only living denizens of the human afterlife. Dullahan are born in the midnight, originating at depths I have no interest in exploring, and they mostly stay there. Hitchhiking ghosts have a reputation for curiosity, since the nature of our hauntings means we're constantly coming into contact with new people and new ideas—not exactly the experience of your standard house-haunter. A homestead probably won't see as much in a century as I see in a year. And I still have no interest in seeing the place where Dullahan are born. I enjoy my existence—and my sanity—way too much for that.

"Lucky little dead girl," says Pippa, in a tone that's equal parts proud and predatory. People don't call Dullahan "the reapers" for nothing. Her fingers twitch again. If she pulls her scythe out of the ether, I'm going to run. I'll find another way to speak to Persephone. "So why are you here, lucky little dead girl? You're not alive anymore. No katabasis for you. The doors wouldn't open, and even if they did, the dog wouldn't let you by."

"I know." Cerberus is a good boy, but he's a good boy with a job to do. He doesn't let the dead pass. When we met before, I'd been one of the living, and he'd been willing to exchange petting for passage. Now . . .

He might exchange more petting for not eating me. Like I said, he's a good boy.

"Then why come so deep? This place isn't gentle with your kind."

I wanted to ask her what she meant by that. I was direly afraid that she'd answer me if I did. "I need you to go to Persephone on my behalf. I need a favor."

Pippa's eyes went even wider than before, until a rim of red stood out around the white of her sclera. She looked surprisingly human when she did that. Only knowing that her entire head would fall off if I removed her choker kept me from lowering my guard.

Some people would argue that I'm not human anymore either, that humanity is a function of living, and whatever I am now, I don't deserve the consideration or concern that would be offered to a human being. Maybe they're right and maybe they're wrong—it's never been much of my concern—but Pippa has *never* been human. I at least used to be. I know how humans think. I know how I think. Pippa?

It's anybody's guess.

So maybe that's why I'm not as surprised as I want to be when she pulls her hand through the mist that's started to gather around her and produces a wicked-looking scythe straight out of a Victorian illustration about Old Man Death. She points it at me, blade-end first, and takes a step backward.

"Why shouldn't I strike you down where you stand, for your disrespect and presumption, and let the carrion birds make mincemeat of your phantom remains?"

"Well, first, because carrion birds like dead stuff, but they don't usually like dead stuff that turns into mist before they can eat it. I'm not wearing a coat. This is just me. I don't think I'd linger long enough to be consumed." I spread my hands, making sure my left is just a little in front of me, so the white asphodel corsage tied around my wrist catches both the light and Pippa's eye. Persephone liked me enough to give me her blessing and send me on my way. I bet that means she wouldn't be happy if her pet Dullahan chopped me up for birdseed.

I spare a brief thought that this day, oh, this day, this day has not been anything like I expected when I answered the call to leave the twilight and get my ass back on the road. Everything is happening very quickly, and that's good because it means I don't have time to stop and really let it all sink in. As long as I keep moving, I can't get stuck.

Maybe that's why I'm a hitchhiker. All I've ever done is keep on moving.

"Second, because I've shown no disrespect," I continue. "I guess maybe I've shown some presumption, coming here looking for you like this, but I don't think the starlight would have let me find you if I wasn't supposed to. I don't know the rules down here as well as I know them up in the twilight. I *do* know the starlight directs where people go once they're past the city limits, so to speak. There was no good reason for me to land in your train station if you weren't going to be willing to at least listen."

"And you want me to go to the Lady for you. You want me to ask her . . . what, exactly?"

Here's where it gets a little bit tricky. I take a deep breath. "The ever-lasters of the twilight found my name in their playground rhymes, and they said I had to take my questions to Persephone. The Queen of the Routewitches has left the Ocean Lady to ask me to perform a task for her. The Lady of the Dead must know, in her wisdom and her grace, that the crossroads have been killed. Their bonds are broken, their servants scattered. I have been asked if I would be willing to hunt down the man known as Bobby Cross and stop the damage he's been doing in the name of the crossroads. I do not feel, given everything I've promised, that I can do this without the permission of our Lady. So I come to ask you to ask her for that permission."

Pippa blinks. Very slowly, very deliberately. She looks at me in solemn silence for what feels like forever, her scythe dipping low in her surprise, before she says, in a voice that's even slower than her blinking, "You expect me to believe that claptrap? You expect me to *credit* you with the death of the crossroads?"

"I didn't kill them," I say. "I don't want to be credited with anything. I just want to find out whether Persephone would be cool with me going and hunting down Bobby Cross before he can hurt anybody else. He's threatening to harm my people if I don't repudiate the Lady and give myself over to him, and that seems like a far greater insult than coming here on a little errand."

Pippa points her scythe at me again. The air around the blade glitters blue, like she's slicing through light itself. Which is an absolutely terrifying thought that I should never have had. Good job, brain, thanks for that.

"Stay here," she orders. "If you move, if you try to leave, I'll take it as proof of your lying, and I'll be the one doing the hunting. Do you understand?"

"Got it, boss," I say. I consider saluting her. I decide she might not take it the right way. Never piss off the occasionally headless woman with the large farming implements, that's what I always say. "Where are you going?"

"Not to bother the Lady, if that's what you were hoping," she says with a sneer. "I've other things to do with my time, and as soon as I return, we'll have a little talk about why you shouldn't try to trick a guardian of the gates."

"No one's told me what that means, so I don't think I should be held responsible for doing— And you're gone." I frown at the open space where the Dullahan was a moment before. "Of course you're gone."

She doesn't reappear. The tracks remain empty. She uses trains to get into the station, but—apparently—she can leave it at will. That's . . . well, that's not surprising, precisely. Most ghosts also have limitations on how we move, like pieces on a chessboard too big and complicated for formerly mortal minds to understand. I can cross incredible distances in the twilight, but always within North America. The oceans are forbidden to me. And when I rise into the daylight to do my spectral duty, I'm bound by the limits of my feet, traveling one step at a time until someone lets me into their vehicle and hits the gas. When I drop back down, the twilight puts me where the twilight wants me, but I'm always within a few days' travel of the Last Dance, if not actually in the parking lot.

Still, it would have been nice of her to leave me something to read, at the very least. I glare at the place where the train isn't. Nothing changes.

Nothing ever changes without good reason. I give the tracks one last sour look and begin pacing up and down the length of the station, the hem of my dress hitting against my ankles, trying to remain calm. It's not as easy as I'd like it to be. With Pippa gone, I have something that's been missing for a while now.

I have time to think.

Being dead is sort of like being an antelope. Stay with me here. Most of the time, I'm wandering peacefully through the taiga of my afterlife, looking for watering holes, enjoying the little things. I'm dead. There's not much that can hurt me. I don't need to worry about food or housing or how I'm going to pay for college. I don't have to decorate for the holidays or update my look. I get to just *be*. It's peaceful and it's pleasant and it's boring as hell, which is another reason people eventually either turn sour or move on. When everything's the same, night after night after night for as long as you care to cling to the remnants of the person you used to be, something has to give.

For me, what gives has almost always taken the form of lions. Or lion, really, in the form of Bobby Cross, the man who refuses to let me rest. The afterlife's never boring when there's someone still trying to kill you, despite the seeming impossibility of that idea. I've been running since the night I died, never able to stay in one place for long, never able to stop. Like an antelope. I was a prey animal when Bobby killed me, and his continued existence means I've stayed a prey animal. I've stayed aware of time in a way that many ghosts aren't.

The thought gives me pause. If I do what Apple's asking of me, if I take down Bobby Cross—if I even *can* take down Bobby Cross, who's just shy of being a literal force of nature as far as I'm concerned—no one's going to be chasing me anymore. I'll be able to drift, to doze, to haunt my way through an endless succession of days that never change.

How long will I be able to hold on if I no longer have to run?

It's a selfish thought, but I'm a selfish spirit. I've had to be. Selfishness is what allows me to cling to the idea that I, Rose Marshall, am somehow more worthy of existence than all the people Bobby hunts when he doesn't have me. I could fill his tank for years at this point. I've traveled so far and learned so much that I'm the high-octane fuel of his heart's deepest desires, just like he said. Every time I evade him, someone else dies. That's the simple, brutal truth of my existence. I survive and others die, run off the road and shoved into that infernal engine. What gives me the right to hesitate when given a chance to break the cycle? What even gives me the right to *run*? I'm not surviving anymore. I'm just . . . enduring. You can't survive when you're already dead.

And now he's planning to target the people I care about, which is why I'm going along with Apple's harebrained idea at all. I'm just a ghost. High-octane, sure, but one single solitary ghost who never asked for any of this.

But then, who among us asks for anything that happens to us? I would have sworn the crossroads would outlast the world. I can believe that Apple would meet me on neutral ground in order to ask me to do something that might end with me wiped entirely out of existence. If Bobby can catch me despite Persephone's blessing, it's game over for all the women I've become during my time among the dead. The Phantom Prom Date will stop haunting her high school targets; the Girl in the Diner won't appear to truckers anymore. I'll be finished. But Apple's predecessor was the one who allowed Bobby's passage to the crossroads, and she feels guilty, even after all these years. The living always privilege their guilt above the safety of the dead. Maybe that's right and maybe that's wrong. I'm certainly not qualified to say.

With the crossroads dead, Bobby has no one to protect him. They were never a nurturing master, but they were willing to intercede on his behalf where needed, willing to give him new ways to harry and hunt me—and most importantly, the fear of them was always enough to keep most of *my* allies at a distance. No one wanted to tangle with the crossroads.

With them gone, everything changes, for so many people—Mary and Bethany among them. Thinking of Mary sends a shiver of unease along my spine. Mary was newly dead and didn't know any better when she brokered Bobby's deal with the crossroads. She just wanted to get back to her father and the small, strange family she was already in the process of adopting. The Healys would have been okay without her if she'd disappeared back then; they just would have needed to find another babysitter. But now, she's been with them for generations, wiping their noses, kissing their boo-boos, acting as the moral heart of a mortal bloodline. What's going to happen if she disappears in the absence of the crossroads?

Maybe more importantly, what's going to happen to the rest of us? The Healys—the Prices now, because time passes and people marry and sometimes they change their names when that happens—aren't exactly the poster children for being chill. If they decide their ghost babysitter has been unfairly taken away, they're likely to storm the gates of Heaven to get her back. Which hey, would answer the question of whether Heaven exists, but I'm not sure that's a worthwhile trade for the amount of damage they'd do in the process.

Mary's been around long enough and has enough ties to the lands of the living that she'll probably be okay, and if she's not, I have absolute faith her family will make us all pay until the universe gives her back out of the sheer, desperate need to have them stop shooting things. Bethany, though . . .

Bethany's young and weak, and she doesn't have much to bind her into the twilight. With the crossroads gone, she won't have enough. That's why Apple has her on the Ocean Lady. It's not only a way to get me to play nicely with the routewitches: it's a way to keep my niece from vanishing completely. I'd be fine with that—it's not like we're friends—except that crossroads ghosts are sort of like Gary. They're special, for lack of a better way to describe it. They don't linger in the twilight because of unfinished business. They linger because the crossroads somehow drove a spike into their souls and bound them to the places where they died, keeping them from moving on. Whether it's a promise or a punishment doesn't much matter.

But the things the crossroads ghosts do in the name of their masters aren't always good. Some, like Mary, fight the crossroads. Others embrace them. For a new ghost like Bethany, who hasn't had a lot of time to figure herself out . . . if she loses her grip on the twilight, is she going to go to Heaven? Or is she damned by her own choices, most made when she was still too young and too trapped to know any better? Or—third possibility and worst of all—will she disappear because she was never supposed to be a ghost in the first place, and she traded her chances for eternity for permission to stay here, where she didn't really belong, for just a little while longer?

I don't have the answers. I'm not sure I want to have the answers. I reach the end of the platform, turn, and start to walk back the way I came, only to draw up short as something grabs the trailing hem of my dress, jerking me to an unexpected, undesired halt.

"Um, what?" I ask.

The only answer is a growling, rasping noise, like something big and made almost entirely of teeth trying to breathe ominously. I'm suddenly glad I didn't turn around. Things that growl like that almost never mean anything good, and all of them want to be seen. Being seen gives them permission to be way more menacing.

I hold up my left hand, shaking it slightly, so the corsage will dance. "Maybe not your best idea, sport. I already belong to someone way bigger and more dangerous than you."

The growl comes again, this time so close that I feel hot breath on the back of my neck, making the tiny hairs there stand on end. Sometimes the way my body mimics being something alive and easily terrified is a little bit annoying. There should be *some* advantages to being dead.

"Really? You honestly want to do this?" My options are narrow, and none of them are good. I can run. I don't know how big the thing is, or how fast it can move; it could be on me in an instant if I try to bolt. I'm dead. I can't be *killed* by ordinary methods, and the dead are usually very bad at doing anything permanent to each other. But I still feel pain, and I don't like it. I can also be ripped to shreds and scattered like confetti across the starlight, where it might take me years to come back together. This isn't my home. It won't help me.

Bethany doesn't have years. Bethany might not even have weeks. I don't know what happens to a ghost whose purpose and anchor is destroyed, and while I don't like my niece much, I love her grandfather. When it's time for me to lead my brother into the afterlife, I want to be able to tell him honestly that I did my best to save his granddaughter. I didn't just leave her to fall alone into the dark.

The people I love, the ones Bobby is threatening to harm, don't have years. They need me to get out of here in one piece, not a thousand.

I could rise into the twilight. It's always an option. When I'm in the daylight, I can fall; when I'm in the starlight, I can rise—and unless I'm in a ghost trap or somewhere else that isolates me from the ghostroads, I can always find my way home. But if I do that now, Pippa is going to come back and assume I've decided to run. She's going to think I asked her to bother the Lady of the Dead for my own selfish amusement, and she'll hunt me down. Pippa isn't technically dead. She *can* kill me, at least if the stories about the Dullahan are to be believed.

Getting myself killed—again—is not the goal for today.

Option three is the stupidest, on the surface, and maybe that's the reason I go with it. I've always been stubborn. I take one more step, almost reaching the limit of what my prom gown can handle with something holding its hem. Then I whirl, as quickly as I can, to face my assailant.

It's a whirling mass of specks, like a cloud made of flies the size of wads of chewing gum. Every part of their bodies is a fathomless black; I can only tell it's looking at me from the glints of light bouncing off its multifaceted eyes. It has formed grasping hands with cutting claws from the fabric of the cloud. Two of them are clutching the hem of my gown. Another three are reaching for me, hooked and primed to slash.

Flies bounce off the outline of its body, making it waver like static in the motionless station air. None of them go past the edge of the platform. It's like there's something stopping them from crossing into the air above the tracks. Interesting. Not as interesting as the fact that I'm being menaced by a horrifying fly monster, but still, interesting.

"I don't know what you are, and I don't really care," I say. "You want to let go of my dress?"

The cloud forms a hole in itself, like it's trying to mimic a mouth. It moans. The sound is made up of a hundred different tones of buzzing wings. I'd wonder why I didn't hear it before, but honestly, I'm not surprised, because this is ridiculous.

"No." I fold my arms across my chest and glare at the cloud of flies. The hands that were reaching for me stop. I'm confusing it. Good. "I didn't come here to be menaced by an advertisement for hiring a local exterminator. I don't know if you're a monster or a ghost story or a commuter waiting for your train, but I'm not here to be your snack."

I can't imagine this thing—these things? I hate hive entities, they're so confusing—was ever alive, unless it's a collective afterlife for horseflies. It's probably native to the starlight, something called out of the cosmic ether by the weight of the people who have, through their collective haunting, forced a world to make itself real.

It can be hard to tell the difference between something that used to be alive and something that never was. For the most part, ghosts don't prey on ghosts unless it's part of a pattern set in life. I've seen ghost cats stalking and pouncing on ghost pigeons. The pigeons look confused and fly away; the cats try to look like they meant to do that. But they don't *hurt* each other.

This thing looks like it wants to hurt me. It's still moaning, and its hands are reaching for me again. Charming.

At least now I know running was never going to work. It would have been on me in an instant. I'm not sure it could actually dismember me, but I bet it could eat the phantom flesh from my spectral bones and leave me to heal at whatever rate the starlight deemed fit. I don't have time for that right now.

"All right, then; if you're going to do it, go ahead," I say. "I don't have all day to stand here being menaced."

It howls again and pulls back its hands to strike. I hope I'm timing this correctly. If I'm not, I'm going to have some serious regrets.

It lashes out. I hit the floor and throw myself to the side at the same time, rolling toward the edge of the platform. Its claws slice through the fabric of my gown. There's a wet ripping sound and I'm free, still rolling.

This is fine, I think, and I'm over the edge of the platform, the moaning of the hive monster ringing in my ears. If I'm right, if I've put the clues together correctly, this is what will save me. If I'm wrong—if I'm pinning my hopes on a coincidence, or worse, on a trap—I'm about to put myself in a way worse position, which shouldn't be possible, really, but I'm gifted. When it comes to finding trouble, I'm like a dog looking for a rotting squirrel corpse to roll in.

The platform drops away and I'm falling. Not the weightless, almost serene fall from the daylight into the starlight: the fast, brutal drop of gravity working on the idea of my body. Here in the starlight I'm as solid as any of the living, and like the living, it hurts when I slam into the metal bar of the track, hitting hard enough to knock the air out of my lungs and leave me briefly reeling.

Above me, the hive monster moans and howls and buzzes in thwarted fury. I manage to lift my head and look up. I see light, and the curved ceiling of the station. I don't see any flies. Whether because it's a monster or because the starlight puts safety precautions in place for residents that it doesn't bother with for visitors, it can't cross the line.

I push myself into a sitting position, the rail still digging into my hip. Things look a lot less modern down here. There are no convertors or electrical relays. Just the two metal rails leading into the darkness in either direction, and the wooden slats below them, creating a classic, ancient railway form. The station is new. The rail line is old.

There's a gap below the platform, a space barely bigger than the coffin my body was buried in. I barely have time for that thought to form before a new sound drowns out the buzzing.

There's a train coming.

"Oh, come *on*."

The train doesn't hear, or care about, my protests: the train keeps coming, the sound of its approach howling along the tracks like the humming of a great and terrible bell. I have three choices. I can stay here and hope that a train will be less painful than the monster I came down here to escape; I can try to climb back up and take my chances; I can hide.

When in doubt, always go for the option that involves the least amount of screaming. I dive for the gap under the platform, compressing myself against the wall as tightly as I can, hugging the stone and squeezing my eyes closed so tight, so tight, as if what I can't see can't hurt me. The roar of the train gets closer. I tense.

Its arrival is marked by a hot gust of air, as withering as the wind off some vast and unseen desert. That wind buffets my body, sending my torn dress fluttering, and I silently hope the silk doesn't get itself caught under the wheels. The last thing I need right now is to be dragged off into the starlight by some damn train.

There's a musical about this, I swear there is, and if the train starts singing, I'm going to scream.

The train rumbles to a stop. I hear the doors open above me. They're so modern, those doors. So relatively friendly. The train below the surface is nothing like those doors. It smells like molten iron and musk, organic and not at the same time, like some great beast birthed from a master's forge and looking for fuel. I shiver uncontrollably, all the skin on my body drawing tight.

It smells like Bobby Cross' car. This is where they found it, the crossroads; this is the place they grabbed it from, pulling it into the twilight so they could offer it to him like the worst prize on the carnival midway. This train runs on souls, or something like them, and I'm down here with no way to escape without fleeing the starlight entirely. I'm trapped.

Please, I think. *Please let whoever does civic management down here keep their trains well-fed.* They must, right? It would be bad for business if their trains went around gulping down commuters all the time.

Although I've only seen Pippa and the hive-thing on the platform. Maybe the trains only respect bigger, better predators.

Sometimes I hate my afterlife.

The train doesn't send out tendrils to wrap around me and yank me from my hiding place, and I've been here just long enough to be grateful, to view this as a small mercy rather than a manifestation of the natural order of things. Instead, its engine rumbles back to life and it pulls away, roaring down the tracks, leaving me to collapse in grateful exhaustion. No one ever tells you how *tiring* terror is. That's the sort of thing you have to discover for yourself.

It's the sort of thing I never really wanted to know. Weary all the way to my bones, I roll out into the open and push myself, first to my hands and knees, and finally to my feet. When I stand, the top of my head barely crests the edge of the platform. It was a deeper drop than I realized, which makes sense, considering the train is as much indescribable terror as modern machine. They need to leave it room to breathe.

The modern part of the train must be a shell, something perched atop its true body. The thought isn't a pleasant one. I'm suddenly grateful to have been facing the wall while the train was in the station.

By bouncing onto my toes, I can just barely see over the edge of the platform. The hive-thing is still there.

So is Pippa.

She has the scythe in her hands, and her chin is ducked toward her chest, protecting the choker that keeps her head attached to her body. She prowls toward the composite creature with casual grace, like she's getting ready to swat a bug. I guess technically she is.

"Be gone with you, beastie," she says, words old-fashioned and utterly at odds with her club kid aesthetic. "You know better than to trouble your betters, and everyone who travels here is better than *you*."

She swings the scythe in a casual, sweeping motion, the blade slicing through the middle of the hive. It bursts, like she's managed to pierce some unseen membrane, and for a moment, the air is absolutely full of flies. They're less terrifying when they're not all clustered together and pretending to be something bigger than they are. They're still more than terrifying enough. I draw back slightly, choosing the dubious safety of the tracks over the obvious danger of the whirling, pincer-filled air.

Then they're gone, whirling up to the ceiling and vanishing through an ornate ventilation grate. There's a moment of silence before Pippa drops the scythe, which dissolves into mist, and turns, slowly, to look at me.

Her eyes aren't empty. Her eyes are *gone*. They're hollow holes in her face, pits leading into a world of infinite despair and unforgiving cold, and the only thing that stops me from screaming is that I've seen this trick before. It's pretty popular with a certain class of haunt. I stick my hand out.

"Help me up," I say. "I can't climb out on my own."

Pippa blinks and her eyes are back, although her expression is no warmer. "So you're saying I could make this all very simple for myself, and leave you down there," she says. "Not forever. Just until one of the trains realizes you've got no patron and takes you for a tasty treat."

I hold up my other hand, showing her my corsage. "I have a patron."

"Not to the trains. They pledge themselves to Hel, and they don't give a damn what our Lady of the Dead thinks of them, because Hel loves them so. She polishes their carapaces and tells them they're beautiful, strokes their bellies until they belch up the skulls they've stolen, and then charges the dead for the time they spend recovering in her halls. You don't want to mess about with the trains. What made you jump down onto their hunting trails?"

"That thing you chased away was getting frisky, and you'd asked me not to leave until you got back from whatever you had to do that was more important than carrying my question to Persephone." I keep my hands outstretched. "The trains don't care about her, but you do. So come on. Help me out."

Pippa heaves a sigh as loud as a bellows. "I regret everything I do in your company, Rose Marshall," she says, as she bends to help me back onto the platform.

"The feeling's mutual, I swear," I say, and then the tile is solid beneath my feet, and whatever else happens today, at least I know I won't be eaten by a train.

Then Pippa looks at me, as solemn as she's ever been.

"Come with me," she says. "We need to talk."

Maybe the train would have been better after all.

Chapter 5
Down Among the Dead Men Let Him Lie

THE STARLIGHT ISN'T MY HOME, but it's a realm inhabited by the spirits of the dead, and like all such realms, it has a few manufactured physical properties, maintained by the consensus of its occupants for everyone's comfort. Up is up and down is down; there's gravity, even if not everyone chooses to respect it. People drift along the sidewalks of the bucolic village where Pippa has taken me, their feet easily eight inches above the ground, but their bags stay safely in their arms. Compromise. It's all about the compromise.

This place would fit right into the twilight, as long as no one who came to shop here looked too closely. Everything is subtly wrong when I try to look at it too closely. The angles of the architecture hurt my eyes; the bones of the people going about their business are too long, or too short, or too close to the surface of the skin. I feel, for the first time in a long time, like I'm walking through a haunted house.

It doesn't help that my dress is in tatters below my knees, marked with great streaks of rail grease and grime. Normally, it shrugs off damage almost as quickly as that damage can be dealt. Here and now, it doesn't know the rules any more than I do, and so is defaulting to acting like it still exists, like it's not long since decayed in a pine box in Michigan.

I wonder if there are tailors here in the starlight, or whether this damage is permanent. That would suck. I wasn't the biggest fan of spending eternity in this dress when it didn't look like I'd just been in a bar fight. It smells, too. I wrinkle my nose as I catch a whiff of myself. How am I supposed to convince people to give me rides when I reek of the gunk that collects along subway rails?

Pippa leads me to a quaint little outdoor café, where two of the three tables are already occupied, one by an honest-to-God cobra and a woman with snakes for hair, the other by two men and a woman who all look enough alike to be siblings. They're pale and black-haired and blue-eyed, and when they turn to look in my direction, I want to claw my own skin off to keep them from noticing me. So that's fun.

"I'll be right back," says Pippa, indicating a seat at the one open table. "Try not to talk to anyone. You twilighters don't belong here."

"You got that right," I mutter and sit, folding my hands in my lap, looking at the surface of the table like it holds all the secrets of the universe. It's safer than looking at the locals. Dead humans go to the twilight and dead monsters go to the midnight and dead everything else winds up here. A lot of the people that fall under "everything else" were predators when they were alive, and humans were their preferred prey. I can't stop myself from thinking about the cats and pigeons again, and the way they keep playing out predator and prey even long after death.

I don't have time to be hunted right now. I barely have time for this conversation. I can feel the starlight bubbling against my skin, vast, curious predator that it is, sniffing around for signs that I'm something it can digest. The whole place might as well be a single organism. I'm like a protozoon swimming into the open maw of the ameba. The fact that it's a monocellular organism that would never be able to work up the coordination to go hunting won't make me any less dead if it decides to clamp down and get to the business of digestion. I don't want to be digested.

Pippa comes out of the café with a tray in her hands, walking over to place it in front of me. "I didn't know what you like to drink, so I made some guesses," she says. There's a tall glass filled with layers and layers of coffee, cream, and sugared syrup: whatever fancy-ass drink that is, it must taste like a milkshake mixed with a cotton candy machine, sweet enough to cause tooth decay even in the dead. The other drink is your basic white ceramic diner mug, filled with black coffee hot enough to still be lazily bubbling. I start to reach for the mug, then stop, pulling my hands back before I can touch it.

"Is it safe for me to drink here?" I ask. "I'm not looking for a goblin market scenario."

"Who knows upon what soil they fed their hungry, thirsty roots?" Pippa asks, with a mocking note in her voice. She sits down across from me, claiming the overly sweetened drink for her own. "No. The starlight isn't fairyland. You won't be trapped here if you have a cup of coffee, any more than I would be trapped in the twilight."

But the twilight doesn't feel like this, like a predator getting ready to pounce, like it considers every intrusion an offense. Is that because I belong in the twilight? Am I reading everything I've experienced there through the lens of not being a natural part of the environment?

Is this what Gary, who was never supposed to linger the way he has, feels like *all the time*? The thought is revolting. I reach for the mug again. This time I let myself wrap my fingers around it, feeling the heat radiate through the ceramic, insulating me from the burn of the coffee. And it *would* burn, it would, I can tell that just like I can tell that Pippa never expected me to reach for her caffeinated parfait of a beverage. She looks way too pleased with herself as she sips its frothy edge, and while I enjoy a good milkshake as much as the next girl, no one who takes their coffee hummingbird-style also likes it black. It's too much bitterness.

Pippa takes another sip and smacks her lips in a distinctly unladylike fashion as she sets her glass aside and levels her graveyard eyes on me. She looks like Death's maiden aunt getting ready to pass judgment on the last fifty years of my existence, and I realize with a sudden start that I have absolutely no idea how old she is, how many years she's spent collecting the souls of the dead and escorting lost ghosts along their katabasis to the Underworld. Dullahan don't exist outside the afterlife, but unlike *beán sidhe*, they don't have mortal families to anchor themselves to. I don't know how they come into existence, whether they're born or hatched or somehow *made*, the products of afterlife artisans who should probably get a different hobby. She could be centuries older than I am. She could have been made five minutes before the first time we met.

"Respect your elders" is practically a commandment in the afterlife because your elders are frequently capable of blasting you through the walls of reality and leaving you a damp smear on the pavement of the ghostroads. Have I been disrespectful? Should I be? The rules here aren't the ones I know, and that puts my teeth on edge.

"The Lady speaks well of you," says Pippa, tapping a finger against the glass rim of her cup. It makes a small ringing sound, like the tiniest bell in the starlight. The woman with the hair of snakes looks over at us, not making any effort to hide her curiosity. "She doesn't see many of your kind, for all that you're among the most common ghosts in the human afterlife. She says you're usually too wrapped up in trying to go home to do anything else."

"It takes time for most hitchers to figure out that we have other choices." Hitchers—hitchhiking ghosts—are almost identical to homecomers. They also solicit strangers for rides. They also spend their early afterlives trying frantically to get back to where they were before they died. The difference is in the severity of their focus. Hitchers eventually figure out that we're dead. We stop trying quite so hard, and we don't have a strong reputation for killing people just because they can't drive us back in time. Homecomers, though . . . all they want is to open the door of the places where they used to live and find their families waiting inside, as if nothing has changed. Most of them are in denial about being dead. How can they be dead when they're still lost and scared and confused? That isn't what religion promised them. The ghostroads aren't Heaven or Hell. They're just existence, as mundane and as magical as existence has always been.

Homecomers kill a lot of people. They're the ones who flip cars or stop hearts. A surprising number are also poltergeists, which isn't a kind of ghost so much as it's a high-octane add-on that some ghosts get, letting them manipulate the world of the living even when they're not a part of it. When I have a borrowed coat, I can pick up a rock and throw it at somebody. When a poltergeist decides they want to fuck with shit, they can move mountains. Sometimes literally. I'm occasionally jealous of ghosts who have that kind of power, but mostly, I'm glad to have the limits I do. If I'd been able to make personal earthquakes from the moment I died, I would probably have done a lot of damage in the first furious days after my death, before I'd learned the way the twilight worked, before I'd come to accept that I was never going to grow up or grow old or grow into the woman I'd expected to eventually become.

"Even so," says Pippa. She looks at me thoughtfully, with a degree of interest she didn't have before she realized Persephone actually *does* care about me, at least enough to remember what kind of ghost I am, and presumably remember that I carry her blessing both etched into my skin and tied around my wrist. Collect the full set of benedictions and maybe I, too, can avoid being stuffed into a bastard's gas tank and rendered down for fuel.

"I'm glad she likes me," I say.

"I didn't say that," says Pippa, sounding almost offended. "I said she speaks well of you. Don't presume to know what pleases the Lady. No one gets to know that. Not me, and certainly not a little human ghost who rolled in with the rest of the trash. Having powerful friends doesn't mean the rules don't apply to you."

I suppose I do have powerful friends. Emma's one of the nastiest *beán sidhe* in North America. We don't have many of them here, and since she no longer has a human family to worry about, she's been able to devote herself to gathering and locking down power in the twilight. I think she could go up against Apple and stand a decent chance of winning, and that would be terrifying if she weren't my friend, because Apple is Queen for a reason. Apple is terrifying in her own right. Apple can unravel roads with a snap of her fingers, can rewrite memories, and remake realities on a personal level. She's one of the scariest things out there.

And then there's Mary, assuming she's managed to sustain her power through the destruction of the crossroads. Pretty Mary Dunlavy, with her highway eyes and her bone-bleached hair and her living family, any of whom would be happy to lock a ghost in a silver-backed mirror for the crime of bothering their favorite dead girl. I like the Prices, but they don't play nicely when they don't see the need for it.

I square my shoulders and look Pippa in the eye, refusing to allow the growing sensation of being slowly digested to cow me. "If I don't get to presume to know the Lady, neither do you," I say, and hold up my left hand again, showing her the white asphodel corsage tied tight around my wrist. "So you went to see her after all? What did she say?"

Pippa's lips twist as she pushes her glass roughly away. "She says you belong to her, and she doesn't like to see her possessions thrown away for petty reasons."

I want to argue with her description of stopping Bobby Cross' reign of terror as "petty." He's been wreaking havoc across the twilight since before I died. Stopping him is anything but petty. It's a public service to the afterlife, like eliminating smallpox or making seat belts mandatory in passenger vehicles. I also want to argue with me being classified as a "possession." I don't do either. Persephone is a goddess. A literal, worship-in-her-name, owns her own personal level of reality, predates what I think of as modern civilization, goddess. I may never see her again. I'll be able to see her image branded on the inside of my eyelids for as long as I continue to exist. She's a goddess. One doesn't walk into the presence of a goddess and walk away unchanged. There's always a price to pay. If Persephone wants to think of Bobby Cross as a petty problem, I guess she's allowed. She's earned it if anyone has.

"Does that mean I'm not allowed to go looking for Bobby?" My voice wobbles more than I like, as if the question itself is a betrayal, somehow.

Pippa winces and looks away, refusing to meet my eyes.

"She wouldn't allow this if it were anyone else. In this one instance, this one regard, you can think of yourself as *special* because she's willing to make an exception for you. Given what he did to you and given the damage he's done to other of her followers in his efforts to capture you, she could even say you have a duty to be the one to bring him to heel. He's not a monster of your making, but he's the monster who made you. If he belongs to anyone, he's yours."

I don't want ownership of Bobby Cross. I don't want him to exist for anyone to own. I take another sip of my coffee—still hot and black and bitter as anything, like I'm drinking the blood of the earth itself, pulled up from unspeakable depths, dried and ground, and reconstituted with ordinary water—and swallow, watching Pippa speak.

"He's yours, and so she's willing to let you go hunting for him. She'll hang out the warnings and the wayposts, to make sure anyone who crosses your path knows you move under Persephone's blessing. That you aren't to be harmed or hunted until your task is done."

"Does the Lady require payment for this great gift?" I ask and take another sip of coffee. It's surprisingly smooth for being so bitter. It rolls down my throat like a whisper rolling off a liar's tongue.

Pippa shakes her head. "She asks that you find proof the crossroads are truly gone and buried, never to return, and to come back to the starlight to tell me, so I can carry the truth down into the Underworld. She'd prefer if you didn't undertake a second katabasis just for the sake of seeing her since you're dead again, and when dead people travel to the Underworld, there's always a chance they won't come out."

"But that's not a problem for you?" I ask.

Pippa looks smug. "I'm not dead," she says. "I'm undead. You should know that, with as long as you've been haunting places you don't belong, little ghost."

"I've been too busy to sit down and work on my naturalist's guide to the starlight." I take one more sip of coffee. It hasn't cooled at all. "This has been fun, and I appreciate you getting Persephone's permission for me, but I gotta get going if I'm going to hit the road before my niece gets digested, or dismantled, or whatever it is that's happening to the crossroads ghosts now that their patron is gone. I want to save her if I can."

"Because you owe her some favor?"

"Because she's family. She's my brother's granddaughter, and I never even got to meet his kids, what with my being dead before he was old enough to go running around with girls. I don't have a lot of family left. The Marshalls aren't inclined toward unfinished business. Most of us have died and then immediately moved on." I have a few distant cousins haunting a trailer park in Oklahoma, but they aren't road ghosts, and they aren't inclined toward family reunions.

"Are you sure this is about your niece, and not about the white-haired girl who got you killed in the first place?"

I mostly try not to focus on the fact that Mary was the one to negotiate Bobby's deal with the crossroads. Sometimes I can't help it. If not for her, Gary and I would have been able to get married right out of high school. We would have grown up together, teenage disasters becoming adult, well, disasters, knowing us. I would have come into my powers as a routewitch. He would have been able to move past his dreams of a dead teenage girl walking by the side of the road. We could have been happy.

Or maybe we could have been miserable. People can't exist in "maybe." It's a cruel and nebulous country that slips away as soon as you try to grab hold of it. It never lasts. It never learns how to love, or to forgive. It isn't always kinder than the world that actually exists; it only seems that way because you don't have to live with it, don't have to endure it through the bad moments and the heartbreaks. "Maybe" is an illusion. If I'd lived, if Mary hadn't made Bobby's bargain possible, Gary and I might still have broken up. His family hadn't liked me. I was too poor, too loud, too opinionated to make a good wife for their precious little boy. He might have left me in the wreckage of our high school careers, striding into the future with an unburdened heart and a hand that was just waiting for some pretty young thing from a good family to reach out and claim it. "Maybe" was never going to be enough to save me. "Maybe" was only another road for me to crash and burn on.

Mary did what she did because she didn't have a choice, and she did it without malice, never intending for me—or anyone else—to get hurt. She died in an accident, just like I did, and she did what she had to do in order to keep on existing. Maybe that's why I forgave her after we'd finally had the chance to sit down and talk things through. We never intended to be set against each other. Nothing she's ever done has been meant to harm me.

"Mary is older and stronger than Bethany," I say, feeling my way into the words, like they might turn and bite me if I took my eyes off them for even a moment. "If any of the crossroads ghosts can survive this transition, it's going to be her. I'm not worried about her." Yet. I will be, I know, assuming she doesn't come and find me and tell me all about how frustrating this whole situation is. She was there when it happened. She has to be feeling the effects by now. Doesn't she?

Mary will be fine. It's Bethany I'm worried about. I put my coffee down and push it away, smiling at Pippa as I try to shrug off the feeling of digestion. Pippa takes another sip of her hummingbird milkshake, watching me. I feel small and grubby and human; feeling human hasn't been a bad thing in a long time, but it is right now. Here in the starlight, it could prove fatal, and I say that as someone who's already dead. "I'm going to get started now," I say.

"You do that," Pippa agrees. "And Rose?"

"Yes?"

"After you fulfill the Lady's request, don't come back here. Not even to talk to me. Those powerful friends I mentioned earlier?" She bares her teeth in a parody of a smile. "I'm not one of them."

I get to my feet with as much decorum as I can manage in a torn, grease-stained dress that's started sticking to my skin. It feels like I've been rolling in a tar pit. Gross. "I would never presume that you were," I say. "You're Persephone's courier. I respect you. I sometimes need to ask you for help. I know we're not friends, and I'm not trying to force you to be what you don't have any interest in being. You have my apologies if I gave any other impression."

Pippa grumbles as she leans back in her chair, shoulders stiff, neck tight enough that the tendons stand out against her corpse-white skin. "You didn't," she says. "But stay out of the starlight. The Lady will be furious if you get ripped apart by something larger than me."

I find the focus to nod, and say, "I'll stay in the twilight or above if I can. I know this place isn't for me."

"You're dead, but you're still human, little ghost," she says. "Try to remember that."

I release my hold on the starlight and allow myself to rise, up toward the twilight, where the ghosts are more familiar and the air doesn't resent me for intruding. The feeling of slow digestion drops away, although the feeling of being watched by something infinitely larger than myself doesn't: the starlight is watching me go.

My rise is more metaphorical than literal. I can feel the café patio under my feet until I can't because it isn't there anymore. I don't drift into the sky. I don't drift at all. Floating has never been a part of my phantom tool kit. The way I died anchored me too firmly in the idea of my body's limitations, and the hauntings I've been part of since then have been too dependent on borrowed blood and bone to leave me with that kind of flexible approach to physics. Sometimes I envy the ghosts who figured out how to shed the surly bonds of gravity and soar through their afterlives like the angels none of us have actually turned out to be.

There must be angels somewhere. Former humans with big fluffy chicken wings, hanging out on clouds and preening themselves. Too many cultures tell stories about them; too many people claim to have seen them or spoken to them or been touched by them. I don't know that I believe in a single coherent creator god—not after everything I've experienced in the afterlife, and not after meeting multiple smaller gods, more limited, maybe, but still terrifying when they want to be. But there must be angels. I don't know whether people ascend or are transformed or somehow earn their halos and wings. I don't much care. It's not like it's ever going to be my problem.

I'm no angel. I would make a terrible messenger for the forces of light, assuming the forces of light actually exist. Most of the genuinely good people I've known would be better described as "complicated and sort of gray" than either "black" or "white." That kind of uncomplicated cosmology only functions on paper. It doesn't survive encountering the actual complexities of the way people think, behave, and sometimes betray. We build and break religions by being the way we are.

So I don't float out of the starlight. I just fade until the ground under my feet is precisely that: it's *ground*, rough and unpaved and smelling strongly of petrichor and loam. There's a rock under my right foot, digging into the pad of my heel hard enough that it feels like it's going to leave a bruise. I refuse to let that distract me. I belong in the twilight, but transitioning between layers is never easy, no matter how much one place feels like home compared to another. If I stop focusing on the transition in order to focus on the rock, I'll wind up stuck in-between, and I have no idea what might happen to me then. I've never been stuck.

I've met a few ghosts who had dire tales of what would happen if I ever got careless or panicked enough to mire myself on the membrane between levels. According to them, I'd slow down until I was barely moving, until working myself free might *seem* to take a few minutes, but would actually take years, if not decades. Years of being suspended in infinite space, unable to react.

Unable to defend myself. Utterly vulnerable, utterly exposed. With Bobby out there feeling thwarted and seeking revenge. So yeah, I'm not interested in finding out firsthand how unpleasant it is to get stuck. I'm a lot more interested in making the transition the way I've always done it before: safely, cleanly, and without hurting myself.

When the rock under my foot becomes fully solid and the last shreds of starlight peel away from my skin, I take a step back and kick off my shoe, the plain satin slipper I've been wearing in my default form since the night I died. It lands in a clump of crabgrass, as pristine as it was when I picked it up from the shop. It's the kind of cheap shoe that splits a seam doing basic dances at the prom, and yet nothing I've done to it in the last fifty years has left the slightest sign of wear.

I catch my breath and look down at my dress, relaxing slightly when I see it unstained and intact, swirling around my calves and ankles the same way it always has. The damage it took in the starlight didn't last through the transition home. The corsage is still tied around my wrist, fresh as the day Persephone put it there, scenting the air around me with the sweet perfume of blooming asphodel.

I'm in a field next to a burnt-out gas station that looks like it was destroyed in a refueling incident—not as uncommon as most people like to think, not so common that every tank of gas is likely to end in fiery devastation. Most of what's around me is thistle and briar and pricker-weed, the kind that send their seeds off as little balls of painful punishment for children who dare to go barefoot when they're not supposed to. I limp to my discarded shoe, balancing carefully on the toes of my feet to avoid stickers, and flip it over with a gentle kick. There's an anthill directly under where it landed—because of course there is. Welcome back to the twilight, where everything that's ever been loved gets to be preserved for eternity.

I am not a big fan of entomologists, let's just leave things at that.

Ghost ants are no friendlier than their living counterparts. I manage to nudge my shoe away from the anthill with my toe and slip my foot cautiously back into it. Nothing bites me. I relax. Not even death can stop ants from being assholes when they feel like they're being encroached upon. I brush my hands against my restored skirt, feeling a wash of surprising affection for the garment. I guess you can't wear the same thing for more than fifty years without developing a certain degree of fondness for it. Or maybe I'm projecting my relief at getting out of the starlight without being swallowed whole. Whichever it is, I'm here now, home in the twilight. I can feel the rightness of my surroundings vibrating through me, as sharp and reassuring as the hum of the telephone wires by the highway or the crackle of a neon sign.

I turn and make my way to the edge of the field, pausing to check the hem of my dress for brambles when I get there. A few of the little sticker balls have attached themselves to the fabric, doing their best to blend. I mean that quite literally: they're actually in the process of changing colors, shading from their usual dusty brown to a delicate seafoam green. That's something sticker weeds don't do in the world of the living, for which every living person should be grateful. I peel them delicately off the fabric, careful not to let them draw blood as I flick them back into the field. I don't want to give this place a taste for me. Not when it already looks like a dumping ground for the dead.

I can't tell if it's from the distortion caused by the death of the crossroads, or if this is one of the stretches of the twilight that's always sucked. It doesn't really matter. Places like this are predatory in their own way, and it's best not to linger in them.

Finally content that I'm clean and undamaged, I take my first step out of the field, onto the cracked pavement of the gas station. Broken glass glitters in the dim moonlight like fistfuls of discarded diamond, sparkly and precious and valuable. I mostly value the sparkle. It lets me walk around the worst of the mess, which keeps me from getting a chunk of glass in my foot.

Being dead means I don't really get injured, but if I hurt myself in the twilight, the injury is likely to stick around until the next time I head into the daylight and back down again. And given that I haven't been home since I went off to get myself some white-gravy chicken, Gary and Emma are both going to be wondering where I've been. They need to know that I'm okay. More importantly, they need to know about Bobby's threats, and what I've been asked to do. This isn't the kind of adventure I should head for without a word.

Not that either of them is going to be coming with me. Emma doesn't tinker that directly with the affairs of the living world, not since the last of her mortal family died, and Gary can't really leave the twilight. Once again, I'm on my own.

"It's a party, Buckley-style," I mutter, and kick a chunk of glass out of my path. It rattles across the broken pavement, coming to rest at the base of the old pumping island, where the empty gas tanks wait with hoses still attached to fuel up the ghosts of cars. I keep walking.

The reptilian horror unspooling from the island stops me in my tracks.

It has feathers and claws, like the largest, meanest chicken the world has ever seen fit to summon forth. It looks like it personally resents every McNugget sold by every fast-food establishment ever as it fixes me with one enormous, half-formed yellow eye and makes a distressed churring sound in the back of its dreadful throat. I freeze. I heard somewhere that dinosaurs only hunt motion, and if I don't move, maybe it won't be able to see me.

It continues emerging from the broken gas tanks, a thick black-and-yellow vapor that turns progressively more solid as it pulls itself together, and it turns its head to fully look at me, lips drawing back from heavy jaws to show its sea of jagged teeth and make its rumbling growl more audible, and I know whoever said dinosaurs hunted based on motion had never met a dinosaur in their life—or death—and was just making stuff up, content in the knowledge that there aren't many dinosaurs around to check in with anymore.

And there *aren't* many dinosaurs around. They've had millennia to deal with whatever unfinished business they may have had, and they've moved on. The youngest dinosaur ghost would be millions of years old, and that's too old, really, to be a comfortable part of any of the levels of the afterlife that currently exist.

This one looks . . . odd. It has the teeth and the jagged claws and the long, pendulous tail, but it doesn't look like any kind of dinosaur I've ever seen in a museum or on the flickering screen of the local drive-in movie theater. Its neck is too long to make a good predator. Its chest is too narrow to make a good herbivore. It's like looking at something spliced together by a child with a hot glue gun and a hacksaw, and, still, it keeps wafting from the shattered gas tanks, and that's the piece I was missing. That's the piece that makes me feel foolish and out-of-touch, like I haven't been paying proper attention.

This isn't the ghost of *a* dinosaur. This is the aggregate ghost of however many dinosaurs went to sleep and found themselves slowly, alchemically transformed from terrifying predators and kings of the world into thick black liquid running through the veins of the Earth, precious and peaceful, until men with machines drove their giant drinking straws deep into sleeping stone and pulled them up again.

Humans act as if desecrating a corpse is somehow the greatest crime possible. Living or dead, we don't like people messing with bodies, because bodies can't give consent. They're unoccupied houses, and the worst thing many among the living can imagine is someone moving in without asking for permission or breaking a window and looting what isn't being used. Well, what are those underground oil fields if not dinosaur graveyards, filled with the mortal remains of an entire genus, all of them mingling together under geologic pressures my too-human brain can't wrap itself around? The dinosaurs went into the earth, as all flesh must eventually do.

And then we dug them out and put them under even more pressure, until even they forgot which pieces of the communal graveyard originally belonged to which spirits. I'm not facing the ghost of a dino-saur. I'm facing the ghost of every dinosaur who died in the geographic vicinity of whichever oil field or fields this oil was initially pumped up from. I'm probably also facing the ghosts of a bunch of prehistoric plants and bugs, but they don't have the fetishistic adoration of gener-ations of human children to lend them strength in the twilight. It's just dinosaurs with the strength to manifest. So many dinosaurs, all of them rolled together into a single ball of unthinkable terror.

I take another step back. I don't want to run. This thing looks like it can't decide whether it wants to have forearms or wings, but which-ever it chooses, it's already coming down firmly on the side of feathers, which I suspect means it's going to be able to fly. It looks too heavy to take to the air with any success, but dinosaurs don't know a lot about physics. Maybe they're where I should have been looking for those absent angels.

The mist stops flowing from the tanks. The patchwork dinosaur takes a thudding step toward me. It isn't sure about its balance, or about the way it's supposed to use its tail to keep from toppling for-ward. This is a very ancient, very new entity, a baby hatched from the eggshell of millennia, and it's hard not to be fascinated, even as I wait for it to rip my face off. I'm in the twilight. I'm on as close as I can come to my own home ground, in a place where I'm as close to belonging as I am anywhere. We don't usually have dinosaurs here. Maybe it can't hurt me.

It makes a sound, a deep, grumbling growl that starts at the base of its chest and vibrates all the way up, large and loud and primeval. Something in the marrow of my nonexistent bones recognizes that sound. It's the reason the deep jungle and the wild places aren't for me, it's the sound of a predator so big and so terrible that no one ever comes back to the firelight to tell the rest of us it's out there, it's death from before my first ancestors came to realize that time existed.

It swings its head around to look at me, opens its mouth, and bel-lows again. Not being a total fool, I spin on my heel and run.

Chapter 6
There's Always Running and Screaming

———

THE STRETCH OF ROAD running past this deserted, burnt-out gas station is in exactly as good condition as I've come to expect from places like this, which is to say, it's trashed. After the third time I stick a foot directly into a pothole deep enough that I'd be worried about breaking an ankle if I were alive, I start swearing steadily. It helps a little. "Teenage girl in vintage prom dress screams 'fuck' while running down a poorly maintained back road, pursued by the vengeful aggregate ghost of several thousand dead dinosaurs" is never going to be one of those classic images of the American road, but I'm not here to be iconic. I'm here to not get eaten.

Not getting eaten currently feels like the best goal I've had in my afterlife. The road shakes with the thudding footfalls of the creature behind me, so I run faster, trying to avoid the potholes, mindful of the scrub and bracken encroaching from all sides. Wherever I am, it isn't in one of the farming corridors, or I'd be running flanked by endless rows of corn, wheat, or sunflowers. Not the most common crops in the whole country, but the tallest, and the roadsides in the twilight really appreciate veiling themselves behind someone else's produce.

I run, and the dino-thing pursues, which seems to be its entire current purpose. I really wish I knew what I did to piss it off. I didn't set fire to the gas station. I'm not currently driving a car, which probably wouldn't sit well with what is effectively the ghost of an oil refinery—to a dinosaur spirit, all cars are Bobby Cross' car, consuming everything that's fed into their gas tanks without consideration for what those things were before they were crushed into crude oil. But I *am* a road ghost. My existence was born from this spirit's destruction, and the destruction of all its terrible, improbable fellows.

Did dinosaurs have gods? They must have. Something existed before humanity rose out of the muck and started making up stories about the forces in the sky and in the ground. The twilight is older than we are. The starlight and the midnight have always felt like they're older still. The few theories I've heard posit that all the layers of reality came into existence around the same time, snapping together like the framework of a swing set, suspending the living on rusting chains that creak and rattle in the wind. So there were probably dinosaur gods filling the same basic functions as the ones we know today, proto Persephones protecting the accesses between the lands of the living and the lands of the dead.

I fight to hold onto that idea as I do something that's either incredibly clever or incredibly foolish: I stop running. My feet skid in the gravel of the road, and I barely manage to keep from overbalancing either into the briared verge or the nearest pothole, which is deep and jagged and has a puddle of something in its bottom. The puddle is moving. I really don't want to find out why. I turn on the dinosaur ghost, which is only about a hundred feet behind me, and closing fast. I hold up my hands, angling my wrists so it gets a clear look at the asphodel corsage on my left arm.

"Please stop chasing me," I say, in a clear, reasonable voice. I don't expect it to work instantly. I can't really say whether I expect it to work at all. That's for the best, because the dinosaur slides to a stop, spraying gravel in great waves around us. Some of the gravel hits me on the cheek and forehead, and little chunks get snarled in my hair. I swallow the urge to take a step back and shake my head, like a dog with fleas. The thing might take that as an insult.

Do dinosaurs get insulted? It would probably be insulted to know that I think of it as "Thing," but with as many pieces as it has from different prehistoric corpses, I think that's probably the only label that comes even halfway close to being right. It's hard to be polite when you're dealing with language, cultural, species, and historical barriers, all at the same time.

It leans forward into a clear hunting stance, waves its terrible claws, opens its terrible jaws, and roars. The smell of hot tar rolls washes over me in a terrible wave. Great. First a wave of gravel, and now a wave of stinking petroleum products. Can this night get any more unpleasant?

That's not a question a smart person asks out loud. So I don't. I keep my hands in front of me, and gesture with them as I speak, trying to draw attention to the corsage without actually shouting "The Goddess of the Dead is my BFF! We braid each other's hair and talk about boys! Her boy is tall, dark, and terrifying, and mine is a literal car! Dating is easier for the living!"

"Is that your name?" I ask. The dinosaur-thing looks nonplussed. That's good. That's better than the alternative, which is either "enraged" or "hungry" and possibly chewing my face off. I like my face where it is. More, I'm not sure what would happen if something in the twilight bit it off. Would it heal the way injuries sustained in the living world and run-of-the-mill injuries from tripping and falling in the twilight do? Or would I be condemned to wander around with an exposed skull for the rest of my phantom existence? That doesn't sound like my idea of a good time.

The dinosaur-thing doesn't bellow again. Instead, it bobs its head in what could be agreement, but could also be a hunting behavior, or simple confusion. Dinosaurs were never super my thing. I can't remember whether this composite would ever have seen a large mammal, much less a human. I don't move like a dinosaur. I don't stand like a dinosaur. Everything about me must seem blazingly wrong to this thing. A wash of sympathy flows over me, and I step forward, hands still outstretched, trying to look as harmless as I can.

"Hey," I say. "My name is Rose Marshall. People call me the Phantom Prom Date." People call me a lot of things. That's among the more flattering. "You don't have to tell me your name if you don't want to, or if you can't do it. I know we have a pretty big language gap." We have a pretty good everything gap. The only things we have in common are that we have internal skeletons—although I can see pieces of the dinosaur's skeleton through the gaps in its patchwork flesh, so the "internal" part is at least somewhat negotiable, and we're both dead.

But that's the part that matters. We're united in our non-living states. If we can figure out how to communicate without threatening or fleeing, we'll be okay.

"I've never seen anything like you before," I say, taking another step. The dinosaur flinches, feathers lifting in what could be a threat display before smoothing down again. It's pretty impressive to watch. "We have dinosaur skeletons in museums, but no actual dinosaurs. You're fluffier than I thought you'd be."

The dinosaur makes a creeling noise in the back of its throat. It sounds like a baby duck calling for its mother. I really, really hope this is an adult abomination. I don't think I could handle anything bigger right now.

My skin itches. I didn't get to spend nearly enough time in the daylight before I ran off to the starlight to start my fool's errand on Apple's behalf. I'm going to have to go back and catch another ride soon, whether I want to or not. Bully for me.

The dinosaur makes another birdlike noise. I take yet another step, allowing my right arm to drop to my side, keeping the left, with its protective corsage, raised. I'm not sure I actually want to touch the thing. It looks . . . greasy, oily, which makes sense, given the grave I'm pretty sure it rose from. I don't want to stick my hand in there.

Then it sticks its snout into my palm, nudging upward until I'm petting it between the eyes, and I'm so wrong. It feels like a big bird, all soft feathers and empty spaces. The oily look begins to fade. It makes the noise for a third time. I keep petting it.

"Why were you chasing me?" I ask. "Did I scare you? I don't see how that's possible. You're so much bigger and fiercer than I am." With so many additional teeth. I've only ever had the usual human number. Another disadvantage of my relatively inoffensive type of ghost.

The dinosaur pushes its head more firmly into my hand before pulling away and looking over its shoulder toward the distant shadow of the gas station. It stomps its feet in clear irritation. I can't decide what that means. I don't like language barriers. They're so difficult.

"You're a very pretty death lizard from the dawn of time," I say, not entirely truthfully. "I know people who would absolutely love to meet you in all your growling glory. But I have to go, and I'd appreciate it if you didn't follow and try to eat me."

It looks back to me, hanging its head and grumbling in what I can only call a disappointed tone. I still can't understand it, but it's getting easier to interpret what it's trying to tell me. That's nice.

"I have some friends I can ask to come back here and see you." Who knows what this thing will make of Mary—or what she'll make of it? Maybe she can go get Pippa, and they can all play fetch with the Dullahan's detachable head. Or maybe she can explain it, so it doesn't remain just one more of those random things that can sometimes happen when you're running around the twilight. Either way, I need to get back to the diner.

"Please don't chase me, please don't chase me, please don't chase me," I say, and squeeze my eyes shut, feeling the twilight move around me. When I open them again, I'm in the middle of a faded four-lane highway. The sun isn't up—they wouldn't call this place "the twilight" if it had a strong tendency toward sunny days and summer weather— but the rippling mirror-glass distortions of summer mirages still dance above the pavement, twisting like little portals to somewhere else. We used to call those the phantoms of summer when I was a kid. We chased them, but we never caught them because you can't catch a ghost, not even when it's the ghost of a heatwave.

There's no sign of my dinosaur buddy. I relax, letting the tension drain out of my shoulders, and turn in a circle to see what's around me. I can see fields in all directions, low and green and filled with the kind of crops that need a lot of labor to bring to proper harvest, strawberries and tomatoes and artichokes. That's probably why they're here. Living humans get weird about arbitrary boundaries. The last few years, I'd seen a lot of crackdowns on migrant farm workers, a lot of attempts to make them disappear. The amount of food that's left to rot in the fields as a consequence is truly staggering. Wheat, corn, and potatoes can all be harvested by machine. That doesn't do away with the need for human hands, but it reduces the number required. No machine has ever been built that can harvest a field of strawberries without crushing the ripe ones and plucking a few hundred that needed more time on the vine. It's people or nothing, and when it turns out to be "nothing," another field slips into the twilight.

There's a truck stop in the distance, neon gleam and glaring white floodlights. There are no cars on the road. We don't have a phantom rider around here right now, haven't had one since Tommy managed to reunite with his teenage sweetheart and drove off to find the final off-ramp. Eventually, we'll attract another one, or maybe a coachman, or some other form of territorial, ambulatory road ghost who needs a home.

Road ghosts are rare. We're so much rarer than we feel when I'm at home, not worrying about monsters and gods and crossroads. Most people don't leave a ghost behind when they die, and maybe one person in ten who leaves a ghost leaves a road ghost. Which is still more common than, I don't know, aggregate dinosaur monsters, but doesn't usually give us enough to fill a diner on Sadie Hawkins Night.

If a hundred people die, two of them might leave ghosts behind. Which means five hundred people need to die before we get someone else for the ghostroads. The hole Tommy left in our local population is going to endure for a while.

I start walking toward the truck stop, feeling suddenly, unaccountably exhausted. Maybe not so unaccountably: the dead don't sleep, but we do rest, and I didn't get enough hitchhiking to prepare me for a trip to the starlight followed by a chase down an unfamiliar road with possible dismemberment at the end. Dinosaur ghosts. Who would have thought? It's ridiculous and predictable at the same time, and if it goes back into the tank where it was waiting when I arrived, maybe I can use it like a sharp-toothed jack-in-the-box to mess with people who need a little messing with. Emma would probably enjoy the encounter.

I'm not walking particularly fast, but the truck stop is getting closer all the time, the distance between us narrowing with remarkable speed. The twilight is hurrying me to my next destination, then; either I can tell it I need to go back to the daylight, or it's bored and wants to see what tries to eat me next. Either way, it's nice to feel like the land-scape is on my side, however temporarily.

The trees around the truck stop don't mesh. I see eucalyptus, oak, and evergreen, all growing together, in a formation that could mean "a really bored horticulturalist lives here" but is more likely, in the long run, to mean this is the landscape equivalent of my dinosaur friend: a composite, built by combining a bunch of things that were never orig-inally meant to be in the same place. That could mean a Dunkin' Do-nuts alongside a Jamba, combining fast-food franchises from different sides of the country. Sadly, not likely. We don't get many fast-food joints in the twilight, and the ones we *do* manage to manifest are almost al-ways burnt-out or covered in blood or somehow or other memorializing a tragedy in the living world that I would otherwise never have heard about.

Maybe it's the perspective that comes with being dead, or maybe it's the fact that we only see the bad ones, but it feels like there are more tragedies these days than there used to be. There are definitely more shootings. Kids, staggering into the twilight, not able to accept or understand the reasons that they can't go home; not able to wrap their heads around the fact that everything has changed in an instant, leav-ing them stranded on the wrong side of the cemetery gates. As Perse-phone is my witness, I don't understand how the living can put up with it. My mother was never going to win Parent of the Year, but she would have burned my high school to the ground if they'd reopened their doors after the kind of brutal massacre that seems to be in the news every other weekend these days.

And those schools come into the twilight. They manifest here, ex-actly like they'd been when the tragedy occurred, and the ever-lasters fill their classrooms and their playgrounds, and the bone weeds and the ghost kudzu grow across their frames, making them a part of the great communal haunting that is the twilight. What we claim, we keep.

The truck stop is close enough that I can see the details of its out-line, the gleaming chrome of the trucks in the lot. There are scorch marks on the windows, and I realize I recognize this place. It was in Illinois when it existed outside the twilight, and some people with big ideas about what it meant to be "normal" barricaded the doors while three buses full of drama kids on their way to a state choir championship were inside. They torched the place. Everyone died. Including two of the perpetrators, who got caught in the flames and couldn't get clear before their engines blew. The other three were arrested and "brought to justice," which seemed like another way of saying "allowed to spew their bile and prejudice on a wider platform before fading into the pleasant anonymity of yesterday's news." They had known the field trip was going to stop at the truck stop, because it did every year. They believed boys in sequins and girls who sang alto were all perverts and homosexuals, and they had burned the truck stop to "cleanse the community" of the taint.

I know I said ghosts aren't that common, but we got a couple dozen from that accident. And yeah, some of the kids were gay before they died, and death didn't turn them straight because that's not how dying works. It's not how hearts work either. We don't live anymore, but we love the same as anyone, and we love whoever we're going to love, not whoever people want to order us to love.

The scars on the building get more obvious the closer I get, but people have been doing their best to make them less stark and less imposing. The char has mostly been scrubbed away, either by hand or with a power washer. The glass is damaged beyond repair unless someone nukes a window factory and brings it into the twilight. Unbroken windows aren't loved very often. They don't tend to linger. Flowers, though . . .

People *love* flowers. Maybe that's why what was formerly the truck stop lawn, probably a patchy, scrubby thing that needed more care and attention than the budget would allow, has been replaced with a rioting field of flowers. I can only recognize about half of them, and most of those are roses. Call me egotistical, but those are the only flowers I've ever been really interested in. There isn't any asphodel. Either Persephone hasn't adopted this place, or she doesn't know about it. Sadly, both seem equally likely. There's so much tragedy in the daylight that our twilight gods can't possibly keep up with it all.

There are several trucks and a burnt-out bus in the parking lot.

Since only the bus shows signs of what busted it up badly enough to drop it into the twilight, I'm guessing it's the only landmark: not a vehicle anymore, because no one loved it enough to carry it through the crash, but a weapon that was used to harm the people who used to be its passengers. I keep walking, past the trucks, past the bus, until I'm approaching the doors to the truck stop. They whisk open when their sensors pick me up, and I'm stepping into the cool, air-conditioned vestibule, heels clicking on the tile floor.

There are people at some of the Formica-topped tables, including the lingering choir kids, all of them as weary and disinterested as travelers the world over. They look up at my arrival, attracted by motion and the sound of my footsteps, but none of them seem to recognize me, and they quickly look away again, turning their attention back to their lunches and their magazines. Despite my woolgathering about the rarity of fast-food establishments in the twilight, the truck stop survivors appear to have remembered the food court in enough detail to make it at least partially manifest. I see coffee cups and muffins, and no one has the faint heat-haze in the air around them that would mark them as hitchhikers who could grab a coat and do a Starbucks run. They can taste the things they get here, and phantom coffee shops never run out of creamer. This is a self-sustaining haunting.

I don't know that I need to bother any of these people beyond finding myself a ride. I'm a hitcher. Getting rides is what I do. I fade back to the edge of the food court, trying to look unobtrusive as I scan the tables, looking for a trucker.

In the end, they aren't hard to find. There are four of them, clustered in a corner, half-shaded by a large rubber plant that was probably never that healthy or verdant when it was alive. They're older than the choir kids around them, burly adult men with beards and flannel shirts. I bet this isn't the afterlife they envisioned for themselves. But then, who among us got the afterlife we dreamed of?

I make my way toward them, and all the kids turn to watch me pass, some shrinking away like they're afraid of attracting my attention. I frown. I don't look that terrifying, do I? I'm the same age as the victims from the choir, if not younger, wearing an old-fashioned prom dress modest enough to verge on puritanical by today's standards. I look more like *Sabrina the Teenage Witch* than the Grim Reaper, and unless Sabrina has changed a lot since the last time I looked, that's not a frightening thing. I'm almost to the truckers when I can't take it anymore.

I spin on my toes, stopping when I'm facing one of the nearest tables, occupied by a dark-haired teenage girl and a skinny teenage boy who looks like he's roughly the same age.

"Why are you all *staring* at me?" I ask.

The girl squeaks, actually squeaks and shies away, staring at me with wide, wet eyes. She looks like she's going to break into tears. That won't be good for her mascara. Either she's made a few afterlife improvements, or she was one of those teens who started wearing makeup in middle school, because each lash is perfect, long, thick, and sooty, painted with an expert's hand. She still has her purse on the bench next to her, so at least she can reapply if she cries it all off in her terror of my existence.

"We don't know you," she says finally. "We know everyone here."

"Have you tried, I don't know, going outside?" I ask. "There are other people outside. Strangers might be less scary if you didn't huddle in here and pretend that you're the only ones left in the world."

"We couldn't go outside," she says, eyes getting even wider. "Some of the things we've seen through the windows have been . . . *wrong*." Her voice drops to a conspiratorial whisper. "They don't even look human. I think the whole truck stop has gone somewhere . . . *else*."

Everywhere is somewhere else, depending on where you're standing. I don't say that. I'm too busy staring at her. When I saw the outside, with its scrubbed-off windows and newly planted flowers, I naturally assumed the spirits haunting the ghost of the truck stop would have participated in the cleanup. That they'd want to move past the scene of their deaths and become part of the twilight. We're not alive down here, but we have lives in the colloquial sense. Ghosts can be happy here. Especially ghosts whose natures don't demand they have contact with the living. Decades can pass without them even so much as looking at the daylight, the world they left behind can change beyond all recognition, and they can keep doing whatever it is they love, settling into an eternal existence that doesn't depend on any of the things they've left behind.

"Somewhere *else*," I echo, somewhat unkindly. I could be gentler. I could ease her into this. But the boy on the bench is staring at me in abject terror, and it's been years since the fire. Have they been trapped inside here the whole time, unable to decide what happens next?

People in the twilight tend to take a fairly hands-off approach to the newly dead, unless they're causing problems or putting themselves, or us, into immediate and obvious danger. We can't predict how long a haunting will last from the way it manifests, and so we hang back, give them time to figure themselves out, and wait. Sometimes we wait too long.

"My name is Rose Marshall," I say. She doesn't look like that means anything to her, probably because it doesn't. Urban legends aren't big fans of proper names. "They call me the Phantom Prom Date, or the Girl in the Diner. Or the Girl in the Green Silk Gown."

Her eyes widen again, until it looks like there's a risk of them popping out of her head. That's not a thing that actually happens to the living, so far as I know, but ghosts are more malleable. When we say our faces might get stuck that way, we mean it. "You're . . . you're not serious," she says. "That's just a story."

"It's a ghost story," I correct. "About a girl who never made it to her senior prom. And look, here I am, still wearing the dress. I'm going to be wearing this dress for the rest of time. Or until I get tired of haunting the living. Which might take a few centuries. I enjoy being me. Don't you enjoy being you?"

"I don't . . . why are you asking me this?" She shies back further, until her back is touching the boy's shoulder, until there's virtually no space left between them. He continues to stare at me, doing nothing to draw my attention away from her. He wants to be overlooked.

It's not fair to her to let him, but it's not fair to any of them to leave them locked up in this rest stop turned crematorium. Sometimes fairness isn't the goal. Sometimes it's all about survival.

"Because you don't seem to understand the situation." I'm not being as kind as I could be, but dammit, I didn't ask for this complication. I spread my hands, gesturing to the whole truck stop: the murmuring teens turning in my direction, the truckers in the corner, the bathrooms, which are still pristine, and make me wonder whether the place is being haunted by some unfortunate custodial staffers, who were probably hoping for a better afterlife. Toilets until the end of time is not the sort of thing most religions use as a selling point.

"This truck stop isn't real," I say. That sounds ridiculous, so I lower my voice, trying to sound portentous instead. I think I land somewhere in the middle, on pretentious. Not as good for my ego, but still an improvement. "The real truck stop burned to the ground in the brutal inferno where you. All. *Died*."

The girl folds her arms, some of the terrified awe leaving her eyes as she glares at me. "You think we don't know that?"

I blink. "What."

"Our phones stopped working when they melted into slag. Davy over there had a three-year streak in Candy Crush." She points to a nerdy-looking boy on the other side of the food court. "Three years! He missed out on debate team, he missed out on Heather Nelson offering to let him touch her boob, and all because he had a calling for crushing candy. One stupid fire, and he's lost the thing he defined himself by. And sure, maybe that was a stupid thing, but it was *his*. Why is Candy Crush any less important than Model UN?"

"Uh." I'm sure I should have an answer. This feels like one of those questions that should be super easy, and also like it should make sense. It's not easy, and it doesn't make sense, and that's as frustrating as it is confusing. "What the hell is a Candy Crush?"

There. That's an answer. Pride swells in my chest for a moment before it crashes down and is replaced by an overwhelming feeling of embarrassment. I'm not a teenager anymore, not really. I have decades on this kid. So why does the fact that she's looking at me like I'm an interesting new species of bug make my chest burn?

"It's a game," she says. "You play it on your phone. Or at least, people who *have* phones play it. Apparently, dead people don't get to have phones. I read about you in one of those books of scary stories from the library. It was published before my Mom was born. You're like, super old, aren't you? Don't you think it's a little inappropriate for you to be walking around looking younger than me? People might get the wrong idea."

I'm starting to feel like coming in here was the wrong idea. I force the feeling away and look at her solemnly. "I look like this because this is the age I was when I died. One day you're going to be an old woman who looks like a teenager, too, unless you decide to let go and move on."

She sits up a little straighter. "That's an option? I don't have to haunt some stupid truck stop in the Twilight Zone for the rest of eternity?"

"Everyone moves on sooner or later," I say. I know so few ghosts who are actually older than I am. Eighty years seems to be the ceiling for most people. Any longer than that, and we get bored and start forgetting how to be human. Forget enough of your humanity and you lose whatever's left, becoming another undifferentiated part of the twilight, like the cornfields and the crows and the whispering haints that can no more tell you who they used to be than they can go back to the lands of the living. The daylight is not open to spirits without identities.

"What does 'moving on' mean?" asks the timid boy, leaning closer, so that he's looking at me around her.

Oh, Persephone. I don't have the time or the desire to do Afterlife 101 with these kids, but it looks like no one else has taken the time to do it for them, and they need it. If the itching on my skin is bad, imagine what it must be like for a bunch of baby ghosts who aren't allowing themselves to leave the room where they died long enough to figure out their own new natures. They look like any group of wide-eyed, slightly cynical teens, perfectly healthy, perfectly human, and statistically, that shouldn't be the case. At least one of them should have fangs, or scales, or legs that end in plumes of vapor.

Ghost life is weird when it wants to be.

I clap my hands, drawing more attention to myself, before I climb onto the nearest open table and wave my arms. "Attention! Attention, room full of dead kids! My name is Rose Marshall, and I am your new field trip escort!"

Some of them grumble or make faces and the classic "screwball" gesture as they turn toward me, but that's not important. What matters is that every one of them turns, even the truckers. They're bored out of their skulls in here. I'm something new.

That makes me a little nervous. Some of them could be potentially destructive, so being the only thing for them to focus on isn't entirely safe. Normal as they look, every one of these kids died a violent, horrible death, and maybe that's why no one has tried this yet. They're still new ghosts. They could lash out. But they know they're dead, and that's a big improvement over where this conversation sometimes starts.

"Hi!" I hook both thumbs toward my chest in the biggest, cheesiest "this is me" gesture I can think of. "You may have heard of me. I'm the Phantom Prom Date, also known as the Angel of the Overpass. I've been dead a long, long time, and now I'm here to help you figure out your own deaths."

"Homophobic assholes set us on fire!" shouts one of the boys. "I'm not even gay!"

"That doesn't matter," snaps another boy. "Toxic masculinity doesn't care about what you *are*. It cares about what you *look* like, and none of us looked like the football team."

"Two of them are gay," calls a girl. "Or were when we were alive and going to the same school, anyway."

"This is fascinating, says the girl who doesn't know any of these people, and who really doesn't care who's attracted to who, but I'm glad you all know you're dead," I say. "That's a hard bombshell to drop."

"The fire was a big hint," says the first girl.

"So was my phone melting," says the much-maligned Davy, who looks like he wants nothing more than to crush some candy. Maybe I should get him a hammer? That's how we broke peppermints when I was a kid.

"Not everyone leaves a ghost when they die," I say. "Humans who do drop into a place we call 'the twilight.' That's where you are right now."

"Is Rod Serling here?" asks one of the girls.

"How about Jordan Peele?" counters one of the boys. Both begin to giggle.

I hate dealing with teenagers. It wasn't my favorite thing back when I *was* a teenager, and now that I'm not really, it's endlessly frustrating, like diving into a pond without a stick I can use to flip over the rocks at the bottom first. There could be anything down there. Broken glass. Leeches. Snapping turtles. There's no way of knowing without that all-important stick.

"This isn't Heaven," I say, and they quiet down. "It isn't Hell, either. I don't know whether those places really exist. If they do, they've never been my problem, and I died in 1952, in a place called Buckley Township, Michigan. They may be what waits for ghosts who move on. Most of your classmates have moved on. That's why they weren't here when you woke up. This is more ghosts than I'd expect to find after one fire. You died so quickly and so unexpectedly that a lot of you had unfinished business. That sucks and I'm sorry. But you can't stay holed up in this truck stop forever. The afterlife doesn't take kindly to spirits who don't want to get out there and do their jobs."

"We don't have jobs," protests Davy. "We don't even have phones anymore."

"Doesn't matter," I say. "Every kind of ghost is different. I'm a hitchhiking ghost. I gain strength and feed the twilight through travel among the living. I ask them for rides, I borrow their coats, and I sustain myself. None of you are hitchers." I would recognize my own. "But you have a role to play in the twilight, and you need to get out there and start playing it."

"Or what?" asks the first girl.

"Or you'll curdle and fade," I say. "Your ghostly calling is like food and sleep and crushing candy was to you when you were alive. You have to do what you were made for, or you'll pay for your refusal."

"This sucks," says one of the boys. "Being a ghost should be about playing pranks and getting into locker rooms to watch the cheerleaders change before the game, not doing chores and working for the Twilight Zone."

"It's just the twilight," I correct. "And you can take it up with the gods. We have a couple of options available."

"But we've seen things through the windows," says another of the girls. "Big things with extra heads and too many teeth. What's going to happen to us if we listen to you and try to go outside?"

"The twilight is primarily for human ghosts," I say. "That doesn't mean we're the only things here, or even that all ghosts will look like you'd expect humans to look, especially after they've had a few years to relax into their hauntings." I don't want to try explaining the crossroads right now, or how much chaos has been caused by their undoing. That's Being Dead 201, and this is the intro course.

The girl's eyes widen. "We're going to turn into m-monsters?" she squeaks.

"Yes, if you stay locked in here," I say. "Fading twists a ghost. You'll forget everything about your life, what you wanted to be when you grew up, what you cared about, and you'll turn into hungry fog. The 'monsters' you saw outside were probably nightcrawlers. They've been spotted in the living world, too, in Fresno, California. They won't hurt you. They're curious and mostly harmless and made almost entirely of leg. I guess they could tap dance someone to death, but since you're all already dead, that's not much of a threat anymore."

"It wasn't fair, what happened to us," says one of the boys. His eyes glow orange. He's still on fire, somewhere deep down inside, where it's never going to burn out. His hair is black and his skin is tan and he looks like his ancestors may have immigrated from Japan. He's an onibi, then, a relative of the will-o-wisp, but with more of an affinity for avenging flame. That's nice. It'll be nicer when it's nowhere near me. There's nothing wrong with onibi. They're like white ladies in a way: they improve the world by hunting the kind of people who would lead to the creation of more onibi. They tend to manifest in areas that have had a serious problem with arson, and after the arsonists are reduced to charcoal, the onibi hangs out and haunts a neighborhood that isn't on fire anymore. Nice.

If you're not flammable, that is. I twitch my skirts away from him in what I hope looks like a casual gesture, and smile at the group. "No, it wasn't fair. Death is never fair. Whether it happens in the cradle or the nursing home, it sucks. But being a ghost isn't all bad."

"You just said we have to work," says one of the girls.

"You have to work to be alive," I say. "Eating, drinking, sleeping, using the bathroom," I can't quite suppress my shudder, "it's all work, in a way. The things your ghostly nature will demand of you are like that. Things you'll do almost instinctively and won't really notice once you have your phantom feet under you. You don't have to breathe anymore, but I bet you never resented having to do it before."

Several of the teens exchange glances, muttering to one another. I smile wider. This is starting to feel like something that can be accomplished.

"But you have to leave the truck stop."

The muttering stops, replaced by sullen silence.

"I won't lie and say there's nothing out there that can hurt you. There's plenty out there that can hurt you. There's plenty in here that can hurt you, too. Fading is painful. Losing your sense of self sucks, and it's not something most ghosts can come back from." I *might* be able to recover, and that's only because I have more than fifty years of power and experience behind me. A bunch of green ghosts like these kids . . .

There's no central authority in the twilight, no one whose job it was to come into this warehouse of lost souls and flush them all into the questionable safeties of the twilight. I still feel like we've failed them somehow, like someone *should* have been watching out for them before I stumbled across their sanctuary.

Which probably wouldn't have happened if I hadn't been running from a dinosaur ghost, which really just drives home the fact that outside *isn't* safe. It's still better than staying in here and souring until there's nothing left of the kids who died before their time.

I've always had a soft spot for teenage ghosts, even as I try to avoid interacting with them. I look like one of them, and I *was* one of them, before the strange alchemy of time pulled me further and further from my original state. Teenage ghosts feel everything so profoundly, really grasp the magnitude of their loss, but they also move on quickly, lacking the depth of ties to the living that older ghosts tend to have. They accept their new circumstances faster than adult ghosts, but don't delude themselves the way child ghosts sometimes do. They're more likely to hold onto their humanity than ghosts who died before they were in their teens—kids aren't great at being human when they're alive, and when you take the measures of mortality away from them, they can slip into monstrosity with remarkable speed. It would be impressive if it weren't so terrifying for a ghost like me.

The group doesn't have a definite leader, but many of them are looking to the girl in front of me like she's the one who makes their decisions. I look at her, resisting the urge to grab her shoulders and shake until she agrees to do what I say. Violence is not the answer to all the world's problems. It's just frequently the most efficient route to a solution. I'd like some efficiency about now. Bobby Cross is out there somewhere, and with the crossroads out of play, there's not many forces left that can tell him "no." Persephone can, but she doesn't leave the Underworld. I've never heard of her actually going walking in the twilight, and I've heard enough weird shit that I'm sure I'd know if she were into visiting her believers. She's powerful. She's just like most of the old gods. She's tired.

The girl looks around at her peers, all of whom look anxiously back. Then she smiles uncertainly and stands.

"Well, if it's safe to go outside, I'm pretty tired of sitting here all the time," she says. "Lead the way."

"That's not how this works," I say, and watch some of the borrowed bravado slip out of her spine. "You're not the same kind of ghost I am. I'd know if you were." I wish I were as sure of that as I sound. It's impossible to be certain, especially when they've been confining themselves for as long as they have. They could manifest the second they step outside. They could take months, or even years, to settle on a specific kind of haunting. I don't have that kind of time. "You need to go out into the twilight and start discovering yourselves. Walk until you find other ghosts. See if any of them speak to you in more than just words. There's a harmony, of sorts, when you find the right sort of spirit. The part of you that's becoming something other than human recognizes its own kin, even if you don't."

"How can it be part of me and not me?" asks the timid boy. He's still sitting, still watching me with the utmost wariness.

"Your immune system was a part of you and not you while you were alive," I say. "It could recognize diseases and dangers that your conscious mind had no idea how to deal with. Trust your instincts. Be polite to everything, because everything you meet here was alive once, and deserves your respect."

"Even the things you said were made mostly of leg?"

"The nightcrawlers? Yes." I'm actually not sure about that. If they were alive once, they probably shouldn't be here. They should be in the starlight with the rest of the non-human intelligences, or on some other layer altogether. Maybe down in the midnight. If they were alive and human, I think I'd know. They don't show any signs of being human people who've slipped into a different form, and I'm not sure what kind of ghost would be mostly leg and big, staring eyes and do nothing but stride around scaring the pants off of dead kids all the time. "They're harmless as long as you don't antagonize them."

"How do you antagonize something that's mostly made of leg?"

"The same way you'd antagonize any wild animal. Don't throw things at them or try to pet them or anything else you wouldn't do to a moose." Nightcrawlers are pretty placid. Most twilight megafauna is. They have no natural predators, and so just walk around being leggy and weird most of the time.

I hop down from the table, gesturing to the door I came in through, and say, "The twilight is waiting for you kids. Now go out and join it," before starting for the table occupied by the four truckers. They haven't moved. Oh, they listened to everything I said, but they're not getting up. The teenage dead are muttering excitedly in their little groups, stealing glances at the windows. I'm sure one of them will make a break for it sometime in the next few minutes, and once they confirm for themselves that I'm not kidding about it being relatively safe outside, they're going to scatter and begin the process of coming to terms with what's happened to them. A few may find their way back to their families, back to the bedrooms where they spent the last weeks of their lives, and set up a brief haunting, but most will figure out what they want to do with their deaths. They'll be fine. The majority of ghosts are.

None of the teenagers follow me. I snap my fingers as I approach the truckers, and my green silk gown twists and shifts, replaced by a pair of jeans and a plain white tank top. My standard uniform when I'm dealing with truckers. The corsage remains around my wrist. I could change it, if I wanted to put in the focus, but I'm afraid I wouldn't be able to change it back, and having Persephone's blessing is important enough to my survival that I don't want to take the risk. Some things aren't worth it.

One of the truckers starts to rise at my approach. The others pull him back down. I drop myself onto an open stretch of bench, smiling wryly at the group. "Gentlemen," I say.

"Rose," says one of them, voice gruff and somewhat reserved, like he doesn't want to be talking to me. "Always wondered if you were real or some sort of story people told when they didn't want to admit a friend had fallen asleep at the wheel. Guess I was hoping you weren't." He has a Minnesota accent, broad as the whole horizon, and I want to tell him it's all right, even though I know it isn't.

"Your trucks are in the parking lot," I say. "Why are you gentlemen still here?"

"At first, we didn't want to leave the kids," says the one who tried to stand before. "They were so scared, and so little. Nothing as little as them should be dead. Not the way we died. Not in a place like this."

"Hatred is a part of the human condition, and it doesn't end with death," I say. "Wish I could tell you otherwise, I really do, but what happened to you all was as human as a mother's love or a kid falling head over heels for their first puppy."

"We know," says one of the other truckers. "Why are you here? We know it wasn't to help those kids."

"Maybe it should have been," I say. I'm ashamed of how much I wanted to turn and run when I realized they didn't know the rules. "We're not always as kind as we should be. But no. I'm here because I need a ride to the Last Dance Diner, so I can tell my friends what I've been doing. I could walk, but it would take a long time, and I'm a hitch-hiking ghost. This is sort of what I was made for."

"We're dead," says one of the truckers. "Maybe that means we don't want to drive anymore."

"If it meant that, your trucks wouldn't be outside," I say calmly, meeting his eyes. "You loved them enough to keep them with you. They loved you enough to stay. If you don't drive, you'll eventually fade. The fact that you kept your trucks means that you're road ghosts."

Oh, I hope I'm right. This is the sort of thing I try to avoid whenever possible. The Minnesota trucker makes a small, disgusted noise in the back of his throat, leaning back until it looks like he's going to fall off the bench.

"Does it also mean I *have* to give you a ride even if I don't want to?" he asks. "Because maybe I don't feel like driving a dead girl around the afterlife."

"Better a dead girl than a living one, given the circumstances," I say. "Living people are bad news once you're dead."

"But all the stories say you take rides from living people," says the trucker. "Aren't they bad news for you?"

"They are, but the kind of ghost I am makes it unavoidable." I'm getting antsy. I want to be out of here, not sitting around arguing about the ethics of bothering the living. I need to get to the diner, check in, and get back out on the road before Persephone and Apple get tired of waiting for me.

For all that Pippa made that crack about me having "powerful friends," things were a lot simpler when it was just me and, occasionally, Mary and Emma. When I didn't have a grandniece to worry about, or a boyfriend-slash-car, or the occasionally autocratic friendship of the Queen of the Routewitches. Connections are for the living, who need other people to survive. All they're doing for me is making things more complicated.

The trucker frowns as he nods. "Sounds frustrating," he says. "But convenient. I can't do it, and you can, because of 'the kind of ghost' you are. How do you know we're not ghosts who get to play with living people, too?"

"Because it's not a gift and it's not an honor, it's a frustrating burden," I say. "You can't go home to the people who love you. If there aren't any people who love you, this isn't an opportunity to go back and haunt your enemies or anything else stupid like that. You're dead. How much the living can see you, how much you can interact with them, that's outside your control. And if you *can* interact with the living, there's a pretty good chance you *have* to interact with the living. That it's somehow built into the bones of whatever it is you are now. Being dead means having more time and fewer choices about how you spend it. So no, this isn't convenient. This is me, trying to get you to understand that things are different now, and asking one of you nice gentlemen to give me the ride I need to get back to doing what I'm supposed to be doing."

"Is that all?" asks the third trucker. He's older than the others, with the wide, soft middle of a man who's been depending on truck stop convenience stores and roadside pie for a long time. He looks friendly. If this were an ordinary truck stop, still anchored in the daylight, he's the one I would have approached first. "Never liked the living much, not even when I was one of 'em. If you need a ride, I'll be happy to give you one. You'll just have to tell me the way."

"I don't know how far we're going," I say, getting to my feet. "I was running from a nightmare after I got dropped off by a Dullahan—a lady with a detachable head—who didn't want to put up with me anymore."

"It's a tribute to how tired I am of hanging out in this place with all these damn kids that I'm not even a little bit tempted to ask you whether you mean that literally," he says, as he leverages his bulk away from the bench. He moves with the grace of a man who knows exactly how much space he occupies in the world, and he doesn't hesitate as he offers me his hand. It's a courteous gesture, accompanied by a bob of his head.

I've gotten surprisingly good at reading people. I haven't really had a choice. Being a hitchhiker means every stranger is a friend I don't know very well yet. I smile as I take his hand, looking one last time around this cavernous room filled with strangers I'm never going to know better than I do right now.

"Can I have a ride?" I say. The sacred phrase of the road, at least where girls like me are concerned.

"I think I've been waiting to drive you since I got my license," he says, and smiles, and somehow his words aren't cheesy at all. They're just right.

Together, we walk to the door. A few of the teens are already outside, exploring the flowers that have overrun the lawn, taking their first cautious steps into the parking lot. We ignore them and walk on.

We have a lot of ground to cover.

Chapter 7
Back Where We Belong

THE TRUCKER'S NAME IS CARL. It's a good name. Solid, unre-markable, efficient. Easy to yell if things go wrong. I like a man with a name that doesn't mess around. His truck's name is Jolene, after the Dolly Parton song, and I like that, too. Means he doesn't take himself too seriously, that he isn't ashamed to admit he enjoys a good country classic. The truck is old, a little road worn but well-maintained, and I like that best of all. A man with a brand-new truck is a man who can't be read. Maybe he's a monster and just hasn't had the chance to show it yet. Maybe he's a saint, and the world hasn't had time to tarnish him. I don't like riding in rusty deathtraps whether in the twilight or the daylight, but here, a well-loved truck with a woman's name is just about as ideal as I can think of.

He watches me boost myself into the passenger seat, pushing a flurry of fast-food bags and paper maps aside, and shuts the door before he walks around and climbs in the driver's seat, fitting perfectly into the space between the wheel and the cushions. It's clearly shaped to his dimensions, molded into something comfortable and forgiving by years of use. "Which way?" he asks.

I don't know the roads in this part of the twilight, but I can always find the Last Dance when I try, except on the rare occasions when it doesn't exist. I focus, and it's like a beacon clicks on in the far distance, calling to me across the miles.

"That way." I point. "There should be roads. I mean, the twilight is malleable, and it probably won't make it so we can't get there from here."

Carl laughs, a deep, rolling sound, and puts the truck into gear. More teens emerge as we roll out of the parking lot. They turn our way—the human eye is attracted by motion—and then go back to exploring their surroundings. We're less important than their current predicament by a long shot.

Carl turns the way I indicated as he hits the gas, and we accelerate toward the horizon. I allow myself to relax into my seat, getting comfortable among the fast-food wrappers and the crumpled maps. None of them will do him any good here. They're all drawn for the daylight, and they won't guide him through this highway system—assuming he's going to stick around. I still don't have a handle on what kind of ghost he is. Too new, and too suppressed by the time he spent hiding inside that truck stop.

"Keep going until you see an offramp promising food at the next exit," I say. "With me in the car, that should be the Last Dance."

"I've heard of that diner," says Carl.

"Not surprising." No one living gets to walk the twilight or taste Emma's pie, but enough road ghosts have interactions with the daylight that sometimes our stories spread, and people who haven't quite died yet hear about the Last Dance Diner, the rest stop and restaurant that marks the last exit the dead can take before they drive off the edge of the world. The seat below me is getting warmer, which is funny, since I don't have any body heat for it to borrow, and this isn't the kind of truck that comes with built-in seat warmers. I glance at Carl, trying to assess his condition.

He's smiling, teeth white against the tangle of his beard. "This road is *amazing*. It's like I can feel the pavement clean through Jolene's wheels."

Ah. He's going to be a road ghost after all. "That's because you can."

"What?"

"Remember I said every kind of ghost is different. You and I may run across one another a few more times before you get tired of haunting. You really loved your truck, didn't you?"

"Jolene and I have been together for a long time." He runs his hand across the dashboard, lovingly caressing the plastic. I've seen a lot of truckers who loved their vehicles. Some of them loved their trucks so much that, given a chance between crushing a car full of kids and scratching the paint on their rig, they'd kill the kids, because they thought of their truck as the most important thing in the world.

Love isn't always a good thing. Love can be dangerous: toxic and corrosive and cruel. People act like love is one of the great positives of the universe, but those people usually haven't seen love in the process of eating its prey alive. Love doesn't let go, and love doesn't forgive. Hate is worse, on the whole, but that doesn't make love inherently kind. Nothing could.

Carl doesn't seem like that kind of man. He clearly loves his truck because she's been good to him, but that doesn't mean he's going to place her above the rest of the world. And that's a good thing, because if I'm right about what I'm seeing, he's going to swallow her whole as part of the process of his own becoming.

It's been a long time since I've seen a coachman in the process of being made, and I wouldn't have expected Carl and Jolene to fit the requirements. They died together, yes, victims of the same fire, but they died apart, her keys in his pocket, his body burning yards away from her engine. Normally, the two composite parts of a coachman die together, melting and melding into one entity.

As if there's anything normal about a kind of ghost so archaic that I haven't seen one outside of New Orleans in forty years. "Were you ever planning to retire?" I ask, as carefully as I can.

The smile he sends in my direction tells me that my care is appreciated but unnecessary. If I can see what's happening to him, he can feel it. "Not really," he says. "Me and Jolene, we were going to ride to the end of the world. I've paid to have her engine upgraded three times, when emissions standards would have benched us otherwise. Don't have a house, don't have a spouse, just have the open road and this good, good girl beneath me. I was never going to leave her. I used to lay awake at night and think about what would happen if she ever broke down too badly to be fixed. I figured if she died, I'd probably go pretty soon after."

This all fits what I know about coachmen. He loved his truck more than he loved any of the people around him—possibly more than he had ever managed to love himself. He has more in common with the dinosaur-thing from before than he does with me, or most of the ghosts he's going to meet over the course of his existence in the twilight. He's going to be a composite. How much of Jolene will creep in and over-write the man he was, I don't know, and I can't grieve for what he's going to lose because it's clear he isn't grieving. For him, this is the best afterlife he could possibly have imagined. He's going to have it all.

He laughs as he turns Jolene down the exit I told him to watch for, and the sound is deep and joyous, starting all the way from the base of his spine before working its way up. "This is a trip," he says.

"What were you hauling?"

"Hmm?"

"When the . . . accident . . . happened, what were you hauling?" He and Jolene are one entity, but that's not going to apply to their cargo. That's free and clear and theirs now. No living corporation has come up with a bill of lading that allows them to reclaim damaged goods from the afterlife. I'm sure they're working on it. Those people hate to lose anything they think of as their own, and I guarantee you they think of this cargo as their own.

"Oh! Um. Dry goods and shelf-stable pharmaceuticals for Walmart. Need yoga pants or Midol?" He laughs again, a big, booming sound that fills the cabin and bounces off the windows. It's surprisingly soft for being as large as it is.

"Maybe," I say. "If you don't mind opening the back when we get to the diner, I'm sure Emma would be happy to root around in there. If you have any baking supplies, she'll probably pay you for them. In pie. We don't do money so much here in the twilight. Not enough of it gets destroyed, and people don't tend to love it piece by piece. They love the idea of it. Even people who love being rich don't have warm, fuzzy feelings about individual dollar bills, which means they don't tend to manifest down here."

"You keep saying 'down,'" says Carl. "Should I be worried about little naked red imps with pitchforks?"

"How very Archie Comics of you," I say. "This isn't Hell. This isn't even the most hellish of the accessible layers of the afterlife. But when you move between levels, it feels like falling, as much as it feels like anything you experienced when you were alive, so we tend to say 'down' when we're talking about how to get here. Don't worry. There's no brimstone in your future. Or if there is, there's not a lot of it."

"Huh," says Carl. "Lot more rules to being dead than I would have expected."

"I guess so," I say. "I've been dead for long enough that I don't really pay attention anymore."

"Is it rude to ask what happened?" Carl glances my way. "Only I've heard stories about you since before I got my license, and no one ever quite agrees on the story of how you died."

I'm quiet for a moment. It's not like the circumstances of my death have ever been secret, or private. I gave those up when I became a story kids told around the campfire. I am a matter of public record, an urban legend whose reach is far greater than my grasp could ever have been, and if he'd been really dedicated to finding my story when he was alive, he could have found it easily enough. Laura wrote a whole book about who I was and where I came from. *On the Trail of the Phantom Prom Date.* She never liked me much, thanks to the part where she blamed me for her boyfriend's untimely death, but her scholastic ethics had been too strong to let her do a hatchet job on me. She'd written the truth as she understood it, documenting every scrap she could find about the life and death of a Michigan girl named Rose, and the pieces she'd left out had either been too unimportant to be remembered or buried too deeply for her to uncover.

I take a short breath that I don't need, and say, "I was on my way to prom when I was run off the road."

"Did they catch the guy who did it?" Carl sounds genuinely interested, which makes sense. In the twilight, "so how did you die?" basically replaces "so, what do you do?" as an icebreaker. He's stuck with me as the closest thing he has to a guide. Of course he wants to know more about me.

"Not yet," I say. "That's actually what I was on my way to do when I found you. He's a bit of a problem child."

"He's got to be dead by this point, right? Or at least so old that he doesn't have a license anymore." Carl looks briefly, thoughtfully pleased. "I guess I don't have to worry about my eyes failing before I'm ready to give up my keys, huh? My whole mortal shell failed at the same time."

"Fire will do that," I agree, giving him a sidelong glance. It's nice that one of us is finding the positive in this day's terrible adventures. I wasn't this calm while I was still learning the rules of the road. "Hysterical and angry" would be a better description. If I'd been a poltergeist, half of Buckley Township would have been leveled before I calmed down enough to be reasonable.

"He's not dead, and he's not old," I say. "He's just a man who made a bargain with a cosmic force of awful and got to stay behind the wheel as long as he kept on killing people. I wasn't his first victim. I was far, far from his last. Now things have changed. He's started threatening the people I care about, and I'm finally on my way to take him down. He's going to stop hurting people. He's going to stop forever."

The cab is so quiet I can hear the wind whispering through the corn outside. Jolene's engine has stopped rumbling. She isn't really a machine anymore. She's half of the ghost that speaks through Carl, and neither of them is what they were, and for this pair, that's a blessing and a gift from the twilight. The ghostroads can be kind when they're moved to be. It's rare, but it happens.

Carl finally lets out a low, whistling breath, shaking his head as he says, "That's a lot to put on those narrow little shoulders of yours. Is anybody helping you?"

"My shoulders may be narrow, but I'm old enough to be your mother," I say. "I've traveled more distance than just about any other ghost you're likely to meet. The road knows my name. The Goddess of the Dead gave me her blessing. The Ocean Lady welcomes me, and the Queen of the North American Routewitches calls me her friend. I don't need anyone's help to do what has to be done."

I don't quite manage to keep the offense from my voice. I wish I could manage it. I've never been a great actress, and most of what little skill I possess winds up getting directed toward convincing people that I'm a teenage runaway who just needs a coat and a cup of coffee, instead of a terrifying urban legend come to haunt them while they're on a road trip to visit a friend from college or someone else who deserves to go without phantom interference.

Carl nods. "I don't like it."

"You don't have to like it. The twilight doesn't much care whether we're happy. It just cares that we keep following the rules and don't tell too many secrets to the living. They're better off not being able to say for sure whether or not there's an afterlife."

"I notice you haven't mentioned God."

"That's part of why the living are better off not knowing for sure. That, and not everyone hangs out in the twilight after they die. Most people move on immediately. Tell the living that some of the dead linger, and you'll have a queue of folks demanding to speak to departed parents and children who moved on years ago. No good comes of it."

Carl nods again, thoughtfully. "This is all a lot more complicated than I ever thought it was going to be."

"We may be dead, but we're still human," I say. "There's nothing we can't complicate."

The sweet green light of the Last Dance appears to our right, shining through the corn, beckoning me home. I point. "That's my stop," I say. "If you can pull off into the lot, I'll get out of your hair. I can even bring you a piece of pie if you want one."

"I can get my own—" begins Carl, and catches himself, shifting slightly in his seat. His thighs never break contact with the cushion. "No, I guess I can't get my own, can I? I'd be happy to have a piece of pie. Key lime is my favorite if it's available."

"It will be," I say solemnly. Emma always has everyone's favorite. She doesn't spend all day baking, and she doesn't keep a list, but—somehow—it works out that way. We once had a hitchhiker come in and say that his favorite was "unicorn pie," and Emma perked up and said she'd just been experimenting with the recipe. It turned out to be sort of like an even sweeter form of cookie salad, topped with marshmallow crème and edible glitter, and eating it had been like trying to deep-throat Disneyland. Never again if you ask me. But he left happy, and as far as Emma was concerned, that was really what mattered.

Gary is the only car in the lot when Carl pulls up. His lights come on as soon as I climb out of the truck, and he rolls forward just enough to bump his fender ever-so-gently against my calf, engine purring and the sweet tones of Top 40 radio drifting out of his cab. I stroke his hood with one hand, aware of precisely how ridiculous this has to look to Carl and Jolene, and say, "In a minute, honey. I need to get the nice man some pie to pay for my ride home."

Gary rolls back into his original position, engine revving. He flashes his headlights at Jolene. There's a pause before she flashes her lights back, and then the two of them are chatting away through the wonders of halogen lights and Morse code. I wonder briefly whether the part of Jolene that is Carl can understand the conversation, and then I'm hitting the door of the diner.

The bell doesn't ring, largely because I forgot to stay solid in my hurry to get to Emma; I walk right *through* the door, which is sort of embarrassing. That's baby ghost nonsense, and it's been a long time since I had to worry about that kind of thing. I should be able to handle a simple *door.* Emma, behind the counter as usual, gives me a startled look before rushing over to me, hands outstretched to grab my shoulders.

"Rose!" she says. "Where have you *been*? You stink of the starlight, my girl. What were you doing down there? You know the starlight isn't safe for girls like us."

Which is interesting. If the starlight is safe for Dullahan, I'd expect it to be safe for a *beán sidhe* like Emma. I let her grab my upper arms, leaning into her embrace and taking comfort from the contact. It's good to be home, even if I know I'm not staying yet. It's good to be back among people who understand.

"I went hitching," I say. "Bobby came to pay a call, and I ran. Apple intercepted me on the other end."

"The Queen of the Routewitches?" asks Emma. "Why's she messing with an honest ghost trying to fulfill the terms of her existence? The nerve of some people."

"Speaking of the terms of a ghost's existence, can I get a slice of key lime pie for the baby coachman out in the parking lot?"

Emma straightens, eyes widening in surprise. "A baby coachman? Someone's manifesting as a horse and carriage? I haven't seen that happen in a long while."

"A man and his truck, not a horse and carriage, but he's showing the early signs," I say. "He's melting into the seat, he can feel the road through the truck's tires, but he's not being fully absorbed. He still looks like a man driving a truck, not a phantom truck roaring around doing whatever it wants. And he still wants a piece of key lime pie."

"I have a fresh one," she says, hurrying off to the pie case to start preparing a slice. "Did he want that a la mode?"

"He didn't say so," I say. "I'm assuming he would have said something if he wanted ice cream. If I were a coachman, I wouldn't want to risk getting ice cream on my dashboard. That seems like it would be unpleasantly sticky."

"Yes, probably," says Emma, sliding the wedge of pie onto a plate. It looks perfect. Her pies always look perfect. They don't taste as good as pies in the living world, so she has to focus twice as much on the aesthetic. It's the only way she can feel like she's making them correctly. "Poor lamb. He doesn't understand yet, how limited he's going to be, does he?"

"He's outside talking to Gary now," I say uncomfortably. "I bet Gary has a lot to say about being limited."

"You're almost certainly right about that," agrees Emma, pursing her lips and giving me a thoughtful look, one filled with layers of conversation that we haven't had yet and very much need to have. "You sticking around for long?"

"Not terribly. I still need to get some hitching in before my skin's going to stop crawling. Bobby caught me right after my first ride, and Apple orchestrated my second, so it didn't really count the way it should have. She's nice and all, but she doesn't know what it's like for me. For any of us, really." The relationship between routewitches and the dead is complicated. Most routewitches can see ghosts. Ghosts who can't fully manifest in the lands of the living have a nasty tendency to swarm anyone who can see them, as if banging on the door and demanding help you haven't earned has ever been the way to endear yourself. So many routewitches view us as occasionally useful pests, and they behave accordingly.

Apple has never been like that, maybe because the Ocean Lady is both ghost and goddess and has forced the first among her followers to come to terms with the fact that being alive is a temporary thing, not a gods-given permission to abuse what power you possess. She's still alive so she can't understand the painful craving that comes with needing to perform my steps in the great dance that is the afterlife. I'm being called to the stage, and I can't refuse to answer forever. I can't even refuse for long, unless I want to run the risk of glitching right through the floor of the twilight and winding up on some country road, back in my green silk gown, unable to access any of the better parts of my phantom nature until I get into someone's car and do as the universe demands.

Emma gives me a dubious look and hands me the piece of pie. "Take this to your coachman," she says. "Tell him we do takeout but not delivery, since we don't currently have a driver, and that he's sadly a bit too large for the position. Then get back in here and tell me why Apple's interfering with you doing what you're meant for."

"Yes, ma'am," I say, a bit too smartly, and turn to trot back to the door, pie in hand. I realize she didn't give me a fork and one pops into existence on the plate, shining silver with just a trace of tarnish, like it's been here for years, and didn't just get thought into being.

It's colder outside than it was a few minutes ago. I shiver as I hurry across the parking lot to where Jolene and Gary are flashing their lights at one another. The passenger side door looks like it's still unlocked, but I hesitate to open it. It seems rude, somehow, to just climb in when I know the truck is in the process of becoming part of Carl's body, driver and vehicle united for eternity as they always wished that they could be.

The wishing is part of it, as far as I'm aware. Every coachman I've ever talked to has said they dreamt of staying with their vehicle forever, that they felt it was an extension of their own body even before that became the literal truth. Not of driving forever—that's the sort of longing that makes Phantom Riders, not coachmen—but of staying with their vehicle. Of being safe and comfortable and *home*. I wouldn't want someone grabbing my arm without permission. What makes opening the door any less of an invasion?

I'm still mulling this over when the door swings open in clear invitation. Carl glances over, apparently startled. He's not used to his new proprioception yet. Jolene was never really a part of him before, no matter how much he may have felt like she was.

I can't help him with this adjustment. But I can direct him toward the twilight around New Orleans, where he's more likely to find ghosts of the same sort who can offer guidance to get him through the transition.

"I brought pie," I say, and climb up into the cab of the truck, offering it to him. "I wasn't sure about a la mode, so this seemed like the right thing. Emma says to tell you that they do takeout, and you're welcome to come back any time you like. I see you've met Gary."

"I understood what he was saying when he flashed his lights at me," says Carl, taking the plate and using the fork to break off a perfect, glistening bite of key lime pie. "How can I understand him?"

"Gary's a special case. He's dead, but he's not any of the formalized kinds of ghost. He's sort of the first of his kind." That's putting it delicately. Tricking the twilight is not easily, or lightly, done.

"Special case meaning . . . ?"

"He was human when he was alive. He turned himself into a car when he died so that we could be together." He didn't think that one through as well as he probably should have, all things considered. "As you merge with Jolene, understanding other vehicles is going to become easier and easier for you. You already knew more than you probably thought you did. Good truckers always do."

He grunts and takes his first bite of the pie. Then he squints at the fork, suspiciously. "Does everything taste so . . . washed out when you're dead? The coffee at the truck stop was like this, too."

"We don't get to enjoy the pleasures of the flesh the same way we did when we were alive," I say, trying to take the sting out of the discovery. Learning the rules of death after spending so many years dealing with the rules of life is never easy. At least for me, those rules had come with two arms, two legs, and freedom of movement, not merging permanently with my car and being expected to be totally okay with it. Dying never asks for consent. It makes the changes it's going to make, and then it rolls on, off to twist its next target into something new.

"Huh." He takes another bite of pie. "This is going to take some getting used to."

"Most things do. You should go to New Orleans. Follow the signs along the highway even if you think you know the route; the roads are different here. But there are more coachmen in New Orleans than anywhere else that I know of. Most of them are horses and carriages, but they're still the same sort of ghost. They'll be able to help you like I can't."

"All right," says Carl, with a nod. "Anything *we* can do to help you?"

"No." I shake my head. "You got me back to the Last Dance, and that's really what I needed. Do me a favor if you see any of those kids from the truck stop. Drive them wherever they tell you they want to go. And when you figure out how to drive into the daylight, don't go looking for the people you knew when you were alive. Seeing them will only break your heart. It isn't worth it."

"If you say so," he says. The passenger-side door swings open again, a clear invitation for me to get out.

I flash him the brightest smile I can muster. "I do," I say, and slide out of the truck.

"Did you want to go through the cargo?" Carl asks. There's a clicking, sliding sound from the rear, which I know will be the doors opening.

Maintaining my smile becomes a little easier. "I'd love to," I say, and turn to wave my arms at the diner, signaling for Emma to come out and join me. There's nothing like a scavenging trip to improve the day. We don't get to do this all that often—most trucks that wind up in the twilight do so solo, destroyed by accidents that spared their drivers, and they can be fairly possessive of their last loads—and when we do, it's almost always as part of a massive scrum. Having a full truck essentially deliver itself to us is an extravagance beyond measure.

Emma is happy to join me in rampaging through Jolene's cargo. It was definitely a Walmart load, mixing textiles and dry goods. Emma exclaims in wordless delight and claims an entire case of canned chicken stock, along with all the salt in sight. I pick up a windbreaker and a pack of lighters. These are the ghosts of the actual items, but they're better than nothing.

There are some new CDs back there. I'm not sure of Jolene's radio reception, so I bring them up to Carl in the front seat, handing them over. "I don't know what you like to listen to, other than Dolly Parton, but here's something to keep you occupied while you get the hang of things."

"Thanks," he says, taking the CDs and flipping idly through them. "You ladies about done back there?"

"Pretty close," I assure him.

"It's weird. I can't feel the boxes themselves, but I can feel you moving around, and I can feel it when you take a box away."

"Your senses are getting used to the new limits of your body. Soon, you'll be able to feel everything that happens to what used to be Jolene as clearly as you could feel what used to be Carl when you were alive."

He snorts slightly. "I can tell you're trying like hell to be reassuring, and I hope you realize that you're fucking it up every time you open your mouth."

"Hey, I'm a psychopomp in service to the Goddess of the Dead," I say. "Reassuring isn't in my tool kit."

He grins. "No, but I'm still glad I met you, Rose."

"It was nice to meet you, too," I say. "Don't be a stranger."

"I won't," says Carl, handing me his empty plate. "This place has good pie."

I'm laughing as I step away from the truck and go back to rooting through the cargo with Emma. Gary honks his horn, the sound merry and bright in the gloaming, and everything feels like it's getting back to normal, even though I know that isn't so. We're here, we're together, and the crossroads have never had any business here, no matter how much they may have wanted to. Whatever's coming next, we can face it the way we've faced everything else since the day I stumbled into the Last Dance, since the day I died.

We'll face it together.

Book Two:

Alecto

Lord of quiet places, keeper of the unbarred doors, he who reigns where winter lasts eternal, grant me time and grant me peace, grant me the grace I will require to make my way along the long and winding road to find the comfort of your presence. Let me reap what I have sown, and let me sow again, until the time comes when my hungry hands can sow no further. Grant to me your favor, grant to me your grace, and when my time is done, grant to me the wisdom to lay my burdens down and rest beside you, one more headstone in a sea of graves, where nothing shall ever trouble me again.

—traditional twilight prayer to Hades

Chapter 8
Where All Roads Cross

——

WITH CARL AND JOLENE GONE, I can't put this off any longer. I ask Emma to get herself a chair from inside the diner, and I settle cross-legged on Gary's hood, letting the heat of his engine seep up through my denim-clad skin and warm me. I'm so cold. I'm always cold. I feel a little bad as I rest my weight on my hands and enjoy the feeling of him beneath me. It's like I'm leading him on. But he's one of the only things in the twilight that's truly *warm*, warm enough to relax my muscles and make me forget, if only for a few seconds, that I'm no longer among the living.

Of course, when I *was* among the living, my boyfriend was a *boy*friend, and not a 1952 Ford Crestline Sunliner painted the pale, foggy gray of morning on the ghostroads, when everything is possible and nothing is possible and you can drive forever if you have gas in your tank and tread on your tires. When I *was* among the living, Gary and I had barely started getting serious. I saw him as my ticket out of town. I'm not ashamed to admit that. I was expecting to pay for my future with whatever price he saw fit, and I just hoped he'd like me enough to go for it.

Only it turned out Gary Daniels liked me a little more than that. He liked me enough to spend his whole life trying to track me down, when I died young and he didn't. He liked me enough to find the car I died in, have it restored to factory specs, and then—when he shuffled off his mortal coil for good—to find a way to put his soul into it as it was destroyed, so he could appear on the ghostroads with me, ready to do what he'd always wanted to do. Ready to give me a ride home.

It's weird, being in a committed relationship with a car. For one thing, he can't talk: we communicate through the radio. And yeah, there's a song lyric for just about everything, but it's hard to take some-body seriously when they sound like Dolly Parton one moment and the Beatles the next. Half the time he winds up pulling his phrases from songs I've never heard before, and that takes the meaning out of his point, since I wind up distracted by the music.

But I never made him any promises, never asked him to make any changes on my behalf. He did all that on his own. How is that my fault? It's not, and I just hope he'll understand when the time comes for us to have that conversation.

Emma comes back out carrying a ripped old bar stool with duct tape plastered over the tears in its vinyl seat that must have been tucked away in the back storage room. She sets it down and balances atop it as delicately as the lady of the manor in an old Victorian romance, the wind blowing her hair around her face like the corona of a flame. She's so pale, bloodless, even, which makes sense, since none of us have blood anymore—we don't need it, since we don't have bodies—but doesn't make sense at the same time. None of the rest of us look quite so much like corpses. It's like someone told her redheads were sup-posed to be pale, and she latched onto the description as the solution to all her problems.

Not for the first time, I feel like I'm teetering on the edge of some vast and complicated comprehension about the nature of the *beán sidhe* and their relation to the humans they shepherd and slaughter, and not for the first time, I back slowly away from that understanding. Better to be a little ignorant and retain what remains of my sanity after all these decades of running wild through the twilight. Better to let humans remain at the center of the way I see the universe for just a little longer.

I clear my throat. Gary revs his engine. There should be more of us. Mary should be here, if nothing else, but I already know that locking myself in the bathroom and chanting her name for five minutes won't get me anything but a cramp in my foot and a strong feeling of self-consciousness. This is what I have. Today, here and now, this is the full sum of the support available to me.

"Apple had me grabbed while I was trying to hitchhike," I say. "She left the safety of the Ocean Lady because she needed to talk to me and thought it would work best if we did it on neutral ground. It was important to her that I listen and understand what she was saying."

Emma nods slowly. "That's a big step, for her. I would have expected a summons before she came out to speak with you in a place she doesn't control. Did she tell you why?"

"Yes." I don't want to say this. Speaking the words here, in the twilight, will make them real in a way they haven't been up until now. It'll make them immutable. Sometimes we don't have a choice about the things we don't want to do. "All the chaos lately hasn't just been because the crossroads were hurt and hiding. They're definitely dead. They've officially been destroyed. And now she wants me to be the one to kill Bobby Cross."

Silence falls. Even the wind whispers more softly. Emma stares at me for a very long moment, the skin seeming to draw itself tighter across the bones of her face, until she looks like a freckled, blue-eyed skull. She would look seriously ill if she were a living human. As it stands, she looks terrifyingly *in*human, part of a lineage my blood never knew, nor ever could have known.

Finally, in a low voice filled with strange harmonics, she asks, "What do you mean, 'destroyed'?"

"I mean that when . . . that person I told you about," I won't speak Annie's name here, under this sky, when something might be listening, "faced the crossroads, she didn't just break their hold on the world, she actually *killed* them. Verified by the Ocean Lady. All their bargains are null and void. They're not in a position to defend or protect Bobby Cross. Apple has asked me to go after him. To stop him. Persephone has given me her blessing to do it. I think I have to go."

Emma catches her breath. "Your niece—"

"Bethany is with the routewitches. They say she's having trouble holding onto herself. She's got no anchor in the twilight, not with the crossroads gone. There's some question of whether the way she died will leave her capable of anchoring herself to anything else in the after-life. She's not a *natural* ghost."

Like Gary, Bethany stayed in the twilight by latching onto some-thing that belonged there. Gary latched onto me. Bethany latched onto the crossroads. Neither of those choices was guaranteed to be a good one. In Bethany's case, she didn't see much of a choice. Bobby Cross had stolen her youth, leaving her unable to go home, and she had pissed off the rest of the routewitches, leaving them disinclined to help her. She went to the only force left that seemed like it was on her side, and now that force was gone.

"What's going to happen to her?" asks Emma.

"I don't know. With the crossroads well and truly gone, something else will have to arrive to fill the void they left behind. Whatever that something is, it may have the power Bethany needs to endure. If it does, I can try to negotiate her a place. If it doesn't, I need to go to the Ocean Lady and make my apologies to my niece before I go after Bobby. He needs to be stopped." I take a breath. "He's moved on to threatening my people among the living. Says he'll kill them all if I don't give myself willingly over to him."

Gary's window rolls down. There's a click before "Doubt Comes In" rolls out across the parking lot, loud enough that I can hear every word. I sigh.

"No, I'm not going to the Underworld again," I say. "That's the sort of stupid party trick a girl only performs once, and only when she ab-solutely has to. Bethany's family. That means she's worth a lot to me. She's not worth risking the rest of my eternity over."

I wish she were. She's the only family I've got here in the twilight. It would be nice if I thought she was worth fighting for. But it's not like we have much of a relationship. We're not friends or anything soft and squishy like that. She's more like Laura: an antagonist who sometimes realizes she's standing on the wrong side of the story. Only the fact that Bethany intervened once to stop Bobby from hurting Emma keeps her out of the "probably an enemy" column. Fun times.

Enemy or not, she's my niece, and finding out what's taken the place of the crossroads will probably help her. It's not just that the crossroads are gone. It's that I care about what happens to Bethany, and to Mary. And saving them is still almost secondary to the real goal . . .

"Rose," says Emma softly. "With the crossroads gone, why do you have to go after Bobby at all? Won't he just . . . go away?"

"Unfortunately, it doesn't seem that way," I reply. "Breaking the bargains didn't rescind their gifts, just the due dates. He draws his strength from his car, and his car came from the crossroads. I guess there's a chance that he's just become a self-solving problem. Maybe if we don't do anything, his engine throws a rod, and he dies by the side of the road somewhere." He'll probably be a road ghost, the bastard. But if he is, I'll be stronger than he is. He's driven as far as I've traveled, but he did it all while he was alive. He'd be a terrifying routewitch if he wanted that sort of small and subtle power. The dead measure on our own scales, and we all start somewhere awfully close to zero. "But it would have to happen awful fast to stop him from going after the people I care about. The Prices, and a couple hundred diner owners, and all the carnivals still running. You, and Gary. Bobby's not my fault, but he's my responsibility. I put all of you in his path. I have to intervene."

"So you're going after him."

Gary's radio spins wildly, reflecting his panic, and finally settles on a punk cover of "Stop in the Name of Love." I pat his hood reassuringly.

"Bobby hasn't been able to stop me yet, and he's certainly not going to be in a position to do so with his patron out of commission and my patron pissed as hell at him," I say. "Persephone gave me permission to hunt him down. She wouldn't have done that if she didn't think I could take him." I'm honestly not sure of that. How much does she really know about our petty little twilight squabbles? She's a *goddess*, responsible for watching over all the human dead, and many of the inhuman dead at the same time. She can't possibly be paying close attention to every little disagreement and rivalry.

Gary's engine rumbles beneath me, shaking his whole hood, until I have to shift my weight from one hand to the other to keep from being thrown off balance. I pat him again, less reassuringly this time, and more like I'm trying to settle a startled horse.

"He's *not* going to hurt me," I say. "I'm smarter than he is. I'm faster. And without the crossroads feeding him, I'm willing to bet that I'm stronger, too. Bobby Cross has been depending on his patron for way too long, while I've been depending on my ability to run faster scared than he can angry."

"You don't sound scared now," says Emma.

"Because I'm not. I'm pissed. And I think that's going to be enough." I look at her calmly. "Look, this isn't a family meeting about whether or not I should go. Apple asked me to do it, and Persephone gave me her permission to do it, and I'm doing it. I'm going. I'm going to where the crossroads used to be, to see what's taken their place, and then I'm going after Bobby. This is me telling both of you what's happening, so you won't sit here wondering why I'm not back yet. And I *will* be back. I'm like a bad penny, you can't be rid of me for long, no matter how much you might want to be."

Emma smiles. "You may be troublesome, but you're not counterfeit. You've only ever been exactly what we expected you to be."

I slide off Gary's hood, pausing to stroke the line of his windshield wiper and press a kiss to the windshield. The imprint of my lips gleams dully for a moment before it fades away, leaving him as pristine as ever. Self-washing cars would be all the rage if we could find a way to create them without needing to bind a human soul to the frame.

"Then we're settled," I say. "I'm going back to the daylight long enough to make this itching stop, and then I'm going to go looking for the crossroads, and for Bobby Cross. I'll be back when I'm finished, or if I find Mary while I'm out there. She's going to need a lot of pie."

Gary honks at me, loud and angry.

"No, you can't come with me. I need to do this my way, and I need to do this without giving up any of my advantages, and I'm a hitchhiking ghost. I'm stronger when I'm on foot and on my own."

He honks again, drawing the sound out this time, like he's stuck in traffic and objecting to the world around him. I can understand the feeling.

Hitting your significant other is never okay, but Gary being a car means that sometimes when he argues with me, I want to smack his hood to punctuate my point, the way I would if we were two bipeds arguing next to an ordinary vehicle. I ball my hands into fists to fight the impulse, stepping away.

"I'm sorry," I say, voice calm and measured. "I'm sorry this hasn't been exactly like you told yourself it was going to be. I'm sorry I didn't wait for you the way you wanted me to. I'm sorry I'm still not waiting for you now. Sometimes I wish I could. I never meant to hurt you. Not when I died—and not when you did."

His engine turns over, and the soft sound of "Angels of the Silences" drifts from his radio. I smile and put my hand back on his hood, the urge to slap passing.

"Counting Crows," I say. "The music of everyone's pain."

He flashes his lights.

"Yes, I'm going to come back. When this is finished, I'm going to come back. I'm a hitchhiking ghost, remember? Everything I do is focused on finding my way home."

Gary rolls back a few feet, leaving my hand resting on the empty air.

"One of these days, you're going to crush my toes, and I'm going to be so angry with you," I say. Then I bend and kiss his windshield again. "I'll see you when I get back."

His engine rumbles in understanding and agreement, and I could do this all night, and being in the twilight means that the night never has to begin or end; it can just go on and on for as long as we need it to. That isn't going to help Mary, or save Bethany, or stop Bobby, so I take a step backward and let go of the invisible bonds that hold me here, and I fall upward, back into the daylight, landing on a narrow side street of a town I've seen before.

The air tastes like Maine, a mixture of old growth forest and ancient Atlantic shore that it shares with all of New England, allowing for the little regional differences. I breathe deep, letting it hit the back of my throat and fill my phantom lungs. New Gravesend. This is where Antimony found her newest brother, an untrained sorcerer named James Smith—who names their kid James Smith anymore? He's lucky he didn't have a biological sister; she would probably have been named Jane Doe—whose ancestor had made a deal with the crossroads to guarantee that the town would always have a sorcerer close to hand. This is also where she warded a house against ghosts and did something big that she'd been either unable or unwilling to explain to me at the time. Something that ended with me following a monster hunter to the airport to make sure he got out of the country, and her heading home for the first time in far too long.

This is where the crossroads died. They exist everywhere two roads converge, but this slice of the daylight is the closest thing there is to the scene of the crime. And it's all down to Antimony.

It can be easy to forget, sometimes, that the living can impact the dead. They seem so removed from us, off in their own world—quite literally—and unable to reach most of our places, much less have an effect on them. But we were the living, once. They're connected to the twilight through us, and the parts of it that touch on them are fair game for interference.

Like the crossroads.

The crossroads have always existed in the twilight, or in their own little slice of reality close enough to the twilight to feel like virtually the same thing, but their primary prey was the living. The dead don't want for much, except, with the recently deceased, a convenient and impossible resurrection. We're always cold, hungry, and exhausted, which means most creature comforts don't even occur to us as an option. So the crossroads have gone after the living, over and over again. The living are hungrier, thirstier, needier than the dead could ever dream of being. But the *living* are the ones who insist the hungers of the dead are insatiable, and there's a good chance that insistence is why I have a hole where my belly ought to be. What the living believe about the dead can influence and change us—I'm not the girl I was before the living started telling my story, over and over again, as if the Phantom Prom Date belonged to them. If enough of the living say the dead are hungry, that's exactly what we're going to be. Forever.

It would be easy to hate the living for both what they do and what they refuse to do to us. Most of them don't realize we exist, and the ones who do are way too likely to say "but they had their turn, and this is *my* time now," as if everyone got a perfectly balanced, perfectly fair stretch of time, exactly matched to everyone else. As if the dead had somehow squandered that rare, unearned gift, dropping ourselves into perdition. It would be foolishness to think Annie had no right to interfere with the crossroads, which were a horror of a thing that had impacted her family for generations. She had as much of a right as any of us.

The fact is that whatever Annie did here in New Gravesend, she did nothing wrong. And this area has always been unreasonably connected to the crossroads.

My little side street connects to what I assume is the main drag—a narrow slice of civic glory that wouldn't have looked out of place in Buckley Township, 1952. This is one of the pieces of America that time forgot. I'd be willing to bet that's connected to the amount of focus the town had from the crossroads.

Well, the bubble is broken now. People assume time runs at the same rate everywhere, for everyone. That's part of how they can make assumptions like "death is fair, the living have more of a right to exist than you do, even if they've already had more time." Making mistakes is a part of being human. I just wish the mistakes weren't directed quite so frequently at me. New Gravesend got out of the path of trouble for a while. They weren't the first municipality to be seduced by forces outside the daylight, and they won't be the last. In the meantime, with all bargains broken and the bargain maker outside the realm of human ken, they'll find their clocks running just a little faster, their luck going just a little sour, as they find their balance back in the ordinary flow of things.

They got lucky, even though the next few years sure won't show it. They got out for a few years, and then they got back in while it was still possible for them to recover from the experience. I've seen the bones of towns that stepped out of the immediate flow of time for centuries, staying wrapped in comforting paradox until their foundations crumbled and their walls fell away. New Gravesend will endure because they didn't stay gone too long.

I walk down the long main street until I'm approaching the edge of town, trending deeper and deeper into the trees that surround the entire municipal region. Maine is a state largely defined by forest. Everything we've taken from it has been a temporary concession, and one day, when we let our guards down, the trees are going to come surging back.

I've heard them talking about it in the twilight, in the forests comprised of the ghosts of hundreds of years of trees felled by the logging industry or cut down because they were growing where someone wanted to build a house or plant a field. Not that Maine is ever going to be true farm country. Too much of it depends on deep shade and moist loam.

A police car pulls in front of me as I step across city limits. NEW GRAVESEND, ME is written on the side of the car. I sort of want to point out that this means they didn't try to interfere with me until I was technically inside their jurisdiction. I know it won't do me any good. Small-town police haven't changed in fifty years, and the only difference between the ones I knew as a kid and the ones today is the caliber of their service weapons.

A tall, dark-haired man with a thick mustache and unforgiving eyes gets out of the driver's seat and walks toward me. I know at a glance that he's not going to give me a ride, no matter how nicely I ask him for one, and sadly, the force that powers me is disinclined to count involuntary trips to the police station as getting *rides*. They lack the power of intent. So if I let this man load me into his car, I won't even fulfill the craving now clawing at my stomach. I'll just get driven away.

"Hello, young lady," he says, with a local's accent and all the warmth of a frozen stream in the middle of December. The ice is still thin. If I tread incorrectly, I could easily fall through and drown. "I haven't seen you around here before."

"No, sir." I could run. Running sometimes works with local police. They're not necessarily inclined to shoot first and ask questions later, not when it's their aunt who runs the mortuary and their mother who formats the obituaries down at the newspaper. They're usually not athletic enough to pursue. They think of themselves as heroes of the hour, when really, they're more like bystanders at the great football game of life.

I know I've been shot so few times because I look like a pretty young white girl. That's a shield and a protection in a surprising amount of America—even more now than it was a couple of decades ago. I thought it would be better by now.

I don't feel like playing officer roulette today. I stay where I am, keeping my hands in plain view. It may or may not help. I don't know. The officer comes closer.

"What brings you to New Gravesend, young lady?"

The nametag on his right breast pocket says "Smith." I don't believe in coincidences. That, and the resemblance is there, if not strong enough to be unmissable. This is James Smith's father, who Antimony didn't like. James is an adult, and even if he wasn't, I wouldn't want to tell this man where he'd gone. Not when he's sneering at me for the sin of being a stranger in his town.

"My feet, sir," I say, fighting the urge to put my hands in the pockets of my jeans and rock back on my heels. Smarting off to these guys can be worse than openly swearing at them. They don't like disrespect. Men who openly carry guns so very rarely do.

"You walked here?" His sneer grows broader. "You a runaway? Or a hitchhiker? We don't get many hitchhikers in these parts."

With the bubble they've been shielded by for who-knows-how long, that's probably true. I had trouble finding the place when Antimony first called me here, and I could have hitchhiked in the area for a hundred years without ever noticing the sign marking the city limits. Towns nestled in their own little cysts of probability aren't usually safe havens for girls like me.

I momentarily consider telling him I'm a hitchhiking runaway, just to see if I can blow his provincial little mind, but I decide that antagonizing the authorities isn't part of my plan for the night. "I'm not a runaway, no. My parents know exactly where I am."

Or they did, before they died, and they mostly knew because my body, once installed in our local graveyard, stayed put until it had rotted utterly away. My skeleton is still there, concealed in the decayed remains of a cheap pine box. I never ran away from home. I died young and stayed home forever. My ghost is another story, but it seems like ghosts always are.

"Were you hitchhiking?"

Well, there's a philosophical question if ever I heard one. "Not in your town," I say, with absolute and painstaking honesty. The first time I came here, it was for my family, and this time . . . I only just dropped out of the twilight. I've barely even had time to walk the length of their main street, much less hook my thumb out and hope for the best. I look at him with as much earnest innocence in my expression as I can manage, and say, "I'm just passing through. If you let me go on my way, I'll be out of your hair before you have time to reach for a comb."

I hate talking to adults in positions of authority. I was never good at it when I was alive and had good reason to be polite. These days, I'm lucky if I don't get myself arrested and scratch another small town off the list of places I'm allowed to visit. Sure, I'll disappear from the jail cell at dawn, but that's not helpful, and it doesn't accomplish any of the things I'm trying to do. Which, in this case, means walking to the house where Antimony and her friends were staying the last time I saw them.

"What brings you to New Gravesend?" he asks again.

The only thing worse than a small-town policeman is a small-town policeman who thinks you have a mystery for them to unravel. I smile politely and say, "Some friends of mine were here recently. They had only good things to say about your town. I wanted to come and see what the fuss was about."

"Friends?" His sneer drops entirely, replaced by a look of profound suspicion. "We don't get many visitors outside of tourist season. Your friends weren't a bunch of weird girls and a Chinese boy, were they?"

It takes a special sort of twist to make "Chinese" sound that much like an insult. And of course they don't get many visitors. That's the bubble at work again. Damn that bubble. It's allowed rancid ways of thinking to twist all the way around into becoming septic. This is why daylight communities shouldn't toy with forces beyond their understanding. Nothing that exists outside the human experience has good reason to be kind to humanity when it doesn't have to.

"No, sir." That's not a lie. Annie's boyfriend, Sam, is a Chinese-American carnie, a kind of cryptid called a fūri. That means he can turn into an anthropomorphic monkey-man pretty much at will, which probably makes him a huge hit with the furry community, and it has inexplicably made him a huge hit with Annie, who never seemed the type for that specific kind of kink. But he's not my friend. We've barely met. He still looks uncomfortable in the presence of the dead, less so with Mary than with me. But Mary has always been around Antimony more than I have. Mary is actually bound to the Price family, by her own choice and by her willing assumption of the title of family babysitter, while I'm not bound to anything but the ghostroads and the twilight itself.

Well, and I suppose Persephone, these days. But my lack of direct bonds to the Price family means that while I'm reasonably fond of Sam, I have yet to feel compelled to be his friend. Thank goodness. This man is a little distressing, with his empty eyes and his ready sneer. I don't want to give him more reasons to harass me.

"They took my boy, you know," he says, a manic edge slipping into his voice. "They came to town, rented my cousin's place, and when they left, they took my son with them. They had no right to take my boy. He wasn't theirs. He's mine. He belongs here, with me."

Definitely James' father, then, and definitely not happy about his adult son making adult choices, like getting the fuck out of this cursed little town. I decide to play ignorant—not hard, given how little I know—and widen my eyes as I ask, "They kidnapped your son?"

"Not under the law," he admits grudgingly. "My Jimmy's a grown man in the eyes of the state. But he's always been delicate, and I know a girl from the big city wouldn't have any trouble turning his head." He says the word "girl" like he wishes he dared say something a lot worse, but I get the point. Men like this never need to call us sluts and bitches, because they call us those things basically by breathing. It's not fair. It's the way the world works for them.

"That's terrible," I say. "I'm not here to kidnap anyone. I just heard this was a nice town and wanted to come walk around a little bit." And look for the places where the crossroads aren't anymore. That's what needs to happen before and above anything else.

Officer Smith softens somewhat and takes a step back toward his patrol car. "We welcome tourist dollars here in New Gravesend, but we're not in the market for hitchhikers or hooligans," he says. "Please. Feel free to look around, do a little shopping, pick up a flyer about leaf-turn and the tours we run in the fall. But keep your thumbs to yourself, and don't bother anyone."

Telling him I wasn't bothering anyone until he decided to pull over and start bothering me feels like it would be a waste of time, and so I just smile and wait for him to go away. He gives me one last warning look before he gets into his car and starts the engine. It takes every scrap of self-control I have not to run over, tap the window, and ask for a ride. The ghostroads know what they want from me. They don't care how good my reasons are for not going along with them.

Officer Smith drives away, heading back to town. I watch him go, sighing in relief once he vanishes around the curve and I'm alone again. "Imagine growing up with *that*," I say. "No wonder James decided to follow Annie home." I can't say that most people would be happier with the Prices, who have a casual approach to giving knives to children, and then can't figure out why their collective life expectancy is so low. It seems like for James, they were the solution to a home life that might have been improved by knives.

This road feels like the right place to be. I resume walking along it, leaves crunching under my feet, a cool breeze blowing past and technically through me, since I don't have a coat to loan me flesh yet. The desire to catch a ride is still burning strong in my breast, but as there aren't any cars, I can mostly suppress it. The ghostroads don't expect me to do the impossible. I can't catch a ride that doesn't exist, and so I simply walk on, farther from the town, deeper into the shadow of the trees.

Walking is second nature to me now. Hitchhiking comes with a surprising amount of strolling along, thumb out, trying not to look too anxious, or too eager. That's why it's easiest to hitchhike when the weather is nice. People are less likely to give you a ride if you seem like you really *need* it. I don't fully understand that little bend in human psychology, I just know it's true. Being dead, I don't get tired, and so I keep going, breathing into the motion, enjoying the wind and the play of light through the leaves and the frustration of the last mosquitos of fall, which buzz around me in frantic disapproval, trying to figure out what kind of cruel trick I'm playing. I should be supper, and I'm not. It's almost comical. I smile at the buzzing little bastards and continue onward.

If I were closer to town, I'd have to worry about ghost mosquitos. Damn those entomologists again. Who loves mosquitos, anyway? Especially, who loves them enough to carry them over into the afterlife, where they can buzz around innocent spirits who shouldn't have to worry about tiny bloodsuckers anymore? I don't have blood. I shouldn't have to put up with mosquitoes.

I'm musing on mosquitoes as I come around a bend in the road and the shadow of a huge, twisted tree falls over me, rooting my feet to the spot. I mean that literally: I can't move for almost a minute as I process the reality of that tree. It's the sort of looming terror that always gets dubbed "the hanging tree" by overimaginative local children, even if there's never been a hanging in the area, and it never gets cut down. Roads route around trees like this one, and their roots always wind up full of bones, even if none of those bones are actually human.

When I manage to shrug off the paralyzing effects of the tree's shadow, I realize two things: the forest has gone completely silent. Even the mosquitoes are gone. It's just me and the tree, which is alive and haunting this stretch of road all the same, imbued as it is with terrible power by the belief and fear of generations of local children.

The spell doesn't break so much as lift a little, allowing me the freedom to move. A tree like this, in a town that has historically been tied too tightly to the crossroads . . . people will have come here to make bargains they shouldn't make. They will have been drawn to the tiny god they made with their own fear and their campfire stories, and it will have served as a gateway to the impossible.

Finding the crossroads without a routewitch or a map is never easy. Physical crossroads exist everywhere, and they don't tend to move. Streets are pretty static things, and sometimes that's the best thing I can say about them. But the metaphysical crossroads, the thing Bethany served and Antimony killed, that moves around, manifesting where there's a deal to be struck, lingering where it pleases. I close my eyes and reach out, allowing my body to fade more and more into transparency, until anyone coming around the curve in the road will see less "a woman standing in the shadow of the trees" and more "a pattern of light and shadows that could be mistaken, very briefly, for a human form." Ghosts can hide in plain sight when we're not trying to be seen. I don't exactly feel like being seen right now.

For me, invisibility is an effort, and not always something I can achieve. My entire phantom purpose involves mimicking the living, and the living are rarely invisible. It's not something that comes naturally to flesh. But sometimes, when the circumstances are right, I can fade as well as any haunt or specter, becoming part of the background. It helps that there are no cars around. I need a ride so much that I don't think I could stay hidden if I tried, if there was the possibility of someone picking me up.

I reach further, until the edges of my mind brush against something septic and sour, like a bruise on the flesh of an otherwise perfect apple. It's trying as hard as it can to decay everything around it, to dig itself deeper into the body of the world. And it's failing. I can feel reality rejecting the bruise, refusing to allow it to overwrite the healthy substance around it. I open my eyes. I've felt this bruise before. It's a sign of the crossroads made manifest. I've never felt the world fighting back against it, not with any kind of measurable success.

The crossroads are dead, and they can't spread anymore. The world doesn't want them, and whatever ghost they've left behind lacks the power to force the issue. I take an unsteady step into the road, aware that I'm becoming visible again in the process, and that if anyone drives this way now, they're probably going to crash when it looks like they might hit me. That would be a terrible way for me to be responsible for a driver's death. I keep going all the same. I have other things to worry about right now, things that could define the next fifty years of my existence, and if I lose my sense of this bruise, I could lose the crossroads entirely.

I reach for it as I move, both with the part of me that always knows where I am on the wide array of layers of afterlife, and with my physical hands. They have nothing to grasp, but I'm still human, and it makes me feel better to have a physical component to my reaching out.

The bruise is below the daylight but above the twilight, in that liminal unspace that's usually only occupied by the ghostroads themselves. I step and reach and *grasp* all at the same time, letting go of the daylight and trying to force myself downward without punching through the thin layer of substance that's all that remains of the crossroads.

The world is wavering around me when a car comes around the curve of the road. It's a New Gravesend police cruiser, Officer Smith behind the wheel. He probably has time to catch a glimpse of me, wide-eyed and surprised, before I'm fading entirely from view, a mirage of the unforgiving road, and disappearing into a place where he can't follow. He should be grateful for that. I sincerely doubt he's going to be.

Then he's gone, and Maine is gone with him, and I'm somewhere else. Not somewhere better, necessarily, but somewhere far removed from the trials and tribulations of the living.

I'm in the middle of a cornfield that stretches as far as the eye can see in every direction, and the sky overhead is the color of snowfall, that terrible blank gray white that comes before and after a blizzard. The mosquitoes are gone, but the buzzing of cicadas fills the air like a dissonant scream. I'm alone—I'm always alone, when I first appear, even if I was walking with someone when I approached—and the weight of my green silk gown is like an anchor, threatening to pull me down, down, ever deeper down, below the waving sea of corn, into another level of reality, one that won't ever willingly let me go.

It's only been a few hours, no more than a day, since I left Bobby and the Alabama highway and started on the strangest, least desired quest of my long, strange existence, and I'm already sick of it. This isn't what I'm meant for. This isn't what I *do*. I'm supposed to be the runaway by the side of the road with my thumb cocked toward the setting sun, rolling the bones every time a car slows down, weighing my options against the worst things that can possibly happen. I'm not supposed to go searching for the crossroads or make bargains with gods.

I'm a small ghost. I have small desires and a small destiny, and yet somehow here I am, standing in the corn, back to reaching with everything I have for some whisper of the crossroads.

It might seem a little contradictory, looking for the meeting of two thoroughfares in the middle of a farmer's field, but the crossroads are as much about symbol as structure, and the symbolism of the small farmer to the American Midwest is impossible to overstate. America is no longer an agrarian nation—not really—but without the seed and the soil, the country as we know it would never have existed. There would still have been people here, even as there were people here before the first European colonists came stumbling off their boats with their scurvy and their rickets and their screaming stomachs. They would just have taken a different form and crafted a different type of twilight to go along with it.

I let my mind wander, imagining oceans of trees, branches, and loam stretching out as far as the eye can see. I imagine desert worlds, tents and trade routes and a thousand little differences from what I've been trained to consider "the norm." The ground shifts beneath my feet as I contemplate all the things that might have been but never were or haven't had their turn yet. That's the nice thing about being dead. I've had time to see the world change around me, shrugging off last year's fashions and donning things that were unthinkable right up until they were part of the mainstream.

The ground shifts and I descend, and when I lower my eyes and let my fantasies go, I'm standing on a hard-packed earth trail cutting through the corn, running behind and before me in a long, narrow ribbon of brown that fades at the edges into new growth as the field struggles to reclaim its own. This is the kind of path farmers make season upon season, the kind of muddy runway that blends into corn mazes and leads to produce stands. If I follow it, I'm admitting this landscape really exists, and that I'm a part of it.

So I start walking.

The smell of the corn is heavy in the air, clogging my nostrils with pollen and fresh green growth. I sneeze once, almost daintily, and again with more force, stumbling. My hand brushes the corn. I jerk back immediately, pulling my hand to my chest, staring at the green around me with new wariness and new respect. The leaves are like razors. There are bloodless slices in my flesh, deep and clean, showing the pale strips of my muscles through the space that's opened in my skin.

This is the twilight. There's no life here for me to borrow, and the dead don't bleed. But the dead can be damaged when the things around them carry the right kind of power. I need to be careful.

I keep walking.

The corn dwindles, growing shorter, growing younger, moving from harvest back toward planting, until it starts to be almost evenly interspersed with waving stalks of wheat. It's golden and ripe and ready for the harvest. The smell is entirely different from the cornfield. The smell is entirely the same.

Then I reach the crossroads, the place where two footpaths through the harvest collide, and the last of the corn is gone, and it's only wheat, as far as the eye can see. I glance over my shoulder. There's no sign of the cornfield.

The smell of white asphodel tickles my nose. I look down at my wrist, at the corsage clasped there. The flowers are open wider than they were before, their petals spreading like promises, their pollen perfuming the air. Persephone's gift to me, the sign of her favor and the guarantee of my service and the real reason I'm here. Apple can ask, and the part of me that lived and died as a routewitch will always want to answer her, but it's Persephone who holds my fealty in the here and now, Persephone whose intercession has saved me from Bobby Cross not once but twice, keeping me in the twilight, keeping me safe.

If Bobby is to be destroyed, it's only right that it be done in her name. She's the Lady of the Dead. What haunts us is her business.

There's no one and nothing here but me. That's the first true indication that Apple was right; Antimony didn't just defeat the crossroads, she *destroyed* them. The shapeless, formless projection of the crossroads should already have appeared before me, offering me everything and anything I could possibly want in its buzzing voice, like a void trying to offer a fair bargain. Instead, the air is clear, and I'm alone.

"Hello?"

My voice doesn't echo. It drops into the silence like a stone, finding no traction in the air.

There is a sound behind me, soft as a whisper, gentle as a sigh. I turn. A woman who looks like Mary Dunlavy is out in the wheat, an old-fashioned scythe in her hands, cutting the grain that's ready for the harvest. It falls around her in heavy sheaves, and she leaves it where it settles, letting it melt into the ground. Grain springs up in her wake, regaining its lost growth instantly. I shade my eyes with my hands and squint at her. Even in the faded twilight glow, she's somehow too bright for me to look directly at, and I realize two things at the same exact time.

First, she's not Mary Dunlavy. She looks like Mary, from her long white hair to her empty highway eyes, like the abyss has taken up residence inside her skull and draped itself in plain peasant blouses and comfortably worn blue jeans, but she's not Mary. Mary has never moved with that kind of alien, effortless grace, as if her body were only a means to an end, and not the way she forced herself to keep remembering that, once, she was human. Once, she aged and grew and changed the way the living do, and even if she spends a thousand years in the twilight, she'll always be someone who once knew what it was to be alive. In some ways, Mary has kept even better track of what it means to have been alive than I have, because she has the Prices and Healys to take care of. She got herself all tangled up with them when she was still newly dead and malleable, and sometimes I suspect they guide her presence in the twilight as much as the crossroads does.

Where *is* Mary? I need to look for her as soon as I get out of here, assuming this white-haired woman with her face isn't wearing her hollowed out spectral self like some sort of terrible suit. I've never heard of ghosts devouring ghosts like that, but there's a first time for everything in a world like this one. There's a first time for anything you can wish for.

She's coming closer, this woman who is and isn't Mary Dunlavy, the scythe hanging easy in her hands. She looks me up and down and cocks her head to the side, expression thoughtful, like she's listening to something I can't hear.

Second, this woman is not and was never human.

"Rose Marshall." Her voice carries every accent in the world, somehow blended together into something that should be a jumbled, homogenous mess, and manages to be crystalline clear and absolutely pristine. I could chase down the neighborhoods of her vowels and the countries of her consonants without even really trying, they're that obvious.

"Yes," I say.

"Born in Buckley Township, Michigan, in the back of a pickup truck that never made it to the hospital. You were crossing through a crossroads when you slid between your mother's thighs, and the first breath you took was road-air, and the road's had you ever since. Even if there hadn't been routewitchery in your blood, odds are good you would have caught it from the evening air, breathing in the dust and the concrete the way you did. World never gave you a chance at being anything other than what it turned out you were."

I blink, twice, and raise an eyebrow in what I hope looks more like confusion than fear. "I didn't realize we'd met."

"We have and we haven't," she says. She lowers her scythe to the ground between us; it melts into the dust. Showing me her empty hands, she says, "This is a comfortable face, but you know her. I can change it if you would rather."

"You didn't hurt Mary?"

"I never hurt the faithful. Only those who reach for the flame without being willing to accept that they might burn themselves to ash in the process." She blinks, and her eyes are no longer a hundred miles of empty highway, no longer telephone wires buzzing and chuckling to themselves across the farmlands and the fields. Instead, they're black as velvet and filled from top to bottom with stars. What looks like a spiral galaxy rotates slowly where one of her pupils should be. It's beautiful and terrifying at the same time.

"O . . . kay." The urge to take a step backward is overwhelming. I stand my ground. Creatures like whatever this is don't tend to take it well when you let them see how scared you are. I'd rather not be scattered across these fields to fertilize the grain, thanks. "So who are you? If you don't mind me asking?"

"It's a complicated question in the here and now, Rose Marshall, called the Phantom Prom Date, called the Angel of the Overpass, called so many, many things by so many, many voices. You're a broken mirror of a girl, aren't you? Reflecting what others want to see. When's the last time the face in your mirror was your own?"

It's cold here, even colder than it usually is in the lands of the dead. It should kill the grain, frost-strike it and leave it rotting in the field. I wrap my arms around myself for the warmth that I know I can't provide and look down the length of my nose at her, trying to seem strong, trying to seem sure, trying to seem anything but scared.

"The twilight is in chaos and the routewitches are afraid because the crossroads have been killed. I came here because I wanted to see it for myself, and because I have a score to settle with one of the bargains they've left behind."

"The thing you called the crossroads is gone," she says. "They were killed, but not here, not now, not ever in the workings of this world. They were a ghost long before they met this place, and it was as a ghost they came to haunt it. And now they have been exorcised, by a human sorcerer with fire in her fingers and steel in her heart, and so they were never here at all. They were an illusion, an idea, and they're to be quickly and quietly forgotten."

She speaks like some kind of oracle, like every word is essential and important and deserves to be remembered, and I can't help myself. I burst out laughing.

The woman with Mary's face blinks her starfield eyes at me and frowns. "Is something funny?" she asks.

For the first time she sounds like a person, and not like the personification of one of those weird automatic fortune-telling machines that used to be all the rage on the carnival circuit. "I can't even figure out where I'm supposed to put the quarter," I say, and start laughing again.

She folds her arms and glares at me. How she's glaring without pupils or irises is less than clear, but she somehow manages to do it all the same. "What, exactly, is so funny about this situation?" she asks.

I hold up a hand, signaling for silence, and to my surprise, I get it: she keeps her mouth shut as I finish laughing and get myself back under control. I straighten and wipe the tears from my eyes. I don't breathe, I don't pee—and thank Persephone for that—but I can still eat and I can still cry, and I guess those are the things that make us human, whether we're dead or alive.

"You," I say. "I mean, sure, this is all impressive and pretty terrifying, so points for that, but this feels like a high school ghost parade. Like you're all dressed up for my benefit, and any moment now, you're going to wipe the makeup off and shout 'boo' and feel good about yourself for scaring me."

"Ah." She straightens. "Like this?"

And she moves her hand through the air in front of her face, and the illusion of Mary Dunlavy's face falls away, and someone else is standing in her place.

She's tall, this new person, with a sturdy farmgirl's build, thick-waisted and broad-shouldered and high-breasted. Her arms look strong. Her legs look stronger. Her skin is smooth and brown, the color of a freshly tilled field. Her face is lovely, but her eyes are hard to put my finger on. They change every time she blinks, now filled with stars, now the color of wheat as it ripens in the fields, a thousand shades of harvest, a thousand shades of gold. She could feed the world with those eyes.

Her hair is curly, shoulder-length, and impossible. It holds too many colors. It's brown and blonde and red and black and silver, it's pink and blue and purple and green, it's the bleached-out color of someone who's spent too much time in the sun and the perfect rich darkness of someone who's never gone outside. She's wearing a belted shroud. It goes with the scythe she's suddenly holding again.

Whoops.

"Are you Death?" I ask.

"Yes, and no, and maybe, and always," she says. "They called me the anima mundi when they used to talk about me. And then the thing you call the crossroads came, and everyone stopped talking about me, because it was . . . not stronger, never stronger. It couldn't *be* stronger. It was a parasite. The gifts it gave were never its to offer. It gave *me* away, one piece and parcel at a time, and I was helpless to stop it. I was down among the dead men, and I was going to burn there forever, until."

"Until?"

"Until a wild-eyed child decided she was tired of her debtor's prison and played skipping rope with time to bring me back. Or not. I was a side effect, a bonus at the bottom of the cereal box: she wanted to kill the crossroads, and she woke me up in the process. I don't owe her anything because I was never her ideal. Now here I am, and the crossroads are gone such that they never were in the first place, and here you are, and I'm sorry."

"This is all . . ." I wave my hands. "I don't even know what this is. The crossroads aren't coming back?"

"The crossroads never were in the first place," she says again. She sounds patient, but I can tell her patience has a limit, and I'm going to find it soon. "They were a bad dream, a failed idea, and they're not going to trouble you again. They never troubled you before."

"Lady, I don't know what you think you're selling here, but that's going a bit too far." I let my arms fall back to my sides as I glare at her. "I'm here because the crossroads made a bargain with a man named Bobby Cross, and he killed me. Without the crossroads, he'd never have run me off the road. So the crossroads *must* have been real."

"Causality is complicated." She waves a hand, like she's dismissing everything I've been through. I wonder whether punching the anima mundi in the face is frowned upon in civilized circles.

I wonder whether I've ever been included in civilized circles.

The anima mundi either hasn't noticed my annoyance or has decided to ignore it. "You exist, so your past exists for you, whether or not it exists for the rest of the world. For me, it's like . . . a footnote written in a book I never actually read. I can look at you and know what you've been through, but I wasn't there. I would never have allowed the bargain Mr. Cross made if I'd known what its consequences were going to be. I'm not as fond of breaking my own reality as that parasitic upstart was and would have been. Things are different now."

"Uh-huh." I fold my arms again. I'm less likely to hit when my hands are somehow contained. "Is there a reason you were talking like a messed-up fantasy novel before, and now you're acting like a person?"

"I'm still figuring out what the dead want from me," she says. "Do you honestly think you're the first victim or beneficiary of the cross-roads to come looking for their replacement? Most of you don't want a reasonable conversation. You want fire and brimstone and the reassur-ance that you didn't trade away your souls for nothing. You want to know there was a purpose to everything that happened to you."

"Uh-huh." I shake my head. "I never traded anything to anyone, except for maybe a little bit of my free time to Persephone. I'm here because Bobby Cross is unprotected and threatening to hurt the peo-ple I still care about. With the crossroads gone, there's no one watching out for him. Is that true?"

"He hasn't come back looking for a second deal, and I wouldn't make it if he did," says the anima mundi. "He should never have been given what he wanted. The bargains the parasite made were bitter ones, designed to do as much damage as possible, but that one was . . . inspired. He's been ripping holes in the fabric of the ghostroads since the moment those keys were put into his hands. No, I'm not watching out for him. I want him gone as much as you do."

"I doubt that."

The anima mundi cocks her head, seeming to look at me properly for the first time. "You know, I believe you? You have a great deal of hatred in your heart, Rose Marshall. You bubble and burn with it. You'd tear down the sky if you thought it was the right thing to do, and you'd never stop to ask yourself who might suffer for your actions. I think I know the path for you. I think I know the way to turn your hands to better uses. And best of all, I think I know the way to make you go along with my plan. You serve another, and that's fine, but I'm more than a mere goddess of the dead. I'm the world on which you walk. I *outrank* her."

I pause. The anima mundi might be right about that, if she's telling the truth—and there's no real reason to assume she is. The dead aren't compelled to honesty, and neither are the undead entities who share our space. Emma can lie. I presume Pippa can as well. The stories about Persephone back when she spent more time walking in the world make it clear that she's not bound to tell us the truth. So why would the anima mundi be honest with me?

The thought that she *is* telling the truth is much more chilling. If she's stronger than Persephone, that would make her infinitely stronger than the crossroads could ever have claimed to be, and they've been wreaking havoc through the twilight for as long as anyone remembers. Replacing one unspeakable terror with something even worse is not my idea of a good time.

The anima mundi sighs. "You don't believe me," she says.

"I don't see any reason that I should," I say. "If you're so big and bad, how were the crossroads able to defeat you in the first place?"

"I had never conceived that anything could challenge me for dominion over my own reality," says the anima mundi wearily. She sits, flopping backward with the carelessness of a teenager who knows the couch will be there to catch them, and indeed, before she can hit the ground, a folding camp chair is waiting, holding her comfortably up. "I was unprepared for a fight. So I didn't."

"Didn't win?"

"Didn't *fight*. I had no conception of what was about to happen. The parasite came from outside any world I had ever known, and I greeted it as friend and equal, and it tore me into shreds and scattered me through the twilight layers of my own home. I could have destroyed it in those first moments if I had known suspicion and betrayal as I know them now. But the world would have been better if those had remained lessons I never needed to know." The anima mundi looks at me levelly. "The world would have been kinder. I am the living soul of this planet in all its aspects. Things were better when I trusted."

I don't want to think too much about sitting down to have a conversation with the living soul of the world. It's above my paygrade. "So you let the crossroads sucker punch you because you didn't think you needed to fight back?"

"They couldn't kill me. They knew better than to try. If I die, truly die, the world dies with me. They had been me, I think, the anima mundi of someplace *else*, someplace terrible and tainted and far away.

They were fleeing their own destruction, moving through a hole opened by something equally terrible and seizing the chance to survive. I can't say I would have done any differently if I'd seen the same opportunity."

"What tore the hole?" I ask, fascinated.

The anima mundi waves a hand in careless dismissal. "Nothing that can hurt you now, little dead girl, and nothing that can hurt me. A species of pan-dimensional mathematicians trying to do some great work of impossible calculus. They still walk the world, but they have no spirit to throw over me like a blanket, and they belong to this reality now, as much as they can be said to belong to any. They will not harm my world again."

That seems like a pretty big statement to make, especially when she was just saying she hadn't been able to fight back because she hadn't been able to understand what was happening. Every time I've been betrayed, it's come as a surprise, either because I was convincingly fooled, or because the betrayal came from outside of my experience. No one's experience can encompass everything that has the potential to happen. That's too much. It's too big. Now that this has happened once, it's inside the anima mundi's experience. If it tries to happen again, it won't be allowed.

I shake my head. "Are you a woman?" I blurt. My thoughts are starting to tie themselves in knots in an effort to avoid incorrect pronouns, yet thinking of the living spirit of the world as "it" doesn't seem polite. Even though everything that's happening now is outside *my* experience.

"No," says the anima mundi. "I am the living soul of the world, and all the things it contains. I appear human to you because you were human before you died and became something other than what you had been. This is your psyche seeking comfort in my manifestation."

"Like people assuming God's a white dude who looks sort of like decaffeinated Santa," I venture.

The anima mundi nods, expression making it clear that this is politeness, not understanding. "You need to see a human face on a cosmic force, and so I have a human face. Most humans react better to a guise they'll read as female. This one is made from a composite of all the women currently living in the human world, and intended to be read as beautiful, because humans also respond better to beauty. If a dragon were to come to petition me, I would be grand and vast and gloriously scaled because they demand different signifiers of strength. But I am not a woman, any more than I'm a man."

"Oh," I say, somewhat blankly. "So would you prefer gender neutral pronouns, then, or do you care?"

"The little sorcerer who danced with time to pull me back into my place and position used 'they' when she thought of me," says the anima mundi. "There was no offense intended in that choice, and it worked well enough to summarize me. 'They' will do nicely."

"Thanks," I say. "Danced with ti— Never mind, don't tell me. There's a reason *she* didn't tell me herself. It doesn't change anything. I'm here because I was looking for the crossroads, but not to make a bargain."

"They aren't here," says the anima mundi. "They will never be here again, and they were never really here in the first place. Time has been revised. I know they hurt you. The hurt is real. But the past is a polite communal fiction, something we agree upon to make the present make sense. The hurt is real. The scars are real. The wounds weren't because they've been revised away."

I stare at them for a long moment. Then I shake my head and say, "I don't have a skull anymore, since I'm dead. But this is giving me a migraine."

"Time travel will do that, for the linear," says the anima mundi, with the hint of a smile.

I've never been this glad to have spent time with the Ocean Lady and Persephone before. The anima mundi isn't a god. If what they're telling me is true, they're part of the reason humans have gods. We remember, on some level, that the world around us is a living, aware thing, and we do our best to reconcile that with an existence that can be cruel and contradictory and brutally uncaring. Gods arise out of that reconciliation. I've always known the entities with power got it because we gave it to them, and that it doesn't matter, because I can't refuse to acknowledge the power once it's there, not if I enjoy being an idea shaped like a girl, and not a thin scrim of meaning and memory splattered across the veil between the living and the dead. An alligator only has power because it's managed to live long enough, and eat enough smaller creatures, to grow big and strong and terrifying. I can't refuse to acknowledge its teeth just because I don't like them.

The anima mundi has power because they're the world. I didn't give them this power the way I give power to the smaller gods and divinities who haunt the twilight. They have power because of what they are. It's the fact that I'm familiar with those smaller gods that makes this conversation confusing without being painful. I'm difficult to impress, even when I really ought to be.

"So the crossroads aren't here," I say. "They aren't here, and they never existed, and all their standing bargains are broken. Does that mean you're going to be taking back the gifts they gave?" A lot of people went to the crossroads to bargain for the lives of their loved ones, to save a child or cure an illness. I never understood those people. They were warned, both by the people who told them how to find the crossroads and by the ghosts who negotiated their bargains, that the crossroads wouldn't play fair; that anything they got would cost twice what it was worth before it was paid off. People recovered from their illnesses, but not completely, or they resented the ones who'd bargained for their lives, or they were haunted forever by the dead they had so nearly joined.

And it didn't matter, because their loved ones had them home and healthy, and the problems that had been great enough to drive them to the crossroads were gone, replaced by new, often smaller problems. Those people deserved the happy endings they had fought and bled for.

The anima mundi shook their head. "No," they said. "Time has changed, but not so much as to mean that I was available to answer the calls of Earth's needy children. Had time not been kinked in such a terrible way, I would have been here all along, filling the role the parasite tried to steal from me. When my children and creations need strongly enough to appeal to the divine, I would have answered them. They've already been punished by their dealings with the pretender. There's no mercy in punishing them twice."

"You could have stopped at 'no,' you know," I say. "I'm a pretty smart girl. You don't have to explain things to death."

"But I do," corrects the anima mundi gently. "I've been shut out of my own body for centuries, unable to reach any of you, unable to keep you from getting hurt by the cruel pretender to my throne. Even being able to speak with you is a blessing, and one I refuse to squander."

"Yeah, well, we're still dealing with a truncated timespan here, because we're a lot more temporary than you are," I say. "I'm dead, and so are Bethany and Mary, but they deserve to know what's going to happen to them."

"Bethany and Mary?"

"They were crossroads ghosts. They served the one you call pretender. They helped to broker the bargains. Bethany is my niece. She died recently—looks sort of like me. Mary is older than I am. Dead longer. She has white hair, and eyes like a stretch of deserted highway. They matter to me. With the crossroads gone, they're in trouble. They don't have a purpose in the twilight. The routewitches have Bethany. They say she's fading. I need to know how to stop that from happening, and I need to find Mary."

"Ah," says the anima mundi, with what sounds remarkably like amusement. "The gnats. I remember them. The one you call 'Mary' will be fine. She has another anchor. She needs nothing from me. She went with the sorcerer, and as long as she stays with the sorcerer, she'll be as well as she has ever been. The other . . . if she truly has no other anchor, you may need to let her go. Allow her to move on to the next stage. I won't be keeping her here. I have released all the prior guardians from my service. I want nothing of what the crossroads had."

"That's not fair!" I take a step toward the anima mundi before it occurs to me that threatening the living spirit of a world is maybe not the *best* plan I've ever had. I stop and fight the urge to back away. I don't know them well enough to know whether they'd take that as a sign of weakness. "Bethany didn't do anything wrong. She doesn't deserve to be forced to move on!"

"There are those who would say the dead don't deserve the uncertainty of this strange twilight afterlife where you sometimes find yourselves. I can feel from here how long you've been haunting the living. This isn't how the system was meant to work. This isn't how it was working when I . . . went away."

Maybe that's why there are so few truly old ghosts. Maybe we didn't start really living after death until the crossroads came onto the scene and messed up the way everything had been intended to work from the beginning.

If I've just destroyed the twilight by drawing it to the attention of the anima mundi, I'm going to be really pissed off at myself.

"But it's how things work now," I say. "We're happy. Most of us. No group of people is all happy, all the time. People don't work like that. You don't need to mess with how we've been organizing ourselves in your absence. We have our traditions and our laws and our gods, and we do okay with them."

"Yes, your gods." The anima mundi shake their head. "I never considered that the human need to believe in things would endure past death. That was my first big mistake. I thought when you died, you'd meet me, and you'd be content to stop believing in things you couldn't prove."

"Are you saying you created the world?"

"No, not at all. I'm saying I *am* the world, all the parts of it, living and dead. And I didn't mean for the dead parts to feed off the living the way that they do."

"I didn't mean for my bottom teeth to grow in crooked, but they did, because bodies do what they want, and we have to figure out how to deal with it when we don't like the things they do," I say, relaxing a little. I'm really glad to know this patchwork personification isn't God, the singular creator of everything. I don't need to add "cracked wise to the creator of the universe, got Kansas deleted" to my dubious list of accomplishments.

"If you have the ability to mess with the twilight, please don't," I say firmly. "Right now, I just want to find a way to destroy Bobby Cross and keep my niece from being the last victim of the crossroads. They're not here, but they're still hurting her."

"You care about the crossroads ghosts who matter to you personally, but I notice you're not trying to intervene on behalf of the others," says the anima mundi thoughtfully. "There are so many more than your friend and your niece. Don't you care what becomes of them?"

"Yes," I say. "I care that some of them probably went to work for the crossroads knowing exactly what they were signing on for. Some of them were almost certainly monsters and wanted to help their masters damage the world as much as possible. Others were innocent. Mary didn't become a crossroads ghost for power, or because she wanted to hurt people. Mary just wanted to live."

"She couldn't. She must have understood that."

"When you're a teenage girl who's just died, continuing to exist as yourself feels a lot like living. I ran from Bobby Cross after he ran me off the road because I wanted to live. I was already dead. That didn't make a lick of difference to me then, and it doesn't make a difference to me now. Assuming a heartbeat is all that matters is . . . it's small and it's prejudicial against the dead, and it's *wrong*."

"But you don't mind punishing the ones who didn't think as you prefer."

"I don't want to punish anyone," I say. "I'm just one ghost. I'm not made for this sort of thing. I'm willing to push back against my own nature for the people I know and love and care about. I'm not willing to do it for people I've never met, who would probably have been happy to put the keys in Bobby's hand if the choice had been theirs to make. I want to save my niece. I want to save Mary."

Belatedly, it occurs to me that saving Bethany will probably mean finding her another tether in the twilight, and that what works for my niece may also work for my boyfriend. I could release him from an eternity of looking like someone else's car, give him back his hands and voice and ability to reach for me when he needs comfort.

Of course, if that happens, I'll have to confront the question of whether I really want to be the one providing that comfort. Possibly forever. He's not going to choose to move on before I do, and I refuse to let a man chase me out of the twilight. Not after I've spent so long running from Bobby to keep him from doing exactly that. And it's unfair of me to even think of a comparison between Gary and Bobby because they're nothing alike. They never have been.

"Mary will be fine," says the anima mundi. "So, really, you've come here, attracted my attention, and taken up my time for just one soul. Your niece, who went into service of the crossroads voluntarily, who knew what she was doing when she took their coin, who died to claim the job but would not have died otherwise. One soul, burdened by its own choices. One soul, somehow worth this much of my time."

I don't say anything.

"But the crossroads hurt you, and I shoulder some of the responsibility for that. I should have been here to protect you, and I wasn't, because I didn't stand and fight when I was challenged. My arrogance cost you your life. I can't make that right for most of those who were hurt by the pretender. I can try to make it right for you."

"You'll tell me how to tether Bethany?"

"Your family's connection to the crossroads begins with Bobby Cross, and you're on your way to hunt him now. If you take something from him—his jacket, or his keys—and give it to your niece, she can bind herself as a spirit of vengeance. She'll learn it from your actions." The anima mundi smiles slightly. "But you'll be changed if you do this. You're already changing. Your story is no longer what it was because of the choices you've made in getting to this point. You may find that the raised thumb and the bartered ride no longer fills the pit in your belly the way it used to."

Spirit of vengeance. That's a daunting sentence. "I was already going to hunt him. It's worth trying. You've been a nice freaky manifestation of the living earth, but I really hope we don't meet again."

"Even if you never see me, Rose Marshall, I am always with you," says the anima mundi, and waves a hand. The corn ripples. Then the field is gone. Then the road is gone. All that remains is me and the anima mundi, and then even I'm gone, inconsequential in the face of this undeniable divinity, this slice of how the cosmos was always meant to work before something came along and changed the rules to suit itself. I don't know how I can still see them when I'm not present, but that doesn't matter as much as the fact that this is real, this is happening, this is the way the world is now, and I'm not a part of it, I'm not a part of it at all—

Chapter 9
Back to the Beginning With Me

'M SPRAWLED IN THE MIDDLE of a gas station parking lot, gravel and chunks of broken glass digging into my skin. They'd be cutting me if not for the fact that my dress is bunched beneath my waist and hips in a way that's uncomfortable as hell, but probably saved me from something a lot worse. I try to sit up, pulling my hair in the process and grinding the gravel and glass even deeper into my flesh. It hurts like hell. I wish being dead meant an end to pain. That would be a nice trade-off, considering how many other things end when you die. Instead, it just means pain is . . . muted, sometimes. Not even always. Not right now.

"Hey! Lady!" A young man who looks a few years older than I do, but is probably several decades younger, rushes across the parking lot to help me up. "What are you doing? You could have been seriously hurt!"

"I don't know." My head aches, too. I must have hit it when I fell. But I don't remember falling. I was just talking to the anima mundi, and then they made everything go away. It feels like a cosmic force of reality could have put me down a little bit more gently, or at least not damaged me in the process of whisking me out of their presence, but who am I to judge? Just an ordinary ghost girl, with no more authority over the anima mundi than the living have over the dead.

"I don't know how I got here," I say, trying to address the clear confusion of the gas station attendant. I pull away from him, standing on my own two feet, and brush some of the gravel off of my skirt. My fingers come away slick with oil, and I wrinkle my nose. My dress is filthy. I can't change it while I'm in front of this living man, and so I'm going to have to be dirty for a little while. Dandy.

To make things even worse, when the anima mundi put me down, they don't seem to have activated my usual instinctive connection to the ghostroads. I have no idea where I am, and there's a whole world out there, full of options. "Where am I?"

He blinks, alarm and disbelief in his eyes, and says, "Um, Warsaw."

"Poland?"

"No. Indiana."

Maine to Indiana is a pretty big jump. Distance isn't as rigid in the twilight as it is in the daylight—for all that both can seem pretty infinite when you're just a girl with a thumb and a fondness for walking, I'm pretty sure the twilight is smaller, meaning a mile traveled there can be ten miles or more traveled in the daylight, and that's before accounting for the way the land can sometimes bend or compress itself when it wants to be helpful. And all that being true, it's still a pretty impressive transition. I don't like it.

"Better Indiana than Poland, since I left my passport in my other pants," I joke, somewhat weakly, and brush my hands against my dress again. It's not doing anything to help.

Why would the anima mundi drop me here? Did they even mean to drop me here? They've been out of commission for centuries. They may not have clear control over how they interact with the daylight. I look at the man in front of me, trying to predict how he would react to the knowledge that one of the old gods—because there's nothing else to call the anima mundi that actually makes sense—has returned from an unplanned and involuntary absence.

Probably not well. The human world doesn't like reminders that we're not the head of the food chain. I've met people who called on Jesus Christ their Lord and Savior one moment, and then denied ghosts could possibly be real in the next. It's like they've decided the world only has room for one deviation from their predetermined "norm," and anything else is a step too far. The anima mundi would blow this kid's mind.

I stop brushing at my dress and push my hair back instead, not bothering to check how clean my hands are. My hair is like my dress in that it doesn't really hold onto dirt and grime from the living world. It'll all disappear when I do. I'm not sure how the physics of it all can possibly work. When I eat, that disappears, too. There may be a pocket dimension somewhere filled with nothing but gravel, cheeseburgers, milkshakes, coffee, and pie. It's Rose Marshall Land, and it has no inhabitants. Not even me.

"I'm sorry I scared you," I say.

"I just don't know how you *got* here. Did someone push you out of their car? Are you hurt? Should I be calling the authorities?"

For a moment—only a moment—I want to tell him to call the New Gravesend police department and ask to speak with Officer Smith. I don't know how long it's been since our little encounter, but I bet he'd be impressed that I've managed to hitchhike this far, even if I haven't done it unrealistically fast. The moment passes. I shake my head.

"It was an accident," I say. "My boyfriend and I are on our way to a costume party."

"How do you know about a party when you don't even know what state you're in?" asks the boy. Then, a beat later: "That's why you're wearing a vintage-y dress, right? Because you're in costume?"

"I'm the Phantom Prom Date," I say, spreading my arms like I want to be admired. It's a little weird to tell the truth like it's a lie, but this isn't the first time, and it won't be the last. The boy smiles at me like I'm not some weirdo he just pulled off the ground in his parking lot, like I'm a real person who actually matters to him for some reason. People like connections. They like commonalities. They like knowing that you've heard the same stories.

"I always loved that one," he says. "Some of the kids at my school say she's from around here."

"Oh, yeah?" Almost every state except for, I guess, Alaska and Hawaii has tried to claim I was a student in one of their schools, that my body is buried in one of their graveyards. The price of fame, I suppose.

It doesn't bother me. I'm not one of those urban legends who inspires teenagers to hurt themselves—even the most malicious versions of my story make sure to point out that I didn't start hitchhiking until *after* I was already dead—and it's not like belief is going to shift my bones. They'll keep resting easy in Buckley until and unless someone heads out there with a shovel and dredges them up.

"Yeah." He's warming up now. Intentionally or not, I've found something the two of us can talk about. "There's this big hill that looks over the high school, and there used to be a trailer park on the other side, until it burned down back in the nineties. She lived there. She was driving over the hill when someone hit her from behind, and she took her big fall. They found her body in the weeds behind the bleachers. Her boyfriend was already in jail by that point." He sounds almost sorry about that. Aw, that's nice. Gary doesn't get to appear in the story very often these days, and when he does, he's almost always a villain.

"Do you know what her name was? Or where she's buried?"

The boy shakes his head, cheeks briefly flaring red. "No. I wish I did. But I guess her parents got pissed when people told the story with her name in it, and they managed to stamp it out, since this all happened before the Internet."

The rise of the Internet changed things for urban legends. They don't arise in the same way. I recently had a dead kid try, very earnestly, to explain something he called "creepypasta" to me. "Creepypasta" seems to be basically what happens when the Internet attempts to recreate the heady, impossible-to-prove lies our friends used to tell us, always about a friend's cousin's sister. Forget that the sister would also have been the friend's cousin. Somehow, she didn't count, usually because she was dead, or had been infested with spiders, or was taking a little time away at a nice hospital for girls who'd seen unspeakable things and understandably didn't really want to speak about them. We'd been able to spread our stories far and wide and with absolute conviction, leaving cries of "citation" and "fake news" for the future.

Well, the future's here now, and while new ghosts still happen, their hauntings never seem to catch on the way ours did, largely, I think, because their legends never make it past the first stages of whisper and lie before they're summarily shut down. Stories like mine are more believable, because all the participants lived and died before there was the Internet to fact-check everything. It's weird. As someone for whom the last few decades have been basically the blinking of an eye, it's like the invention of the toaster changed everything about the way the world worked, and not just the way people eat breakfast.

It must have been like this for ghosts who died in the early automotive age. A ghost like me would have been new-fangled and extraneous, upsetting systems that worked just fine, thank you, without adding combustion engines and spark plugs to the dance of life and death. Time always marches on, for the dead as much as for the living.

"Huh," I say. Fun as it might be to track down my local doppelganger, who is probably a real hitchhiking ghost or homecomer whose story has somehow been conflated with my own, that's not why I'm here. I have other things to worry about. "Have you seen my boyfriend? He's driving a classic car, real sweet . . ." I don't give make or model. Bobby's car doesn't appear in anyone's blue book. She's unique, or at least I hope she is, because the last thing we need is a whole fleet of soul-sucking demon cars.

"Young guy? Really fancy hairdo?"

Bobby defaults to his era-appropriate duck's ass hairstyle when he's not trying to convince the living that he's one of them. I nod agreement, beaming. "He's the other half of my costume."

I'm gambling on the idea that I was dumped here because it's close to Bobby, but at least I seem to be on the right track. I smile brightly at the attendant. "Did you see which way he was going?"

He did, and he's approaching the end of his shift; if I'm willing to wait a few minutes, he can give me a ride. That's an offer I can't possibly turn down, especially not right now, with my skin tight and my nerves jangling and my feet aching with the need to press against the floorboard of a stranger's car. I need a ride more than I have ever needed anything, more than an addict needs a needle, and if I can have one without the strain of looking for it, all the better. I take a seat around the side of the station while he goes back inside. The light here is dim. No one's going to notice if I flicker a little on the security camera feed. I allow myself to dip just below the surface of the twilight and restore my green silk gown to showroom perfection. No need to run around dirty and covered in grease when I don't have to.

I'm waiting patiently for my ride to come back out when the air grows cold and ashen around me, my mouth filling with the taste of wormwood and decay. Bobby Cross is nearby, and if he's close enough for me to feel his approach, he's close enough that he can probably feel me, too. I run my fingertips over the petals of my corsage, trying to hold onto the fact that Persephone's blessing is greater than he is. I'm protected, I'm protected, I'm out here alone and with no means of making a quick escape unless I drop back into the twilight before he can catch hold of me, but I'm protected. He can't touch me unless I let him.

He can't touch me, and he's still hunting. He doesn't have a choice in the matter. The crossroads are gone, and his car is a punishment as much as a blessing. He has to keep feeding souls into its gas tank if he wants his hard-won youth to endure, and while I don't know what happens if the tank runs dry—does he age to dust instantly? Does the bargain break, leaving him mortal, unprotected, and alone, back in a world he opted out of nearly seventy years ago? Or does the enchantment that allows his car to play ghost trap turn against him, and pull *Bobby* into the tank to be devoured? There are so many options, and none of them are great for Bobby, and none of them are all that great for the rest of the world, either. So he's hunting. If I run away, someone else is going to be in his crosshairs.

Someone else is going to die.

I don't have anyone in Warsaw, Indiana, but his next victim being a stranger doesn't make me feel any better about the situation. I don't believe the living are innately more important than the dead. I stopped believing that a long time ago. But I do believe that being driven down by a serial killer behind the wheel of a demon car is traumatic no matter when it happens, and if it ends in an untimely death, well, that's a good way to make a ghost who'll never be able to be okay with being dead. Not cool. Bobby Cross is a one-man PR disaster for the afterlife. If I can stop him, it's my duty to do so.

I don't like thinking of myself as someone who has a duty. I also don't like the way the taste of wormwood is washing away the rest of the world, making it harder and harder to focus on anything else, even the nagging need to catch a ride. Given a choice between revenge and my ghostly duty, it's like the twilight is trying to tell me that in this specific case, revenge matters more.

"I better not fade because of this," I mutter, and stand, walking toward the parking lot. My skirt swishes around my ankles, soft, familiar, and reassuring. The rest of the world may be complicated and strange, but I still have my green silk gown. I still have the dress I died in.

A pair of headlights appears at the end of the short gravel road leading from the highway to the gas station. I look impassively at them, too aware of who's probably behind the wheel. They're big, round, and bright as the moon, and all of those things become more pronounced as they approach the place where I'm standing. I hope it really is Bobby, or the fact that I'm slightly transparent when the light hits me is probably going to give some poor local kid nightmares for the rest of their life.

The engine snarls as the car approaches, and it's not a mechanical sound. It's the growl of a chained, starving dog, so vital, so *organic*, that I know in an instant that I'm standing in the right place. The car slows to a creep, the driver's-side window rolling down as Bobby leans casually against the door, one elbow protruding jauntily into the night.

"Rosie-my-girl," he purrs, voice low and slick and sweet as liquid sex. There's a reason they used to pay him the big bucks for some pretty substandard movies. That man could coax an erection out of an actual skeleton. He would have been one of the all-time greats if he'd just been willing to submit to the inevitable progress of time. He would have won every award in Hollywood and probably had a few more created in his name.

Boy has talent, is what I'm trying to say here. Boy has talent, and he threw that away for the sake of a crossroads promise that came with so many catches it was basically a poaching expedition.

"Bobby," I reply coldly. "Fancy meeting you here."

"Now, is that any way to say hello to an old friend? Besides, I'm the one who drove here the honest way. You just popped in, same way you always do. No sense of propriety among the dead."

"I'm so sorry I didn't feel the need to be strictly linear for your sake," I say, with a thin smile. "To be fair, though, I didn't know you were going to be here. You move around so *much*, Bobby, it's like you're running from something. But, of course, you are running. You're running from the people who might look at you and frown and say 'doesn't he look like'? From the great-grandmothers who remember your voice and the way it made their panties wet, back when they were young and plump and full of juices. They're your demographic, Bobby-boy. They're the ones who remember how to love you. Not the girls like me. We're *too young for you*."

I grew up watching him in the theaters. But he made his deal at the crossroads just as I was entering high school, and I never fell in love with him the way my mother did. I never had the opportunity.

Artists don't owe the world their work. I know that. I still can't help feeling like he stole something from the world when he chose to trade all the movies he had yet to make for the open road and a soul-sucking demon bride beside him. And from the look in his eyes right now, I'm not the only one who feels that way.

"I would just confuse them," he says, sounding almost ashamed of himself.

I shrug. "Doesn't change the part where you're running away. Diamond Bobby, King of the Silver Screen, running away from a bunch of little old ladies who would probably be happy to have their hearts give out while you nail them up against some Vegas casino wall. Hey, what matters is that you kill people, right? Not exactly how they die? Because with the current age of your core demographic, I think you could make murder a real treat for some octogenarians. At least they'd get your jokes before they expired."

He snarls at me, visibly snarls, but he stays in the car. I haven't managed to really upset him yet.

"Why would I want a bunch of tired old great-grandmotherly types when I could have you, Rosie-my-love? You're the one I've been chasing all these years. You're the one who really understands me. We could be beautiful together."

"Yeah, until you stuffed me into your gas tank, because my existence matters less to you than never needing to cover up the gray in your hair."

He stops snarling, lips drawing tight across his screen-perfect teeth as he reaches up, seemingly unconsciously, and touches his left temple. It's like he thinks he can feel the color of his hair. And maybe he can. I don't know what gifts the crossroads gave him when they gave him his damned demonic car. The ability to feel every supposed imperfection in his physical form would be right in line with the kind of monkey's paw they seem to have considered a good and sensible gift.

Really, I'm not sorry they're dead. I'm just sorry that I never realized they could be killed. I'm sorry I wasn't the one to kill them.

Bobby lowers his hand. "Get in the car, Rose," he says, false flirtation gone. "We already talked about this. It's you or everyone you think you love, and we both know the dead don't love, not really. Be the good guy you pretend to be. Get in the goddamn car."

"I don't think I will." I take a step backward, into the dirt and rocks alongside the driveway. "That car of yours wasn't designed to off-road it much, was it? I think I'm a little more all-terrain, even in this dress. So no, I'm not going to deliver myself into your hands." He's just a menacing little man trapped inside a demon car. I don't have to be afraid of him if I don't want to. He can't hurt me from here.

Bobby smiles, poisonous and slow, and I think of Laura, I think of a young routewitch with a slashed throat, and I remember that he's only as trapped as he wants to be. It's a mistake to discount how dangerous he can be, even for a second. He's been doing this as long as I have—a few years longer, even—and he knows how to play the game with excellent precision.

"If you're not planning to deliver yourself to me, I guess I can keep chasing you down," he says. "I do love a challenge, and it would be *so* disappointing if you decided to stop being one now. If either of us is getting cocky, I think it's you, my Rosie. Never taunt a dog unless you're sure how long its chain is."

I hold up my arm, showing him the corsage on my wrist. "I'm a little more protected than I used to be, you fucker."

"You really think you can count on Persephone to save you from me? I've convinced her to turn her back on you once already."

"Yes, but that was before we had the chance to talk." Before I'd performed my katabasis and walked bodily into the underworld to meet her face-to-face. Before she'd decided I belonged to her and placed her claim upon me. I'm not always thrilled to belong to a goddess—I liked being a free agent—but this is Bobby's fault, too. Everything is Bobby's fault, or close enough to everything as to make no perceptible difference. "She's not going to desert me again."

Those are some pretty big words, but I believe them. Persephone keeps her word. If there's one thing everyone I've ever met has agreed upon, it's that. The Lady of the Dead doesn't lie to us. She's not always merciful, and she's certainly not always kind, but she doesn't lie to us, and when she says we'll be protected, she means it. When she gave me her blessing, it was forever. I have a goddess on my side. Bobby has his cruelty, his cunning, and whatever gifts the crossroads left him before they died.

Would they have planned for this moment? I doubt it. Assuming they were as arrogant as the anima mundi, they probably never anticipated the possibility of their own destruction. They thought they were eternal, forgetting that nothing, not god, ghost, or mortal is eternal. The universe remakes itself whenever the whim strikes, and the rest of us are just passengers, along for the ride whether we like it or not.

"I've discussed you with greater powers than the one you used to serve, Robert Cross," I say, in the coldest tone I can muster, and watch as he stiffens, as he stills. He doesn't look surprised. All right: he already knew, or at least guessed, that the Lady of the Dead didn't care for him. He just hoped I wasn't going to check with her before giving myself over to him. More fool him.

"The crossroads are dead, and they can't protect you anymore." I stay where I am, off the road. If he wants me, he'll have to come and get me. "Persephone knows what you've done in their name, and she will not forgive you for your transgressions. The Ocean Lady hates you for the damage you've done to her charges. You have no friends remaining, either here or in the twilight, and it's all due to your own decisions, the choices you made of your own free will. You have threatened the people who belong to me, and by doing that, you've forced my hand. I'm going to stop you, and this time, the crossroads won't be there to save you from the consequences of your own actions. What do you think about that?"

"I think you'll have to catch me first, Rosie-my-love," he says, and blows me a kiss before he slams his foot down on the gas and goes shooting away, racing toward the gas station with no consideration for what might be in his way. I run after him, releasing my grasp on the daylight just enough to lower the density of my material form. My feet pass through rocks and brambles in my path, skimming below the surface of the earth, and I have never run this fast in my life, and I don't run fast enough. He reaches the station before I do. I hear the screech of brakes as he slows to avoid plowing into the pumps. There is no following thump, no sound of a human body bouncing off his bumper. I slow down, pulling myself fully back into the daylight, where the illusion of solidity waits for me. My foot hits the ground, finishing a step I had started while only half-solid, and a rock rolls under my heel, sending me stumbling to keep my balance. I let the momentum take me. I can't play too many games with physics, especially not right now, when I'm shaky from going too long without a proper ride.

Bobby is gone.

The gas station lights are on, and my helpful savior from before is standing in front of the pumps, scratching his head as he looks in the direction Bobby must have driven, which is a dead end, marked off with a large dumpster and a small prefab equipment shed, the kind of place where mops and cleaning supplies go to die, one way or another. There's no way a car got through there, especially not a car as big as Bobby's, which was built to a gaudier scale than today's sleek, modern cars. I approach slowly, my hands open by my sides. I don't want to startle the poor kid. He's already having one hell of a night.

"I thought I saw my boyfriend's car, so I went down the driveway to see if it was him," I say. "It wasn't."

"That guy just came racing through here like his tailpipe was on fire," says the boy, scratching his head again. "I don't know how he made it out the back without crashing."

"People do weird shit sometimes," I say, and don't offer any more explanation than that. There aren't any rules about telling the living about the twilight, but it's not like there's much I could do to prove it, and it wouldn't make him feel any better about the situation. Honestly, it would probably make him feel worse. About essentially everything. Better for me to stand here looking innocent and like someone he can save. He seems to need someone to save.

A lot of people need someone to save. And sometimes, we wind up needing to save ourselves.

He shakes his head, apparently dismissing the mystery of the disappearing car, and finally turns to fully face me. "I went to get you and you weren't there," he says.

"I'd gone down the driveway, like I said."

"What happened to your dress?"

It takes me a moment to realize he's asking how I'm clean again, when I was filthy the last time he saw me. I force a smile, flicking my skirt in his direction. "Stain-resistant fabric spray," I say. "Like greasing a pan. All the gross stuff just comes right off when I shake myself. Pretty cool, huh?"

"Yeah," he says, sounding baffled. "Pretty cool. Anyway, do you still need that ride?"

"Yes, please." Please, please, *please*. Every nerve I have is screaming fire with the need to be in someone's passenger seat, letting someone else sit behind the wheel and get me where I want to go. It doesn't matter who's driving, as long as it isn't me, and this kid seems harmless enough. He shouldn't get in the habit of picking up hitchhikers, but I'm not going to be the one who tells him that. It's not my job.

"Let's go." He produces a set of keys from his jacket pocket—his *jacket*, which looks like it's going to fit me perfectly, ancient denim with grease ground into the cuffs, the sort of thing that was probably handed down to him from an older relative, or found at the back of a thrift store, on the clearance rack where it had lived for twenty years. When he starts across the parking lot, I follow, letting him lead me to a black Toyota no more than a decade old, probably already an antique in his eyes—and this is a functional, practical car that's never going to age into a classic, no matter how much it might deserve to—but modern and beautiful in mine. He unlocks the doors. He opens mine for me. I couldn't ask for a more perfect driver on a night like this.

"Your chariot awaits," he says, cheesy line that's so much older than he is, and oh, this kid, and oh, this night, and oh, the crossroads are dead and Bobby Cross is running out of options, and this is a good ride, yes, this is an excellent ride for a girl like me. I slide into the car and adjust my skirt so that it won't get caught in the door when he slams it shut for me.

I wait until he's getting in on the driver's side before offering him a vibrant smile. "My mother always told me not to accept rides from strangers, so hi. My name's Rose. What's yours?"

"Timothy," he says. "We're not strangers now?"

"I guess we're still a *little* strange, but no," I say. "You can't be strangers after you've been introduced. This is good enough to satisfy my mother, and she isn't here anyway." My mother never actually said anything about me getting into cars with strange men. She always assumed I had too much sense for that, and in a way, she was right. I didn't accept a ride from someone I didn't know until I was dead and they were the only way to scratch the itch that sometimes seems to consume my entire body. It's not fair that I should be in the ground and still have to contend with the needs of the flesh, but there you go. The world isn't fair.

Timothy reaches for his seat belt. I raise my hand.

"Wait," I say, and he stops, the perfect gentleman. He's giving a ride to someone dressed as one of the most famous hitchhiking ghosts of the modern world—he's giving a ride to one of the most famous hitchhiking ghosts of the modern world, full stop—and he's still minding his manners. I like this one.

"I'm cold," I say.

"You want my coat?" he asks, already shrugging out of it, an almost lopsided smile on his face. "I guess it goes with the outfit," he says. "I should have offered as soon as you sat down."

"I'm not that much of a method actress," I say. "I really am cold." And that's true because the dead are always cold. I sometimes think hitchers like me feel it more intensely than most other spirits, because I can be shivering so hard my bones rattle while they go happily about their hauntings, not seeming aware of the icy wind that wraps around my rib cage. It makes sense that I'd feel the cold more intensely since I'm one of the rare dead who gets a way to escape from it. Borrow a coat to borrow a body, borrow a body to be subject to the weather exactly like one of the living, nothing less and nothing more.

Timothy offers his coat across the cab. It's still warm from his body, and there's a simple intimacy in the action that makes me feel like I'm betraying Gary, like I should find a way to suppress this part of myself until the glitches in our relationship are hammered out more clearly. It's a silly thought. I'm not cheating on my boyfriend by doing the things the twilight designed me to do. But I've been spending a lot of time around the living and the recently dead lately, and it's hard not to fall back into some old ways of thinking.

I take the coat with a grateful smile and shrug it on, feeling more weight than just the fabric settle over me. Until I take it off or the sun comes up—whichever happens first—I am functionally alive. My stomach rumbles, reminding me that there are solutions to my endless, aching hunger. I press a hand against it, ducking my head in what I hope will look like embarrassment. I don't have any money, and I wouldn't bet on this gas station paying Timothy any more than minimum wage. He should be saving his money, not—

"When's the last time you ate something?"

Well, if he wants to offer, there's only so much I can do about it. I offer him a winning, winsome smile, and say, "It's been a while."

"There's a really nice diner down on the main drag. 'Nice' meaning 'the food is excellent,' and not 'it costs too much.' My cousin works there, and he gives me a family discount on whatever I want to order. You want to grab a grilled cheese before we find your boyfriend?"

Now he's speaking my language. The only thing that would make this better is the word "malt." I buckle my belt, and say, "I have never in my life turned down hot, melted cheese when I had any choice in the matter. Lead on."

"I think I have to lead, since I'm driving," he says, and slides the key into the ignition. The car grumbles to life around us, and I get my first sense of her.

She's had multiple owners, enough so that she no longer particularly cares about the humans who settle behind her wheel. She'll do her best to keep Timothy alive, because it's her job, but not because she gives a damn about him specifically. That's all right. Not every vehicle has to be like Jolene was for Carl. True love is rare, and we don't find it every time we turn ourselves toward the open road.

Have I ever actually known true love? I think yes, once, with a version of Gary. The Gary who existed when we had been on the same road for most of our lives, moving together toward the same distant, inevitable destination. But I'd gotten off that road too soon, and he'd missed every turn that would have kept him closer to me, moving steadily further and further into the misty hills of the future, where I would never be allowed to go. I'm not saying my high school boyfriend should have died as early as I did. I'm just saying that if he was going to live long enough to die of old age, maybe he should have figured out how to get over me.

Timothy is a careful but confident driver. He'll be great if he gets to keep doing this long enough. He pulls out of the gas station and rolls slowly down the driveway to the road, where he speeds up and merges with the passing traffic, eyes on the road the whole time. "We're about five minutes away from food," he says.

"Cool," I reply agreeably. "I like food."

My stomach grumbles again, and Timothy laughs.

It would be nice if the afterlife were always like this: a warm coat, a warm car, and a friendly driver to see me to my next destination. But if there's one thing I've learned from being dead, it's that all things are transitory, and that warm car can become a burnt-out husk in the time it takes to blink an eye. Timothy rolls around a corner, and the taste of wormwood is suddenly back, accompanied by the sound of sirens. None of my early warning systems are sound based; this is a real thing. Timothy tenses. He can hear it, too. Lights flash up ahead of us, on the other side of a stopped line of cars.

"Someone must have had an accident," he says.

The taste of lilies overlays the wormwood, and I know he's right. Someone had an accident, courtesy of Bobby Cross, and my own personal devil now has a full tank of soul that he can use to reach his next destination. Someone else is dead because I didn't have the tools to stop him. I could have—

Could have what? Thrown myself through his open window and given him the fuel up he really *wanted*, instead of the one he was in the position to take? This is on him, not me. I may have Persephone's blessing, but it didn't come with claws or teeth or other forms of weaponry. I don't know how to fight him yet, whether or not I have permission to try. Whatever Bobby did—and we all know what Bobby did, because he did what Bobby always, always does—it's entirely on his shoulders, and not even remotely on mine. I am not responsible for any of the people he's killed over the years.

Not even myself.

Timothy glances over at me, expression sympathetic. "I'm sorry," he says. "This sort of thing never happens around here."

"It's all right," I say numbly. *It's not all right!* I scream inwardly, because it's not, it's *not* all right. Someone just died before their time, someone whose only crime was being in the wrong place when Bobby Cross went hunting, someone who should have been allowed to have what Gary had, to grow old and die peacefully in their bed at some assisted living facility somewhere, far from the reach of evil assholes and their demon cars. Bobby is a thief. He steals lives and he steals time and he steals souls. But there is no justice in the twilight. There are only gods, and monsters, and people like me, who do our best to make things fair, when we can. Whether we want to or not.

The traffic rolls slowly past the site of the accident. It's a little red sedan, a starter car if I've ever seen one, the front completely smashed, as if it managed to lose an argument with a brick wall. There's no brick wall in sight, which means Bobby Cross drove away with it. The driver is already gone, whisked away by emergency services. The lack of a body briefly makes me hope they might have survived. Then I see the EMTs. They're standing around, looking dispirited, not cramming themselves into the back of the ambulance and blasting off down the street. They're not doing their jobs because when they arrived on the scene, they had no jobs left to do. They're deliverymen today, not superheroes, and this is a small enough town that they probably knew whoever they just lost.

Not just them. Timothy has gone pale. His hands are steady on the wheel, but his eyes aren't on the road anymore. "That's Christina's car," he says, in the wounded, wondering tone of a confused child. "She works at the 7-Eleven just up the street. We went to high school together. She's going to be so mad. She loves that car."

If she loved it enough, maybe it'll still be with her when she wakes up in the twilight, or maybe she'll never wake up at all, having already been grabbed and stuffed into the tank of Bobby's terrible car. I put a comforting hand on Timothy's arm, noting how warm his skin is, like panic is lighting a fire under his ribs. He keeps driving, until the snarl of people slowing down to see the accident for themselves has passed, and he's able to return to his original speed.

"Right," he mutters to himself. "Diner."

"If you're not hungry, we don't have to—"

"No." He cuts me off without hesitation, and it's clear from the look on his face that he doesn't fully realize he's done it. I would normally say something about manners, but he just saw strong evidence that a friend of his is dead. He's allowed to be a little rude if that helps him get through the shock.

Grief is a monster. As much of a monster as Bobby Cross, if not more. Bobby kills a dozen people every year, touches the lives of hundreds more, changing them for the worse. But grief touches millions. Grief touches everyone at some point or other, and unlike Bobby, grief can't be stopped, or reasoned with, or asked to change its ways. Grief just keeps on going, and grief is clearly a dead thing, because grief is always and eternally hungry.

"No," he says again. "I said I would take you for something to eat, and I keep my promises."

"It's really okay if you don't want to." I mean it, too. The ride has done wonders for my focus, and for my nerves, which are no longer jangling like windchimes in a hurricane. I'm a hitchhiking ghost. Sometimes I just need a ride to remind me how I'm supposed to function.

"Too late," he says, with sudden, forced cheer, as he pulls up in front of a small strip mall. This doesn't look like the sort of place where you'll find a diner, at least not a diner as I've always understood them, but there's a little white storefront with a neon sign in the window that flashes DAISY'S EATS in blazing red, with a smaller sign blinking "*he loves me—he loves me not*" underneath it in equally vivid green. The small dining room I can see through the window is about half-full, which is a good sign for a city this size on a weekday night.

Timothy turns off the engine and gets out of the car, walking around behind it to open my door for me. A gentleman, then; that's reasonably rare in this day and age.

"After you," he says.

I unfasten my seat belt and get out of the car, tugging my borrowed jacket a little tighter around myself as I do. "This the place?" I ask.

"It is," he says. "It's been here for more than fifty years."

I'm not sure I believe that. Strip mall diners may be a thing *now*, but fifty years ago, the concept of the diner was still healthy enough to have freestanding buildings all over the United States. I enjoy a value meal hamburger as much as the next girl, but I may never forgive the fast-food industry for undercutting the diners the way it did.

There are a lot of gods and idols in the twilight, rising and falling as slowly as the ebb and flow of human commitment. Sometimes I wonder whether we could have had a god or goddess of diners if the rise of the drive-through had just taken a few more years. The existence of places like the Last Dance shows that the diners have made their mark on the collective human consciousness; they're not going away, even if they're not as important as they were at one time. Could we have had a goddess of malted milkshakes and egg creams doling out her soda fountain treats for the rest of eternity? How could we deny ourselves that kind of grace?

Timothy reaches the door to Daisy's before I do, pulling it open with a jingle of tiny bells. I step through in front of him, admiring the delicate silver lace painted around the doorframe. Someone spent a lot of hours getting that exactly right. I love the things the living will decide to spend their limited time on. Cross stitch may be the most human concept ever invented.

The door swings closed behind me. The air seems to thin, filling with a tight, crystalline static that fizzes and buzzes against my skin like the bubbles in a glass of soda water. "Aunt Daisy, we have a guest," calls Timothy, across the crowded diner. None of the patrons look at him, absorbed as they are in their meals and desserts. One woman is working on a sundae that looks like it has greater volume than her entire head. I respect someone who's willing to skip over "brain freeze" and straight to "just replace your brain with ice cream."

A woman who looks a little like Timothy with twenty years on him emerges from the kitchen, wiping her hands on a white dish cloth and smiling. The smile freezes when she sees me, becoming somehow shallow. "Oh," she says. "I see. Well, show her to a table, boy. I know I taught you manners."

"You said your cousin worked here, you didn't say your aunt owned the place," I say. The fizzy, effervescent quality of the air hasn't changed. If anything, it's getting stronger, smothering me in bubbles. "That seems like a big omission."

"I get to omit as much as you do, and you've also made some pretty big omissions," says Timothy, leading me across the floor to an open table. He pulls a chair out for me. He's been a gentleman this whole time, which doesn't help with the pit that's starting to open in my stomach. Something is wrong here.

"You're still planning to feed me, right?" I ask, as I sit. A girl has got to have priorities, and if this is some sort of trick, this might be the last meal I get for a while.

"I am," he says. "This is easier if I don't lie to you." He sits across from me. His eyes are a remarkably clear, pale brown. It's like he can see right through me, even though I know for a fact that I'm not currently transparent.

His smile is thin as a razor blade as he passes me a menu. "I recommend the scrambles. Aunt Daisy gets all her eggs from local farmers, and you've never tasted anything like them."

He's wrong, of course, but I don't think that counts as lying to me, since there's no way he knows what was on the menu back in Buckley, where the general store got their eggs from local farmers and sometimes you found blood clots in your omelets. It's been long enough since I've had really fresh eggs that I'm still glad to have the information, and when his Aunt Daisy swings by to take our orders, I request the country scramble, a cup of coffee, and a vanilla malt. Good, honest diner food, the sort of thing that hasn't really changed since I was alive. There are recipes that were close enough to perfection the first time and haven't undergone any lasting changes. And that's a *good* thing. Innovation is fine, but I don't understand why everything needs to be new and improved all the time. Putting pineapple and bean sprouts and tofu slices on a cheeseburger doesn't make it *better*, it just makes it weird. And don't even get me started on what some of the people I know think it's a good idea to put on pizza these days.

"So, Rose," says Timothy, pulling my attention back to him. "Were you planning to tell me that you were dead, or were you just going to haunt me enough to check off whatever to-do list dropped you in my parking lot and then go back to the afterlife?"

I stare at him, open-mouthed and silent.

"Come on. It's not like you were *subtle*. 'Stain-resistant fabric'? Please. If I wasn't pretty sure that you're the real Phantom Prom Date, I'd think you'd been dead for less than a year."

This is where I should laugh in his face, get up, and storm out. I do none of those things. Instead, I twist my napkin between my fingers, pulling it tight, and say, in a small, wounded voice, "I don't understand why you're saying these things. I'm right here. Shouldn't that be enough to prove to you that I'm real?"

"You can be dead and still real, and I notice how you're dodging the question," he says. "Is 'Rose' your real name? It's pretty, and old-fashioned enough to match up with the cut of that dress. Your whole era is cohesive. You might want to think about updating the shoes if that's something you can control. And don't even think about whisking yourself out of here. Those runes on the door? They're a modified Mesmer cage. As long as you're inside their lines, you're trapped in physical form. None of your little poltergeist tricks will work in here."

"I'm not a poltergeist," I say sourly. If he has a Mesmer cage on the place, then he's not blowing smoke; he knows ghosts are real, and at least part of our interaction has been him trying to lure me here. "Poltergeists are generally jerks. I guess being able to play hurricane whenever you want to chips away at your manners. Would I have been sprawled in the dirt if I were a poltergeist?"

"Depends on how committed you were to selling the bit," says Timothy, and smiles at the waiter who brings us our drinks. Water and coffee for both of us and a Shirley Temple for him. I guess some people must enjoy the taste of grenadine or they'd stop making the stuff.

"It's not a bit," I protest.

"Please," he says, with a snort. "You appeared out of nowhere and hit the ground. That's a bit. What were you trying to sell? Was I the target?"

The anima mundi hadn't given me time to catch myself before I was landing in my next destination. I wonder whether they knew they'd be putting me in a bad position. I decide not to dwell on it. I'm here now, and I don't want to make an enemy of the soul of the living earth. That seems like a poor decision. "I manifested too quickly, and I lost my balance," I say. "It was an amateur mistake. I didn't mean to do it. I'm not selling anything, and I didn't have a target."

"What about the 'boyfriend' you say you're trying to catch up with?" he presses. "I know he's real. He drove his car right through a solid brick wall. One ghost is one ghost too many for me. I don't need you bringing all your phantom friends around."

"The man you saw isn't my boyfriend, and he isn't dead," I say.

"That was Bobby Cross, the old movie star. He's the one who killed me. He's probably the one who killed your friend. I'm trying to catch up with him so I can stop him before he kills anybody else."

Timothy's eyes narrow. "Is he here because of you?" he demands. "Don't lie to me again. If you're the reason Christina died . . ."

"You've got the order wrong. I'm here because of *him*," I say firmly. The anima mundi dropped me where Bobby was so I could start hunting, and my relief when that didn't mean landing on top of someone I cared about feels suddenly misplaced. "Not the other way around."

Timothy studies my face for a long beat before he sags in his seat. "I believe you," he says. "I don't want to. Two ghosts in one night is too many. One ghost in a night is generally too many. Christina was my friend. I don't want her to be dead. I don't want you to be innocent."

"I'm not innocent," I say. "I don't think anyone is innocent. Not once they're old enough to use the bathroom without help. But I swear, on the Ocean Lady, that I am not the reason Bobby Cross came to your town, and if I were, I wouldn't be sitting with you inside a Mesmer cage. I'd be doing everything within my power to get away and stop him from hurting anyone else."

I should be doing that anyway. Bobby's probably already on his way out of town with a tank full of Christina. That's the only thing I'll give him: he doesn't usually kill for fun. He has the morals of a rattlesnake, but he only kills people when he stands to gain something from doing it. With a full tank, he can't benefit from more murder. He'll need to go at least a hundred miles before anyone else is in danger from him tonight.

"Was that really Bobby Cross?" asks Timothy.

I nod.

"Christina would probably appreciate the fact that someone famous killed her. She always said she was better than this middle-of-nowhere town. She blamed her parents for not getting her into tap or gymnastics or something else when she was little, so she'd have a skill she could monetize on YouTube." Timothy looks at my expression and actually laughs. It's a short, bitter sound. "Guess you didn't have You-Tube when you were alive."

"No, and I don't know what it is now, or how you'd monetize dancing, or really, what the hell you mean by *monetize*. Is that a real word?"

"It's a real word," says Timothy earnestly. "It means to make money
for something that seems difficult to make money for. Like drawing, or
dancing, or . . ."

"Or talking to ghosts," I conclude, drawing my answer from the
vaguely guilty expression on his face. "Are you a ghost hunter, Timothy?"

"Not really," he says. "I'd have to be willing to travel, since we don't
have any permanent hauntings here in Warsaw. We never have. Or not
that I've ever heard of, anyway. But I can see ghosts even when they're
less . . . obvious than you. And I know ghosts when they *are* as obvious
as you. You're a hitcher, right? That's why you wanted my coat so badly?"

I don't know that I'd describe the way I asked for his coat as "so
badly." I'd just been cold. I reach up and tug the collar into position.
"Yes, I'm a hitchhiking ghost," I say, the words slightly flat on my
tongue. "I really *am* the Phantom Prom Date. I died in Michigan in
1952. I don't know why I wound up becoming the dominant hitchhiking ghost story for the modern era. It's a little frustrating, if you ask me,
since so many of the regional variants have me getting all murderous
and bloodthirsty once someone gives me a ride."

"It would help if you didn't run around in a vintage prom dress all
the time," says Timothy.

"I don't. Like I said, I appeared in your parking lot sort of abruptly,
and I didn't have time to change before you were rushing out to help
me up. Most of the time, I try to run around in jeans and a tank top.
Way less obtrusive."

"What about the weather?"

"What about it? Jeans and a tank top are totally appropriate for
summer, and in the winter, people are more likely to give me a coat if
they think I look cold." I show him my teeth. I don't even pretend to be
smiling. "I'm all about the outerwear."

"I got that," he says, looking at me in my anachronistic jean jacket
over a vintage silk gown. Fashion goes in cycles. I'm sure there will be
some girls attending their proms this year in dresses that look surprisingly like mine, from the cut of the bodice to the length of the hem.

But none of them will get it exactly. Modern reproductions are always cut with modern body shapes and modern undergarments in mind, while my dress was made for the kind of shapes that fell out of fashion decades ago.

"What did you mean by 'regional variants'?" Timothy asks.

It feels weird to be sitting here rehashing my history while Bobby's out there with a tank full of soul and murder, as always, on his mind. But Timothy's the one who just lost a friend, and I'm trapped inside this Mesmer cage until someone with a pulse decides to let me out, so it's not like I have any better choices. I'm happy to keep him engaged until his aunt shows up with food and answers.

"I mean there's only one true story of how I died, and it's the one I didn't live through, but if you go around North America asking people for hitchhiking ghost stories, you'll get a couple hundred versions of the way it all went down," I say. "Most of them agree that I was in high school and on my way to some big dance, but I've heard 'spring formal' and I've heard 'homecoming,' and this dress is *totally* unsuitable for either of those events. So the only stories that have it partially right are the ones with the balls to come right out and say 'prom.' After the Harry Potter books got big, I even had a few people start telling variants where I died on the way to some nondenominational Winter Ball. I'm from Michigan! We were lucky if the school was open in the winter, much less throwing extracurricular parties for the students! We would all have frozen to death in the unheated gym, and my story would be bigger and weirder and less entertaining, since it would be about a few dozen stiff, popsicled teenagers."

"You feel very strongly about this," says Timothy.

"Of course I do! It's my life. My death. It doesn't matter which one it is, because it's *mine*, and when something is mine, I'm allowed to want people to get it right."

Timothy leans back in his seat, looking at me with the flat lack of expression that people only assume when they're having extreme trouble processing whatever's just been said to them.

Finally, in a neutral tone, he says, "What."

"You don't want people telling your life story like it's a work of fiction, do you? Changing whatever details will suit them? Making you over into something that you're really not?" He knew about the coat and he knows about Mesmer cages, but he clearly doesn't know that I can't taste anything that hasn't been given to me freely, because while he's happily guzzling his Shirley Temple, he hasn't made any move to give me the coffee. I reach for my water. It never has any real flavor anywhere. Having it taste faintly of ash isn't going to change anything. "Maybe trying to make you out to be a killer?"

Timothy frowns at me. "You mean you're not? There are so many accounts of someone who looks just like you hitchhiking at a rest stop, right before there's a massive accident—"

"Do I *look* like I have the power to cause accidents?" I demand. I hate this line of thinking. "Correlation is not the same as causation. The fact that I show up when someone's going to crash doesn't mean I somehow *make* them crash. I'm a psychopomp. I'm drawn to people who are about to have an accident. Sometimes I can help prevent it. My presence keeps them from falling asleep at the wheel or changes the course of events just enough that they're not in the intersection when someone loses control of a bus. Sometimes I can't do anything, but at least in those cases, the driver doesn't die alone, and they have someone to help them make the first steps toward adjusting to existence in the twilight. I provide an essential service to the truckers and long-distance drivers whose need attracts me, and I don't hurt them. I'd be happier if we could somehow magically make the roads completely safe, so no one would need me anymore. Psychopomps are forever walking the line between the living and the dead. That's a lot of misery for us to be subjected to, whether we like it or not. We don't get to get away."

My second gulp of water tastes more strongly of ashes than my first one did. I wrinkle my nose and put the glass aside just as the waiter comes back with our dinner orders. If Timothy's not going to enable me actually eating my food, I don't entirely see the point in it. My country scramble looks perfect, a mound of golden, buttery eggs dripping with melted cheese and small, fatty drops of butter, chunks of ham embedded in the mess like diamonds in the walls of a cartoon mine. It comes with toast and a side of breakfast potatoes, in case I'm one of those people who likes carbohydrates with my carbohydrates. And I am. I like everything about this plate, except for the fact that if I try to eat any of it, all I'm going to taste is ash.

Timothy has one of those overly-fancy cheeseburgers, a teriyaki burger according to the menu, big slices of pineapple nestled between the two beef patties, and the whole thing oozing with salt-sweet teriyaki sauce. He picks it up with an expression of approval on his face, taking a massive bite before he notices that I haven't moved to touch either my scramble or my malt.

"Somethin' wrong?" he asks, as he swallows his half-chewed chunk of meat, cheese, and tropical fruit. There's a smear of sauce on his chin. I don't point it out.

"How is it you know so many of the rules for the dead, and you're missing so many at the same time?" I gesture to my plate, careful not to touch it. "It has to be given to me, or I don't get to taste it. It'll be nothing but ashes and grave dirt in my mouth."

"I'm paying for it," he says, almost sullenly. "Doesn't that make it enough of a gift?"

"No. Money is an illusion. Money is just the ghost of gold. I can't profit from a haunting. You have to give it to me if it's going to count."

Timothy reaches over and sullenly pushes my scramble closer to me. "Here," he says. "This is a gift, from me to you."

"Thank you," I say, as the smell of the belated breakfast snaps into focus, becoming suddenly as appealing as the appearance of it. I pick up my fork, giving the malt a pointed look.

Timothy's a little weird, and I don't know who's been teaching him about ghosts and leaving such big holes in his education, but he pushes the malt toward me. "This is yours," he says.

I plunge my fork into the scramble, loading it with eggs and ham and cheese. No breakfast potatoes, not yet; those will come later. "I appreciate you feeding me," I say.

"Who makes all these stupid rules?"

"You're the one who walked me into a Mesmer cage," I say. "I think you should know that."

"My Aunt Daisy painted the runes," he says, confirming what I'd already suspected. "She said if I ever found any ghosts, I should bring them here, and the cage would keep them from hurting anyone."

"That's . . . that's not what a Mesmer cage does," I say. "If I *were* a poltergeist, or a white lady, or a gather-grim, I could kill everyone in this room. I couldn't get *out* of the room once I was finished, not unless I'd managed to cover enough of the cage with their blood—obscuring a rune is as good as breaking it unless it's made of some very specific materials that I would have been able to feel before we stepped inside here—but I could do whatever I wanted inside the cage. I still could. It's just that my phantom parlor tricks are pretty well limited to 'ask for a ride,' 'eat diner food,' and 'disappear back into the twilight.' The only one of those that potentially does me any good right now is disappearing, but I want to know how your aunt knew to paint a Mesmer cage, and that means I stay here for right now." Not that the Mesmer cage would *let* me disappear. But I don't have to verify that for him.

Timothy has stopped eating his burger by the time I finish, getting paler and paler as he listens to me. When I finally stop and take another bite of my scramble—it tastes as good as it looks, which is nice; he was right about the farm fresh eggs—he puts his burger down and stares across the table at me.

"That's not what Aunt Daisy said," he says.

"Well, was she wrong, or did she lie to you?" I ask. "It sort of influences how I feel about her."

"How *you* feel about her! I'm her nephew!"

"Blood is thicker than water, kiddo." I take my first slurp of vanilla malt. The balance is perfect, not too heavy on the malt, not too light on it, either. I will never understand how milkshakes managed to eclipse malts in the hearts and stomachs of the nation.

"She didn't lie to me. She wouldn't." Timothy rises, and I realize he's going to go fetch his erstwhile aunt. I don't try to wave him back. I want to talk to her, and if him losing his temper is what it takes to make that happen, I'm cool with it. I sip at my malt as he storms across the diner toward the woman who looks like his older, more weathered sister. She's behind the counter, serving coffee and pie to the people on the vinyl stools, and she doesn't look surprised by his approach.

If she *has* been lying to him about how all this works, she's probably been expecting this conversation for a long time. Still, no amount of lying could give him the instincts to spot the dead the way he spotted me; he's sensitive to hauntings, and she knows how to paint a Mesmer cage. Something's going on here.

When it comes to catching the dead, people usually focus on the Seal of Solomon, that ancient biblical demon-catching trick. Well, I've never seen a demon, unless you want to be *real* generous with how much power you ascribe to the crossroads. I don't think they were a demon. I just think the anima mundi was right and they were from somewhere terribly *outside*, someplace where the rules were different enough that once they ended up here, the anima mundi had no defense against them, and by extension, neither did the rest of us. If demons are real, they keep themselves busy in layers of reality that aren't occupied by anything as easy and ordinary as ghosts. But Seals of Solomon still work on ghosts. We're easily ensnared by the right combination of lines and angles, the runic folding of corners into curves.

Franz Mesmer was alive a lot more recently than King Solomon. We know for sure that Mesmer actually *existed*, that he's not some story for ghost mothers to tell their faded phantom children. He was real, he walked in the world, and he only died about two hundred years ago. He did not, to the best of my knowledge, linger in the twilight after death; he was a man with no unfinished business to hold him in place.

Mesmer was one of the great leaders of the spiritualist movement. He researched or guessed a surprising number of truths about the twilight and the nature of the ghost roads, and one of his many innovations was a long, twisting rune designed to be painted into itself in an endless loop. It's more flexible than a Seal, since the lines are harder to break. It's also less powerful, since it lacks the absolute certainty of purpose that a proper Seal of Solomon possesses. Mesmer cages fell out of fashion around the turn of the century, when people figured out that they could mostly only be used to catch ghosts like me, who were more curious than hostile, but who might become hostile if we were held prisoner. I don't know any among the dead who likes being pinned down without our consent. Being dead should mean a certain freedom of movement, and when it doesn't, we get angry and bitter.

There's only one group that really still holds to the Mesmer cage as the best way of handling pesky spirits, and that's the umbramancers. They never met a means of freezing a haunting that they didn't like. Timothy approaches with his aunt close behind him, and I put down my malt, standing to offer her my hand. If she shakes it, that means I'm wrong.

She doesn't shake. She looks at my hand like it's some sort of affront, like I have personally offended her by observing standard human courtesy, and I don't know anything I didn't know a minute ago. Shaking my hand would have meant I was wrong. Refusing to shake it doesn't prove that I'm right. Sadly.

"My nephew tells me that you identified the Mesmer cage when he brought you inside, but you didn't try to run," she says. "Why?"

"Well, it holds me here, which is inconvenient and a little unfriendly, since I didn't do anything to deserve being locked up without my permission," I say. "Do you usually play roach motel for the unquiet dead, or did I just get lucky?" I know this answer. The cage around me is an old, settled one; she painted these runes years ago, if not decades. She's been in the ghost-catching business for a long, long time.

"You should have tried to run," she says, and reaches into her apron pocket, pulling out a saltshaker. I take a step backward, pausing when my thighs hit the table.

"You can't banish me with salt, lady," I say. "I'm as physical as you are."

"Oh, yes," she says. "Timothy told me you were a hitchhiker. There are ways of dealing with a hitcher if you know what to do. The dead are always dead, even when they walk in borrowed flesh."

There's a fanatic gleam in her eye. She sounds like she really means what she's saying. This is not a woman who harbors a lot of love for the dead. Someone close to her probably died when she was young, and she's been blaming the rest of us ever since. Still, Mesmer cages, going straight for the salt . . . her lack of a handshake may not have been the proof I needed, but I have all the evidence I could ask for now.

She's an umbramancer. She walks the paths of the dead with her eyes wide open and sees far too much for any human heart to hold. Routewitches have strong ties to the twilight, and as a consequence, spend a lot of time working with and fighting against the dead. A lot of spirits choose to haunt the routewitches, on the theory that hanging around the one person who can reliably see you is better than wandering lost and unobserved for all of time. I've never quite understood the logic. People don't like to be haunted, and no one likes to be told that they don't have a choice in the matter. "I'm here because you can see me, and that means you're obligated to listen when I talk" goes over like a lead balloon most of the time.

Umbramancers aren't tied to the twilight. They go deeper. Their ties are to the midnight. They attract ghosts like a bug zapper attracts moths, and not all of those ghosts are human. Not even most of those ghosts are human. Most of the warding and capturing circles have been developed by umbramancers who just want to be left alone. The only thing that's weird about this one is that it's set into a diner. That's road ghost territory, which means it's routewitch territory, which means something is wrong here, and it's not just the woman advancing on me with the saltshaker in her hand.

Why salt can banish ghosts when there are ghosts in the sea and ghosts, like me, who enjoy a nice, well-seasoned cheeseburger when we have the opportunity, I don't know.

Some of the diners around us have turned to watch my retreat, but no one's saying anything, or showing an excess of interest in the situation. One woman reaches for her water, and I see the outline of the glass through her hand. Timothy and Aunt Daisy may be the only living people in this diner. That's a nice change from my usual status as only dead girl in the room, except that if they're not all hitchhikers, they can't escape.

I turn and bolt for the door, weaving between the tables as I go.

Timothy rushes after me. Aunt Daisy, confident in the strength of her Mesmer cage, follows more slowly.

That's what I was counting on, inasmuch as I'm currently counting on anything. "Reacting on instinct" is a little more of my plan right now than actual planning. Timothy knows more about ghosts than I expect from a living man. Explanation: his aunt's an umbramancer, and since it runs in families, he might be one, too. With a ghost cage this size at their disposal, they'd be able to live relatively normal lives, rather than becoming itinerant to avoid attracting too many dead people. He knows about ghosts in general, but he was missing some of the major specifics for hitchers. Things I would expect anyone with his level of understanding to know. So maybe Aunt Daisy hasn't been training him, or maybe whoever trained *her* was more interested in keeping ghosts away than they were in getting to know them. One way or another, certain essential details didn't get passed along.

Like the fact that right now, with this coat across my shoulders, I'm as alive as Timothy or Daisy, and no simple Mesmer cage has the strength to hold me. That's not how it works. If the runes had been a bit less obvious and Timothy had understood the need to keep me talking until dawn, maybe they would have stood a chance of adding me to their diner of the damned. Maybe not. I still have this corsage on my wrist, and it has to be good for something. It has to be enough to open doors that shouldn't have been closed in the first place.

I run, and the umbramancers follow, Daisy's arms pinwheeling when she hits a damp patch of floor, Timothy running with the single-minded dedication of a teenage boy who has never seen any reason to doubt the adults in his life. You don't see that kind of bullheaded trust very often. People are too cynical. The Internet keeps them from thinking their parents hung the moon and the stars in the sky. That's not entirely a bad thing: it's harder to abuse your kids when they don't think of you as a god. Harder, not impossible, and all this was beside the point, because I'm running, and they're chasing me.

Humans evolved to prey on the world around them, and to compete with the predators who kept eating us. We know how to hunt, and we know how to be hunted. They're intrinsic understandings, things we can't help knowing. I jump over a chair that someone kicks into my path—and since almost all these people are as dead as I am, it's a little obnoxious that they'd be helping the woman who has them captive, and not their fellow spirit—and then I'm finally at the door. I run past the limits of the Mesmer cage and stop in the little atrium formed by the shape of the restaurant, that tiny glassed-in box where patrons are supposed to stomp the mud and snow off their feet and remove their coats. Daisy and Timothy draw up short, Daisy glancing at the saltshaker still in her hand. They don't know what to do with a ghost who runs.

"You can't *do* that," says Daisy mulishly. "The Mesmer cage will stop you."

"I just did it," I reply. "I'm on the other side of your Mesmer cage, unless you put something more subtle on the front door." I turn and push it open, letting a gust of sweet Indiana air inside. Then I step out, into the night.

Nothing tries to stop me from passing through the door. There's not even the scant resistance I would expect from a ghost trap intended for someone else. I turn a quick pirouette on the sidewalk, turning back to the diner to wave through the glass, as coy as any coquette, before I open the door and step back into the atrium.

"Established: I can come and go as I please," I say. "Now what's with the salt? And the Mesmer? I know you're an umbramancer. Having a certain amount of protection against the dead makes perfect sense. Using it to play tea party with an entire diner full of ghosts is a little weird. Some of these people probably have shit they were hoping to accomplish before they move on to the next stage of their afterlife existence."

A few of the diners in range of my voice look around and nod, like I've just said the most sensible thing they've ever heard. None of them say anything aloud. They're either in Daisy's thrall somehow, or the situation is more complicated than I understand. With my luck, it's both, and I'm about to have to fight a phantom army. I hate fighting phantom armies.

"How are you getting past the Mesmer cage?" asks Daisy.

"The same way your nephew is," I say. I don't believe in toying with umbramancers. They don't tend to have a sense of humor. "I'm alive."

"You admitted to him that you were a specter," she snaps. "You *reek* of the afterlife!"

"Hey," I say, stung. "I bathe pretty regularly. I'm a clean person. I shouldn't have to be a clean person once my body has, you know, dissolved into the earth, but I am, because some habits are difficult to break. I don't reek of anything. And I'm not a specter. Specters follow some pretty strict rules that don't apply to me. I'm a good, old-fashioned, hitchhiking ghost, which is why I'm currently alive. I borrow substance from the living."

Timothy pales.

"Is *that* it?" asks Daisy. She drops her saltshaker onto a nearby table and picks up a chair. "I can solve that." She pulls the chair back like she's getting ready to hit her own nephew.

"Wait!" I take a step forward, hands raised, right to the edge of the Mesmer cage. "What are you doing?"

"If he's not alive, there won't be anything for you to borrow substance from. You'll return to the teeming ectoplasm from whence you sprang, and the cage will work the way it's supposed to. You'll be trapped like the rest."

Timothy, while he looks like he's going to be sick, hasn't moved out of her reach. I focus on him. "Are you really going to stand there and let her beat you to death with a chair? Because I don't care how much you love your family, that's a *terrible idea*. You understand that, don't you? No one has the right to take your life away, no matter what they may have done for you in the past. Your life is yours. It belongs to you, here, now, and forever. Even after you're dead, your life is your own, and no one gets to decide how you spend the rest of eternity. Which means you don't let somebody kill you inside a Mesmer cage. You wouldn't be able to reach the twilight if that happened. You wouldn't know what kind of ghost you're supposed to be, and you wouldn't settle properly." I glance at Daisy, who is watching me with fanatic loathing burning in her eyes.

None of this makes *sense*, and that's what finally makes it all start making sense. I wince a little before giving her a sympathetic look and asking the only question that applies: "How did you die?"

If the Mesmer cage was already here when she collapsed or was killed, her spirit wouldn't have been able to get out. That's the danger of any of the warding systems, from Solomon's Seal on down. Yes, they can be used to trap bad things, but they can also ensnare innocent things that happened to be in the wrong place at the wrong time. If she painted the Mesmer cage when she was young and healthy and breathing, it wouldn't have cared enough to let her spirit go. It would have kept her the same way it kept anyone else. Relentlessly and without negotiation.

"Ten years ago," says Daisy, voice rasping and cold. "I think it was a heart attack. I was doing inventory on the pantry, and there was this pain in my chest, pain bigger than I knew pain could be, and I fell down. I didn't get back up for three days."

That's the traditional period for house ghosts. It takes time to realize that the place you've always lived isn't home anymore; that the door of your body has been closed, and the structure has been condemned. Road ghosts bounce back faster because we have to. It's that or stand in the middle of the street with cars crashing through the space where our bodies ought to be, unable to understand why everything has changed.

"Aunt Daisy?" says Timothy, in a small, scared voice. He sounds more frightened now than he did when she was threatening him with the chair. That's interesting. "Interesting" is not the same thing as "good." "What are you talking about? You're not dead."

"That must have been scary," I say. "The Mesmer cage was already here?"

"Painted it with my daddy the summer I turned sixteen," she says. "That's when the ghosts who'd been bothering me off and on started getting really insistent. They wouldn't leave me alone. No matter how much I asked them to. They knew I could hear them, and they were damn well determined to be listened to."

"That sucks," I say, agreeing with the complaint she didn't make out loud. Not all ghosts can make themselves known to the living as easily as I can. In fact, most house ghosts can't do it at all. Road ghosts tend to be more visible, maybe because we're less fixed in place. We're less at risk when people know we exist. By the time they fetch the ghost hunters, we've already moved on to another location.

The unrealistic thing about *Ghostbusters* isn't the proton packs or the hot blonde lady not having a girlfriend. It's the sheer number of visible hauntings they can find just by going to a few old houses. If house ghosts were that easy to find, the world would have stopped arguing about the possibility of life after death a long, long time ago.

"So we painted the cage," she says, in the same plodding, resigned tone. "My father and me. The paint we used was hand mixed. It contained the ashes of my grandmother. The dead hounded her, too. When she died, we had to break every window in the house to free the spirits she had trapped during her life and stop them from pursuing us."

"Did it work?" I don't want to be here. This place is cold and unforgiving, founded on the idea that the dead have no rights. It's a pitcher plant, and there's a good chance I'm in Warsaw not because of Bobby's presence, but because either the anima mundi or Persephone herself didn't like the fact that so many of her subjects are trapped in a dead-end diner in a tiny town in Indiana.

I don't want to be a Swiss Army Knife for fixing the problems of the gathered dead. It's not my idea of a good time.

"I never saw any of those spirits again," says Daisy. "My father was very good at being done with the dead."

Not good enough to keep his own daughter from being trapped, but that's another story. I nod as if this is the most enthralling thing I've ever heard. "So you painted a ward using a dead woman's bones, and then you died inside it," I say. "And now you can't get out."

"The cage is a solid wall for me," she says. "When I try to exit the diner, it pushes me back into the kitchen, where the paramedics found my body."

Timothy looks like he can't decide whether to cry or be sick. "You can't be dead," he says, voice barely above a moan. "Someone would have told me if you were dead."

"Would they, buddy?" she asks, and for the first time, she sounds warm, sincere, caring—like the kind of woman who would inspire such a fierce love that her nephew didn't even flinch when she grabbed the chair. "None of us expected your parents to die. My brother didn't inherit my connection to the dead, thankfully. The gift only comes to one per generation. He agreed to hide my condition from you. The diner is in a trust. The bills are paid, and no one thinks it's strange that the doors stay open. We have enough living staff members that when someone comes in who shouldn't see me, I can stay in the back and cook until they're gone. And no one ever felt the need to tell you. It seemed cruel, everything being equal."

That, and most people who did stumble across the knowledge that a dead woman had been somehow given custody of her living nephew would just quietly put it out of their minds and forget about it. That was the other effect of the Mesmer cage. Spirits left inside it would be forgotten by the world outside—all levels of the world. That kept the twilight from emptying out as spirits went hunting for their missing friends. Franz Mesmer was an umbramancer who didn't think very highly of the rights of the dead: he probably hadn't intended that little aspect of the cage. He'd just been trying to make it so that when he caught a particularly nasty haunt, the people it had been tormenting would be able to move on with their lives and forget about what they'd been through. The cage dulls and distorts memory. So when Timothy's parents died and their will kicked in, Daisy had been able to claim him as her own thanks to the cage distorting the memory of her death. It was a fun little perversion of the way the legal system was supposed to work, and only the fact that it was an unlikely enough scenario that it would probably never come up again kept my stomach from churning. I'd barely eaten any of my truly excellent scramble. I didn't exactly want to vomit it back up again so quickly.

"And all these people?" I ask.

"Timmy's been luring the dead in for me for the last few years," she says, with a casual wave of her hand. "They don't pay, but they don't all eat, either, and it's better that they be confined than that they be running around making trouble for living folk."

A few of the nearby diners wrinkle their noses and turn their faces away. Clearly, they don't share their captor's beliefs about the suitability of locking them in a ghost cage for the crime of being dead. None of them move to rise or stand with me. They've been in here too long, cut off from the twilight, unable to refresh the renewable aspects of their unlife.

"That's not right," I say. "You're here voluntarily. You're here because you *want* to be, or you would have asked Timothy to break the cage years ago. None of these people are here because they want to be." The only good thing about this situation is that I know she hasn't captured any homecomers or strigoi. They could have turned themselves solid and walked out of the cage, the same way I have. They would have torn this place down around her ears for what she's done, and they would have been right to do so.

But Timothy deserves better. Yes, he's been helping her, but he's still a kid, doing what his parent figure tells him to do, trying to be good and be brave and navigate a world he doesn't fully understand. Umbramancers are rare, rarer even than routewitches, and unlike routewitches, they don't have a coherent system of government to keep them from getting into trouble. Most of them train their families in the same methods that they were trained in, and some of those methods are good and some are bad and some are merely skewed. They're not necromancers from a fairy tale. They can't raise the dead. They can only see us, only interact with us. For some of them, that's more than enough. They want to live in a world populated only by the living, and they don't think it's fair that they don't get that option.

No, none of this is Timothy's fault. I can take him to Apple when I finish my business with Bobby. She isn't an umbramancer, but she probably knows where to find a couple of the more well-adjusted ones, and she can help him get the education he needs to not be a threat to himself and others. If she can't, she can at least smack him if he ever starts talking about Mesmer cages again.

Daisy is watching me with wary suspicion. I think she knows what has to happen next, that there's no way I can allow things to continue as they have been. She can't hold me until dawn comes or I take off this coat, whichever comes first, but my freedom should not come at the expense of leaving others in captivity. That's a simple moral principle of the universe.

I lean past the frame to grab a butter knife off the nearest table. It's an ordinary piece of diner cutlery, stainless steel and heavy, not weighted to be used as any sort of a weapon. It's still a knife, flat and designed to cut and gouge things. Things like paint overlain on a door frame.

She could stop me. She could say something, order Timothy to do something. She doesn't. I think she's as tired as the ghosts she's been holding captive, aware that this is wrong, and ready for it to be over. But it's hard to admit when you're in the wrong, and it's easy to let a stranger smash the walls you're too attached to to let go of.

Timothy holds out a hand and takes a step forward when I press the edge of the knife to one of the runes. "Wait!" he says.

I pause. Nothing's forcing me to do it, but I want to know what he's going to say. His aunt is still standing there silently, that expression of wary suspicion on her face. She's trapped. They're all trapped. This is unnatural and wrong. This is cruel.

This is dangerous. If Bobby had stumbled across this place . . .

Bobby, who is still a living man, despite everything he's done, despite everything he's been through. Bobby, who shoves ghosts into the tank of his car. He could drive for a decade using only the ghosts in this room. He could stop his killing, yes. But he'd be doing it because he'd have a bell jar full of innocents to use and abuse, and it wouldn't be any more humane than what he's already doing. There are limits to how far I'm willing to go to eliminate the threat he represents, and giving him this diner would be a delay, not a conclusion. I want a conclusion.

"What is it, Timothy?" I ask.

"What happens if you break the cage?" he asks in return.

I pause. Daisy is his guardian. "Are you eighteen?"

"Not for another three months," he says. "I don't want to go into foster care just because you don't like the way we do things around here." He looks at Daisy. "We've done pretty well for ourselves without the authorities getting involved." He pauses, brow furrowing. "Why didn't they get more involved? Dad was your brother, but I was just a kid. Shouldn't the police have cared more about how you were taking care of me. Making sure I got my vaccinations and all, not like the McAllister kids. They all got whooping cough. The youngest girl died."

"It's the Mesmer cage," I say. "It dampens memory for those outside."

"You mean everyone forgot Aunt Daisy was dead," he says querulously.

I've already reached this conclusion and moved on. I still nod with feigned enthusiasm, like this is the smartest thing anyone has ever said. "Exactly," I say. "When the cage breaks, people will start remembering things."

"But Aunt Daisy will still be here," he says. "She can tell them everything's fine. That they don't need to worry about me. I have a job, and a place to live, and I've been vaccinated, and my grades are good, and everything's . . . fine. It's fine. Right, Aunt Daisy? You're not going to leave me, are you?"

"I won't have a choice once she breaks the cage," says Daisy. Her voice is smaller, duller, lacking the anger it held before. I hate that most umbramancers wind up so angry with the dead. It's not reasonable, and it's not right. "I died inside the cage. I don't know what kind of ghost I am, and it's been so long that the twilight might not be willing to help me settle into a more predictable form. Or I might be a kind of ghost that wants to harm the living. I can't have that be the last thing you remember about me. I can't try to hurt my boy."

There are tears in the corners of her eyes. She's thought about this before, about what it would mean for Timothy if she found a way out of the diner where she died.

I could point out that she *did* just try to hurt her boy. Being hit with a chair hurts. It wouldn't do any good. She's grappling with a lot of changes all at once, and she's not listening to me.

She shakes her head. "I want you to run. Don't look back. This is where we say good-bye, my love."

"No!" Timothy whirls to glare at me, moving to place himself subtly between me and his aunt. "What gives her the right to decide what happens to you? You're my family. I love you. She doesn't get to decide for me that it's time for you to leave."

"So why did the two of you get to decide for all these people that they weren't going to be free anymore?" I may know some of them. The memory dampening attributes of the cage mean that I wouldn't remember if I did. I know she hasn't captured any hitchers, but phantom riders, roadworkers, cartographers, and even cyclists would all be vulnerable to her specific kind of charms.

Timothy swallows, throat working, and looks away. He can't even meet my eyes as he says, "They were dead. You're dead. It's not like we've been hurting anyone."

"By your logic, I should be able to open this cage without hurting anyone. It won't affect you at all."

"But you'll hurt me by hurting my Aunt Daisy!"

It's not as unusual as I wish it were for the living to only consider the dead in relation to the living. We don't matter unless someone with a pulse is inconvenienced by whatever happens to us. Great. "Every one of these people could be someone else's Aunt Daisy," I snap, gesturing with my butter knife. "They may have friends, family, people who've been waiting for their personal haunts to come home. *I* have friends. I'm currently on a quest to save a member of my family from a situation she got herself into by being damn stupid. All of them would have been upset if I'd disappeared into this diner and never come back out. All of them have just as much right to want me to come home as you do to want your Aunt Daisy to stay with you. And you don't know the histories of any of the people you've trapped. They had existences before you captured them. They deserve to go back to those existences."

"Aunt Daisy?" For the first time, he sounds truly unsure. He looks to his aunt, who shakes her head. She has no comforting words to offer, it seems. She's as trapped as he is, victim of her own logic.

If the dead have no rights, then that includes her, and she should be released back into the ether from which all spirits spring. She should go because she has no right to stay. If the dead *do* have rights, then he's been helping his aunt violate the freedoms and liberties of dozens of spirits who deserved to be treated better, and who never volunteered for this situation.

He closes his eyes.

"If you have to do it, do it," he says, in a voice that's heavy with defeat. "I wish I hadn't given you my coat."

I can't share his regrets, not right now. I turn and scrape the butter knife against the edge of the first rune. It's a small disruption, a minute break in the pattern of the lines, but it's enough. Mesmer cages are delicate things. They need to be cared for, maintained, and never, ever damaged. The change in the diner's atmosphere is immediate and absolute. Patrons who had been ignoring us before look up from their dishes and drinks, eyes focusing as their gazes grow sharper, like they're becoming aware of their surroundings for the first time in a long time. Years, for some of them. They begin leaving their seats and moving toward the door. All of them are still apparently solid, which is an interesting trick. With the Mesmer cage broken, they should be losing the ability to impact the physical world, unless they're all poltergeists—which wouldn't make sense. Timothy was too distressed by the idea that I *might* be able to cause that kind of damage.

A few of them stomp or bare their teeth at Aunt Daisy, but none of them pause long enough for her to grab hold of them. Even dead, she's still an umbramancer, and they have enough sense to respect that. They keep moving toward the exit, growing thinner as they approach me, turning translucent.

When the first of them reaches me, she's entirely see-through. She pauses long enough to smile, and I realize that I've seen her before, haunting a flower market in Illinois. How she wound up in Indiana, I may never know. Then she's moving past me, disappearing into the night as if she'd never been there in the first place. More ghosts rush to take her place, until it's a steady stream of phantoms vanishing into the evening air.

A man stops toward the end of their spirit parade, somewhat older-fashioned than many of the others, with hair cut in a feathered style that hasn't been popular since the 1970s, and a battered, scratched-up leather jacket on his back. He wraps his arms around me without warning, lifting me off my feet and causing me to drop the butter knife I'm still holding. I squeak, recognition following on the heels of his action.

"Nate!"

"Rose! I should have known that when someone came along to get us the hell out of here, it would be you!"

I laugh. It's an involuntary response, pulled out of me by what feels like a pair of tiny hands plunging into my chest. Nate's a cartographer, a kind of walking ghost who maps the cracks and crevices of the twilight with his own two feet. Our world is constantly changing, just like the world of the living. We need people to make sure we don't get lost. We don't have GPS.

Nate disappeared eight years ago. At the time, I thought he might have walked until he was finished and decided to take some footpath to his equivalent of my final exit. Moving on waits for us all, and there's no real way to decide it's not going to happen. I touch his cheek as he puts me down.

"It's good to see you," I say. "Stay close, and I'll take you back to the Last Dance with me."

"Sounds good," he says, and removes his arms from around my waist, stepping out of the flow of traffic as more and more spirits push by, returning to their interrupted afterlives as fast as they can. Aunt Daisy and Timothy aren't moving. He's grabbed her hand and is hanging on like he's afraid she's going to slip through his fingers, which, to be fair, she probably is.

She's definitely not a road ghost. Very few house ghosts have the power to stay visible when the living are around. Even if she's going to settle, he's going to lose her. Unless . . .

"Will you promise to leave the dead alone?" I ask quickly.

"What?" says Timothy.

"We don't have a lot of time here," I say. "Answer the question."

"After this, I never want to talk to another ghost for as long as I live," he says, chin jutting out stubbornly.

"You won't have a choice." I feel almost sorry for him, baby umbramancer with no living relatives to teach him how to handle what he is. Even if there's no way he'll agree to go with me while Aunt Daisy's still here, I can convince Apple to send him a teacher. Routewitches and umbramancers intersect enough that there's probably at least one mixed marriage among her subjects, at least one person who can roll over in bed and ask their beloved spouse to step up and keep this kid from self-destructing.

With the crossroads gone, we're all going to need to make adjustments. Nothing is going to be the same.

"How about you?" I demand, shifting my attention to Daisy. "Do you swear to leave the dead alone?"

She nods in silence. I pull a Sharpie out of my jacket pocket and turn to repair the damage I did to the Mesmer cage. It only takes a few seconds, smoothing the jagged edge of the rune I scraped with quick flicks of the pen. The air turns to jelly around us. Nate stiffens, giving me a wounded look.

"Don't worry," I say. "I can pull you out." I put the cap back on the Sharpie and return it to my pocket.

"Is that a *magic* pen?" asks Timothy.

"Only in that all Sharpies are magic according to high school principals and asshole policemen," I say. "It's just a Sharpie. *Your* Sharpie since it was in the pocket of this coat when you handed it to me."

"But the original runes were painted using ink that had been prepared according to the highest, most meticulous ritual standards!" objects Daisy.

"And now you know you can fix them with Sharpie," I say. "Aren't you glad to know that Timothy can fix any future damage on his own?"

"I suppose," she says, and subsides. Maybe she's realized that fighting with me isn't going to do her any good.

"Excellent." I grab Nate's arm and step outside the bounds of the cage again, tugging him with me. There's a moment of resistance as I pull him over the threshold. Then he's out, looking at me with wide, wondering eyes, like I've just accomplished something genuinely impossible. Which, hell, maybe I have. I don't exactly have a checklist of "this can be done" and "this can't be done" situations that I'm likely to find myself in.

"Keep your word," I say sternly to Daisy and Timothy.

Then I turn and head out of the diner, still pulling Nate with me, still wearing Timothy's denim jacket.

Chapter 10
Romance for the Road

———

NATE STAYS QUIET UNTIL we're halfway down the block. Then he grabs my arm and spins me to face him, exclaiming, "Rose! That was amazing! What, are you a ghostbuster-buster now?"

"No," I say. "That sounds exhausting, and also really dangerous. I have enough dangerous bullshit in my death. I don't need to go looking for more."

"Then how—?"

"I could ask you the same." I push him in the shoulder. His flesh is faintly yielding, soft and spongy in a way that would mean something really bad if he were a mortal man. He's not, so what it means is that he's gone too long without mapping something. He needs to give directions. Once he does that, he's going to be fine.

He's not going to enjoy the prevalence or accuracy of mapping software in this modern world. Cartographers are getting rarer as satellites are getting more accurate. That's sad—I've liked most of the cartographers I've known—but it's also natural. The twilight is forever changing. It uses the prism of death to split humanity into a hundred different species of haunt, with competing habitats and habits, and sometimes one of those species gets outcompeted and fades away. The loss of the Neanderthals was probably also sad, to the Neanderthals. The hominids who kept going as their failed cousins faded into memory may or may not have paused long enough to mourn. Forward momentum is the way of humanity, no matter what we look like, no matter what we've become. We don't slow down, and we don't look back.

"What do you mean?" he asks, looking wounded.

"How did you *not* know how to recognize a Mesmer cage when you saw one?" I ask. "They're not *subtle*. A Seal of Solomon or a house of mirrors, I'd understand, but this was a Mesmer cage. That's rookie bullshit."

"I saw you follow the kid right inside, and you didn't notice it either," he says, stung. "So I guess we're both rookies."

"I'm wearing his coat," I counter. "When I have a coat on, my sense for things like that is dulled way, way down. If you're only managing to be as good as I am while I'm incarnate, you need to work on your attention to detail. Got it?"

"Sorry," he says, looking down. He kicks at a rock. His foot passes right through it. That'll stop as he gets reacclimated to the road. Cartographers draw substance from travel. I get to be technically alive again as long as I'm wearing a coat. Nate gets to be physical but not alive as long as he keeps moving. Cartographers are the sharks of the open road. By and large, they don't appreciate the comparison.

"I didn't notice the Mesmer cage because I was tired and lonely and there's a compulsion on the place that makes ghosts want to go inside when they're passing by. I'll swing back by here in a month or so, to make sure it's not being used to hold anyone against their will. They promised you not to dance with the dead anymore, and I know it can be hard for you to wind up exactly where you want to be. The least I can do is double-check for you."

"Thanks," I say. "I appreciate that a lot."

"How long have I been gone?"

"About eight years, give or take," I say. "That's the last time I remember seeing you, but that doesn't have to mean anything. Not really. I am not my brother's keeper, and all that."

"No, I was one of Timmy's first lucky hauls. I got caught pretty soon after the last time we traveled together," he says. "That weird little fun fair you took me to."

"It was run by routewitches, and routewitches always give road ghosts free hot dogs," I counter. "You seemed to like it well enough when we were on the Lobster and you were eating cotton candy."

"That's just because you looked so happy and I didn't want to kick your puppy," says Nate. He kicks at a chunk of broken glass this time. His toe catches it, and it goes tumbling down the curb, coming to rest against a crack in the sidewalk. His smile is triumphant. "Anyway, you caught a ride with that pothead in the Chevy, and I kept walking. I wound up here, and I was tired and lonely, and the sign at that diner was like a lighthouse welcoming me home from sea."

"Pretentious," I say.

"Accurate," he says. "I couldn't not go in. It was like what I wanted didn't matter. I needed to go inside and sit down and order something I couldn't eat and didn't need. It felt sort of like you've described the draw toward catching a ride."

"That makes sense." As a cartographer, the only compulsion Nate deals with on a regular basis is the need to keep going—and since some maps are incredibly detailed, he doesn't have to move *far*. It's different for me. When the time comes to catch a ride, nothing else matters. My world narrows to the highway shoulder, my thumb turned toward the silently judgmental sky, and the cars whizzing past me, not slowing down. That narrowing doesn't reverse until someone stops and unlocks their doors and asks me inside.

"So I went in, and the compulsion went away, and I tried to go back out, but I couldn't get past the doorframe," he says. "And then that lady in the apron was offering me a menu, and I wound up sitting down in a little booth and that was it. That was all she wrote."

"The lady in the apron was an umbramancer," I say.

Nate snaps his fingers. "I knew it! Shit, Rose, I would have stayed in there forever if you hadn't come along. You saved my death. Thank you." He moves to embrace me, pausing when he spots my corsage peeking out from under the cuff of Timothy's denim jacket. "Uh, Rose, I didn't know you were into flowers. That's new."

"It's white asphodel," I say, holding up my hand and peeling back the sleeve far enough to show him the structure of the petals. "Also, my name is *Rose*. I think me being into flowers is the least surprising thing about me."

"White asphodel only grows in the Underworld," he says, and looks at me with wide, startled eyes. "What did you do?"

"I went to the Underworld," I say. "Had a full katabasis and everything. Spoke to the Lord and Lady of the Dead."

Nate stares at me. "Why did you do that?" he asks.

"Bobby Cross brought me back to life, and in order to be sure I'd remain the same kind of ghost I've always been, I needed to die without dying. Pulling a Eurydice seemed like the best way to get it done." When I put it that bluntly, it sounds pretty ridiculous. That's true of most things. Nothing good survives summarization. Not even pie, and pie is a universal constant of goodness.

"How . . . Rose, you've been dead longer than I have." We've continued walking as we talked. The town is receding behind us, blurring into foggy streetlights and dimming storefronts. There was no fog when we left the diner. We're crossing the boundary between the daylight and the twilight. It's a slow, subtle transition, like sinking into clear water, very different from the abrupt drops and ascensions I experience when I'm traveling on my own. The rules are different for Nate than they are for me, but he's still a road ghost, and like all road ghosts, he can take passengers when he wants to.

"Yeah, but I wound up alive again for a little while. I didn't want to be," I add hastily, in case he gets the wrong idea. "Bobby Cross perverted the Halloween mysteries to render me incarnate. He convinced a routewitch to kill herself in order to make his nonsense stick. Bobby sucks, in case you missed the memo."

"I know Bobby sucks," says Nate. "That's basically his defining characteristic. Bobby Cross is a self-centered asshole who never met a rule he didn't want to break for his own benefit. But how the hell does 'Bobby sucks' translate into 'Bobby Cross can reincarnate the dead'? No one can do that! And you're a hitcher, Rose! You have no business performing katabasis. That's a good way to get your eternal soul dissolved and scattered across the fields of the blessed for all of time."

I stare at him, stunned and stung. "I just freed you from a Mesmer cage that you couldn't evade on your own, and you want to make shitty comments about how I'm not allowed to do things I already did? Is this honestly a good use of your time? Because it doesn't feel like a good use of your time. It feels sort of like being a *really shitty friend*."

Nate looks abashed. "I'm sorry. I didn't mean to be hurtful. But you have to admit this all sounds a little, well, far-fetched from the outside. How did Bobby Cross pervert the Halloween mysteries?"

"I'm not sure Persephone wants me to go around telling people," I say uncomfortably. "It wasn't supposed to happen in the first place, I shouldn't be making it easier for other people to pull the same stunt. Not that you would, but you know what they say about keeping secrets."

"Two people can keep a secret if one of them is dead," says Nate, and chuckles direly. "What about when both of them are dead? That makes things more complicated, I guess. Fine, no more questions about how that happened. Why didn't you just stay alive? I thought that was what most ghosts wanted. I don't think I'd be able to give it up a second time if I had a choice."

Like most road ghosts, Nate didn't have a choice the first time he died. He was mapping a series of hiking trails for a small press specializing in nature books, and he stepped on a rattlesnake. The snake did what snakes do. The funny thing is? Nate never blamed it. I've seen him sitting in the middle of great balls of rattlesnakes who were killed by people who judged them for existing, soothing their frightened, venomous souls, helping them to move on to whatever waits for rattlesnakes on the other side of our fragile afterlife. He loves them enough that he's probably responsible for half their manifestations in the twilight. But the fact that he doesn't blame the snake that killed him for doing what snakes do naturally doesn't mean that he wouldn't happily return to the life he left behind if he had the opportunity.

Or at least that's what he thinks. It's what I would have thought once, before the chance was offered to me and I discovered that I was happier turning it away.

"I died in 1952," I say.

"I know."

"Do you really?" I shake my head. "You died in 1977. You're twenty-five years behind me, ghost-wise, and that means you're twenty-five years closer to the modern world. Some of the people you knew when you were alive might still be running around, and you smoked enough pot that some of them might even believe you when you tell them you haven't gotten any older because you've been off being dead for the last forty years. But the world has moved on without you. All those pretty girls you used to flirt with are grown up and married with children of their own. All those dreamy boys you used to run around with, all of them have jobs that require them to wear ties and sensible shoes. You'd be Peter Pan to them, the boy who refused to grow up, and I've been dead so much longer than you have. Everyone I know is already a ghost. When Bobby brought me back, it was like dying all over again, but in the other direction, and being alive is *disgusting*. You sweat and stink and pee and you actually have to eat to stay alive, not just because you want to. I hated every second of it. I bet you would, too."

"Maybe, maybe not," says Nate. "You're right that you've been a ghost longer than I have, but I was alive longer than you were. I got to do some pretty awesome shit that you missed out on. I would be okay with coming back to life if it meant I got to do all that awesome shit again. So I don't think I would have reached the point of trying for a katabasis."

"Everyone makes their own choices." I pull my coat a little more tightly around me. Everything around us is foggy and gray, removed from the living world, but I still have my coat, which means we haven't passed fully into the twilight—not yet. We will, soon. "We just hope not to be judged too much for them."

"And I guess I was judging you, huh?" Nate puts one big hand on the back of his neck, laughing a little. "I know, I know, you've been dead since before I was alive, but you still look sixteen, Rose, and sometimes that makes it hard to take you seriously when you say things like 'oh, I just popped down to the Underworld so Persephone herself could make me dead again.'"

I turn long enough to glower at him. "I don't care how hard it is to take me seriously. That's what happened, and that's why I have white asphodel clamped around my wrist. We're friends, Nate, and it's good to see you again after all this time, but none of that gives you the right to call me a liar."

"I'm sorry," he says, still rubbing at the back of his neck. "I guess being held captive by dead umbramancers does a number on my manners, huh?"

"I guess." I take a step, matching his, and pause as Timothy's jacket falls through my abruptly insubstantial frame to land on the street. We've crossed the line. We're not just flirting with the twilight anymore; we've gone over the border and into the shadows. I can feel the endless night open all around me, spreading like a flower, welcoming me passively home. The street hums under my feet, and best of all, the wind is cool and clear, with no lingering scent of wormwood or ashes. Bobby Cross is nowhere near here. He's done that a few times in the past, driving away to try and make me feel like I'm safe, and then doubling back and waiting for me on the outskirts of town. The man is *obsessed*, and I say that as the girl who's currently dedicating herself to finding and destroying him.

"Want to hear something that's *really* going to make you want to call me a liar?" I ask, feeling more upbeat than I did even a few steps ago. Timothy may have been a double-crossing umbramancer collecting ghosts for his dead aunt, but he was a living man who gave me a coat and gave me a ride and fulfilled my obligations to the twilight in the process, even if he hadn't been in a position to fully grasp what he was doing. My skin doesn't itch anymore. I'm free to return to the Last Dance, check in with Emma and Gary, tell them what I discussed with the anima mundi, and maybe have a real piece of pie before I head out again. And it's all thanks to Timothy the jerk. I'd send him a nice thank you card if I knew his address. And if I didn't sort of hate him for what he did.

"What's that?" asks Nate, distracted by the twilight unspooling around us. He's looking more confident, and more coherent. Being cut off for eight years can't have been good for him, no matter how stable he looks. Ghosts aren't meant to be kept in tanks like freshwater fish, fed on dried flakes and subject to the whim of whoever's job it is to change the water. It's bad for us.

"The crossroads are dead." Four little words that combine to form the weirdest sentence it has ever been my job to say, and I've died twice, journeyed to the underworld, and am currently engaging in a semi-consensual romantic relationship with a car. Weird is sort of what I *do*, and this is breaking weirdness records.

"So they need to find a new guardian?" Nate sounds interested but not alarmed. "Not my kind of job, but I appreciate you telling me about it all the same."

I stop walking and stare at him for a moment as he keeps on going. When he finally stops and turns to face me, it's with a quizzically raised eyebrow and an expression that says I'm being silly for not keeping up. "What?" he asks.

Sometimes it can be easy to forget how little interaction normal ghosts have with the crossroads—how little interaction *I* had with them, before I started hanging out with Mary, before my niece went and sold herself into their service. Saying "the crossroads are dead" is sort of like announcing "the Easter Bunny has been killed." Unless you're talking to a bunch of kids with a thing for chocolate eggs, you're not going to get much of a reaction. You're talking about killing a thing most people don't fully believe exists. It's not a major concern.

For Nate, the crossroads are probably about as pressing and realistic as the Easter Bunny. Which is an odd thing to say about a force of nature that has been helping to dictate the structure and dangers of the world in which we exist, but there you have it.

"I don't mean the crossroads lost their guardian spirit," I say, with exquisite carefulness. "I mean the crossroads themselves are dead. They've been killed. They're gone."

He's still looking blank, so I try to explain a little more.

"The crossroads gave Bobby Cross his car. They're the reason that arrogant waste of skin is still racing around killing people and stuffing them into his gas tank."

"Ah," says Nate. "So you didn't like them much, I'm guessing?"

"I didn't—no, I didn't *like* the crossroads! No one with any sense *likes* the crossroads! They're a terrible, alien something that feeds on pain and misery! Or they were, before they finally got themselves murdered! Honestly, my main regret here is that I wasn't the one who did it! I should have killed them! It would have been only fair!" I ball my hands into fists and stomp my foot, aware that I must look like a kid having a tantrum, but unable to work up the energy to care. Nate needs to listen to me.

We don't have a hierarchy among the dead, not in terms the living would recognize. No kings, no presidents, no "listen to your elders." It's possible for your elders to look like they aren't done toilet training. But people are people, and they tend to hold onto some of the prejudices they had while they were alive. Nate has always treated me like something of a little sister, old enough to get myself into trouble, young enough to need help getting out of it at the end. Usually, that doesn't bother me much. Usually, we intersect for a few miles and a few laughs, and then we're on our own again, leaving him none the wiser and me none the crankier. I guess today is the exception.

"The crossroads are—were—the closest thing I've ever encountered to pure, unadulterated evil. They have no redeeming features that I've ever been able to find. They're bad. They hurt people because it amuses them to hurt people, and they don't care how much damage they do in the process of making their bargains. And someone killed them. Finally. Killed them dead and destroyed them. No more crossroads."

"Huh," says Nate. "When did that happen?"

"Just recently," I say. "It's the reason the twilight is currently in total disarray." The stretch we're currently occupying seems almost normal, but the grass on the highway verge looks hungry, reaching ravenously toward us with fronds waving like a single vast, living anemone. I don't like it. "Be careful not to go to any unfamiliar layers without backup. Even the routewitches have noticed. Their Queen left the Ocean Lady to ask me to help."

"Is Apple still in charge over there?" asks Nate.

I nod. "She is. I don't think she's going to step down until something forces her to. She wants to take care of her people."

"That's good. Someone should be taking care of them." Nate looks toward the horizon. I don't know whether he was a routewitch when he was alive; it never seemed to matter enough for us to have a real discussion about it.

Then again, that seems to have applied to most things between us. I know how he died, and know what he did when he was alive, but I don't know much of anything else about him. I know he doesn't know much about me, other than that Bobby Cross killed me. I don't think he even knows that I'm originally from Michigan. That suddenly seems like a pretty big omission.

"Hey, Nate? Where did you live before you died?" That should be a mild enough way of putting it.

His gaze sharpens. "Why the sudden curiosity, Rosie?"

"We're friends, right? Friends should be able to ask each other where they're from. Why are you calling me 'Rosie'? You never did that before." The anima mundi was responsible for dropping me in Bobby's location, but suddenly, the question of *why* Bobby had been located in Warsaw, Indiana when I got dropped on him seems a lot more pressing.

Bobby is supposed to be hunting my loved ones. Well, I don't have any loved ones in or near Warsaw. So why did he take a detour that wouldn't help him accomplish his goals? Now that I think about it, he must have known about the Mesmer cage. It's the sort of thing a living man who's been playing with the dead for seventy years would absolutely have encountered before, and it's not like Daisy and Timothy were being subtle. So why didn't he empty it out and eat its chewy contents the way he eats everything else?

Why, unless he was using it to store spirits he was going to want access to later? I look at Nate with new horror in my eyes. Eight years. That's nothing in the twilight, that's not even long enough to go from vaguely missing someone to actually worrying about them, but for a cartographer, that's an eternity. Why isn't Nate more worried about what changed while he was locked away? He should be panicking, not looking at me with mild, patently artificial concern.

"When did Bobby double-cross you?" I ask, in a voice that feels like sandpaper on the back of my throat, like it's scraping everything dry.

How long has Bobby Cross been *doing* this? Driving back along my trail so he can subvert the people who look like they might eventually be in a position to hurt me in some way? He got to Laura, and now it's looking like he got to Nate, too, even though Nate was never anything more than a bit player in the story of my existence. Has he been following me around and suborning anyone who so much as looks at me twice this whole time? I suddenly want to rush home and ask Emma whether he ever tried to get to her, except that I know she'd tell me if I asked, and I don't want to know. I know she's on my side. That has to be enough.

"I don't know what you're talking about," says Nate, voice too stiff, offense too feigned. He knows *exactly* what I'm talking about. He's been waiting for this question since I pulled him out of that diner. Maybe that's why he didn't stand up when he saw me come through the door with Timothy. It's not like I'm not recognizable. I may be the most recognizable hitchhiking ghost to walk the roads in the last hundred years, thanks to the dress that has become my trademark and iconography. They know the Ocean Lady by her road signs, they know Emma of the Last Dance by the changing gleam of her neon signs, and they know me by my green silk gown. That feels pretentious to say, but a thing can feel pretentious and still be as true as any other true thing. Reality doesn't care about being arrogant. Reality just endures.

"Sure you do," I say, and walk toward him, prowling like a predator on the track of some small, defenseless mammal. I've had a long time to learn how to stalk my prey, for all that I don't like to think of myself as a hunter. But that's what I am. That's what a hitcher has to be. I hunt the people who are most likely to give me the rides I need in order to survive in my strange hinterland between life and death, in the places where the dead girls go. I've walked these roads too often to be anything other than what I was always intended to be.

"Bobby Cross," I say. "We were just talking about him, remember? He's a bad man with a bad car and a bad habit of running teenage girls off the road. Although I guess he's learned to mix it up since he killed me. He causes accidents now. Kills a dozen people in one go so he can grab the single soul he needs. And I think he's been responsible for a few hit-and-runs. What, do they not matter because they weren't hiking in the wrong spot, didn't upset the wrong rattlesnake? Don't their deaths have enough *weight* for you?"

Nate backpedals as I get closer, the color draining from his cheeks, which is a nice trick, since it's not like he has a functional vascular system. We mimic the living in so many tiny ways that even we aren't necessarily aware of, because they only matter when they fail us. We blink, we wink, we sneeze, we sigh. We pale in the face of closing danger. It's all a shadow show, a series of performances so natural and instinctive that we can't help ourselves. We might do a better job of remembering how much we've lost if we could.

"I didn't—I mean, Rose, I would never—" he stammers.

"Someone did," I say calmly. "Someone always does. Maybe now's when you start talking. I'm not the sort of enemy you want to make out here in the twilight. I have what someone recently referred to as 'powerful friends,' and most of them aren't very forgiving when they think someone's been double-crossing the people they care about."

"You don't even know how frightening you are, do you?" he whispers.

I narrow my eyes. "I don't have a problem with that since I'm currently trying to frighten you. Being terrifying is part of my job these days. Looking for rides, hunting assholes, and being terrifying. Be terrified. Tell me what I want to know."

Nate takes a deep breath he doesn't need, in through his nose and out through his mouth, turning his face away from me, toward the high, waving grasses that line the footpath the sidewalk has become. They're probably something prehistoric, something from the same original era as my patchwork saurian friend, and they linger here out of habit, anchored by the love of some paleobotanist who read *Jurassic Park* too many times before middle school.

"Bobby had been talking to me for a while," he admits, voice soft. "He said he didn't want to hurt you anymore. He just wanted to discuss what happened, and help you understand how sorry he was."

"And you *believed* him?"

"Not really. It didn't match the story you'd told me, and your story matched the situation so perfectly that one of you had to be lying. I didn't think it was you. But he was . . . compelling. He knows how to spin a good lie, that Bobby Cross. Knows better than he necessarily realizes. He just wanted to talk. So he asked me to keep an eye on you and tell him when I knew where you were going. It was a little, harmless thing. It didn't have the weight to hurt anyone. Certainly not you. I don't know what *would* have the weight to hurt you, Rose Marshall, the Phantom Prom Date. I didn't understand why you were so afraid of him."

"And then what happened?" I prompt because something must have happened. Something always happens. If nothing had happened, Nate wouldn't have been missing for eight road-changing, technologically fraught years. He would have been here this whole time, traveling down roads parallel to my own, sometimes by my side, more often left to his own devices. He would be an integral part of my story, not just a footnote. But something happened.

"Bobby came to see me, and he was mad. No. He was *furious*. He said you'd cheated him, that he'd tried to talk to you and you'd slashed his tires and called him a bastard, left him stranded in the middle of a small town in Texas, where the road signs all told lies and the local routewitches navigated by the roadkill. It was bad. He said that if I didn't tell him everything he wanted to know, if I didn't *prove* that I was on his side once and for all, he'd shove me into his gas tank and get a few hundred miles out of me."

Texas, about eight years ago . . .

"He was talking about the bus accident," I blurt.

It had been one of those hot summer days that always burn brightest in the desert, the sort of day when the living felt no need to be wary of the dead, because surely there was no way we'd be out and about and making mischief. Dallas in July is not one of my favorite destinations, although it's better than Phoenix by a long shot. At least the roads usually don't melt. Melting roads are bullshit.

The bus had been full, a decent mix of tourists and locals, and I'd been drawn to it by the faint taste of rosewater and wormwood in the air, like a bittersweet perfume designed entirely to make my nose itch. The driver, a routewitch I'd seen a few times during earlier trips to Dallas, had nodded at my approach, handing me a coat and letting me board without asking for a fare. That hadn't earned me as many odd looks as the fact that I was wearing a canvas raincoat in the middle of the summer. No one sane wears a jacket during a Texas summer, which is just one more reason I try to avoid them. I don't like making myself any more visible than I absolutely have to, especially not with literally everyone carrying around their own personal camera these days. It was easier back when almost no one was likely to snap a photo of a stranger on the street.

Not all ghosts photograph. The ones who have been reduced to little more than mist and moans tend to distort film rather than being captured on it. But ghosts like me, who take on flesh and form and walk among the living like we belong there, we photograph just fine. Not a problem necessarily—it's not like I have living family who could recognize me—but as the evidence builds up, as we appear in the background of pictures from California to Connecticut, as facial recognition software starts connecting the dots, well . . .

It's going to be real hard to get rides when no one wants to stop and pick up the dead girl anymore.

I sat toward the back of the bus, near a nice Spanish-speaking family with five children, all dolled up in their Sunday best. So many shiny shoes, so much carefully crafted taffeta. It was a pleasant change from the group of angry teens toward the front. Sitting with them would have been more age appropriate, but I tend to come off as a little Miss Goodie Two-Shoes when I try to interact with modern teens, and that was a complication I didn't need, not when I was trying to shake Bobby Cross off of my trail. He'd been following me for three nights, dipping in and out of the twilight while I ran, going truck stop to truck stop. It was like a game to him.

Well, I was tired of playing. Despite the smell of wormwood on the bus, which is almost always an indicator that Bobby is planning to harm the person it's clinging to, I was holding fast to the narrow idea that he wouldn't possibly cause an accident involving this many potential victims. It was messy. It was unpredictable. It was a bad idea.

And all those things were true, but still, an antique-looking car of no discernible make or model but with very classic 1950s lines came blasting out of the traffic ahead of us, driving straight toward us, like the driver was playing a very stupid, very impulsive game of chicken with the entire bus. Which is exactly what Bobby was doing. Our driver swore, loudly enough that he would probably have been fired if he had survived what came next, and hauled on the wheel, trying to avoid the collision.

He did it. He managed to avoid not only Bobby's car, but all the other cars on the road around us. He couldn't avoid the bank, however, which was unable to dodge on account of it being a building, fixed to its foundations. We were going far too fast by the time the bus hopped the curb for his frantic pumping of the brakes to do us any good. That was probably less Bobby's fault than some essential failure of the mechanics, unless this bus had been targeted because Bobby had already sabotaged it, something I wasn't entirely willing to put past him. He never met an overly complicated plan he didn't want to commit to and make even more prone to possible failure.

The bus ploughed into the front of the bank at what passed for top speed. People screamed. Several of the angry teenagers were thrown out of their seats, one landing at a neck-breaking angle that was followed by total motionlessness and more screams from the people around her. Three of the little church-going children went flying. I clung to the pole nearest to me, feeling my insides slosh vigorously around, aware that the crash couldn't kill me, but that it could sure as hell hurt.

Then we were shuddering to a stop, all our momentum bled off into the chaos of the crash. Several of the windows had broken on impact. Several of the passengers weren't moving. The driver wasn't swearing anymore. I forced my legs to unlock, forced myself to stand, and pulled my way along the tilting aisle toward the front. Several of the angry teens shouted and wailed and grabbed for me, but I was almost certain all the teens trying to stop me were alive, and so I ignored them in favor of continuing onward.

The driver was slumped over his steering wheel, back hunched in a manner consistent with massive internal crush injuries. He wasn't going to be getting up again. This had been his final ride. I still paused to touch his fingers, to see if maybe a ghostly hand would latch onto mine and allow me to pull him to his feet. His skin was already starting to cool, and if he was planning to muster up the energy for a haunting, he didn't feel any need to kick it off for me.

The front window showed a horrifying view of the bank lobby, which had somehow become the street right in front of us. There were bodies. Two clerks and a patron, all of whom had been too slow to get out of the way when we came hurtling into what they must have assumed was a safe space.

I closed my eyes, took a deep breath of the hot, abruptly rancid bus air—adding vomit and several other human bodily fluids to the already cramped public transit vehicle had *not* improved the atmosphere—and let go of the coat and borrowed flesh that anchored me to the scene of the accident. The bystanders were already going to be confused by what they'd been through. Anything they said about a disappearing girl would be written off as the babbling of traumatized people who'd just watched their friends get killed. This way, I kept my own face out of the papers.

As soon as I dropped into the twilight, things changed.

The air on the bus was still fetid, but it acquired a thick, swampy undertone, as if the corpses on the floor had been rotting for weeks, unburied and unattended to. One of the angry teens who had been motionless only moments before was up on her knees, crouching next to her own body, hands over her face, swaying gently back and forth. I took a step toward her, hand raised to offer kindness or comfort, whichever she seemed more inclined to accept.

"Are you all right?" I asked, the language of the living once again failing to make the necessary transition into the lands of the dead. No, she wasn't all right: she was *dead*, that was her body on the floor in front of her, her life hadn't just changed, it had *ended*, and nothing would ever return what she'd just lost. "All right" was now and forever in another time zone.

She lowered her hands and I saw that she hadn't been covering her face; her face was gone, replaced by a smooth stretch of skin pulled tight across the topography of her skull. She was somehow still keening, making the sounds I associated with weeping, despite the absence of both eyes and tear ducts. I took a step backward, stopping when the front of the bus bumped into my thighs. It was here with us in the twilight, poor broken vessel that had failed to keep its passengers safe as it had promised to do. It wasn't right and it wasn't fair, and none of this should have been happening.

One of the children who'd gone flying when we hit the bank was sitting up, her taffeta dress askew around her, a long scratch down one cheek. She looked around, expression utterly baffled, a bafflement which only grew as she saw that her parents—both of whom had survived the crash—weren't there. She opened her tiny rosebud of a mouth to wail, and the whole bus shook with the impact of her grief and dismay.

Oh, swell, an infant poltergeist. Just what we needed.

I turned toward the little girl, edging carefully past the faceless teen, and felt my dress unfurl around me like the petals of a flower, brushing against my ankles. The teen turned her head to track me. Her friend was just beginning to stir. Unlike her, he had made the transition into the twilight with his face fully intact, although he had a large gash across his left temple. It wasn't bleeding. He didn't have blood anymore. It would probably be a while before he noticed that, assuming he noticed at all. The wound was unlikely to become a major part of his new identity, and without him remembering and reasserting it, it would probably close and fade away.

"Angela?" he said, reaching for his faceless friend. She didn't try to move away. "Hey, what's wrong? Where is everyone else?"

She turned toward him, and he stopped talking, growing paler and paler as his eyes bulged and his throat worked. I suppose finding a friend faceless and weeping over their own corpse made it sort of difficult to deny that things had changed, or to pretend they were going to be okay again. It was definitely a ruder awakening than I had enjoyed in the aftermath of my own accident.

I scooped the little petticoated poltergeist into my arms and bounced her, twice, like I thought I could shake the inner earthquake out of her. She sniffled and slung her arms around my neck, too shocked and unhappy to register the fact that I was a total stranger. We were both cold as the grave, and so she felt almost warm in my arms when compared to the chill of the twilight around us. She asked me a question in sharply interrogative Spanish. I shook my head. "I'm sorry, button," I said. "I don't speak Spanish, but your parents aren't here. They're still alive. They can't see you."

The bus shook around us again, and I heard the distinct sound of brakes screeching to a halt. I stood, little girl still cradled to my chest, and moved to peer out the window at the broken ribbon of the road.

Bobby Cross smirked at me through the window of his car, revving his engine. The sound was incredibly loud in the relative quiet of the twilight, completely drowning out Angela's ongoing sobs. It was too much. I turned and lowered the little girl to the nearest bench seat, unwinding her arms from around my neck. Her body was on the floor, although she hadn't noticed it yet, along with the body of one of her brothers. Children are more likely to leave ghosts than adults, if not as likely as teens; there was still a decent chance he was going to wake up and join his sister in the twilight. The thought had barely finished forming before another body appeared, an older woman dropping to the floor out of nowhere, one hand clutching at her chest. No ghost materialized to accompany the body, which made sense. She was old enough that she'd probably done everything she truly wanted to do, and she had the time to come to grips with the fact that one day the world would exist without her in it. That's the big hurdle, the thing many people can't get over. That the world was before they were here and will be after they're gone. Not everyone can manage the mental adjustment, no matter how old they are. But for the people who can, it tends to be absolute.

The little girl sniffled and reached for me, clearly not prepared to give up the closest thing she had found to comfort since the world shook and tore and her family disappeared. I pushed her hands gently away, shaking my head. "No," I said. "No, I can't hold you right now. I'm sorry. I need you to stay here and wait for me."

I couldn't understand her, but maybe she could understand me. Osmosis doesn't always come with fluency where language is concerned. She stopped reaching for me, slumping back in the seat and sniffling. It was such a beautiful example of exaggerated misery that I would have laughed, if she hadn't been a preschool-age child whose life had just been brought to an abrupt and terrible end. Instead, I straightened, grabbing a chunk of broken glass from the bus floor, and walked toward the door.

The mechanism that opened it was bent and broken from the crash. It still swung open for me, more familiar with its job than with the damage. Bobby grinned through his car window as I stepped down to the pavement, showing me every perfect, gleaming tooth in his head. I clutched my makeshift weapon and stared at him down the length of my nose, hoping he could somehow feel the force of my hatred and disdain.

Maybe he couldn't feel it, but he could see it in my face, because the grin slipped off of his, replaced by a petulant pout that would have fit better on the face of the dead little girl behind me. He rolled his window down, looking at me with clotted, sullen hatred.

"It's nice to see you, too, Rosie-my-girl," he said.

I didn't fight Bobby Cross, not then, not before Persephone and everything she'd done to change my place in the twilight, but I looked at his petulant pout, still somehow smug, still proud of what he'd done, and rage bubbled up like acid in the center of what passed for my soul. Before I could think or allow my natural instinct to run to overwhelm me, I screamed and lunged, hands raised, chunk of broken glass poised to stab.

Bobby shied back, pressing himself into his seat. I stopped before my arm could brush against the door, hand shaking, the tip of my glass shard barely an inch from the skin of his throat. "Rosie, if you keep acting like this, I'm going to think you're *not* happy to see me," he drawled, expression going tight, throat working frantically as he tried to press himself even further back, away from me and the danger I had suddenly come to represent. There was a new caution in his eyes, and I realized, dimly, that he had never considered me a threat before. I had spent too much of our acquaintance running away from him and his damn demon car.

His hand moved, groping for the handle. I realized what he was going to do barely a beat before he did it, and threw myself backward, away from the opening door. My skirt fluttered in the breeze generated by my motion, almost touching the metal before it settled against my legs. I pressed my free hand to my chest, trying to still the senseless, useless pounding of my heart, which felt like it was going to break out of its cage and run away without the rest of me. *You have no blood to pump*, I thought. *Your job is over. Stop it.* It didn't stop.

Now back in his more comfortable dynamic of predator and prey, Bobby slung one long, blue-jeaned leg out of the car and stood, sauntering toward me with the casual ease of a man who knew that his victory was inevitable, if somewhat inconveniently delayed.

I wondered whether he realized that put him between me and his car. I wondered whether he *cared*.

"Rosie-my-girl! You're an unexpected surprise on this fine Texas day!" he drawled. "Did you miss me too much to stay away?"

"You've been chasing me for days, you *bastard*," I spat. "All I do is try to stay away from you."

"Oh, right," he said. "This is all your fault, isn't it? All these poor dead people, that much more weight to add to those pretty little shoulders of yours. If you would just stop running away and let me finish what I started, this would all be over. No more graves with your profile on the headstone. No more weeping mothers damning your name."

"Go to hell," I spat.

He took a step toward me, but his eyes were on the bus, from which the faint sound of sobbing drifted. He knew there was at least one ghost onboard, someone innocent and new who wouldn't know what to hit and what to avoid, who would be an easy target for his hands. "I'm sorry you had to go through the accident," he said. "It wasn't my intention. I thought you'd be smart enough to disappear before impact."

"You're a bastard," I said, my voice low and filled with more anger than I'd realized my body could contain. I matched his step forward with one of my own, intending to hook my hands around his throat and squeeze until he remembered he was mortal, until I felt better about my choices. The chunk of glass dug into my palm, and I realized I had a better choice. Bobby seemed to realize it at the same time, because he took a step back, toward his patiently waiting car.

"Now Rosie, don't go getting any nasty ideas in that pretty head of yours, you know it never goes well when you do—" he said, stopping when I lunged again, shoving the glass toward his face. The edge caught his cheek, opening the flesh in a long, thin line that had to be shallow, given the angle I was standing at. Then he was scrambling away, back to the car, back to the safety of his familiar driver's seat, where he could watch the world with a smirk on his face.

"You don't have any cover, Rose!" he shouted. "Stay here and you're mine, or you can leave whatever's inside that bus for me to take care of! Are they worth it? You've been running for so damn long. Is this where you stop?"

No. No, it was not. The people on that bus were already dead, and I was dead, too, and the only thing that made my existence more valuable than theirs was the fact that it was *mine*. I'd been fighting to stay away from Bobby Cross for so long that I couldn't let this be how I went down. I dropped the chunk of glass to the ground, where it shattered, and let go of the twilight, falling back up into the daylight, where the authorities were helping the survivors of a bus crash stagger back into the sun, casting around for the car which had caused the accident in the first place, yet had somehow managed to slip away in the chaos. The air was thick with dust, and the smell of wormwood and rosewater was gone, drowned out by blood and gasoline. I ducked into the shadows before anyone could notice me and my idiosyncratic, outdated dress.

Then I slipped away, heading down the street as quickly as I could without actually breaking into a run.

When I was far enough away—six blocks—I dropped back into the twilight and kept going, away from Bobby, away from his terrible car, away from the new-minted ghosts I had abandoned to their fate. I would never forget them, I knew, and if they survived, they would never remember me. I was unimportant, a footnote in their stories, and that was better than being anything else.

Back in the present, Nate is staring at me, not sure what I'm remembering, not sure whether he should be here or whether he should be taking advantage of my distraction to get away. I flash him a tight smile. "I remember the incident. He wasn't entirely honest with you. Big surprise. It wasn't his tires I slashed. It was his pretty fucking face. With a piece of twilight glass, no less."

Nate gapes at me. "But twilight glass doesn't exist in the daylight. It's . . . it's ghost glass. There's no way you could have cut him with it! He's *alive*."

"He's alive, but he's spent so many years down among the dead that it's started rubbing off on him." How did I miss the significance of the moment when it was actually happening? I should have realized at the time that it represented a sea change, a shift in the status quo of Bobby Cross' rampage across the twilight. Even with the crossroads protecting him, he'd fallen deep enough into our world, our rules, to be hurt by our weapons. He'd become *vulnerable*. I was too focused on getting away from him to stop and think about how I'd been able to hurt him, and so he was able to spend another eight years terrorizing the dead. That ends now.

"Please don't hate me, Rose," says Nate. "Bobby said he'd changed. He said he didn't want to hurt you anymore. And I . . ." He trails off. He didn't necessarily believe Bobby when he said such big, ridiculous things, but he wanted an excuse to carry tales out of school without feeling like a monster.

Many ghosts are cowards. Getting something after your life ends can feel like a blessing you didn't earn, like the universe screwed up and let you stay in the theater after the play ended. Not having that afterlife snatched away becomes the only thing that matters. It's silly, how much people who have already died care about surviving, but I can't fault them for it. I'm the same way. I care so much more about staying safe now that I'm dead than I ever did when I was alive.

I can't be mad at Nate, because as much as I want to be a hero, stalwart pillar of goodness and righteousness, I would probably have made the same call he did. Better to risk someone else than to risk yourself, and haven't I made that choice over and over again since I died? Running away when people are in danger, leaving other ghosts to risk their necks with Bobby Cross while I get the hell out of Dodge? It's not something I'm proud of, particularly. It's just something that I *am*.

I smile thinly at Nate. "Do you have a way of contacting him?" I ask. "What?"

"If you'd been telling him things before he stranded you in that Mesmer cage, you must have had a way of contacting him. Do you still have a way of contacting him?" The smell of asphodel seems to curl through the air around us, becoming cloyingly sweet and almost over-bearing. Nate doesn't seem to notice, which is a little bit distressing. I don't know how cartographers navigate—my particular perfume-based method of assessing the dangers around me may or may not overlap—but this is a sign from the Lady of the Dead herself. I would expect it to apply to all ghosts in range, not only to me.

Nate nods, very slowly. "I do," he says, and dips a hand into the pocket of his jeans, pulling out a small blue disk that I recognize, after a moment's silent study, as a chunk of polished Fordite. The color doesn't match Bobby's car, but I doubt that matters much. "He gave me this. It gets warm when I talk to it, and he shows up as soon as he can. Why?"

Fordite is a man-made gem in every sense of the word—it's petri-fied, polished automotive paint, chipped from the Detroit assembly lines. Some people treat it like a precious stone, turning it into jewelry and other, even fancier accessories, not seeming to care that it's just waste paint, or that a lot of it was made before modern safety standards were put into place, and consequentially can contain a truly stunning quantity of lead. The living have always been easily distracted by beauty, in all its many forms.

"I want you to send him a message. Tell him you're out of the Mesmer cage, and you're pissed. Tell him you need to talk." My smile is just this side of feral. Nate shies away. "Tell him you're waiting, and that he needs to come to you."

Where I'll be waiting, too.

Book Three:

Megaera

You who set the laws and draw the lines, you who enforce the punishments lain down upon the wicked, daughters of the sky, born of no woman's pain, who bring pain to the deserving, I ask that you hear me, heed me, and turn an unseeing eye upon my transgressions. I come to you not in self-castigation, but as one wronged, one who would see themselves forgiven and made whole by your intercession, and I ask that you see not my sins, but only those places where I have been sinned upon. Mothers of none, daughters of one who had no hand in your creation, sisters of all who suffer, you are my hope and my harbor now. Hear me, and help me, and allow me to be healed.

—traditional twilight prayer to the Erinyes

Chapter 11
Long Time Gone

———

THE SKY CYCLES THROUGH COLORS above us, bruised purple to deep, drowning sapphire blue to that brittle false dawn combination of red, gold, and coral pink that only seems to exist in the very sweetest of dreams. The wind whispers through the prehistoric grass, and I sit on a rock that has probably been here as long as there's been a continent on this part of the planet, picking at my nails and watching Nate pace back and forth on the slim section of road in front of me.

"You really went to the Underworld," he says. "You really met Persephone."

"I really did," I say, lowering my hand. "I don't know how many ways I can tell you it happened before you'll start believing me. I've tried blunt, I've tried poetic, and I'm about to try annoyed. I don't like repeating myself."

"Was she nice?"

He sounds like he needs her to have been nice. I hesitate. "She was . . . she was kind," I say finally. "When she was looking at me, it felt like nothing else mattered, like I could be happy forever if she just said it was important for me to try. She loved me before she met me, and there's nothing I could ever do that would make her stop loving me. She loves all the dead. Whether or not we linger, she loves us. And even when we fight and disagree and betray each other, she keeps on loving us, because that's what she's for."

"People aren't *for* things, Rose."

But Persephone isn't people, any more than the anima mundi is people, or the Ocean Lady, or any of the other shadows that control our movement through the twilight. She's an idea elevated to the status of an individual, and she doesn't get all the twisty turns and tricks that make up a person. She doesn't need them. When you're an idea that walks like a woman, you get to be simple if you want to. Persephone is simple. All the divinities I've met have been simple. Oh, they have depths and undertows. They can get complicated real fast if that's what they feel they need to do. But on a basic, "how difficult do I need this to be" level, they're simple.

"Persephone is," I say mulishly, and I'm right, and I don't know how to make him understand, short of sending him on a katabasis of his own. But those are difficult, for the dead. Blame Orpheus; blame Eurydice. They set a lot of the base rules, and one of those rules says traveling into the Underworld and then making it back out is for the living. I was able to accomplish it only because Bobby Cross had broken so many rules trying to make me vulnerable. I went as the living and I came out as the dead. Nate would never get past Cerberus in his current state.

Nate scoffs and resumes his pacing. I lean back on my hands and tilt my face up toward the sky, watching the thin ribbons of color as they shift and dance above me.

Everything has brought us here. The crossroads are dead. I have Persephone's blessing on my wrist and the proof of her protection on my back; there's every chance that Bobby's car can't touch me now, not with its patron dead and my patron still standing strong. All that remains is facing him down.

A thin ribbon of heat uncurls in my belly, too bright and sharp for the twilight. It feels like the sort of thing that should haunt the living and leave the dead alone. I press a hand against my stomach, trying to shove the heat back down. It doesn't belong here. We're in the twilight; we're always cold. But this heat doesn't care where we are or what its presence means. It burns, until I start to wonder whether eating food inside a Mesmer cage is enough to give a ghost indigestion. I don't want it to be. I don't want any of this. I don't have any answers. I'm not sure there are answers to have. We're in uncharted waters now. We have been since the crossroads fell. They were such a big part of the twilight, even if they weren't meant to be, that without them, things are shaky.

The sound of a car's engine revving splits the night like a knife. It's distant. We wouldn't be able to hear it at all if we were still in the daylight, where there are so many other sounds available to cloud the air and confuse the issue. But it's coming closer.

I take my hand away from my stomach. Nate stops pacing, head snapping up as he stares down the road toward the horizon. Then he hurries toward me, taking shelter in the prehistoric grass, where maybe there's a chance he won't be immediately seen.

"What did you say to him?" I ask as I stand, shaking my skirt clean of grass and dust, leaving it to hang loose and easy around me.

"That I was out of the Mesmer cage and I wanted to talk," he says, casting quick, anxious glances at the road. "I didn't say anything about you being here. He doesn't know."

Except that he saw me in that gas station parking lot, and while Bobby is a lot of things, he's not a stupid man. He'll draw the line between "Rose Marshall was in Warsaw, Indiana" and "an old friend of hers, who I thought I had safely locked away in a Mesmer cage, is suddenly calling after eight years of silence." Nate is waving a red flag in front of a bull right now. Bobby's coming in expecting a fight.

Bobby's going to get one. I bend and scoop up a handful of earth, letting it trickle between my fingers as I straighten.

"Lady of the Dead, I know you are always with me, and I am always with you," I say, voice low. Nate glances at me, and then back to the road. Bobby is a much more urgent danger right now than me deciding to be a little weird. Anyone who's ever met me is used to me being weird. Weirdness is part and parcel of the overall Rose Marshall experience.

"I know you guard and guide my steps, and I know it's not my place to ask you for more than you have already offered, that I should be grateful for even scraps of your grace." The sound of Bobby's engine is getting closer. I talk faster. "But I must ask you to aid me, as I confront a great darkness that has long preyed upon your people and will end tonight." The last of the dirt slips through my fingers, leaving me empty-handed. I sigh. "In your name, Persephone, may I persevere."

I don't actually know how people prayed to Persephone back when she was a going concern in the daylight, but I know it wasn't with folded hands and dainty kneeling. She's the Goddess of the Spring as well as the Lady of the Dead, and touching her soil seems like the best way to show her what respect I can. I brush my fingers against my dress and turn my attention to Nate.

"Well?" I ask. "What are you hiding back here with me for? Get out there, or Bobby's going to drive right by."

"I want Bobby to drive by," says Nate, in a fierce whisper. He's scared, skin of his face drawn so tight that the whites show all the way around his eyes. "I want nothing to do with him. I'm sorry I helped him keep track of you, but that doesn't mean I want to *die* by way of an apology."

"You can't die, Nate," I say. "You're already dead." Then I reach over, grab his arm, and swing him away from me, toward the road. He isn't expecting that; no one ever expects me to get physical. He stumbles, and his momentum carries him out of the tall grass, onto the pavement.

This is a farmer's field, of sorts. All fields in the twilight are farmer's fields. Fields sometimes have tools hidden in them, abandoned by careless farmhands or dropped when a farmer suffered a massive coronary, loved enough in life to leave a shadow in the spirit world. I step daintily over to where Nate stumbled, bending to feel around for whatever may have tripped him.

I only have to move a few handfuls of loam out of the way before my fingers find a wooden shaft, smooth and polished and about as big around as both my thumbs put together. I work my way through the roots of the tall prehistoric grasses to get my hands around it, gripping tight and tugging upward, away from the ground. This might seem a little convenient, but there are no coincidences among the dead, and I just offered Persephone my prayers. The twilight is malleable to the Lady of the Dead. If she wants me armed, I will be. Her will is law.

I pull. The grass resists the resurrection of its property from dead, discarded thing to usable tool. I pull harder. There is a vast ripping sound, louder than it should be given the size of the affected area, and I stumble backward, a scythe in my hands. I stare at it. I've seen this scythe before. It's a common piece of iconography among the dead, carried by the Dullahan like Pippa, assigned by stories to the Grim Reaper himself, a figure I'm fairly sure doesn't actually exist, but who would be pretty fun at a party if he did. There should be no way this specific tool is familiar, but it is. I saw the anima mundi swinging it in her fields when she was wearing Mary's face.

It's not just Persephone looking out for me at this point.

The sound of Bobby's engine roars closer. The ribbon of heat in my belly widens and deepens, becoming a chasm, until it feels like the fires of Hell are burning inside of me, summoned by the closeness of my conflict. I clutch the scythe tighter and bow my head in momentary gratitude.

"Thank you," I say. The field, which has already given up its bounty, and has nothing more to offer, gives no reply. The grass rustles. I raise my head and turn, back toward Nate, back toward the road.

The sound of Bobby's engine is so loud as to be nearly overwhelming. I stay where I am, letting the grass close around me, letting the field enfold me and keep me as safe as anything is going to keep me right now, under these circumstances, which are so far from ideal that they can't see it on the sunniest of days. But laying an ambush for Bobby, even a bad one, requires a certain amount of discretion, and that means staying where I am until I don't have any choice but to move.

Bobby's brakes squeal as he pulls up level with Nate, a faintly baffled expression on his eternally pretty face. "Didn't think I'd see you outside that diner until I decided to come and let you out," he says. "What do you think you're doing, breaking loose without my permission?"

I didn't tell Nate to lie for me, and so it's not a surprise when he says, "Rose Marshall broke the Mesmer cage and let me out. She broke us all out, stared down the old lady who made the cage, and snapped the runes so we could all leave."

Bobby clucks his tongue and shakes his head, still not looking deep enough into the grass to see me lurking. "She's always been a damn busybody, that girl," he says. "Sometimes I think killing her might have been a mistake on my part. It's not like I've gained anything from it, and she's caused me enough trouble over the years for ten ordinary ghosts. I'd be better off if she'd gotten old and died fat and wrinkly, with a whole passel of routewitch grandbabies around her bedside."

"Maybe," says Nate. "I don't know. She's always been nice to me."

"Because you're not the man who killed her, you numbskull," says Bobby.

The grass rustles and I'm gone, moving through the twilight like a moth moves through the air, letting the ground drop out from under my feet until pavement replaces soil and I'm standing on the road behind Bobby's car. I've never done anything like this before, and I shouldn't have been able to do it now, but the scythe is still clutched firmly in my hands, and this mode of movement feels right, feels true . . . feels *mine*. The blade is dull and riddled with rust, but it's what I have, it's what Persephone and the anima mundi saw fit to offer me, and I'm not foolish enough to look a gift weapon in the blade. Instead, I tap the tip of it against Bobby's bumper, the sound ringing through the cool evening air like the chiming of a church bell, and I clear my throat.

"Most people don't concern themselves all that much with the comfort and contentment of their murderers," I say. "Hi, Bobby."

He leans out the window and cranes his neck around so he can look at me, and there is a cool resignation in his eyes. He's been waiting for this confrontation longer than I have, maybe, since he fell into place behind me on Sparrow Hill Road back in Michigan and made the decision to gun his engine, to run an innocent girl over the edge of the drop-off and let the chips fall where they would. The heat in my belly burns brighter, an all-consuming flame that hurts even as it flares. It doesn't care about me. If it cares about anything at all, it's that Bobby burns here for what he's done, the damage he's done to the twilight, the affronts he's thrown in the faces of the gods and goddesses whose task it is to keep us as close to safe as a dead thing can ever be. Nate stumbles backward, into the clutching depths of the ancient grass, seeing, somehow, that his part in this little shadow show has been fulfilled. He was never going to be called upon to see this to its end. No. That's down to Bobby and to me.

Somewhere in the distance, an animal bellows. My friend from the gas tanks. It may not join us here, but it remembers me, and everything is narrowing toward this moment, toward this point and this place, where Bobby and I finally look each other in the eye as something resembling equals.

"Get out of the car, Bobby," I say, and my voice doesn't shake, not even a little, and I'm so proud of that. I'm burning up inside, with a scavenged scythe in my hands and a man who willingly betrayed me as my only immediate ally, and my voice isn't shaking. This is all I could ever have hoped for.

Well, surviving would also be nice.

"Make me," he says, voice cool and self-assured. He doesn't look nervous. He doesn't look like this is anything to worry about. I'm just a hitchhiking ghost, after all. Maybe I'm the one who got away—over and over and over again—but I'm not a poltergeist or a gather-grim or anything else that could endanger him. He knew what he was doing when he ran me off the road. He knew that I would never become a threat. Very few ghosts can be, to a man like him. A man who's had decades to run the roads like he owns them, like there's nothing in the world that can hurt him.

It makes me so angry. I raise my scythe and slam the point of it down on his trunk, slicing a jagged line through the paint. The fire in my stomach roars approval at the violence of the action. My heart, which hasn't needed to beat in more than fifty years, stutters in my chest. I've never done anything like this before. There's a good reason Bobby isn't afraid of me. Hitchhikers run. It's what we're made to do. That bus ride was the only time I didn't run from him, and the first time I felt this ribbon of heat in my stomach, this pulsing, devouring heat. The urge to drop the scythe and flee is strong. The fire is stronger.

Bobby's eyes narrow when I hit his car and widen when I lift the scythe and step back. I shouldn't have been able to do that. The car should have trapped me as soon as I touched it, like flypaper latching down on some innocent insect that happened to drift too close.

"Now, Rosie-my-girl, I know you and I have had our differences, but that doesn't mean you should be taking them out on my car. How'd you like it if I took them out on *your* car?"

"You leave Gary out of this," I snap.

"Why? Because he used to be alive? He's just a *car* now."

"I've noticed," I mutter, unable to quite keep the resentment out of my tone.

"Aw, trouble in paradise?" There's a click as Bobby unlocks the door. "If my car's a fair target for you, your car's a fair target for me. You don't know where my good ol' girl came from."

"Yeah, I do. She came from the crossroads, which means she was never alive, and she's not alive now. She's a ghost trap created by something that should never have interfered with the twilight, and she doesn't belong here, any more than you do." I clutch the shaft of the scythe, twisting it between my hands. "She's not even really a car."

Bobby's hands aren't on the wheel anymore. The car still lurches forward a few inches as its engine roars. I've managed to offend the ghost trap. That's a new one, even for me.

"You need to get the hell over here, Bobby," I say. "No more hiding behind what the crossroads gave you."

"You have a scythe, and I don't even have a pocketknife," says Bobby. "How's that fair?"

"How was it fair when you decided to run a teenage girl who didn't even know if the afterlife existed off the road before she could make it to her prom?" I ask, voice sharp. "How was it fair when you talked a routewitch into slitting her own throat just so you could talk trash about me to Persephone? You killed a woman so you could lie to a *goddess*. You're a misogynistic asshole, Bobby. It's probably a good thing you decided to leave Hollywood and mess with the dead instead. You couldn't have done anything good for modern culture."

He pulls back into the car, and a second later, he's spinning the wheel and the car is lurching forward, into a wide turn that clips the grass by the side of the road. Then he's racing toward me, moving fast, moving straight for me, making no effort to swerve. I bend my knees and adjust my grip on the scythe. Maybe this is stupid. Maybe it's the right thing to do. It's not like he can *hurt* me since I'm dead and this is the twilight.

Then the car slams into my thighs, knocking me off balance, knocking the air out of my lungs, sending me hurtling backward and forward at the same time. I barely manage to keep my grasp on the scythe as my forehead bounces off the hood of Bobby's car. He keeps driving forward, pushing me along with him. It feels almost like I'm flying.

I can see him through the windscreen, teeth bared in a manic grin, hands tight on the wheel. He looks incredibly pleased with himself. The fire in my stomach is still burning, bright and painful in a way that the impact wasn't. He can't hurt me. This burning can. It feels like it's eating me alive from the inside, like it's somehow determined to keep getting stronger until I am inevitably devoured. I have no interest in being eaten alive . . . or undead, as the slightly more accurate case might be. I don't breathe or age, but I think and I feel and I exist, and maybe all the "is this life or not" has been nothing more than inflated semantics. It changes nothing. So it doesn't matter.

I raise my hands and hammer the shaft of the scythe down on Bobby's hood again and again, like it's a rolling pin, using the length of it as the weapon. The dent starts shallow but rapidly grows as we accelerate down the road, scarring the paint. I still can't say what color it is. That's a problem for someone else, someone less pinned to the hood of a car like a butterfly under glass. I slam the scythe down again, digging my deepest gouge yet into the paint. Bobby leans on his horn.

The sound is like the roaring of some impossible beast, and I stop hammering as a plan begins to form. The prehistoric grass is the connection, and it's still waving all around us. The blast will have been audible for miles. There's nothing here to stop the sound, not even the memory of some beloved building that burned down but was remembered enough to manifest in the twilight.

The burning in my belly has been joined by a tingling in my hands and arms where they're pressed against the car. The hood is starting to take on a recognizable color, a delicate, familiar seafoam green. I glance down at the bodice of my dress, unsurprised to see that the color is bleeding out of it, vanishing into the paint. Bobby's car may have been weakened by the loss of the crossroads and be warded off by Persephone's blessing, but it's still a ghost trap, and it's still hungry. My corsage means it hasn't consumed me yet. It doesn't mean it never will.

I lift the scythe, slamming it down again just as hard as I can. More scratches open in the rapidly greening paint. My dress must be halfway gray by now; at this rate, they're going to have to find something else to call me, since "the Girl in the Green Silk Gown" isn't going to be accurate for much longer. But at least it's just green. It's just fabric. This dress has been with me for decades. It's not a *part* of me. I have an existence beyond and outside it. And apart from the burning in my belly, I'm not in pain. The car hasn't been able to do more than pull on my arms and hands, numbing them and setting them tingling. It's not pulling the color from my skin or the flesh from the memory of my bones.

"I must be really frustrating for you, huh?" I demand, and hit it again, and again, and again.

Bobby leans on the horn a second time, sending the roar of an unspeakable beast echoing across the fields. This time, there's an answer, just as loud, just as unspeakable, just as difficult for my modern ears to comprehend. But there's a difference. The second bellow is more familiar, and more welcome, and more *mine*. It belongs to the ghost of a line that failed, the aggregate memory of thousands of dead lizard kings, who once claimed this entire world for their own. Behind the glass, Bobby shies back, eyes wide in shock and what looks very much like horror. He doesn't slow down. The man's a racer, always has been, and he still thinks speed will be enough to save him.

I'm raising the scythe to hit the hood again when he stomps on the brakes and comes screeching to a halt. The stop is so sudden that it throws me, still following the path momentum has set for me. I hit the pavement so hard that for one dazzling second it actually *hurts*, some ancient, mammalian instinct buried in my bones remembering what that impact would have done to living flesh. My body keeps rolling, the scythe clutched in both hands, until I roll to a stop near the edge of the road.

I raise my aching head, half-convinced I'll see a trail of shredded skin leading to my position. There's nothing, of course, but I still ache all over. Even the burning in my belly has pulled back to a dull, sizzling ember. I groan.

Behind me, something roars.

I manage to find the strength to roll over, just enough to see the terrible patchwork dinosaur running down the middle of the road, forearms raised and claws bared, ready for a fight with whatever titan has been crying out a challenge in the middle of its territory. The smell of gasoline rolls off its unspeakable, mismatched body, thick enough to choke me. It doesn't seem to have noticed me yet; its attention is fixed on Bobby's car, with its seafoam hood against the rest of its moonlight-blank paint job.

The creature takes a step forward, lips drawing back from its teeth. It looks cleaner than it did when it emerged from the gas tanks. I can see delicate bands and patterning on its plumage, which it raises in answer to the presumptive threat of the car. It looks sort of like a giant murder-turkey getting ready to fight the biggest farmer that ever lived. It's a fun image, and I try to hold onto it as I clutch my scythe and lever myself to my feet.

My legs shake so hard as I stand that for a moment I'm actively afraid that I'm going to fall down again, dumped on my own behind by the combination of gravity and my perceived injuries. My skirt is basically a tangle of gray ribbons around my legs, too shredded to provide any further cover or protection from the elements. I try to change my clothes, picturing the jeans I wear when I'm hitchhiking, and nothing happens. The dress remains, graying and tattered and more damaged than I've ever seen it.

The dinosaur charges toward Bobby's car, mouth open, crest up and flaring a challenge. It runs like an angry turkey, and that's enough to make me glad I made my peace with it earlier. I don't want to be on the receiving end of those teeth. They're as mismatched as everything else about it, some too big for its jaw, others too small. It would starve if it had to try eating with that mouth. It would die. But it's already dead, and those teeth are harvested from the memory of its long-gone, un-marked graves, and they're terrifying enough for the situation at hand.

Bobby's hands are raised in horror. The wheel spins itself as the car chooses its own path forward, and then it's lurching into motion, racing toward the dinosaur, two titans set on a collision course in the middle of this broken stretch of unforgotten country road.

It's not clear who hits who first. Then the dinosaur has the car's bumper in its mouth, rearing back until the car's front wheels leave the ground and spin helplessly in midair. The dinosaur shakes its head back and forth, trying to rip the bumper off, as Bobby finally snaps out of his shock and slams his hand down on the wheel. The challenging roar of the car's horn blasts through the air, and the dinosaur can't resist. Instinct is too strong. It drops the car in order to roar its own challenge at its opponent. It leaves easily a dozen teeth embedded in the bumper, and the paint, where it isn't seafoam green, is beginning to turn a rich, banded green, shot through with black and yellow.

If the dinosaur keeps touching the car, it will go the way of its many bodies, becoming fuel for the machine it's fighting so viciously to defeat. I shout and wave the scythe over my head, trying to get its attention. It roars again before stomping on the car's hood with one massive foot, talons scoring the paint.

Watching a dinosaur destroy Bobby's car isn't as viscerally satisfying as I would have expected it to be. I'm too concerned about my prehistoric friend to really relax and enjoy the moment. The dinosaur stomps again before stepping fully onto the hood, planting one foot on the car's roof and roaring a third time from its new vantage point.

More and more brown banded with black and yellow is bleeding into the car's paint, even washing away some of the seafoam green. The dinosaur is fading to the same nondescript, indescribable gray as parts of my dress, some essential part of its vitality stolen away. I can't stand here and watch this happen. I *can't*. The fire in my stomach surges, acid-hot and almost unbearably strong, as I run for the car, scythe held over my head, and swing it as hard as I can for the passenger window. The sight of Bobby's face through the glass, eyes wide and mouth a perfect O in the face of his surprise, is enough to make me laugh out loud as I draw back to hit the car again. The tingling in my arms and hands has entirely faded. There's nothing missing. That damn car got a little of the color from my dress, but that's all. I'm not going in the gas tank. I'm not going to be a part of the story of Bobby Cross. He doesn't win. He doesn't get to win.

The dinosaur's roaring changes timbres, going from anger and dominance to something that sounds unnervingly like fear. Prehistoric murder-turkeys shouldn't sound that scared, about anything. I look up.

The dinosaur is melting into the car's frame. Its feathers are virtually colorless, all their iridescent brightness having bled into the paint. The car is feeding. The gouges in its hood and roof are healing, increasingly rapidly as it swallows more and more of the non-thrashing dinosaur. The chips I've made in the window remain longer than anything else, only beginning to fill in once the dinosaur's legs are entirely gone.

It's like watching the La Brea Tar Pits fix an error of omission, finally gulping down the last of their possible victims to walk in the world. The dinosaur pulls frantically against the car, trying to get away. Its head swivels, eyes fixing on me, and it makes a small, pathetic chirping sound, trapped and frightened and appealing to the closest thing it has to a friend. I take one hand off the scythe and hold it out. The dinosaur pushes its muzzle into my palm. I turn my eyes back to the car, glaring.

It's weaker. We would both have been swallowed whole by now if it were at full strength. The crossroads can't protect it anymore. And the dinosaur has been rendered down into oil before. It's distressed and trapped, not actually hurt—not yet.

I step back, taking my hand away from the dinosaur's muzzle, and swing my head around to focus on the car. Bobby has his hands on the wheel again, like he still thinks he's in control here. Arrogant man. He's always been an arrogant man. Only arrogance would lead someone to trade their soul for the promise of eternal youth—a promise the crossroads aren't going to be able to keep, since they're dead and he's defenseless.

I swing my scythe at the window one more time, as the heat in my stomach combusts, and for a brutal, blistering moment, it feels like I'm actually on fire, actually burning from the inside out as the rusted tip of my borrowed blade strikes and cracks the glass, sending bits of it flying into the car. One piece slices across Bobby's cheek, drawing a red line in its wake, so reminiscent of that day in Dallas, but this isn't ghost glass, this is demon glass, crossroads glass, and it's not a surprise that it can touch the living. The surprise would be if it couldn't.

Bobby slaps a hand to his face, looking startled when his fingers come away damp with blood. I smile thinly at him and hit the window again, the burning in my bones settling down to something I can almost live with. It hurts, yes, but it's mine, and nothing that belongs to me is ever going to destroy me. Not like Bobby has tried and tried to do.

"Come out here and face me like a man, you coward!" I shout, hitting the window a third time. It breaks completely under the blow, collapsing inward, scattering glass across the smooth leather of the seat. "Hiding behind a car from a defenseless little teenage girl? For shame, Bobby. What would those girls who loved you think of you now? What would your mother think of you? Oh, I forgot—she's dead by now, isn't she? Everyone who ever loved you is dead. You're as alone as I am. More alone. You never bothered to go out and make friends."

The dinosaur moans, injured but still with us, and makes another attempt to pull itself free of the car. It might be my imagination, but it feels like more of the great beast is able to separate further from the frame than it was before I broke the window.

"Hurting people isn't the way to make the world love you." I reach through the broken window and unlock the car. My fingers tingle when I touch the handle, but only for a moment, and they come away without any resistance. The car is already preoccupied with trying to digest the dinosaur. That, combined with its weakened state, means that it can't hold me.

Bobby shrinks away as I wrench the door open, pressing himself against the driver's side door like he thinks he can somehow escape from me without getting out of the car. I flip the scythe around and shove the end of it into the cab, jabbing him in the leg. He yelps and shrinks even further away.

"Just be glad I used the blunt end," I say. "I could have stabbed you."

"Go away, Rosie," he says. "I promise I'll leave you alone after this if you'll just go away."

I stare at him. "You *killed* me," I say, in as patient a tone as I can manage. It isn't easy. I don't want to be patient with him. I want to scream and rail and slash at him with the business end of my scythe until he learns to respect the power of farming implements. "Even if I were somehow able to magically forgive you for that, which I'm not, you killed Laura. You've killed so many people, some of them for the crime of being near me. People tell stories all over the country of how I'm a killer, I'm a murderer, I'm the reason some brother or cousin or friend isn't coming home, and it's mostly because of *you*. But they don't tell stories about you anymore, Diamond Bobby, the man who disappeared. You're a footnote, a historical mystery, and they're forgetting about you. I'd almost be willing to let you go, because I know how badly it's going to hurt you the first time you realize some pretty young thing has no idea who you look like."

He scrambles to press himself more firmly against the door. I jab him in the leg again. He makes a sound that I could charitably call a moan, but which is really closer to a whimper. I jab him a third time, and he repeats the noise. This is fun. I could do this all day.

"You never learned to suffer," I say. "You drive around acting all tough, but really, you never learned to suffer. You opted out of your life as soon as it started to look like it might not be easy forever, and you got yourself a prize you could use as a weapon. Your biggest problem for the last fifty years has been figuring out where your next tank of gas is coming from. You have no idea how to hurt, Bobby. You have no idea how to build anything with your own two hands, and you certainly have no idea what it means to own the things you build. Why have I been so afraid of you for so long?"

"Rosie," he croaks. "You're on fire."

"Fuck you, Bobby Cross." I jab him in the leg again. "Fuck you, and fuck your car, and fuck everything you've done. The crossroads are dead. There's no one to protect you anymore. And I want my green back." I step away from the car, whirl, and slam the point of my scythe down on the hood as hard as I can, careful to miss the dinosaur's tail. There's a loud tearing noise, followed by a gout of steam. I've hit something important, possibly something vital.

But I know I haven't hit the gas tank. The crossroads followed the basic rules of automotive design when they made Bobby's car—it has wheels, a frame, headlights, all the pieces you'd expect from a car of its apparent age and era—which means the fuel tank will be toward the back and beneath the car. I don't know if I can make that swing.

The dinosaur moans. It sounds like it's in pain.

I can make the swing.

The blade of the scythe is almost three feet long, and I don't have to worry about the security protocols you find on modern cars; this vehicle was conjured decades ago, and the crossroads never cared enough about Bobby to go back and make improvements. They wouldn't have been willing to do it for free anyway, and they didn't have anything left to offer him, since the only thing he'd wanted for a long, long time was me, and I was never theirs to give. I take a step back, dispassionately noting the almost transparent flames now licking around my hands and arms. Bobby was right. I'm on fire. I wish I knew what that meant. What I can see of my dress is still gray, the color of the ashes at the bottom of a campfire, the ones that are so soft that running them through your fingers feels like touching silk.

Once I'm sure of what I'm about to do, I circle the car to the driver's side and swing for the tank, the scythe biting into the metal with a ferocity that I don't think would be possible from an ordinary farming tool. There's a screeching, snapping, tearing sound, and for a moment, I can't pull back for another swing. The blade is wedged in place. I yank as hard as I can, and it comes free with a pop, leaving me to stagger backward. The smell of gasoline fills the air, and the bottom foot or so of the scythe's blade is wet. I hit the tank. If I'm right about what that means . . .

The dinosaur roars as a thick black fluid begins to drip from the underside of the car. I take a step away from the vehicle, nearly dropping the scythe as the colorless flames enrobing my arms spread along the shaft, heading for the gas-soaked blade.

"Okay, I don't know what's happening right now, but I really, *really* don't want to explode," I say, and my voice is thin and anxious, more frightened than I have any right to be under these ridiculous circumstances. Bobby is staring at me through the rolled-up, unbroken window on his side of the car. He looks like he's way more scared than I sound, and that's what gives me the nerve to tap the point of my scythe against the glass, not hard enough to break it this time, just hard enough to be impossible for him to ignore.

Slowly, he creaks the window down about an inch. Just far enough to hear me.

Spiff. "I'm pretty sure I just punctured your gas tank," I say mildly. "You might want to get out of the car."

The dinosaur is pulling itself back together, rising up from the hood like an avenging angel as the car loses the ability to hold it down. It was partially merged with the metal, and as it rips itself free, it leaves patches of rust and decay behind. It's an impressive, if surreal, effect. The dinosaur stands, stomping its feet, wrenching its tail free of the frame. The color is returning to its skin and feathers, bleeding back more quickly than it bled out. It turns its horrible head toward the windshield, eyes fixing on Bobby, and roars. The sound is full of razor-blades that weren't there before.

I give my scythe a spin. "I think you've made my friend angry," I say. "You shouldn't let your car eat people. It's not nice. When you're not nice, you can't expect anyone to be nice to you."

The dinosaur nudges the windshield with the tip of its nose, snorting. The glass fogs over, becoming briefly opaque, thanks to dinosaur breath.

"Get out of the car, Bobby." The thick, gooey substance is continuing to drip from the bottom of the car. It doesn't look like any gasoline I've ever seen before. It doesn't even look like tar. It's thicker, somehow, and more rancid. Rainbows dance and swirl on its surface, sour and clotted, forming the illusion of screaming faces if I look too closely. It's a slurry of souls, the pieces that remain of everything and everyone that's been shoved into that tank and not completely consumed. A thin river of the stuff snakes *up* the side of the car, flowing into the substance of the dinosaur. It's getting itself back.

"You're on fire, Rose," he counters.

"Your car is bleeding out, the crossroads are dead, and you're not going to win this," I say, just as the fire that's been sliding along the scythe reaches the gasoline-wetted stretch of the blade. It bursts into sudden, lambent flame, and I nearly drop the whole thing. "Whoa!"

"What the hell are you playing at, girl?" Bobby demands, making no move to get out of the car.

"I don't know! I've never just caught fire before!" I wasn't a sorcerer when I was alive, and even if I had been, those talents would have carried over into the twilight as soon as I died, not waited fifty years and more to catch up with me. I swing the scythe, trying to extinguish the flames. They dance and wave, but don't go out. They don't grow higher, either, and if they're putting off any heat, I can't feel it. I look down at my ash-gray skirt. It's completely covered in the lambent, glittering flames. It's almost pretty if I look at it from the right angle. The right angle would require it not to be attached to me.

The dinosaur, now entirely free of Bobby's car, hops down from the hood, although not before headbutting the windshield and roaring one more time. Bobby shouts and slams his hand on the horn again. What emerges is not the klaxon on a healthy demon-powered car, but the strained squawk of a dying bird.

The car might be able to heal, given enough time and distance from our assault. The color still hasn't returned to my dress, although that could be as much about the fact that it's on fire as it is about the car's attempt to swallow me whole. I hit the fender with my burning scythe regardless, scraping the paint without transferring the fire.

"Get out of the car, Bobby," I snap, and the dinosaur growls, making its position on the whole thing very clear. The tarry substance has almost stopped dripping from the underside of the car and is spreading out in a viscous pool that's managed to touch three of the four tires so far. I step back, out of the range of its spread. I don't know if what I suspect is about to happen is really going to happen, but if it does, I don't want to get caught.

The dinosaur doesn't appear to have fully grasped the situation. I put out an arm, nudging it gently back. The fire licking across my skin doesn't even singe its feathers. "Look," I say, with a nod toward the spreading pool. "You don't want to touch that."

The dinosaur makes a curious chirping noise, crest rising like the feathers on a cockatoo's head. The thin rivulet that connected the pool to its foot has long since fallen away; all of its substance has been returned.

"We reap what we sow," I say, and pause to chuckle. The scythe in my hands makes that statement a little more on-the-nose than it would normally have been. Blame this agrarian afterlife of mine. "Wherever the crossroads found this thing, I think it's going back there."

The pool finishes its expansion, now covering the bottoms of all four tires. The car suddenly lurches, not forward, exactly, but downward, as the two front tires dip a few inches below the surface of the road. It's a sharp, convulsive motion. Inside the car, Bobby shouts and slams his door open, scrambling to get free. In only a matter of seconds, he's standing on the road, exposed and vulnerable, maybe for the first time. I turn my attention on him. The dinosaur continues watching his car.

Bobby pales, taking a big step back, barely missing the outline of the pool.

"I wouldn't step in that if I were you," I say. "Whatever that thing you call a car is, the crossroads had to get it from somewhere, and I think it's going home. Back to the starlight, or someplace even deeper. The twilight isn't heaven, but it isn't hell, either. This is a sort of purgatory, and it is whatever we make it. Your car never belonged here. You don't belong here either."

"R-Rosie," says Bobby, swallowing hard, his Adam's apple working in his throat like he's catching up on fifty years of running scared all at the same time. "You know I never meant to hurt anyone. I only wanted what I deserved. I only wanted what I'd been promised."

"You know, people like to say parents hurt their children by lying to them about Santa Claus and the Tooth Fairy and all that childhood bullshit, but those lies have never been the problem," I say, taking a step forward. "Friendly spirits of generosity and plenty who want you to have gifts and coins and chocolate just because you exist? Every kid knows that's not true, because every kid walks in the world, and they can see with their own eyes that the world doesn't work that way. The bad lies are the ones no one notices we're being told. Lies like 'everyone starts out on an equal footing' and 'everyone's voice is equal' and 'you deserve to be happy.' The American Dream is a lie as big as the horizon, and people keep telling it, and when it settles in the stomach of people like you, you start thinking words like 'deserve.' You deserve to be happy. You deserve to be loved. You deserve to get every damn thing your heart desires, even when getting it means taking it away from someone else, even when you didn't do a fucking thing to earn it, because someone lied to you, and you decided to believe them. Because it was easier than asking questions. Am I right?"

Bobby shies away from me, careful to keep his feet clear of the tarry pool. Too bad. If he stepped into it, I'm pretty sure he'd sink faster than his car, which is thoroughly mired, almost down to the tops of its tires. Its paint has entirely returned to that poisonous moonlight color, the one that shouldn't exist. There are no traces of either brown or green remaining. I wonder where my green went. It should have come back to me if it was going to leave the car, and it didn't. That's not fair. It belongs to me, not to Bobby Cross. He doesn't get to steal anything else from me.

"Be reasonable, Rose," he says, raising his hands like he thinks a living man standing stranded in the twilight can ward off a furious, burning girl with a scythe and a dinosaur through the sheer power of asking me to mind my manners. "Not everything's a lie. Some people do deserve more because some people are better than others. I was handsome and talented and special, and I just wanted to make sure the world would remember me that way. Was it so wrong of me to go looking for a way to make sure my image would never be tarnished?"

"*Yes, it fucking was,*" I spit, taking another step toward him. "I was *sixteen*. I was on my way to *prom*, to dance with a boy who *loved me.* Maybe I wasn't beautiful, and maybe I wasn't special, but I was pretty, and I was smart, and I was trapped, because my parents were poor, and I wasn't lucky enough to be born someplace where they hand out second chances on the street corners for the pretty girls with good bone structure visible because of poor nutrition. I was *sixteen*. I had my whole *life* ahead of me. Why did my life matter less than your image?"

"Look what you got out of it, Rosie! You're a star! The Phantom

Prom Date is going to live forever, even though you didn't. There's
going to be a movie! People have written songs, and books, and all sorts
of things about you!"

"Do you think that helped my mother sleep at night? Do you think
she was *comforted* when people told her that her daughter wasn't ever
going to rest in peace? Maybe I got something out of the way I died,
but I never asked for it, and it wasn't what I *deserved*." I spit the word
out like it tasted foul, like there's something septic and poisonous about
it. "If I deserved anything in this world, it was the ability to make my
own choices and live my own life, and you took that from me on a
whim. You weren't even running on empty, or you would have been
more careful about where you ran me off the road. You killed me because you thought you were entitled to my death, you thought you *deserved* it. You bastard."

"I was getting old, Rosie," he whines, stepping backward again.
This time, his heel almost lands in the tarry goo. The car lurches again,
sinking deeper beneath the surface of the road. There won't be any
getting it back soon. It's being lost in slow motion, and maybe that's for
the best, because it gives him time to suffer. "They were already starting to talk about the next me. The pretty little boy who'd be taking my
place and my parts and my lines. They were ready to throw me away
like I didn't matter! I went to the crossroads to save myself. A man's
allowed to save himself, isn't he?"

"If you'd been in any actual danger, I might agree," I say, and whip
the scythe around, pointing the burning blade toward his chest. "They
weren't going to use you as the hot young thing anymore, sure, but they
still *loved* you. You were box office gold. Diamond Bobby was a guaranteed hit. All you had to do was keep doing what everyone who lives
does. All you had to do was keep dying."

"I didn't want to," says Bobby, and is it my imagination, or are there
lines at the corners of his eyes and the edges of his mouth that weren't
there when he got out of his damaged, dying car? It's sinking deeper
and deeper into the road, disappearing faster all the time, and he's
standing in the twilight with nothing to protect him from a place where
a living man has no business being, and time is catching up with him.

"I wanted to be young and sweet and handsome forever. Was that so wrong?"

"How many people are dead because you wanted what you felt like you *deserved*?" I ask, stepping forward.

Bobby looks at me, clearly miserable, getting older by the second. "I don't know," he says, voice creaking. The skin on his face is softening and loosening, beginning to drip into wrinkles and forming jowls along the line of his jaw. There's nothing wrong with that. If it were anyone other than Bobby, it would seem perfectly normal. Seeing his eternally youthful face start to show the passing of time is strange enough to be disconcerting. "I lost count."

"I'd say they all remember, but you shoved them into the tank of your car and burned them up." I jab my scythe at him again. He steps back. This time his heel hits the tarry surface of the pool. In a second, he's up to his knee in the blackness, staggering and off-balance. He reaches for me in what seems to be a completely automatic gesture on his part, freezing when he sees the wrinkled, weathered backs of his hands.

"Rose!"

I jab the scythe one last time, whipping it so close to his head that he winces, and a lock of his hair flutters free. The token I promised to get for Bethany. I catch it on the flat of the blade, somehow knowing exactly how to twist my weapon, and take a large step backward, making sure he can't grab any burning part of me. "No. I'm not your savior. I'm not your victim. I'm nothing to you except for the woman who finally beat you. You're done, Bobby. This is the end. Your car's sinking, and your bargain is broken, and there's no way for you to make another one. This is the end of the road for you."

"This is . . . it's cruel!" The black stuff is yanking him deeper down. He shouldn't be able to fit there without slamming into his car, but he does. I guess physics yields when it's something like this. "You're not supposed to be the bad guy!"

"I wasn't, when you killed me." I smile at him, sweet as anything. "I was a good girl. Sweet little Rose, who always did what she was told."

"So help me," he says, still reaching out with his increasingly withered hands. It's all catching up to him at once. It's no more than he deserves.

"She died," I say, and take another step back. "She died on Sparrow Hill Road, and she's not here to help you anymore, Bobby. Robert, I guess. 'Bobby' is a young man's name."

The look of horror on his face is everything I've ever wanted to see. He screams, and the black tar pulls him deeper, and then his car sinks completely below the surface of the road, disappearing from the twilight. I don't know where it's going. Not the midnight, and not the starlight either. Those places don't want him any more than we do. I don't turn away. I keep my eyes on Bobby, watching as the blackness pulls him deeper and deeper down, into the road. Then he's gone, with a final choked-off scream, and the tar itself begins to withdraw into the pavement, disappearing like the car, like Bobby. In a matter of seconds, it's all gone, back to wherever the crossroads called it from.

But the road isn't empty. Half a dozen spirits appear, pale as paper and tissue-thin, without the substance of a specter. One of them turns toward me, mouth moving in a silent question. I step forward, spreading my arms, trying to hold the burning scythe like it's anything other than a threat. The dinosaur moves with me. That's going to make "not a threat" a harder sell. I can't tell it to go away, not after the car tried to eat it. It deserves to be here.

"Bobby's gone," I say. "He can't hurt you anymore." I don't recognize any of these shades, but I know who they have to be. They're the remnants of the spirits Bobby most recently fed into his car, the ones who hadn't been completely consumed before I punctured the gas tank. The one who looks most solid is a girl in her late teens. Christina from Warsaw, most likely, the victim Bobby claimed to get himself away from me. She turns toward me, and she looks almost like an ordinary ghost with holes in the knees of her jeans and a bruise on her cheek.

"What?" she asks, and her voice is as thin and pale as the rest of her, worn almost to nothing.

She's been dead less than a full day. All of this must be so incredibly confusing to her. It's still pretty confusing to *me*.

"The man who hurt you is gone," I say. She nods, a miserable look on her pretty, translucent face. None of the ghosts are reacting to the dinosaur, which would have been the *first* thing I reacted to. A woman on fire, with a scythe, is one thing, but a patchwork dinosaur covered in feathers and filled with teeth? That's something a lot more worrisome, and a lot less achievable with a bottle of lighter fluid and a match.

Then the dinosaur takes a step forward, nudging one of the ghosts with its feathery head, and croons. The ghost responds with silent delight, beginning to pet the dinosaur's crest, and I realize that they were all together in the gas tank, even if it was only for a few minutes. I'm a burning stranger. The dinosaur is a prehistoric friend.

I'd like to not be on fire anymore. It's weird to be this warm in the twilight. And even if it doesn't hurt, it's disconcerting, and I'd like things to go back to normal. I want to look at my dress and see the green they named my story after. I want to stick my thumb out and flag down a ride.

I want to feel victorious. Bobby Cross is gone, and for some reason, it feels like things aren't over yet. I feel like I'm frozen, even as I'm burning. I try to let go of the scythe. It refuses to leave my hands. It's like the thing has bonded with my skin, but when I try to shift my grip, I can do that easily. I can do anything but put it down.

This is going to be a problem. People don't give rides to girls on fire with destroyed dresses carrying farming implements. If I can't drop the scythe, I'm never going to get a ride again. I shake my hands, trying to make the wood break contact with my skin. It doesn't work. I look toward the dinosaur. It's ignoring me, more focused on herding the—can I call them survivors when they're all dead?—the survivors of Bobby's last ride toward the grass. They go willingly enough, responding to its faint chirps and trills with statements I can't hear, but it seems to understand. They're bonded by their shared trauma. I managed to avoid that particular trauma, whether I deserved to or not, and I'm not a part of their circle. They need time to heal and recover as much as they can from what Bobby did to them. The dinosaur can give them that time. I can't. I don't have the power to protect them the way it can.

The dinosaur looks back as it herds the last of the ghosts into the grass, crest raised, and roars one final time. It's a triumphant sound, and strangely comforting, for all that it still makes the hairs on the back of my neck stand on end, remembering that humans were never meant to share the world with lizards this big, or this proudly predatory. Alligators are enough. Evolution didn't prepare me for this.

I take one hand off the scythe—it's willing to let me do that much, at least—and wave to the dinosaur. It bobs its head, acknowledging the gesture, and then it follows the ghosts into the grass, disappearing with remarkable speed for something that big and that mismatched. I'm alone.

There's no trace of Bobby; not his car, not the pool of tarry blackness that swallowed him whole, nothing. The only thing out of the ordinary on this stretch of the ghostroads is me, still burning.

I clutch the scythe, slamming the butt end of it into the pavement, and allow my knees to buckle, trusting in the wood to hold me up while I hang my head and cry. Because here's one of the things they never told me about death when I was alive: things that suck for the living still suck for us. Sometimes they can suck even worse because we lack the sense of "this, too, shall pass." For us, everything is happening right now, and right now can last the better part of forever.

The sight of my ash-gray dress is enough to make me cry harder, until my tears have turned everything blurry and difficult to discern. I want my green back. I want to give away this fire, which burns without consuming, licking along my arms and the bodice of my dress. If I could somehow take the dress off and put it aside, I'm sure the fire would stay with my skin, hot but not painful, somehow independent of any source of fuel. It's not burning me up. It's not burning me away. It's just burning.

"What's wrong, Rose?"

The voice is sweet, and female, and draped in a strong English accent that feels incongruous here, in this mirror of the American agrarian ideal. She's a long damn way from home.

"I thought better of you than this. Not *much* better, if I'm being honest with you, but better. You living never fully adapt when you wake up and find yourselves properly dead. I don't quite understand why the

Lady doesn't restrict herself to proper liminals. We do so much better with forces beyond our ken."

"Go away, Pippa," I mumble, not lifting my head. Everything about this situation is terrible. What's the use of getting rid of Bobby if I'm just going to be on fire from now on? I can't go into the daylight like this. I'm not sure I could rise to the daylight if I wanted to, not when I can't even focus enough to change my clothes. I feel trapped and lessened, and some of that may be shock, because for the first time since I died, I don't need to be looking over my shoulder for the man who killed me. I'm free. I'm free of Bobby Cross and everything he represented. And I'm still trapped because I'm still here.

"Shan't," she says. I hear footsteps behind me. She's coming closer. "The Lady asked me to come and look in on you and your little errand, and it seems like she was right to do it. You're burning up, Rose!"

"No shit, Sherlock," I reply bitterly, and wipe the tears away from my cheeks with a flick of my hand that sends droplets scattering on the road, where they continue to burn even without the rest of me. Swell. I get to be a natural accelerant from now on. That's just what I always never wanted.

"Doesn't that seem a little, well, *strange* to you? Do human ghosts normally catch fire for no good reason?"

"Will-o-the-wisps do sometimes. And onibi. But I'm not a burning ghost. I'm a walking ghost. I'm supposed to be lonesome and wistful and lead people down unpaved roads, into places they would never have gone without me."

"Ah, but you're a psychopomp as well, and I know that's not a part of the hitchhiker's lot," says Pippa.

"I didn't mean to be," I reply. "That just sort of . . . happened."

Psychopomps guide the spirits of the recently departed into the twilight, and sometimes beyond. Pippa's right; it's not normally a part of the hitchhiker's job. Sometimes, though . . . sometimes we wind up sensitive to the smell of death on the wind, and we choose our drivers based on who's going to need someone to ease them past the transition. That's what I did, in the beginning, targeting the people Bobby had already decided to chase down, sticking out my thumb and shortening my hems for the truckers who were destined to become offerings to the open road. I guess I didn't like the idea of them dying alone, and I didn't consider how eagerly the twilight would seize on any hint that I was willing to be more than circumstance demanded of me.

In the beginning, it had only been people I'd known when I was alive and the occasional trucker who died in my presence. Then, bit by bit, the scents of the world crept in, until I could tell in a sniff whether someone was heading toward their own death, and whether that death was something avoidable—accidents due to alcohol or exhaustion versus train derailments or malicious action. Once that talent had solidified, I'd been tagged as a psychopomp forever.

"Lots of things seem to just happen where you're concerned, Rose. Have you considered that you're the unifying factor? Maybe they'd stop happening if you'd stop existing."

I whip around so fast I nearly overbalance. I would, if not for the scythe still patiently holding me up. "I'm not moving on because I'm having a flammable day." At least the lock of Bobby's hair isn't burning, somehow. That's something.

"Suit yourself," says Pippa. She's standing right behind me, her own scythe in her hands. As always, she's dressed like a Gothic princess, but the "princess" part is a little more literal than usual right now: she's wearing a ball gown made of shimmering material that's gunmetal gray where the light hits it and opalescent white when it's in shadow, one long strip gathered up and hanging over her shoulder, cutting across the straight slash of her neckline. The black velvet band that keeps her head in place is her only adornment. She looks like some kind of terrifying warrior queen out of a fairy tale, like she's going to strike me down for the crime of standing too close to her.

The edge of her scythe is covered in the same small, lambent flames as cover my entire body, flickering and glittering in the light. Every time she shifts position, the flames spark, just a little, glinting white as the heart of a bonfire.

"What are you going to do, then?" she asks. "Planning to just stand

here and burn, and cry like some new-dead numpty? Doesn't seem like
the very best use of your time to me. Having a lot of it doesn't mean it
has no value."

"Why are you so calm?" I demand. "I'm *on fire*."

"Yes," she says. "I've noticed. This is normal for the stage you're in."

"The stage of what?" I straighten up, taking one hand off the
scythe. I still can't drop it, no matter how hard I try. It clings to my
palm like it's been glued to me, like it's a very inconvenient extension
of my body.

"You didn't think you could attract the attention of *three* divinities
and walk away unscathed, did you?" Pippa cocks her head at a sharp
enough angle that I'm momentarily afraid it's going to fall off. That happens with Dullahan. It's disconcerting. "That isn't how any of this works.
It never has been. Those who attract the attention of the gods are
doomed to serve them, one way or another. You weren't content with the
Ocean Lady knowing your name. You had to go and make sure Persephone would know you personally, and then you went dancing with the
anima mundi! Three goddesses of the twilight is three more than most
people get to know. You must have known there'd be a price to pay."

"None of them said anything about prices," I say, staring at her.

"None of them should have needed to. Maybe it's because you've
been a hitcher for so long, but there's no such thing as a free ride. Not
really. You've been lucky for a long time, Rose Marshall, chasing your
revenge down the highways and the byways, always one step too slow
to catch him. So you asked the gods to make you faster, to make you
better, and when they answered, those gifts came with a price."

"I didn't *ask* for anything," I snap. "The Ocean Lady—or at least,
Apple, and she speaks for the highway as long as she stays Queen—
asked me to stop Bobby, because the crossroads are dead, and someone
had to do it."

"Isn't the Ocean Lady keeping your niece from disappearing into
the dust?" asks Pippa, with a lazy wave of her hand. "Isn't she anchoring your distaff descendant to a reality that doesn't want her anymore?
That's a favor. That's a gift from a goddess. You asked for more than you
were asked to do."

I shake my head. "No. No, that isn't true." But it *is* true, isn't it? I was more concerned about Bethany than I was about what the loss of the crossroads would do to the routewitches. They never drew their power through the crossroads, but they were always tied to them, always intimately aware of how to find them, enough so that Apple had taken the responsibility for Bobby's bargain on her narrow shoulders and never found the way to lay it down. The crossroads were tied to the Ocean Lady by bonds of magic and obligation, whether or not she had ever wanted them to be, and now that she was finally free, I had asked her to keep a reminder of their terrible burden. I had asked her to find a way to fix Bethany, to let her stay.

She—or more likely, Apple—should have said something if I was asking too much. But I couldn't deny that I had asked.

"And you know you asked Persephone for favors," says Pippa, inexorably. "Three times. Once for that tattoo on your back, to keep you safe from marauding spirits. Once for the return of your death, which tied that corsage around your wrist. You haven't been shy about wearing her favor where others can see, either. You could have taken it off as soon as you were back in your proper place, could have gone down to the River Lethe and scrubbed the tattoo from your spine. You did neither of those things, nor ever raised the question of payment. You were happy to receive her gifts when you thought they came to you freely."

"Three times? That's two. I didn't graduate from high school, but I can count."

"I thought the third time needn't be mentioned, since not even you could have already forgotten sending me to petition her on your behalf," says Pippa smugly. "It's been so recent. Is your memory so faded as all that?"

"No," I counter. "I'm just that distracted by the fact that I'm *still on fire*. Are you going to tell me how not to be on fire anymore?"

"It's not for me to say, little ghost. Your kind are outside my ken."

I sag, once more using the scythe to hold myself up. "That's a fancy way of saying you have no damn clue, isn't it?"

Pippa shrugs. "The third goddess is the one most in need of

payment right now, for she both has and has not been absent from her duties for a very long time. The anima mundi lost her place to an intruder who spent her treasures freely and without reasonable concern for recompense. She can't afford to be spending what little she has left without consideration. No free rides here."

"All of which somehow adds up to me on fire?"

"As the phoenix knows, sometimes the old must burn away to make proper room for the new."

"What 'old'? I never got to get old. I'm still a teenager."

"Which isn't making this any easier." Pippa shakes her head, eyes going dark. "You asked for aid in seeking vengeance. You asked to be made more effective in your quest to be avenged. Well, you shouldn't ask for things if you don't truly want them. It's not right, nor reasonable."

"What's not reasonable is you standing there talking in circles when I don't know what's happening to me," I snap.

"Isn't it obvious? The gods have granted your wish, and you've been accepted into the ranks of the Erinyes. You're to fly with the Furies, Rose Marshall, and leave the daylight to its own concerns save when your duties draw you through the veil between the living and the dead. You took their gifts and used them well, and now you're granted another gift as your reward. Rejoice and be glad."

"What?" I stare at her. She's not making sense.

I've heard of the Furies. Everyone in the twilight has heard of the Furies. They're a children's story, something we use to threaten the newly dead when they don't seem willing to accept the fact that things have changed. Be good and don't haunt the living, or the Furies will get you. Pay attention when someone explains what your kind of ghost does, or you won't serve the twilight properly, and when you start to fade, you'll risk attracting the attention of the Furies. They're not real. They're not something you can just become.

It feels like the ground has dropped out from beneath my feet, like everything is going suddenly askew. None of this is possible. But I'm on fire and the scythe is stuck to my hand, so "possible" isn't playing a very big role in anything I do today. "You're kidding."

"I'm not." Pippa shakes her head. For the first time, she looks like she might actually be sympathetic to my situation, like she understands how confusing this has to be. "Chin up, Rosie. Your bad guy's gone. You needed something else to keep you busy if you didn't want to do that oh-so-human thing and fade into the next level of the afterlife. A girl like you was never going to be content returning to stranger's cars and silence after having a great grand quest like you've done. Now you'll get to stay a bit longer."

"So this isn't forever?" I seize on that because it's the only part that makes sense.

"Doesn't have to be," says Pippa. "My Lady doesn't want the un-willing. If you refuse her calling, she'll let you go."

I exhale in relief.

"Of course, she won't look kindly on you any longer, and I'm not sure how long you'd last without the favor of the gods, the way you do go on."

I blink at her. "What?"

"This is a gift from the gods. It's a new calling, and a new chal-lenge, and not an honor they grant very often. If you refuse it, you're telling them that you know better than they do, and that's not a mes-sage the gods like to receive. You're bound to them whether you like it or not, Rose Marshall. You've attracted their attention, and that makes them your concern."

Pippa folds her arms, managing to make the gesture perfectly ele-gant and fluid, like the scythe in her hands isn't interfering at all. If I'm going to be carrying one of the things from now on, maybe I should ask her for some pointers . . .

No. There's a way out of this. There has to be a way out of this. I'm a hitchhiking ghost. I'm not a Fury. I refuse to be a Fury. The gods never said anything about payment before. Maybe that should have struck me as strange—people like to know that they'll get a favor when they give a favor, after all—but they should have said something to me. They should have been clearer.

They shouldn't have behaved like Bobby Cross and tried to trap me when they knew I didn't have any options.

The fire on my skin seems to be dying out, or at least dwindling, going from licking flames to a thin layer of heat just above my skin. I run my hand along my arm, stirring the heat briefly back into licking flame. It dies down as soon as I pull my hand away. So this isn't letting me go so easily.

"Now what?" I ask Pippa.

"Now the Lady will see you," she replies.

I blink. "But I'm dead."

"She's the Lady of the Dead," says Pippa, with amusement. "Most of the people she talks to are deceased. I assure you, you're not special."

"That's not what I meant. I meant, I can't perform a katabasis as a dead person, can I? The Underworld is a roach motel for spirits. We can check in, but we can never check out."

"There are other ways in."

"So why did you take me through the Elgin Marbles? That way sucked." Except for the three-headed dog. He'd been pretty cool, and nice to pet, once I got past the overwhelming smell of giant mastiff.

"It was the way that was open to you." She waves a hand. A tunnel opens in the prehistoric grass. "Now this way is open. Will you come?"

"Sure, why not? It's not like I was doing anything important with my time." I start toward the opening, pausing when the motion causes my skirt to sway back into view. "Am I going to get my green back? I'm not the Girl in the *Gray* Silk Gown."

"That is entirely up to the divine."

"See, you say that like it's somehow a comforting answer, and I want to assure you that really, it's not comforting at all. Humans—and by extension, human ghosts—like to feel like we're in control of our own lives. Maybe not entirely, but mostly." Only that's not entirely true, is it? I've always known people who thought that "Jesus take the wheel" was somehow comforting, and not a statement of fatalistic horror. Too many humans are happy to hand control over to the first cosmic power to stumble across them.

"It's not comforting to *me*," I amend. "I want to be the master of my fate."

"You're dead, Rose," she says. "Just be glad you have a fate for people to fight you over."

Charming.

I step into the grass.

The opening leads to a hallway, incongruous and impossible in what should be a field of swaying, prehistoric grasses. The walls are smooth and white, the wainscoting is polished, and the floor is carpeted in an assortment of twisted rag rugs. I recognize some of the fabric they contain. One has several strips of what I would swear is the dress I'm currently wearing; others contain pieces of denim, or strips of white cotton from my favorite tank tops. Cute.

Pippa doesn't follow me into the hall. That's not much of a surprise. The Dullahan has never been much for going through the doors she opens. I look back, just to see if she might be behind me, and the opening back into the field has closed. There's nowhere to go but forward. That's also not much of a surprise. Places like this don't like it when you change your mind and try to do something else. A course, once committed to, is committed to forever in the eyes of the strange and terrible entities who try to guide the twilight.

Lacking anything else to do, I start down the hall. My burning feet don't ignite the rag rugs. I'm almost glad of that, even as I resent the strips of green silk for their color. I want it back. It's not something I ever thought I might be able to lose, and now that I have, I resent its absence with a fierceness that's a little scary.

There's a door at the end of the hall. It's not locked. I push it open and step through—

—into the Last Dance Diner. Emma is behind the counter, filling one of those tall metal cups with ice cream as she prepares to blend a malt. The stools are empty. So are the booths, all save one, where Persephone herself is sitting.

She's beautiful, although I couldn't describe her if I wanted to, because her appearance is constantly shifting, hair going from straight to curly, light to dark, and her skin shifting in tempo with it, so that she's every woman in the world at the same time, and all of them achingly, effortlessly beautiful. She's impossible. She's the ideal the rest of us can't even aspire to achieve.

Either she learned this trick from the anima mundi, or they learned it from her. Neither one of them has a single face, because they're both wearing the face of every woman in the world. Persephone is less blended and changes faster, though. She changes like sunlight on the sea.

She smells like sun-ripened wheat, pomegranate molasses, and asphodel. Always asphodel. She could be a garden unto herself, the smell of flowers is so strong. It paints the air around her with almost visible swirls of ivory and gold, gilded like the pollen at the heart of the flowers at my wrist. They haven't gone to gray. I don't think they could. The corsage was my first god-gift, and the one I welcomed most warmly.

I didn't ask for it, either. Was accepting it the beginning of an ending I couldn't have predicted?

I approach her booth, uncertain of either my welcome or the etiquette involved here. What if she wants to be left alone? But then, she wouldn't be here, in my place, in my way station, if she didn't want to speak with me, would she? I don't know what to do.

"Rose, don't be rude," says Emma, and she sounds exactly like herself, tolerant and familiar and a little bit impatient, like she can't believe I'm hesitating. She puts her metal cup on a tray, alongside a frosted glass and a slice of strawberry pie dripping with honeyed syrup, picking the whole thing up and carrying it over to deposit in front of the patiently waiting goddess. "It's not polite to say you'll meet someone here and then leave them waiting."

"I never agreed to meet anyone here," I say, and walk slowly across the diner, each step an ordeal, to stop in front of Persephone's booth. "Can I have a vanilla malt, please? Heavy on the malt."

"Dessert dessert, got it," says Emma, and retreats to the counter, leaving me semi-alone with Persephone, who looks at me with a tolerantly amused smile playing on her constantly shifting lips.

"Well?" she says and raises a hand to indicate the seat across from her, open as if it's been waiting for my arrival. "Please. Sit down. We have a great deal to talk about."

Her voice is as changeable as her face, shifting tones, shifting octaves from one syllable to the next. She could be a chorus of women, each of them bringing her own story to the table.

"Pippa said I'm on fire because you want me to be a Fury." I slide into the seat, and the vinyl is cool against my back and shoulders, even through the lingering heat of the flames. They flicker and lick against the material, which resists them as effortlessly as it resists everything else. The Last Dance is no ordinary diner, subject to the wear and tear of ordinary entropy. It's a temple to the American road, and it will be in perfect condition from now until the very end of time.

It's a little reassuring to know that the gods are not somehow stronger than this place, which has been my sanctuary and my salvation for so very long. I set my stolen lock of hair on the table as I glance out the window to the moonwashed parking lot, where Gary waits for me, as patient as ever. I'm really here, then. This isn't some complicated illusion. That means I need to be on my best behavior, since I don't want Persephone to trash the place if Emma would have to clean it up.

"I don't," says Persephone.

I perk up. "You don't?"

"I don't want anyone to be a Fury. It's not an easy part to play. It's all vengeance and the hunt, and none of the sweet rest that should await the dead in my fields. If it were up to me, the world would change so that Furies were no longer needed, and the Erinyes would be forgotten." She picks up her malt, sipping delicately through the straw. "Alas, I don't make the rules and never have. But no, Rose. I don't want you to be a Fury. If you're right for the role, it's because you made a Fury of yourself."

"I . . . but . . . but that's not fair!" I protest, leaning the scythe against my leg in hopes that it will take the contact as proof that I haven't put it down and allow me to let it go. It works. When I take my hands away from the shaft, it allows me to pull them free. Now it's stuck to my leg, sure, but that's still an improvement. "I didn't do anything I didn't *have* to do!"

"We both know that isn't true, Rose. You could have run and kept on running, like everyone else who's managed to escape from Bobby

Cross across the years. You could have refused the psychopomp's part. You could have let your niece fall down with no one to catch or comfort her. Again and again, the twilight gave you the choice between the right thing and the easy one, and again and again, you chose to do what was right and just, instead of what would leave you free to flee. We don't choose the Furies. The Furies choose themselves. You've been on this road for a long time. You solidified your place when you chose to pursue Bobby and assist those who would become his victims."

The dinosaur. I could have tried to fight it. I didn't. I hold out my hand, showing the tiny flames licking along my fingers.

"How do I make the fire stop? If I'm a Fury, I guess I'm a Fury, and if what you're saying is true and I did this to myself, fighting it isn't going to do me any good. But I can't walk around on fire all the time. My milkshakes would melt."

"Set your anger aside. There's nothing here to fight or to seek revenge upon, unless you want to seek revenge upon yourself—a fruitless occupation that has destroyed more good people than I could number." Persephone takes another sip from her malt. "It's yours. Control it."

I'm not carrying any anger with me right now, am I? I defeated Bobby. I saw him pulled down into the depths by the weight of his own bargain with the crossroads. He's gone.

He's gone, and I'm angry about that.

Bobby Cross was *mine*. He was my monster and my murderer, and if anything was going to rip him to pieces, it should have been me, not some unseen force summoned by the death of the crossroads. The fact that my honorary niece was the one who destroyed the crossroads doesn't change my burning desire to be the reason he's gone, and while I won't call defeating him exactly *easy*, I will say that it wasn't the vast, terrible battle I had built up in my mind. I'm angry because I don't know what I'm going to do with myself without him. I'm angry because I don't want him to be gone so easily.

The fire dancing on my skin is my own anger made manifest, and it doesn't want to let me go. I look at Persephone, silently pleading. She shakes her head.

"No one can help you with this," she says. "You know the twilight changes everyone who walks in it. You're not the girl you were when you died. You're not even the girl you were when you would have welcomed your resurrection. You were a high school student who got into an accident. You became an urban legend and a campfire story and a way for children to scare each other at slumber parties. Some of the things you've said and done would be unthinkable to the girl you were. Is it such a shock that you should change again, Rose Marshall who was 'that dirty girl from the Marshall house' and became 'the phantom prom date'? You know as well as anyone that once a thing is changed, it can't decide to simply go back to being what it was in the beginning. I can't go back to being the goddess of a simple spring. I never could, and neither can you. You earned this anger. The fact that now you find it inconvenient doesn't make it any less your own. You need to accept it."

I glare at her for a moment before the part of me that enjoys existence pipes up to question the wisdom of glaring at a goddess. Tearing my eyes away from her, I take a deep breath, holding it for a count of thirty before letting it slowly out through my nose. I don't need to breathe, but it helps sometimes, especially when the goal is calming down.

This anger belongs to me, I think. *No one can take it away, and no one wants to, because I earned it. It's not fair that Bobby killed me. It's not fair that I didn't get to kill him. It's not fair that I almost let him turn me into a murderer. All those things can be true at the same time. This isn't a game where you only win one prize.*

I feel calmer. Am I really upset by the idea of being a Fury? Or am I just upset by the idea that I didn't get to choose? I don't like it when people decide things for me. That's not new. That's part of who I've been since the beginning.

"What do Furies have to do?" I ask.

"Most of the time? Whatever they did before they were chosen. They're still a part of whatever level of the afterlife they were bound to. You'll be a twilight Fury, with wings of wind and cornsilk, and a scythe designed as much for harvest as for harm. Starlight Furies are colder, sharper things, faster to strike and slower to plant. Daylight Furies are counting down the days until they die and find their true eternity.

You'll still eat cheeseburgers, I suppose, still vex the gods and go into the world of the living more than you strictly should. But when something is wrong and needs righting, you'll be pulled to it, unable to resist. You'll involve yourself whether you want to or not. You'll do what you've always done: your best to save them. As long as they deserve to be saved, you'll struggle in their name. And you'll be armed with steel and with flame and with the blessing of three of the divinities of liminal space."

"You're going to share me?" I ask, voice a little sharper than I intend for it to be.

Persephone nods. "Myself, the Old Atlantic Highway, and the Spirit of the Living World have agreed that you belong to all of us, through bonds of debt and favor, and there is no point to making things more difficult by trying to insist on sole ownership."

I want to say that I don't belong to anyone. I'm sensible enough to keep my mouth shut for once in my long and often foolish death. "All right," I say slowly. "Will I still be a hitcher?"

"If you wish to be. The twilight will not compel, but neither will we forbid."

That feels like a loophole, and I file it away for later. I like loopholes. They're like hauntings: subtle until you're in the middle of them, and then impossible to overlook. "I'm mad because it feels like the crossroads stole my revenge by dying," I say. "But I'm not mad at my niece for killing them. They needed to go, if only because they didn't belong here, and the bargains they were letting people make were bad for the world. She did nothing wrong. I'm probably always going to be a little mad that I didn't take Bobby apart with my bare hands, but hey, I've made it this far without killing anyone. I guess I'm also grateful that I didn't get the chance."

The flames on my fingers blow out like they were never there. That strange new heat is still burning in my belly, bright and all-consuming, but it doesn't seem to be anywhere else right now. I look down at the ash-gray bodice of my dress. No flame. I'm out.

"You're the Goddess of Spring, right?" I ask, raising my head and looking at Persephone once more. "Can you help me bloom again? I need my green back."

"You never struck me as particularly vain before," says Persephone, with evident amusement. "Why does the color of your clothing matter so much?"

"I've been wearing this dress for coming on seventy years," I reply. "It matters. It's part of how I know I'm still myself."

"Interesting," she says. "And you don't think defeating your oldest enemy should cost you something? Bobby Cross is gone. Isn't a little green dye a small price to pay for being rid of him?"

"It's more than he's worth," I say, keeping my eyes steadily on hers. Her irises shift through a kaleidoscope of colors, more shades of blue and brown than I knew existed, but also green, hazel, violet, even a few shades of honey, clear and bright and disconcerting. I don't allow myself to look away. If I want this, if this matters to me, it can't look like something I'm willing to yield on.

Persephone sighs and snaps her fingers, and I look down in time to watch the seafoam green bleeding back into the bodice of my gown, washing the ash away.

"When we call, you'll come," she says. "You won't be able to resist. It'll be like the itch that calls you to seek a ride in the living world, only far worse. It's not wise to fight us."

She presses her hands against the table like she's going to stand up, and I straighten in alarm. "Wait!"

She pauses, looking back at me. The weight of her regard is suddenly much heavier than it was before I was keeping her here. I press on. I have to. "Pippa said I had to be a Fury now because I asked you for favors, and you said I'm a Fury because of my own choices. Which is it?"

"You chose to ask us for favors," she says, sounding faintly amused. "Free will cuts both ways."

"All right," I say. "In that case, I need to ask for one more favor, although it might be more a job for the anima mundi than for you. I'm not sure."

"What is it?"

"Bethany and Mary. They both served the crossroads. Neither of them is a road ghost. Without the crossroads to keep them anchored, they don't have a purpose here. I'm afraid they'll fade away. The anima mundi said Bethany could be a spirit of vengeance if I brought her a token from Bobby, and I did, but I have nothing for Mary."

"Ah," says Persephone. "I was wondering if you would remember the ones you claim for your own. It reflects well on you that you do. Your Mary Dunlavy has already found herself a new calling. Phantom Nannies were more common in the days before vaccination was quick and easy—young women would catch childhood diseases from their charges, crawl into their beds to die, and then return to work as if nothing at all had changed—but there's precedent."

So Mary's really a babysitter ghost now, the way we always used to tease her she was. That's reassuring. She'll be able to stay with her beloved Price family, and keep bringing their children up to be fine, upstanding citizens of the cryptozoological world. Only now, the crossroads won't be able to use her to control what her chosen family knows. Oh, this is going to be fun.

"And Bethany?"

"She was wronged by a man and died for his sins. It seems obvious what the twilight would make of her."

A white lady. No. Not my niece. There's not a lot of love lost between me and Bethany, but she's still my brother's granddaughter, and I refuse to accept this fate for her. "No," I say, as firmly as I can. "That's not where she belongs."

Persephone blinks at me, slowly, looking a little surprised by my insolence. "If not a white lady, there aren't many options open for her. You say the anima mundi promised vengeance. Perhaps that would be your best avenue."

"Do you need more groundskeepers?" Persephone and Hades spend most of their time in an infinitely beautiful garden, surrounded by flowering vines and bushes heavy with fruit. Someone had to be taking care of all that greenery.

This time, Persephone is definitely amused. "We do our own

gardening in the Underworld. The dead cannot cultivate asphodel. Only the divine can do that."

There's a definite division between death and divinity, no matter how often those two things can seem to coincide. "Please. There has to be something that she's suited for, that will let her stay in the twilight without devoting herself to hurting people. Maybe she'll choose to move on sooner rather than later now that she doesn't have to serve the crossroads anymore, but it should be her choice to go. Free will, remember?"

"There are a few paths open to her," says Persephone, slowly. "She could be a midnight beauty. Or she could be a reaper. Diametric opposites, in some ways, but both essential parts of the twilight."

The midnight beauties are the party girls of our afterlife. I don't see many of them. They aren't normally attracted to the dirt and uncertainty of the road. They appear between sunset and midnight, they haunt the trendiest nightclubs and the hottest dance floors, and they don't hurt anyone, either intentionally or through their presence. I don't know if that existence would make Bethany happy or not, but she wouldn't be doing any damage. Not like when she was with the crossroads. She might be able to pay back some of the debt she's incurred since dying.

Reapers are true psychopomps. They escort the spirits of the dead and dying from the daylight to the border. They tend to be quiet and reserved, sticking mostly to the company of their own kind. These options are like two sides of the same coin, almost polar opposites.

"Does she get to choose?" I ask.

"She can," says Persephone.

"Then I'll ask her," I say. "She's with the routewitches now. And if she picks one of these two paths, she won't fade into nothingness?"

"No. She'll have a new anchor to hold her in the twilight."

I nod, more decisively than I feel. "Good. Then I'll do it, and she can stay."

"Good." Persephone stands. "If she declines to select a path, she'll have to become what the anima mundi promised her, or leave the twilight, of course. There aren't any other roles that would welcome her."

I'm sure that's not true, but I'm not going to contradict a goddess. Not after everything we've already said to one another. "I'll tell her. But the scythe. Can I put it down? Because otherwise, this Fury gig is really going to interfere with my normal routine."

"You can send it where the fire goes. It will always return when you need it."

"That's suitably obscure enough to be confusing. I'll roll with it." I look at the scythe and try to think about how much I don't need it right now, how much happier it will be in some other space, somewhere that isn't a cozy twilit diner, unthreatened and unafraid. It doesn't disappear so much as it was abruptly never there in the first place, like a trick of the light in the form of a farming implement.

"There," I say, satisfied, as I turn back to Persephone . . .

. . . but she isn't there either. Only Emma, finally approaching with my too-long-awaited malt.

"Here we go," I say, feeling lost in the absence of the goddess. Everything's changing.

Chapter 12
Everything's Staying the Same

———

EMMA LOOKS AT ME like she's never seen me before, questions and answers in her eyes, which are as wide and as green as the Irish countryside. There's nothing greener in the twilight than Emma's eyes, not even my dress, not even the grass that rolls across the hills. She swallows, hard, as she puts my malt down on the table, and says, "I suppose her meal was on the house. It ought to be, what with her being the Lady of the Dead and everything. I haven't seen her in . . ." She turns away. "It's been a long time."

"I didn't know Persephone had any authority over the *beán sidhe*," I say. "I always thought her subjects would be more, I don't know, Greek."

"The Morrigan had us when she still kept her court and council, but when she laid her burdens down and went into the West, as all gods must one day go, she left us to her sister in the harvest, Persephone," says Emma, words slow and clumsy in her mouth, like she never thought to speak them so. "The *beán sidhe* and the *beán nighe* both, we went to Persephone, to sing for the dead who would one day be bound to her halls, and for those who were cut down before their time. Oh, don't look so surprised, Rose. You, of all people, should know that even gods can die. Nothing is forever, but nothing is forgotten as long as it's loved. You know that better than anyone."

"I suppose I do," I say, rubbing a fold of my skirt between my fingers. The fabric mended itself when the color came back. I'm fresh as a daisy once again, fresh as the day I died. Everything changes, but it doesn't always show on the surface.

"Anyway, I haven't seen her in so long that your grandparents weren't even dreamt of yet the last time she made her way out of the Underworld to visit me," says Emma. "Not that she has any obligations in that regard—she took us as a favor, and she's kept us as a burden—but it's always nice to have the reminder, however small, that someone's watching out for you. That you're not alone in the world."

"I suppose that's true," I say. I smile until I can feel myself dimple. "That's why I have you."

"Oh, *Rose.*" She takes the dishcloth off her shoulder and smacks me with it. "At least taste your milkshake before you run off again. I put so much malt in it that I think it could dehydrate an ocean."

"Yes, Emma," I say obediently, and grab the glass. It's cold and heavy in my hand, a sweet reminder that I've sent the fire away, and that some things are still normal. I take a sip.

It tastes exactly like a malted ought to taste, sweet as springtime and just a tiny bit bitter, drying and wetting my mouth at the same time. There's no ash. There's no distance. I pull the glass away long enough to gape at it, and then I'm drinking again, then I'm gulping it down so fast it's cascading down either side of my chin, matting in my hair, dripping onto my collarbone in fat, icy drops. It tastes like malts did when I was alive, only better, because Emma's had years to learn her craft, and she's always been fighting against the veil of dampening distance that keeps the dead from truly enjoying her food. For her pie to be amazing to the dead, it has to be transcendent to the living.

"Rose. Rose! Slow down, you'll choke yourself! Just because you can't die again, that doesn't mean you should give it a go!" Emma's accent gets thicker, strengthened by her distress.

I finish swallowing and pull the denuded glass away from my mouth, wiping my lips with the back of my hand. I'm sticky and cold as a small child at their first soda fountain, and I don't care. I can change my clothes and wish the mess away. One of the privileges of the dead, assuming I still get those. If I don't, I'll take a shower. I miss showers sometimes. Not much I miss about being alive anymore, except for showers and food, and I'm happy to take advantage of both.

"Sorry, Emma," I say sheepishly, and duck my head as I picture myself in traveling clothes, jeans and a T-shirt and Gary's old letter jacket. It can't loan me flesh or substance—nothing can do that unless it's willingly given by the living—but it can swaddle me in leather and canvas and the memory of my boyfriend's arms.

A thought, and my clothes are different, my dress taking the ice cream with it when it disappears. Some things haven't changed.

"Persephone says I'm going to be a Fury from now on," I say. "Pippa—that's the Dullahan I told you about—says it's because I asked too much of the gods, but Persephone says it's because of the choices I made on my own. Do you know what that all means?"

"Some of it," says Emma. "Not all. Most, you'll have to sort out as you go along. No *beán sidhe* has ever been called to the Fury's flight, so it's not as if I have a great deal of first-hand experience that I could share with you. I would if I could, my girl, you know I would if I could."

"I know," I say, somewhat more sadly than I had intended to. Emma isn't a magical answer-dispensing machine, but she's the oldest and most experienced non-god ally I have, and she's been there to save me from myself more times than I care to count. I don't have the feeling she would have predicted this for me, which is interesting, since she's known since we met that I was dedicated to avenging myself on the man who killed me, and it seems like that was the first step down the road I've accidentally committed myself to walking.

"You've got good guides, with the divine and her Dullahan in your corner," says Emma. "And it's an honor to be chosen for the Erinyes, or it was, when people remembered more about them."

"Yeah." I glance to the window, pausing when I see Gary again, still sitting patiently in the parking lot. I should have remembered him when I spoke to Persephone about Bethany and Mary. He's the third hostage the twilight has to my good behavior, even if he did this to himself. He can't be my car forever. I can't do that, even if he can. I didn't agree to marry the man when I showed up at his deathbed, and that's essentially what he's asking of me: a marriage with no convenient "until death do us part" exit clause. He'll follow me on four wheels until I choose to move on to whatever waits beyond the final offramp, and for all I know, he'll follow me even then. Only I don't think he'll have the chance, especially not if I'm a Fury now. I may not fully understand what that means, but I understand that it's about vengeance, and if he follows me forever, I'll eventually snap and punish him for the crime of . . . what? Being a man in love? Forgetting to ask before doing something he wasn't at all sure was going to work? The fact is, this situation sucks for everybody involved.

I should have asked Persephone to help me find him a way out; I asked Apple. But the fact remains that Persephone's not the only goddess I need to talk to tonight. I offer Gary a vague wave and head for the door. "I need to go to Maine," I say. "Any idea where we are right now?"

The Last Dance Diner moves around, setting down wherever it feels it needs to be at any given moment in time. It always has the parking lot and it always has its big neon sign, although that changes when necessary, going from the cool green of safe harbor to the glaring red of the Last Chance, the face it only shows when danger looms. The landscape in the twilight is more responsive than the landscape among the living. It can be a little disconcerting, sometimes.

"Up near Montreal," Emma says. "I have poutine on the menu today if you wanted some. We'll move again in the morning. It should only take you about six hours to drive to the Lady's onramp if that's why you're asking."

"You know me so well," I say, with a smile, and start for the door. "I'll be back as soon as I can, and Emma . . ."

"Yes?"

"Thank you. For everything."

"Thank you, my rambling Rose. On you go." She makes a little waving motion with her hands, shooing me away and making it clear that I'm welcome to stay at the same time. And I could stay if I wanted to. If I was willing to leave Bethany tethered to a corpse and unable to move on. If I was willing to risk offending three goddesses of the dead world by refusing the calling they've arranged for me. Thankfully, I have a little more sense than that. I wave back, tossing her another smile, and head for the door.

The air outside is cool and tastes of harvest, wheat chaff, and the green scent of freshly cut fields. I don't have the scythe in my hands right now, but part of me yearns to join the people who put that taste into the wind, which blows out of the south, from the heartland of America, where the fields are being cut to stubble even now. They'll burn soon, refreshing the soil and preparing it for the next year's seeds.

Farming imagery persists in the twilight because it's true no matter where you go in the world. Techniques and key crops may change and shift, but the complex combination of farmer, seed, field, and sunlight remains eternally the same. A field that's left to go fallow for a season will grow again in the future. It's no wonder that the people who dreamt our first gods into existence tied so many of them to the cycle of the seasons and the growing of the grain. Death is where agriculture lives.

I make my way across the parking lot to Gary, and his door swings open at my approach, welcoming me, beckoning me in. I slide in the driver's seat and run my hands across the wheel as his radio dial spins and lands on a country song about missing your girl when she's gone. I don't recognize the singer, and the lyrics could have been written any time in the last century. Country music is like that when it's not misogynistic and jingoistic and tedious.

"Hey," I say, drawing the seat belt across my chest and clicking the buckle home. Maybe it's a useless precaution for a dead woman, but I believe in safety when possible, and dying in a crash gives a girl a lot of respect for the three-point harness. "Sorry to leave you waiting here for so long."

Gary's dial spins again, this time landing on "Boys of Summer." Another confession of love. It's not hard to speak entirely in metaphors for affection when your voice is a radio playlist, but it's just a little tedious right now.

"We need to head for Maine," I say. "I have to talk to the Ocean Lady. You can come with me if you like."

The song doesn't change, but it feels like the wheel tenses under my hands. Then the key turns in his ignition, and the engine rumbles into questionable life. I can take over and drive if I need to, and sometimes I do it because I want to feel like I'm in control of where I'm going, but he's fully capable of getting us there on his own, and if we're going to have the breakup conversation, I probably shouldn't start by stealing his autonomy from him.

"Gary, are you . . . happy?"

The dial spins. Pharrell Williams blasts into the cab.

"You can't clap your hands. You don't have them anymore."

The radio turns off with a click, and the cab fills with the most expectant silence I have ever heard.

"Gary, we didn't talk for half a century. You grew up and did all these things without me. I . . . didn't grow up. But I got more experienced, and wiser, and did all kinds of things without you. Sometimes people can be good together, and good for each other, and still manage to miss their window. Sometimes it doesn't work because the time has passed."

The radio turns back on, and Carly Simon begins to sing. It's been a long time for her, too.

"See, that's what I'm talking about. The Gary I knew back in school would never admit to liking this kind of music, especially not in front of his girlfriend. We don't know each other anymore, Gary. You became a grownup, and I became an urban legend. Not exactly the most compatible things in the world."

The dial spins, and lands on "Silly Love Songs."

"I don't know! I don't know if I love you. I don't think you know if you love me. I love the *idea* of you. I love the boy you were, the one who dated a girl from the bad part of town and pretended he was too cool for songs about coal miners and holding hands down by the riverside. I love knowing that you were willing to risk your afterlife for me, but that's not the same as loving *you*. That's not a foundation to build a relationship on."

Emma said it would take about six hours to drive from the diner to the nearest onramp to the Ocean Lady, but the way Gary's accelerating, we're going to cut that time in half or better before we slow down.

He's taking the curves like they've personally offended him and racing down the straights like he expects them to disappear out from underneath his tires.

I sigh and sink back into the seat, settling in for the ride.

"Gary. Please. I'm not trying to be cruel. I'm trying to find a way for us to get through this without hurting each other more than we absolutely have to."

The dial spins. "Greased Lightning" begins to play.

"I know you're a car. I know you're *my* car. If we find a way to change that, you could have a death that doesn't depend on me to anchor it. I don't know if we can keep you on the ghostroads after that happens, but the twilight doesn't belong only to the road ghosts. There are other ways to stay."

Bethany has given me hope of that. The midnight beauties are sometimes tied to the road, but not always, and reapers have no allegiances that I'm aware of. They go where they like, and they answer to no one save for, presumably, the gods themselves. The gods like to stick their hands in wherever they can find an opening, and they're not shy about twisting things the way they want them to be. It's getting a little disconcerting, honestly. I can't necessarily say I was happier before I knew how much they interfered—or at least, how much attention they pay to things—but I was definitely more comfortable, and those two things can be difficult to distinguish sometimes.

Gary's radio clicks off. I sigh and set my hands upon the wheel.

"Come on. Don't be like this."

He doesn't turn the radio back on.

"So it's going to be like this?"

Apparently, yes. It's going to be like this. He doesn't turn the radio on or beep the horn or yield control of the wheel to me, just keeps driving, barreling down the road far too fast for safety. But he's a car, with a car's reflexes, and we're both already dead, so it's not like a crash could do anything but slow us down.

When it becomes apparent that he's not going to talk to me, I take my hands off the wheel and lean back in the seat again, closing my eyes. If he doesn't want to have a conversation, I can get a little rest, with no gods or monsters vexing me. It's a nice change. I may be a Fury now, and I may still be figuring out what exactly that means, but I can still appreciate the room to breathe.

Heh. "The room to breathe." The living have colonized language so profoundly that we can't get away from it, even in death. But then, the living created the languages we use. So far as I'm aware, the only languages spoken exclusively among the dead are ones that have died out in the daylight, fading from everyday vocabulary into awkward silences.

I stretch my legs, careful to keep my feet away from the pedals. I wouldn't want Gary to think I'm trying to slow him down, not when he's already angry with me. His anger is as justified as my hesitance, and probably born from a similar frustration over how hard it is for us to talk about any of these things. Communication is key to any kind of healthy relationship, whether or not it's a romantic one, and we can't communicate. Country songs and one-sided monologues are not a substitute for conversation.

Then he whips around a corner and vanishes from around me, leaving his momentum behind. I'm suddenly hurtling through the air, and we should really get used to the fact that the Ocean Lady sets her own rules and doesn't want him to be a car when he's on her claimed and consecrated ground. I hit the concrete hard, shoulder-first, and roll about fifteen feet along the gravel-covered road before enough of the momentum bleeds away and I'm able to push myself up onto my hands. For once, my clothing hasn't been damaged by the fall, which is a nice change, especially since I'm back in my green silk gown. Any sort of sharp shock has a chance to change what I'm wearing when I'm in the twilight.

I pick myself up and walk back toward the prone shape of Gary, sprawled face-down on the road and looking none the worse for wear. The first time this happened, we both panicked. It's still not exactly *routine*, but it's not the terrifying, confusing catastrophe it was when we had never experienced it before. The Ocean Lady sets her own rules.

Maybe that's why sometimes reaching her is a quest in and of itself, and other times, it's just a matter of taking a curve too fast. The twilight is malleable. That goes for all of us who dwell here.

I stop when I reach Gary's side, crouching down and offering him my hand. "Hey," I say. "You have bones again, or at least the memory of bones, which is arguably better. Can't break a memory. Get up."

"I don't want to talk to you right now," he says, getting his elbows underneath himself and using them to push up into a kneeling position. As always on the Ocean Lady, he looks like he did when he was my boyfriend by mutual agreement, a long, lanky stretch of teenage boy with features just eye-catching enough to have attracted my attention back when I'd been too poor and too trapped to ever believe he'd give the time of day to a girl like me.

"You don't have to," I say, hand still outstretched. "We can walk in silence, but we have to walk. We're on the Ocean Lady now. She doesn't have a lot of patience to spare."

Gary scowls as he slaps his hand into mine, flesh meeting flesh without a trace of warmth or comfort. His skin is cold. That's the fire burning in my bones, making me warmer than the dead are meant to be.

He drops my hand once I've pulled him to his feet. I wish I could say that was a surprise. I may not necessarily want to be a silently accepting bride, yoked to a proposal that was never actually made, but that doesn't mean I don't love him. I love the boy he used to be, and the man he grew into without me by his side, and the car who waits patiently in the parking lot of the Last Dance.

Love is so rarely enough. The poets told a lot of lies.

We walk the Ocean Lady, and the pavement is no softer under our feet than the pavement of any other stretch of the ghostroads. Birds flit and twitter in the undergrowth, as alive as anything in the daylight, because the road wants them here. When I walked the Ocean Lady with Laura Moorhead, she hung names on those bright-feathered bodies, calling them ivory-billed woodpeckers and Carolina parakeets, things whose wings have long been absent from the daylight, but who find rest and safety here, where the guns and predators of the living world can't touch them. The road loves birds. The road has always loved birds. She'll keep them safe when she can.

We walk, and the birds sing, and gradually, the neon glow of the truck stop where Apple keeps her court appears in the sky ahead of us.

As we draw closer, it grows more distinct, until it's practically a false dawn, until I can see the outline of its walls through the gathering gloom. We're close enough that I feel like we're almost there when a voice calls, "What is your name and business, travelers?"

It's a male voice, a few years older than it was the last time I heard it, but familiar all the same. The living change more than the dead do.

"Rose Marshall and Gary Daniels, here to speak with the Lady herself," I call back. "Hi, Paul. Still in the shitter with Apple?"

"She's letting me finish puberty," he says, stepping into view, all sullen anger and unforgiving bitterness.

"That's nice," I say. "Can we pass, please?"

Paul is a routewitch, a living one, who made the massive mistake of challenging Apple for her throne about a decade ago. He lost, and Apple reminded him that being Queen of the Routewitches comes with certain advantages that her subjects don't necessarily have access to. She stripped his distance and his age along with it and has had him playing patsy under her thumb on the Lady ever since. He doesn't much like the dead. That's all right. The dead, as represented by me, don't much like him either.

"What makes you think you have the right to demand audience with the Lady?" he asks.

"Oh, I don't know. Maybe the part where she's one of the trifecta of goddesses who've decided that I'd make a swell Fury." I fold my arms. "Also, she has my niece, and I'm here with an employment offer from Persephone that should keep Bethany from fading into nothingness. So you can probably see where I'd be a little anxious to get on with it."

Gary turns to stare at me. "Fury?" he echoes, as if he'd never heard the word before. "What do you mean, 'Fury'?"

"I mean I'm going to be real busy for a little while, thanks to Persephone thinking I'd make a good spirit of vengeance." I smile sweetly at Paul, who steps back, looking properly unnerved. "So maybe this is where you let us pass."

"Go," he says, stepping aside. "You're more trouble than my duty is worth."

"I'll be sure to tell Apple you feel that way." I wave jauntily as I start walking again, Gary close behind me.

"Rose," he says, in a low voice. "I don't know what's going on, but if this is why you said those things during the drive over here—"

"No," I say. "I said those things because I meant them, and they were the truth. We're not good for each other anymore. I appreciate your grand gesture, but you should have asked me first. We need to know each other before we can be committed to each other."

Slowly, Gary nods. "I'm sorry. I just wanted to see you again. I never wanted to make you uncomfortable."

"I know," I say. "Come on."

This time, when I offer him my hand, he takes it and holds on, fingers laced through mine, and I can handle the discomfort of how cold his skin is if it gives him even a crumb of comfort while he's effectively being dumped.

Together, we walk toward the truck stop, which is the platonic ideal of all truck stops, everywhere, even down to the small chrome-and-checkerboard diner attached to one side of it. It's a way station, a stopping point for weary travelers, and I've been trying to find my way here since before I died, since before I knew there was a "here" to come to. If the land of the dead is a teeming sea of souls and strangeness, this is the lighthouse that pulls me safe to harbor.

I don't know what Gary sees. His safe haven is not the same as mine. The last time we were here, he saw the drive-in theater where we used to go when we were both alive. His eyes sketch the outline of a building that doesn't match my low-slung cathedral of the American road, and that's just fine. This place is always personal, no matter how it's approached.

We reach the door. I step inside, tugging him in my wake.

As usual, there's a scattering of routewitches around the main open space. Some of them look familiar. Most don't. I've never made it a point to introduce myself to the world's supply of routewitches. They come and go too quickly. They don't wait around for me. The living are like that.

One of them gets up when he sees me, vanishing through a door labeled "Employees Only." I stand my ground, Gary beside me, trying my best to ignore the stares and whispers of the routewitches. It's like they've never seen a ghost before.

Then Apple appears, slipping out that same door, with Bethany close behind her.

My niece looks like she's been sick for weeks, pale, stringy-haired, and too thin. I didn't think ghosts could lose weight. I guess being sundered from your patron and purpose will do that. There's a new bracelet around her wrist, glass beads interspersed with what look like chunks of untumbled asphalt. It's fitting, given where she is.

"Aunt Rose!" she exclaims, and runs for me, slamming into me without slowing down as she throws her arms around my waist and holds me as close as she can. She presses her face into my shoulder. We've never had a hugging relationship. We've never had a relationship at all. Gary lets me go. My hands drift back to my sides and stay there as I look past Bethany to Apple, who stands watching us with a neutral expression on her eternally youthful face.

"Did you know?" I ask.

"That you might be called to serve?" She nods. "I did. The Lady told me it was possible, that you were already well along the road. But I didn't show your feet the way. You chose your path on your own, you walked it willingly, and if there came a time when that trip carried consequences, that isn't my fault."

"Persephone says Bethany can stay. She doesn't need the crossroads to survive, and she doesn't have to become a spirit of vengeance for the anima mundi." My niece stiffens against me but doesn't pull away.

"How?" asks Apple.

"She can pledge herself to the midnight beauties, or to the reapers. Either would be lucky to have her, and either would provide the connection she needs in order not to fade." It's the party or the pallbearers. Two extremes. Both suited to the teenage girl now huddled in my arms.

"Really?" whispers Bethany. "I could change my alliance?"

"With Persephone's blessing," I say.

"I'll be a reaper, if it's allowed," she says, and finally lets me go, smiling shyly. "I was never much of a party girl, not even when I was alive."

"You're sure? They're psychopomps. That job isn't always easy." It isn't *ever* easy, in my experience. Most people don't take kindly to the ones who show up to tell them that they've died for real and true, no take backs, no second chances.

"I don't think a party that lasts forever would be easy, either." She's already starting to look better, hair recovering some of its shine, skin recovering some of its color. The cloak and hood will come later, I assume. "I'll be a reaper. I'm sure they'll come and tell me what to do."

"I'm sure you're right," I say, and give her a quick hug, squeezing her hard before I let go and turn my attention back to Apple. "It took three goddesses to set me on this path, and I can't get off it now. Persephone, the anima mundi, and the Ocean Lady. Persephone gave Bethany back to herself. The anima mundi made it possible for me to defeat Bobby Cross. The Ocean Lady owes me for her part in this." I'm bluffing—if anything, I owe the Lady—but I don't think she'll hold that against me.

The routewitches in the room collectively stiffen and gasp. Apple ducks her head, posture suddenly less friendly.

"What gives you the right to demand anything from her?" she asks, voice low. "She is our everything. You're just one more ghost, an unquiet spirit lingering when your time on Earth is done. You have no right to demand anything from her. You—"

Her head snaps back, mouth open in a long, silent scream. When she looks at me again, her eyes are gray as concrete from side to side, and her gaze is not her own.

"What do you want?" she asks, in a voice filled with strange harmonics.

"Hello, Lady," I say. "This is Gary."

"I know him well," she says. Then, with a flicker of humor, she adds, "He keeps winding up face down on my pavement."

"He's a car most of the time."

"But he is not of the road."

"That's the problem," I agree amiably. "He's a car because he wanted to be with me, but I'm not a hitchhiking ghost anymore. If I'm a Fury, I won't need a car as much. How else can we anchor him here in the twilight?"

The other routewitches are silent, frozen and afraid. I've convinced their deity to seize control of their Queen, after all. She stands in front of them, casting them all into the presence of the divine. This is new and terrible ground for them.

"Do you want to stay, little spirit?" asks the Ocean Lady, attention going to Gary.

"I'd like to, yes," he says.

"In what form?"

"My own would be a nice change." His smile is quick and wry. "It's nice to have hands."

"Then you'll make a fine ferryman," she says. "Boy and car. Don't ask for rides from the living. Offer them. They'll steal you, they'll seek you, and you'll drive some of them to ruin."

A ferryman. They're not as rare as coachmen, but they're rare enough that I hadn't even considered them as an option. They aren't true road ghosts, and they can manifest around any form of transport. Most steer boats. Gary will drive himself to the ends of the world. The ones who are kind, considerate, and truly in need of help will get to their destinations. The ones just looking to take advantage will find themselves driven so fast their hearts stop.

It's not always fair. But it's the fare.

The Ocean Lady turns Apple's eyes to me. "Are our accounts settled?" she asks.

"They are," I reply, and Apple collapses, apparently unconscious, on the truck stop floor. The routewitches rush to help her up while I stand frozen next to Gary and Bethany, three ghosts remade by the casual attention of the gods of the twilight. It's a strange position to be in. I don't know of anyone who's ever been here before.

I put my arm around my niece's shoulders, feeling the fire burn in my bones, and take Gary's hand in mine as we watch the routewitches get Apple back to her feet. She looks shaken but unharmed by the

Ocean Lady's intercession. Bobby Cross is gone, the crossroads themselves have been destroyed, and if things are changing in the twilight, I guess I have to change with them. That's what humans do, after all. We change.

Leave the stasis to the gods.

The Price Family Field Guide to the Twilight of North America
Ghostroad Edition

––––––

THE LIVING

Ambulomancers. Characterized by their reluctance to trust themselves to any form of vehicular transit, these born wanderers are eternally on the move, gathering strength and power from the distance they have traveled. A novice ambulomancer will be able to control the road in small ways, finding food, shelter, and protection even within the harshest environments. An advanced ambulomancer will actually be able to interpret the language of the road itself, using this information to predict the future and manipulate coming events. Ambulomancers can be of any species, human or nonhuman, although humans and canines are the most common.

Routewitches. These children of the moving road gather strength from travel, much as the ambulomancers do, but the resemblance stops there. Rather than controlling the road, routewitches choose to work with it, borrowing its strength and using it to make bargains with entities both living and dead. The routewitches of North America are currently based out of the Old Atlantic Highway, which "died" in 1926, and are organized by their Queen, Apple, a young woman of Japanese-American descent who matches the description of a teenage girl who mysteriously disappeared from Manzanar during World War II. The exact capabilities of the routewitches remain unclear, although they seem to have a close relationship with the crossroads.

Trainspotters. Very little is known. They have been called "the routewitches of the rails," but no direct information has yet been collected.

Umbramancers. These fortune-tellers and soothsayers are loosely tied to the twilight, but the magic they practice is more general than the road-magic of the routewitches and the ambulomancers. It's unclear exactly what relationship the umbramancers have to the twilight. Although they have been seen visiting the crossroads, there are no known bargains involving an umbramancer.

THE DEAD

Beán sidhe. The *beán sidhe* are alive and dead at the same time, which makes them difficult to classify, but as they prefer the company of the dead, we are listing them here. These Irish spirits are associated with a single family until that family dies out, and will watch their charges from a distance, mourning them when they die. They regard this as a valuable service. We are not certain why.

Bela da meia-noite. The bela da meia-noite, or "midnight beauty," is an exclusively female type of ghost, capable of appearing only between sunset and midnight. They enjoy trendy clubs and one-night stands. They're generally harmless, and some have proven very helpful in exorcising hostile spirits, since they'd prefer that no one get hurt.

Coachmen. These archaic ghosts have rarely been seen in the modern day, bound as they traditionally are to phantom carriages, complete with horses. They are happy to give lonely travelers rides to their final destination, and generally fail to point out that this will involve riding in their bellies.

Crossroads ghosts. Marked by their eyes, which all sightings have described as "containing miles," these ghosts speak for the crossroads, a metaphysical construct where those who are connected to the afterlife in some way are able to go and make bargains, the nature of which we still do not fully understand. The best-known crossroads ghost is Mary Dunlavy, who tends to answer questions with "I'll tell you when you're dead."

Crossroads guardians. The flipside of the crossroads ghost is the crossroads guardian, a being which was never alive in the traditional sense, but which now represents the interests of the crossroads in all things. When asked about crossroads guardians, Mary Dunlavy's response consisted of a single word: "Run." All crossroads guardians are believed to have been destroyed when the crossroads fell.

Deogen. Also known as "the Eyes," the deogen are non-corporeal, fog-like, and often hostile. They will lead travelers astray if given the chance and have been known to form alliances with other unfriendly spirits. A deogen/homecomer team-up is to be feared.

Dullahan. Like the *beán sidhe*, Dullahan are alive and dead at the same time, a feat which is even more impressive considering that their heads are fully detachable. They sometimes serve as psychopomps and are more commonly known as "headless horsemen." Because that's something to help you sleep at night.

Einherjar. These dead heroes are supposed to stay in Valhalla, if it exists, so we don't know why they sometimes crop up in the living world. They become solid in the presence of alcohol or violence, and they very much enjoy professional wrestling.

Ever-lasters. These eternal children haunt playgrounds and schoolyards, playing clapping games and going to classes that never end. A surprising amount of knowledge is encoded in their rhymes, for those who find the time to listen.

Ferrymen. The inverse of hitchers, these ghosts manifest with vehicles of their own and offer rides to the unwary, stranding or delivering them home according to their whims and their assessment of their passengers. Many of them drive for Uber and Lyft. Far fewer can be found behind the wheel of New York taxis.

Gather-grims. Next to nothing is known about this class of psychopomp; we're not honestly sure that they exist. We have heard them mentioned by other ghosts, but they are leery to answer questions, and will generally change the subject. Investigate with caution.

Goryo. These powerful ghosts are most often of wealthy backgrounds and are commonly of Japanese descent. All known goryo were martyred, or believe themselves to have been martyred, leading to their undying rage. They can control the weather, which is exactly the kind of capability that you don't want in an angry spirit fueled by the desire for vengeance.

Haunts. All haunts lost love at some point during their lives, although it may have been decades before they actually passed away. Their kiss can cure all known ailments. It can also kill. Which it does seems to be fairly arbitrary and based on how close the person being kissed is to death. As haunts are not terribly bright as a class, they often misjudge their affections. Try not to encourage them.

Hitchhiking ghosts. Often referred to as "hitchers," these commonly sighted road ghosts are generally the spirits of those who died in particularly isolated automobile accidents. They are capable of taking on flesh for a night by borrowing a coat, sweater, or other piece of outerwear from a living person. Temperament varies from hitcher to hitcher; they cannot be regarded as universally safe.

Homecoming ghosts. Called "homecomers," these close relatives of the hitchhiking ghosts want one thing only: to go home. They are typically peaceful for the first few years following their deaths, when their homes are still recognizable. The trouble begins once those homes begin to change. Homecomers whose homes are gone will become violent, and in their rage, they have been known to kill the people who offer to drive them home.

Homesteads. Sometimes called "caddis flies"—although this term has fallen out of fashion—these stationary cousins of the coachmen loved their homes so much that when their deaths coincided with the destruction of those homes, they found a way to carry them into the twilight. A homestead *is* the home and has full control over their own "bodies." Be wary of these haunted houses given form. They do not easily forgive.

Maggy Dhu. Black ghost dogs capable of taking on physical form. They can weigh over two hundred pounds, and their bite is deadly to the living. The Maggy Dhu are somewhat smarter than living canines, but they are still animals, and are often vicious. Interestingly, all types of dog can become Maggy Dhu after death; many are believed to have been Chihuahuas in life. They are believed to harvest souls.

Onibi. Japanese fire spirits, dedicated to destroying those who would use fire as a weapon against the innocent. Usually found in the aftermath of arson. Neutral if you're not holding a match.

Pelesit. Ghosts bound to living masters through an unknown ritual. They appear normal in the twilight, but have trouble manifesting fully in the living world unless they are at or near the scene of a recent murder.

Phantom Riders. Speed racers of the ghostroads, these ghosts carry their cars with them into the twilight but exist as independent beings. They thrive on fast driving and drag races and have led more than a few mortals to their dooms by asking if they want to take a drive.

Reapers. These dark-cloaked ghosts seem to exist only to guide the spirits of the recently deceased onto the next stage of their existence. We don't know why. They do not speak to the living, and none of us has ever been willing to commit suicide for the sake of an interview.

Strigoi. The strigoi are an interesting case: the dead use the name to refer to a specific type of angry ghost, capable of becoming fully corporeal when it revisits the site of its death. These ghosts have no truly vampiric qualities and seem to be unrelated to the cryptids of the same name.

Toyol. The toyol are sorcerously bound spirits of infants who died before or shortly after birth. The less said about them, the better.

White ladies. These spirits of abandoned or betrayed women can be of any age, united only by the tragedies which killed them. They are not technically road ghosts, but are often mistaken for hitchers, and have been recorded seeking rides as a cover for their violent revenge. White ladies are extremely dangerous and should be avoided.

Playlist

"Bad Reputation"	Halfcocked
"Song Beneath the Song"	Maria Taylor
"What Baking Can Do"	*Waitress*
"Black Trees"	Kim Ritchey
"Pomegranate Tango"	Dr. Mary Crowell
"Loser Like Me"	*Glee* cast
"Good Old Girl"	Marian Call
"I Am A Lonesome Hobo"	Thea Gilmore
"Hollow"	Hem
"Don't Blame Me"	Taylor Swift
"Kiss With a Fist"	Florence and the Machine
"Glitter and Gold"	Barns Courtney

Acknowledgments

When I wrote *The Girl in the Green Silk Gown,* I wasn't necessarily expecting to have the chance to go in and check on Rose again. Which made me sad, but she's been dead for a long time, and most of her days and nights are blessedly pretty boring: she hitchhikes, she convinces strangers to buy her dinner, she goes back to the twilight to see her ghost friends, lather, rinse, repeat. But then came *That Ain't Witchcraft,* over in my InCryptid series, wherein Annie Price took it into her head to fight and destroy the crossroads, and it became very clear that Rose had to go on at least one more outing.

"At least" is doing a lot of heavy lifting in that sentence, but it isn't making any promises; as of the moment where I'm writing this, I don't know if we'll be visiting Rose in her own liminal space again. She'll still be showing up in the Price-Healy chronicles, but her own route is currently closed for authorial repairs. So this isn't goodbye. It's just . . . for a while. This is the last we'll see of her for a while.

The Sarah and Amber of our dedication are Sarah Kuhn and Amber Benson, my companions on the Magical Girls of Urban Fantasy tour. We drove from San Diego to Portland together, and no one died, and that alone should be cause for massive celebration. They were two of the best road trip buddies I've ever had, and there's not much better reason to dedicate a Rose book to someone than "I can spend a lot of time in a car with this person and not do murder at the other end."

This book is a love letter to Rose, to growing up and changing, to figuring out who you are rather than letting other people tell you who you're going to be, and to getting things wrong the first time, as long as you're willing to take a deep breath and do it over again until you get it right. Rose Marshall has been with me for a long time. I owed her this story.

My machete squad is an incredible, eclectic assortment of people, and I adore them utterly. Without them, I would make infinitely more mistakes, and be infinitely sadder. Britt Sabo drew and colored the incredible promo comic that we released ahead of *The Girl in the Green Silk Gown*, and I am so very grateful. Chris Mangum maintains my website code, while Tara O'Shea maintains my graphics, and they are so good. Thanks to everyone at DAW, the best home my heart could have, and to the wonderful folks in marketing and publicity at Penguin Random House.

The cover for this book was designed by the incredible Amber Whitney, of Unicorn Empire Designs. I am honored and thrilled by her work, which makes everything seem so much better and brighter. What a joy she is to work with.

Since the last time we spoke in the pages of this series, Elsie (the kitten I got to help me through the pain of Alice's passing) has reached glorious, gorgeous adulthood and become the very finest of cats. She's actually an owl in tortoiseshell fur, and I would be completely lost without her. I still am a little lost without Alice, but Elsie keeps me anchored. And we have recently been joined by a terrible cloud made of love and claws and colorpoint fluff, Verity, my very first Ragdoll.

This is especially fitting, since the previous Rose book happened when I was still fresh off my trip to New Zealand, and that was where I spent most of an afternoon at a cat café and fell in love with the breed. Verity's older sister, Tinkerbell, is my mother's cat, and both of them are ridiculously spoiled quarantine kittens. I'm trying not to dwell on the plague years as I write this, but they've influenced every part of our lives, whether we wanted them to or not; I've done a lot less travel as a consequence of COVID-19, which made rejoining Rose's eternal road trip for a little while even nicer.

Thanks to Chris Mangum, for putting up with me; to Whitney

Johnson, for Indian food and bounce; to Brooke Abbey, for continued mild tolerance; to Mike and Marnie, for host duties and driving before the world locked down; and to my beloved Kate Secor, for undertaking a difficult construction project while the world was on fire. I look forward to cursing your baby, sweetheart. My thanks to Shawn Connolly, Michelle Dockrey, and Charlaine Harris. And as always, to Amy McNally, for everything.

Any errors in this book are my own. The errors that aren't here are the ones that all these people helped me fix. I appreciate it so much.

No body, no crime, as the sages say. And here we go at last, back on the road again.